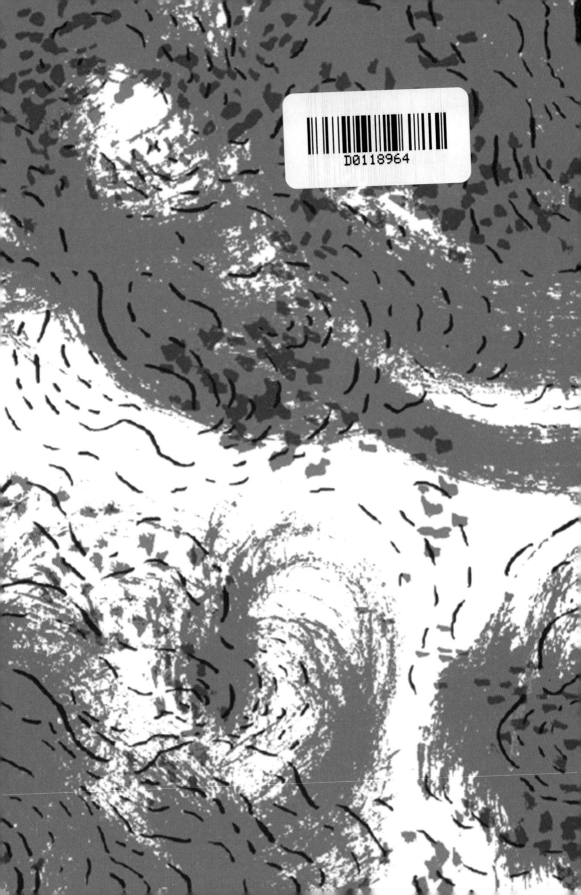

D0118964

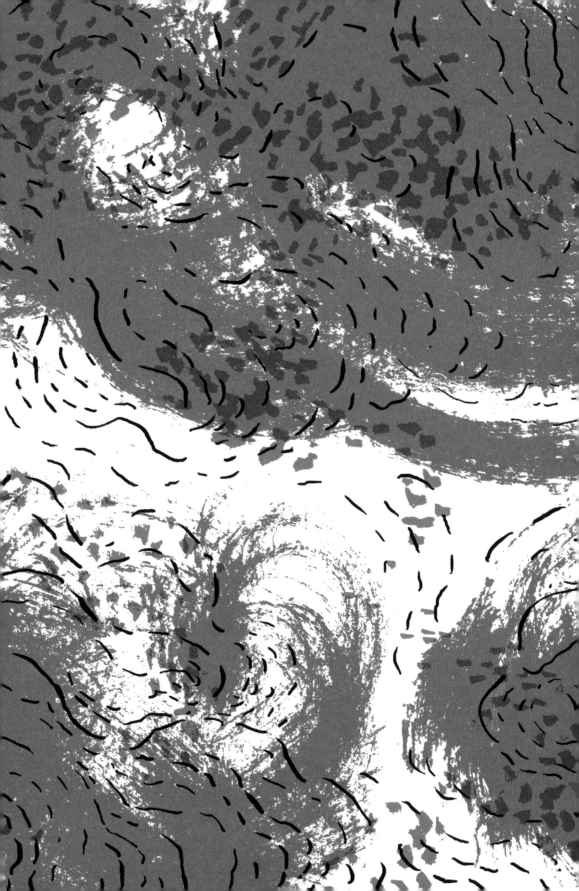

Sylvia Ofili
Birgit Weyhe

German Calendar
No December

CASSAVA REPUBLIC

GERMAN CALENDAR NO DECEMBER

First published in 2018 by Cassava Republic Press
Abuja - London

A CIP catalogue record for this book is available from the National Library of Nigeria and British Library.

ISBN (Nigeria): 978-978-55979-4-3
ISBN (UK): 978-1-911115-61-8
eISBN: 978-1-911115-62-5

Editor: Bibi Bakare-Yusuf
Editorial Staff: Layla Mohamed & Emma Shercliff
Artistic Directors: Bibi Bakare-Yusuf & Johann Ulrich
Cover Design: Junior Ba
Production: Thomas Gilke
Project Concept: Marc-André Schmachtel
A project of the Goethe-Institut Nigeria

GOETHE INSTITUT

KULTURSTIFTUNG DES BUNDES

Funded by the TURN Fund of the German Federal Cultural Foundation

Distributed in Nigeria by Yellow Danfo
Distributed in the UK by Central Books Ltd.
Distributed in the US by Consortium Books

Printed and bound in Great Britain by Bell & Bain Ltd, Glasgow

This book is dedicated to my family. Thank you for being my steadfast companions on my various adventures. German Calendar, No December!
Sylvia Ofili

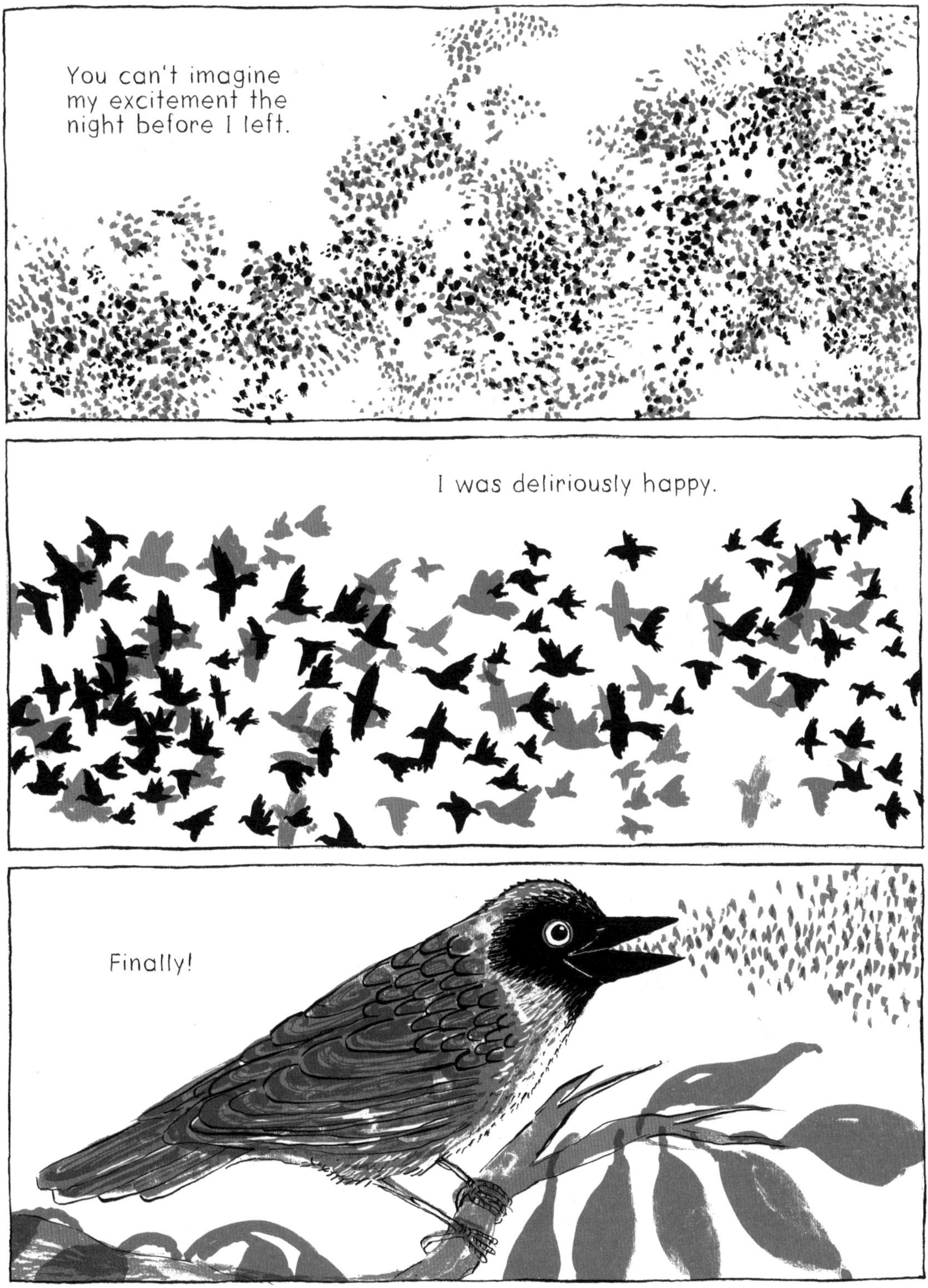
You can't imagine my excitement the night before I left.
I was deliriously happy.
Finally!

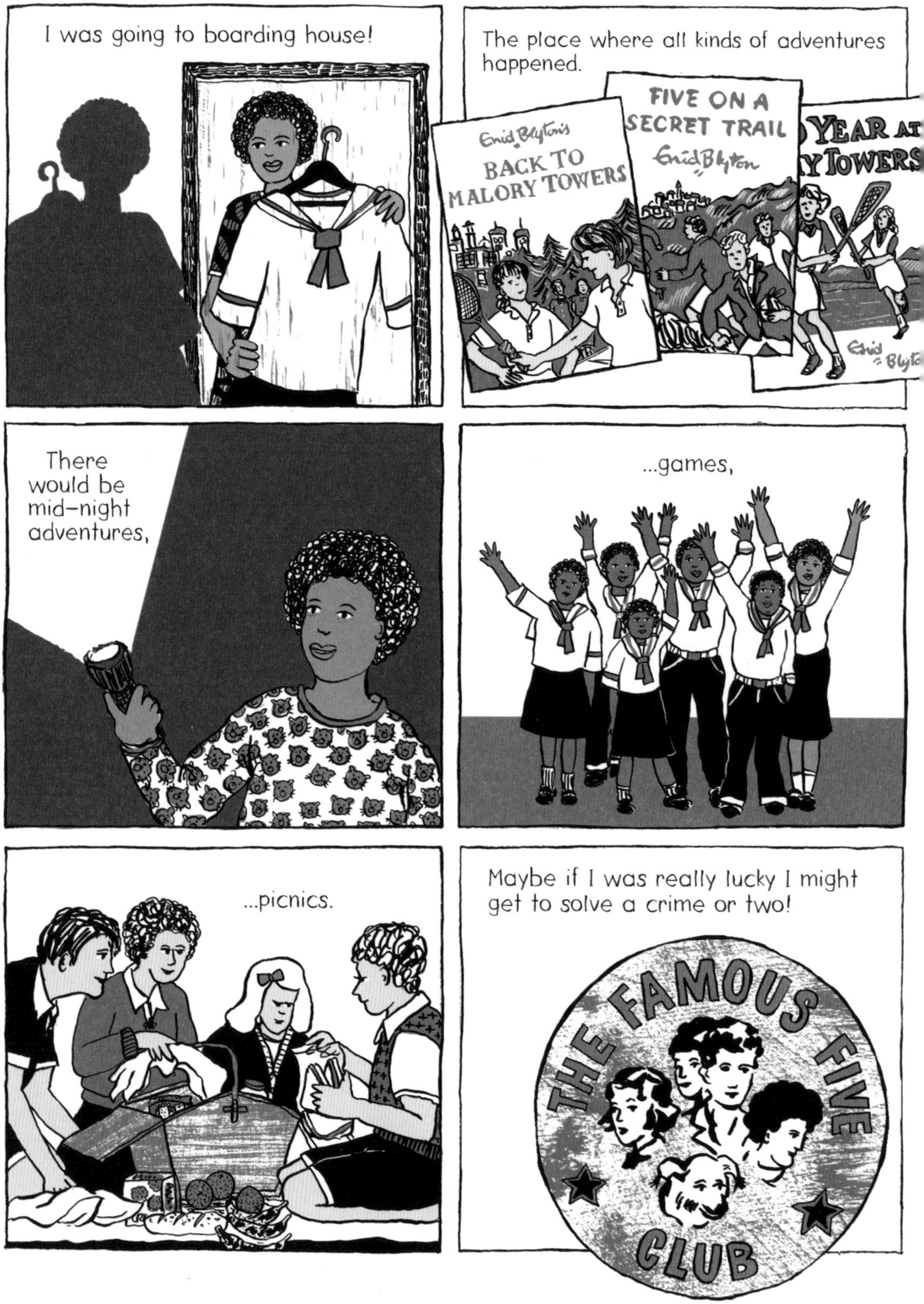
I was going to boarding house!
The place where all kinds of adventures happened.
Enid Blyton's
BACK TO MALORY TOWERS
FIVE ON A SECRET TRAIL
Enid Blyton
YEAR AT
There would be mid-night adventures,
...games,
...picnics.
Maybe if I was really lucky I might get to solve a crime or two!
THE FAMOUS FIVE CLUB

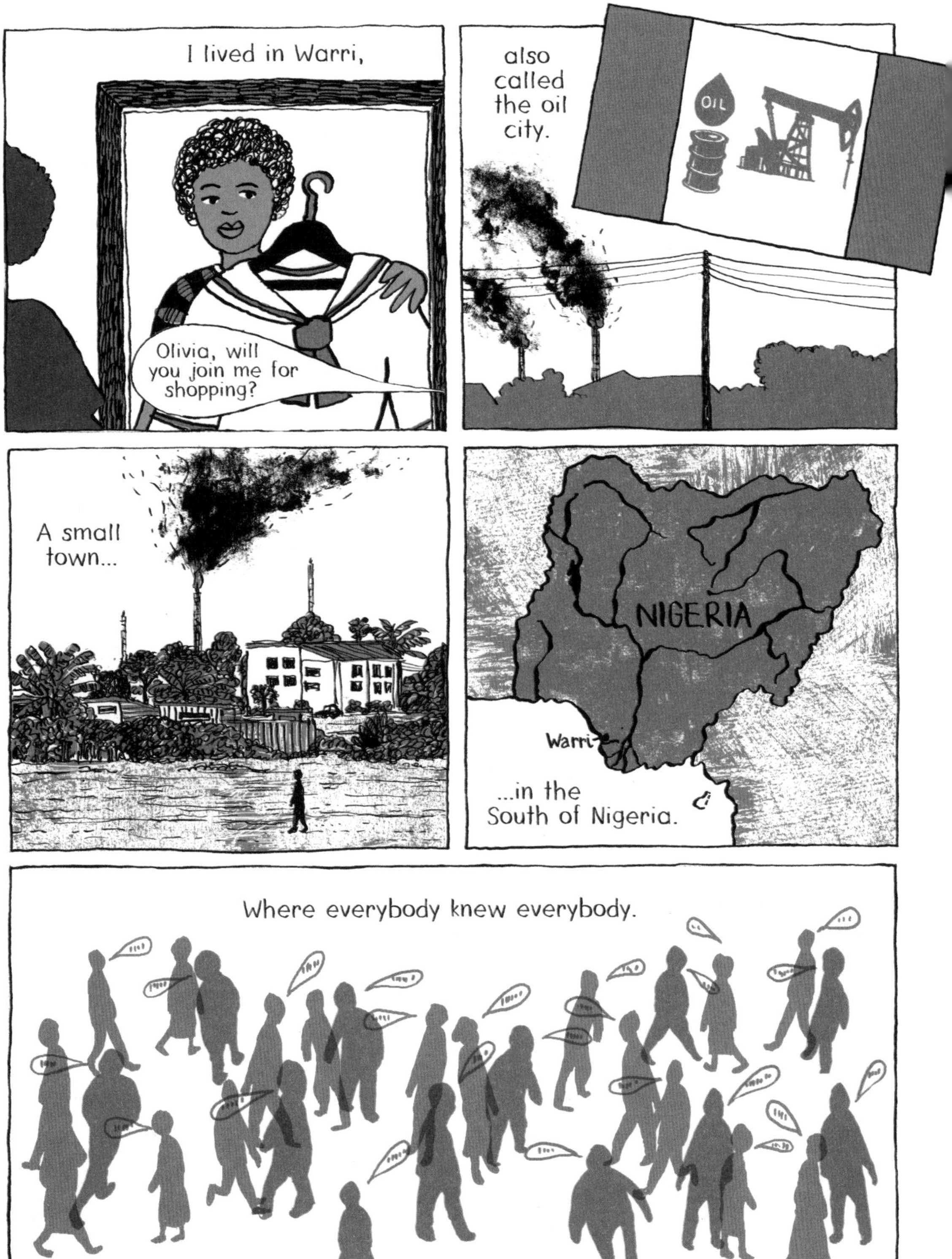
I lived in Warri,
Olivia, will you join me for shopping?
also called the oil city.
OIL
A small town...
NIGERIA
Warri
...in the South of Nigeria.
Where everybody knew everybody.

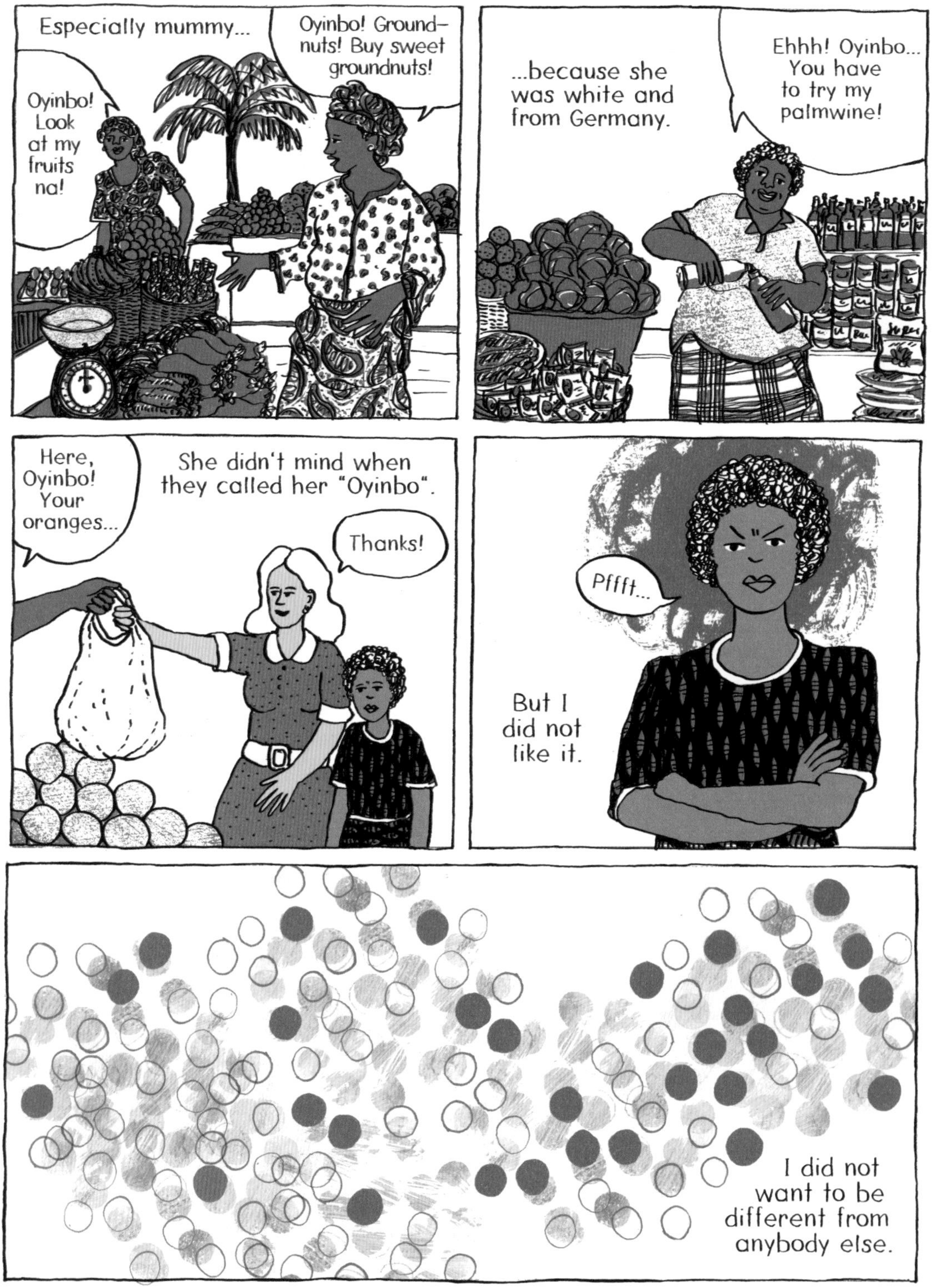
Especially mummy...
Oyinbo! Look at my fruits na!
Oyinbo! Groundnuts! Buy sweet groundnuts!
...because she was white and from Germany.
Ehhh! Oyinbo... You have to try my palmwine!
Here, Oyinbo! Your oranges...
She didn't mind when they called her "Oyinbo".
Thanks!
Pffft...
But I did not like it.
I did not want to be different from anybody else.

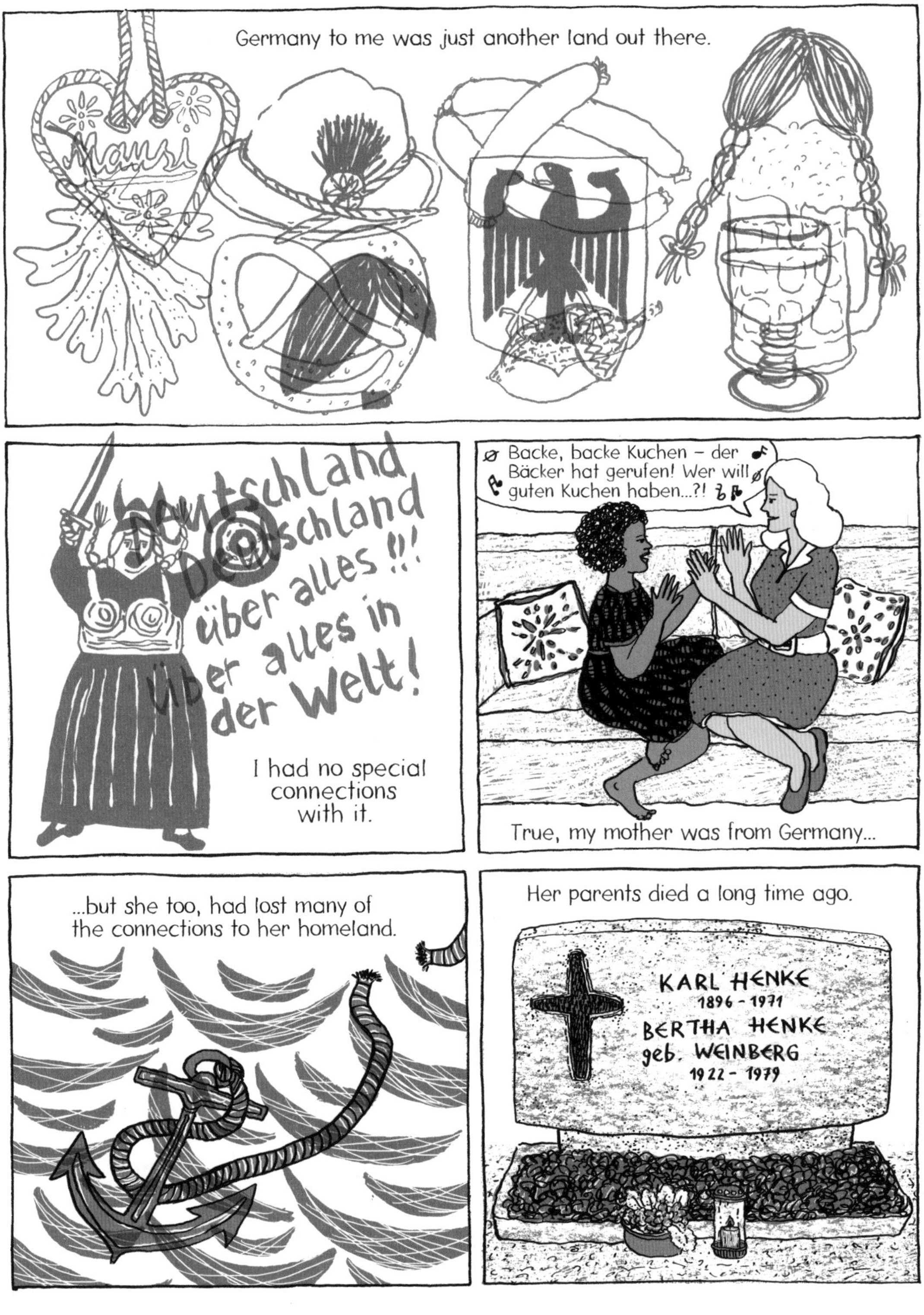

Germany to me was just another land out there.
Mausi
Deutschland Deutschland über alles!!! über alles in der Welt!
I had no special connections with it.
Backe, backe Kuchen – der Bäcker hat gerufen! Wer will guten Kuchen haben...?!
True, my mother was from Germany...
...but she too, had lost many of the connections to her homeland.
Her parents died a long time ago.
KARL HENKE
1896 - 1971
BERTHA HENKE
geb. WEINBERG
1922 - 1979

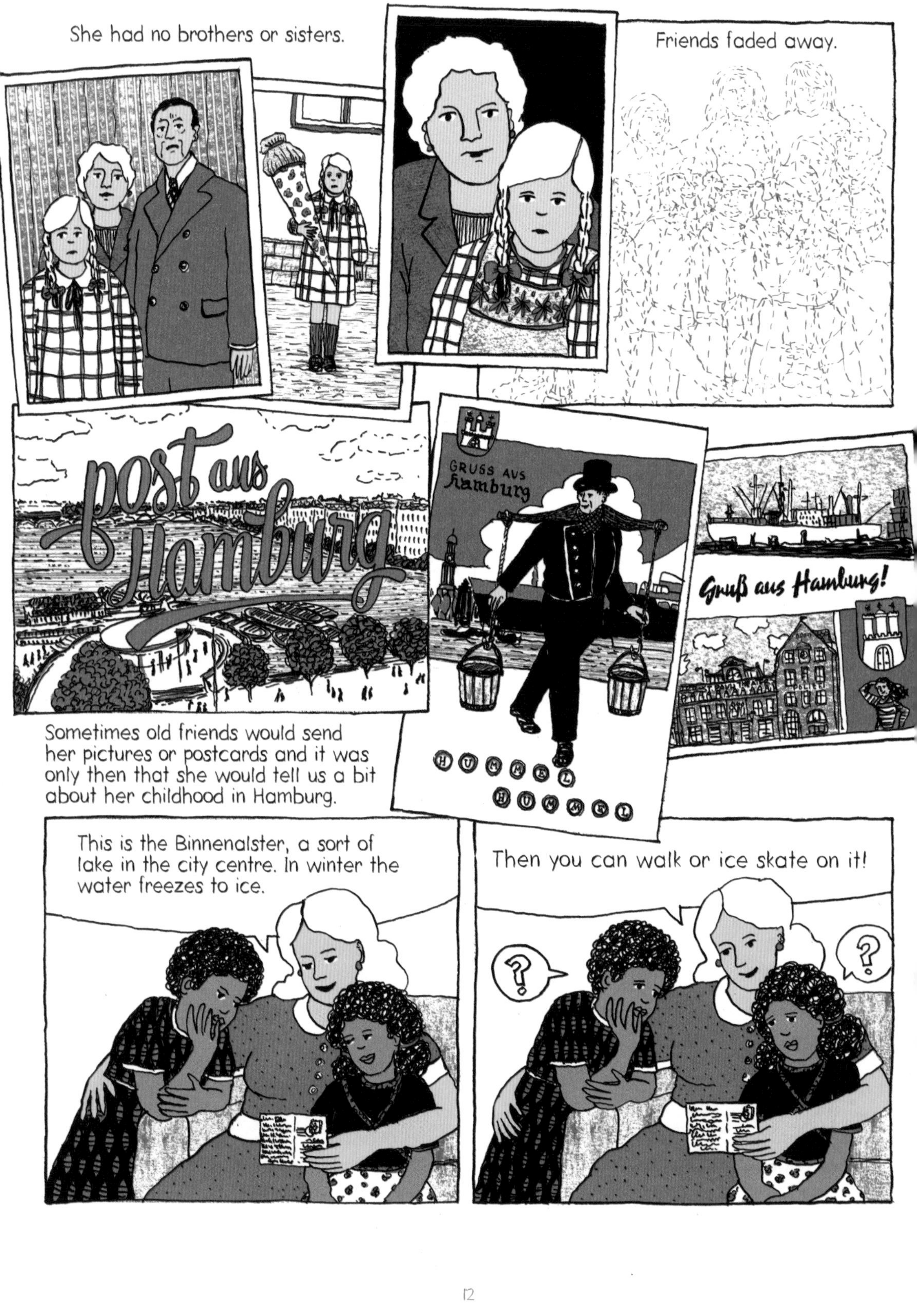
She had no brothers or sisters.
Friends faded away.
post aus Hamburg
GRUSS AUS Hamburg
HUMMEL HUMMEL
Gruß aus Hamburg!
Sometimes old friends would send her pictures or postcards and it was only then that she would tell us a bit about her childhood in Hamburg.
This is the Binnenalster, a sort of lake in the city centre. In winter the water freezes to ice.
Then you can walk or ice skate on it!
?
?

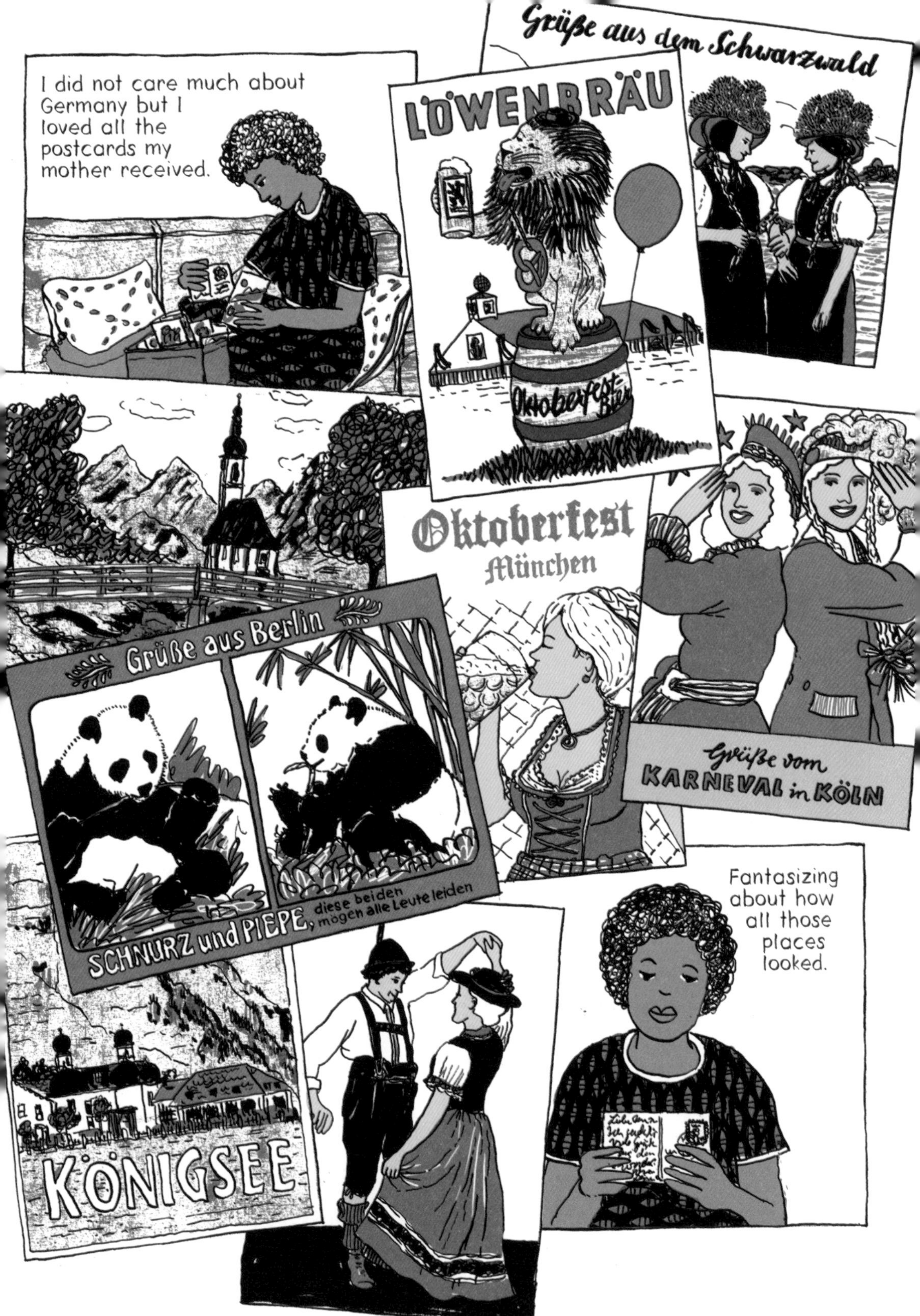
I did not care much about Germany but I loved all the postcards my mother received.
Grüße aus dem Schwarzwald
LÖWENBRÄU
Oktoberfest-Bier
Oktoberfest
München
Grüße aus Berlin
SCHNURZ und PIEPE, diese beiden mögen alle Leute leiden
Grüße vom KARNEVAL in KÖLN
KÖNIGSEE
Fantasizing about how all those places looked.

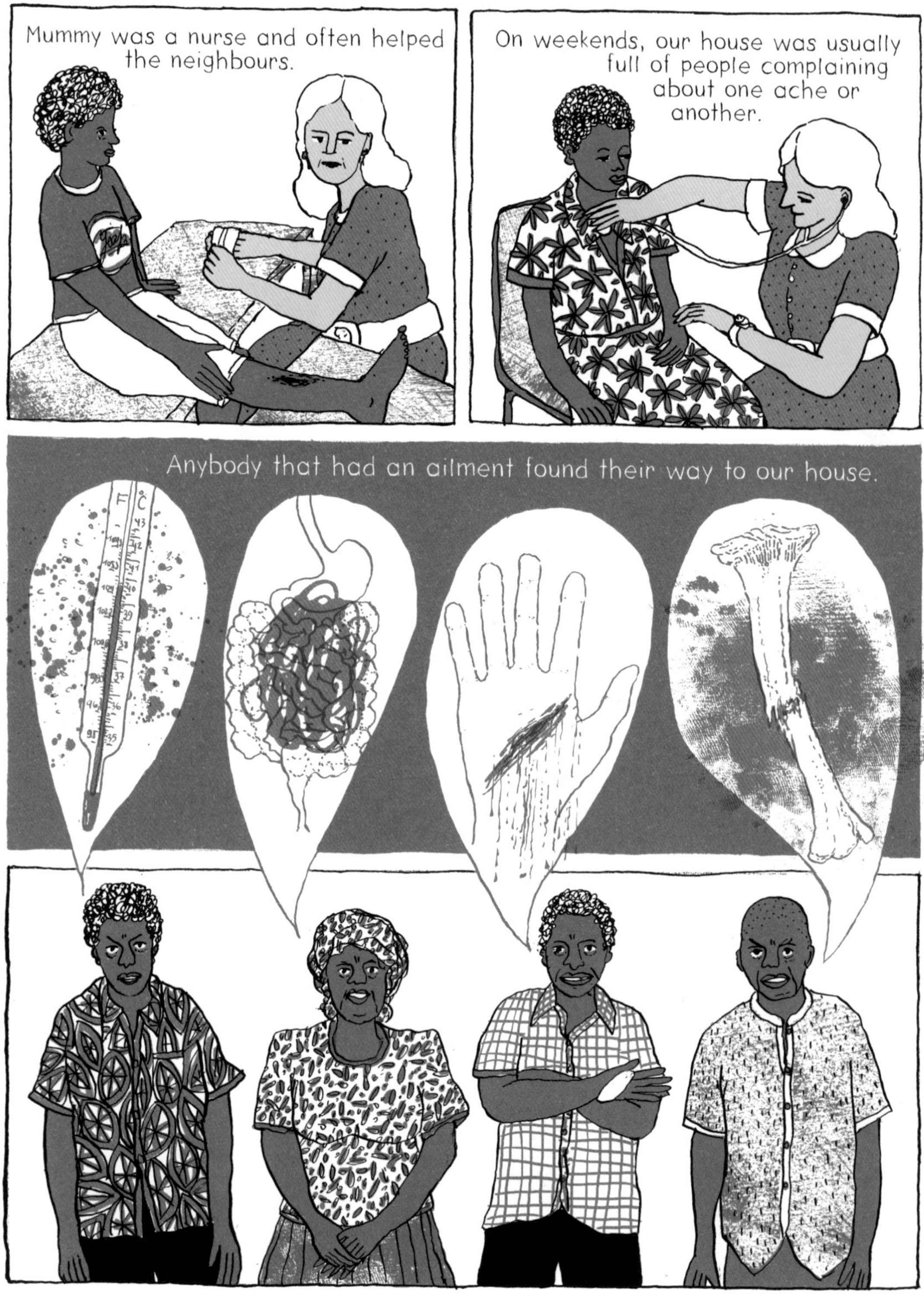
Mummy was a nurse and often helped the neighbours.
On weekends, our house was usually full of people complaining about one ache or another.
Anybody that had an ailment found their way to our house.

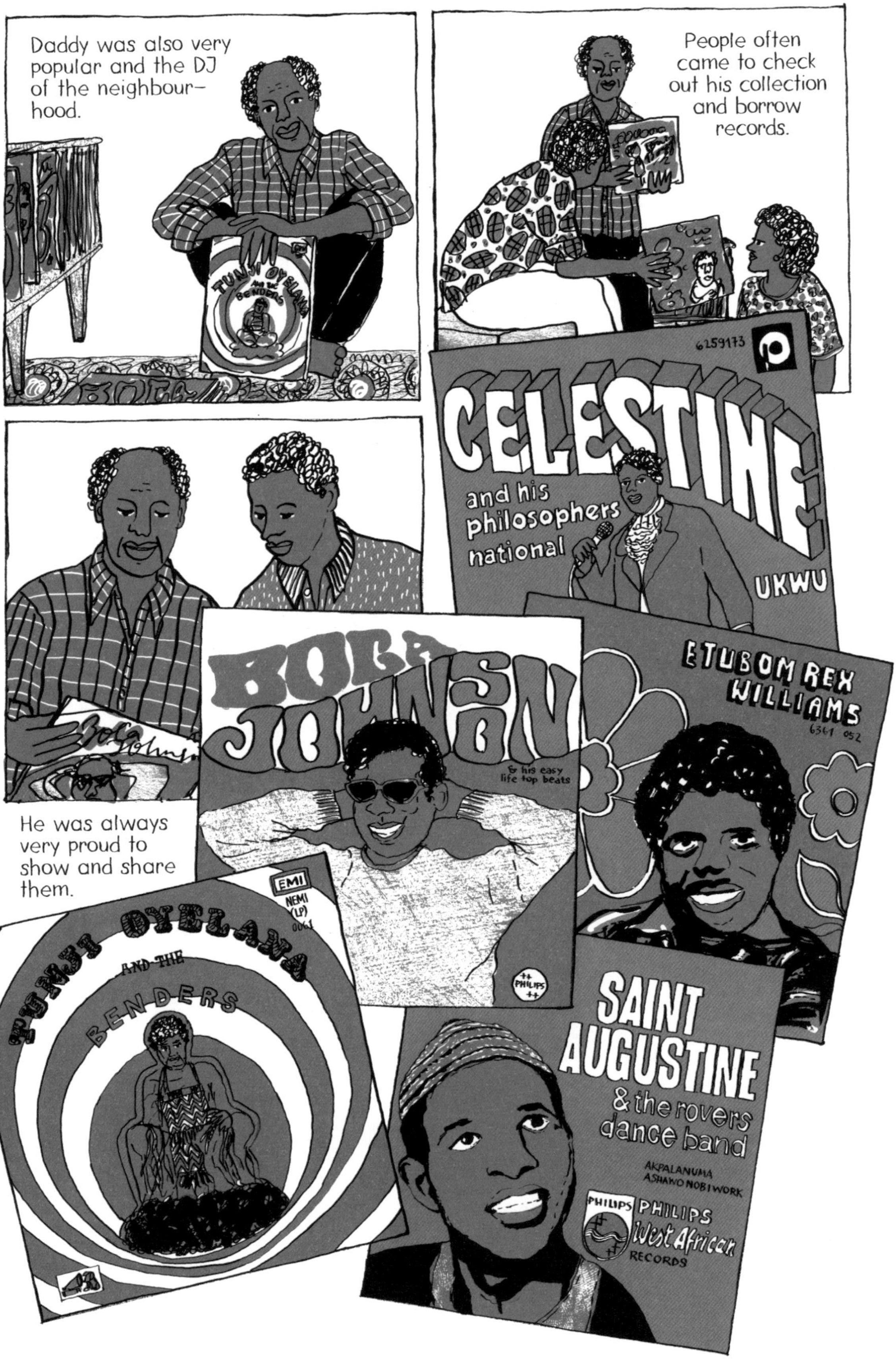

Daddy was also very popular and the DJ of the neighbour-hood.
People often came to check out his collection and borrow records.
6259173
CELESTINE
and his philosophers national
UKWU
He was always very proud to show and share them.
BOLA JOHNSON
& his easy life top beats
PHILIPS
ETUBOM REX WILLIAMS
6361 052
EMI
NEMI (LP) 0061
TUNJI OYELANA
AND THE
BENDERS
SAINT AUGUSTINE
& the rovers dance band
AKPALANUMA
ASHAWO NOBI WORK
PHILIPS
PHILIPS
West African
RECORDS

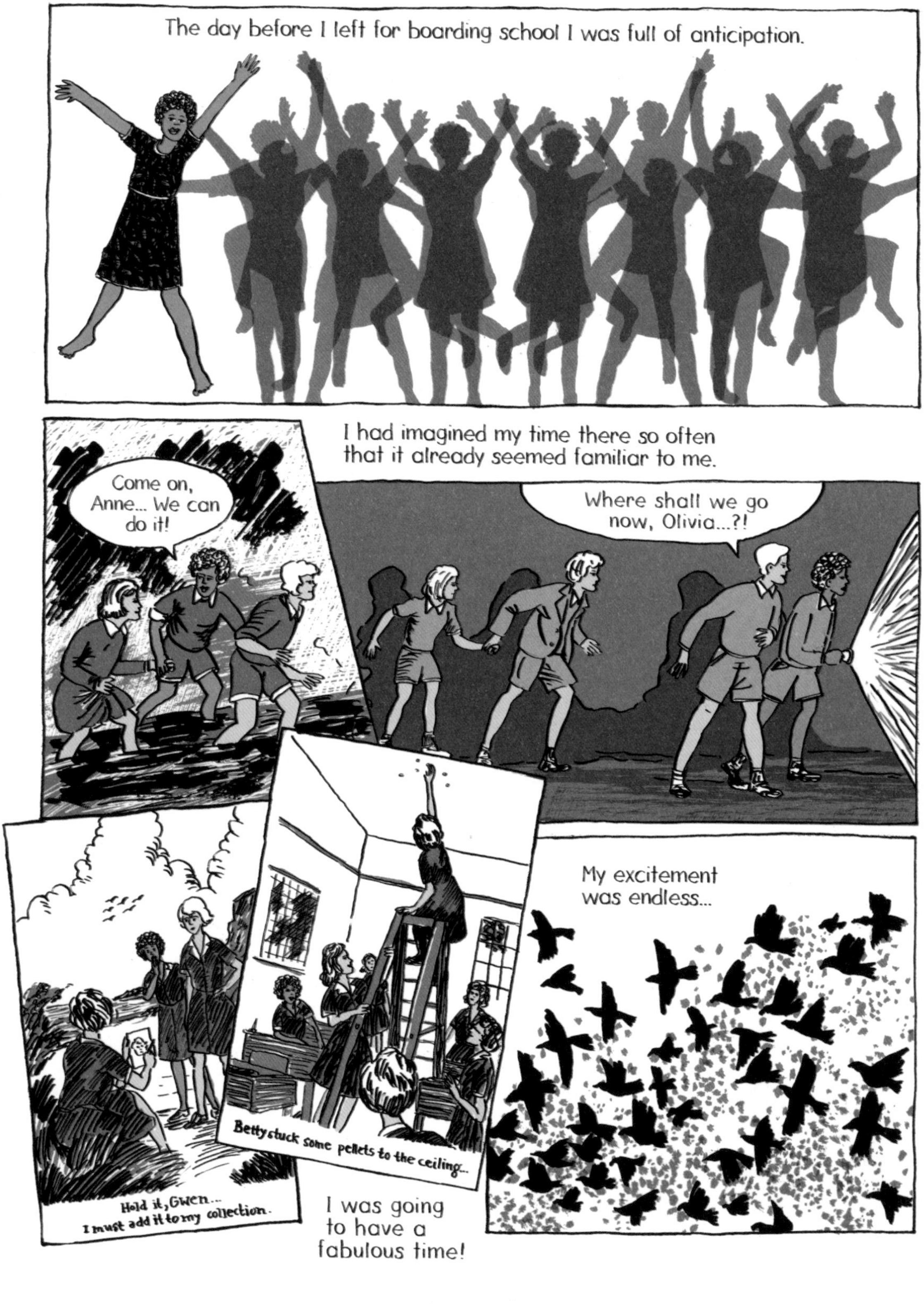
The day before I left for boarding school I was full of anticipation.
I had imagined my time there so often that it already seemed familiar to me.
Come on, Anne... We can do it!
Where shall we go now, Olivia...?!
Hold it, Gwen... I must add it to my collection.
Betty stuck some pellets to the ceiling...
My excitement was endless...
I was going to have a fabulous time!

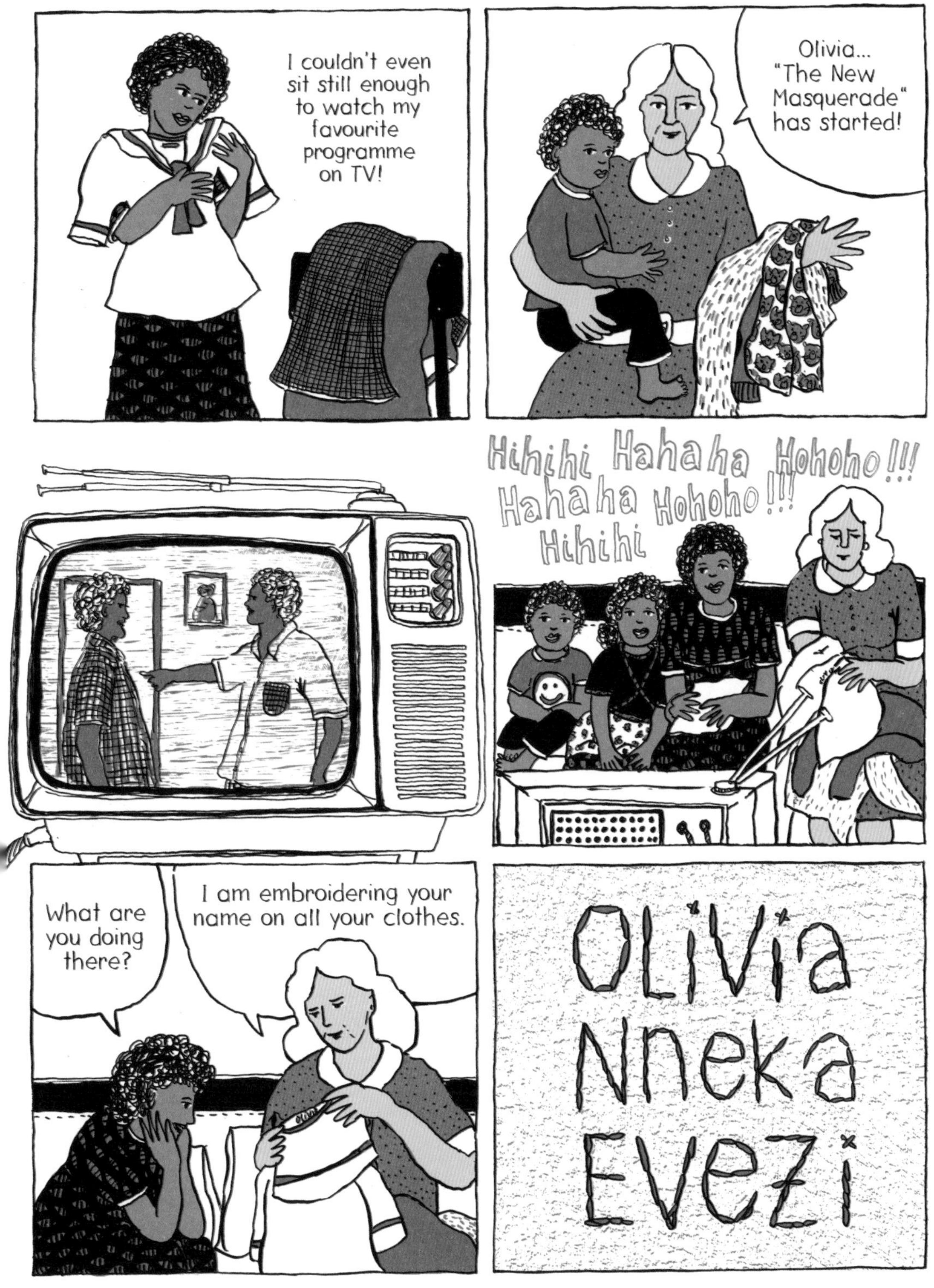

I couldn't even sit still enough to watch my favourite programme on TV!
Olivia... "The New Masquerade" has started!
Hihihi Hahaha Hohoho!!!
Hahaha Hohoho!!!
Hihihi
What are you doing there?
I am embroidering your name on all your clothes.
Olivia Nneka Evezi

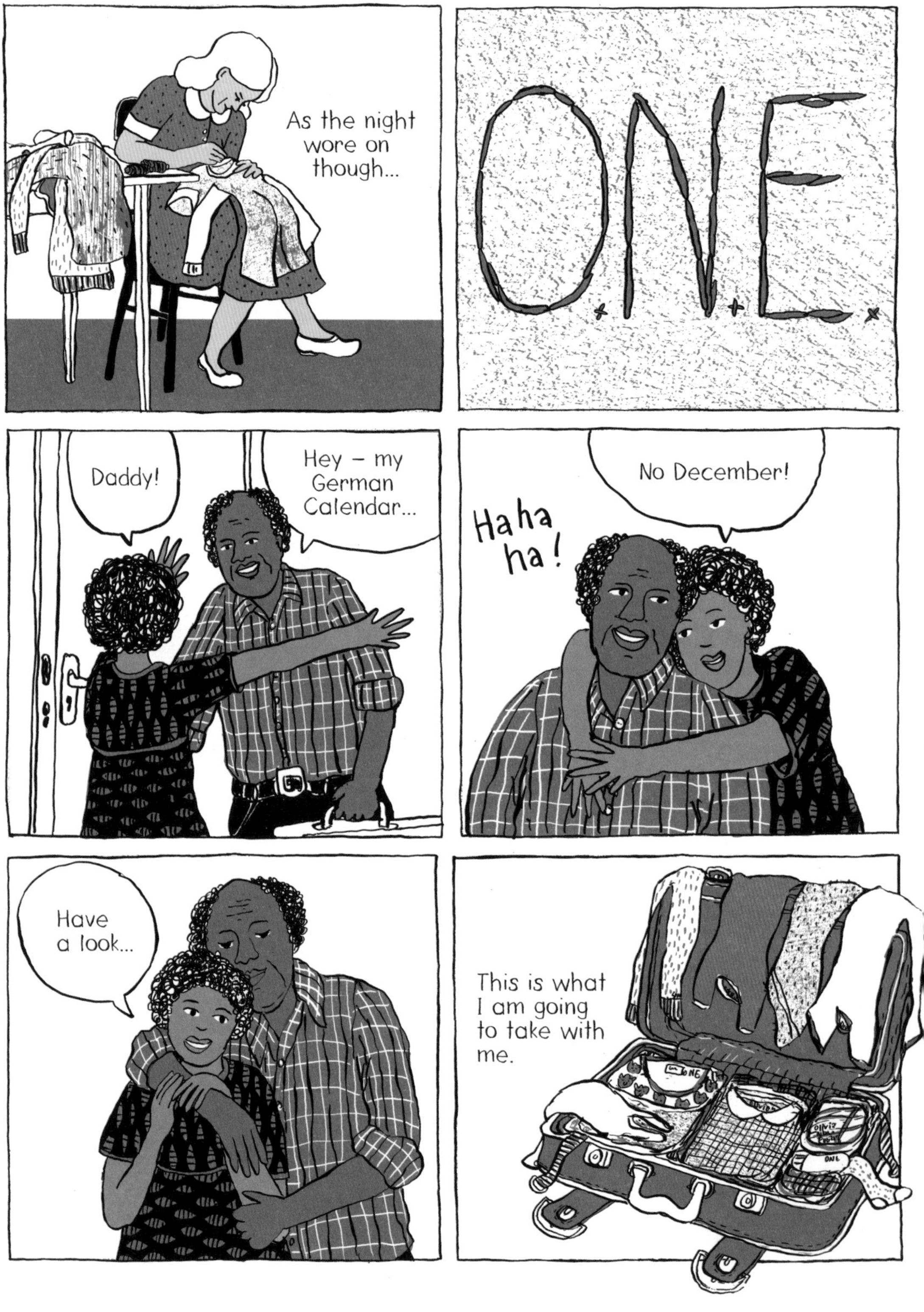
As the night wore on though...
O.N.E.
Daddy!
Hey – my German Calendar...
Haha ha!
No December!
Have a look...
This is what I am going to take with me.

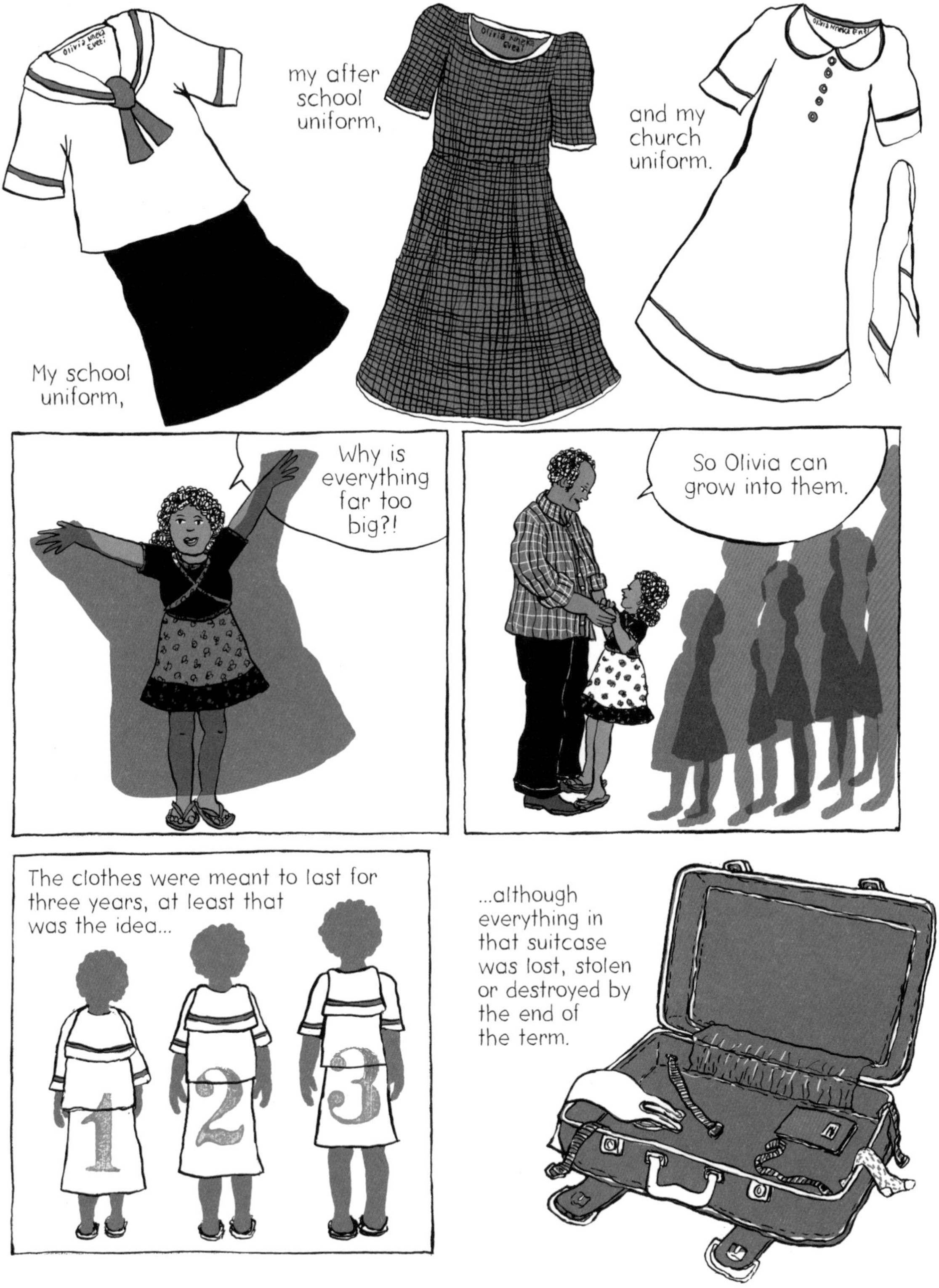
My school uniform,
my after school uniform,
and my church uniform.
Why is everything far too big?!
So Olivia can grow into them.
The clothes were meant to last for three years, at least that was the idea...
1
2
3
...although everything in that suitcase was lost, stolen or destroyed by the end of the term.

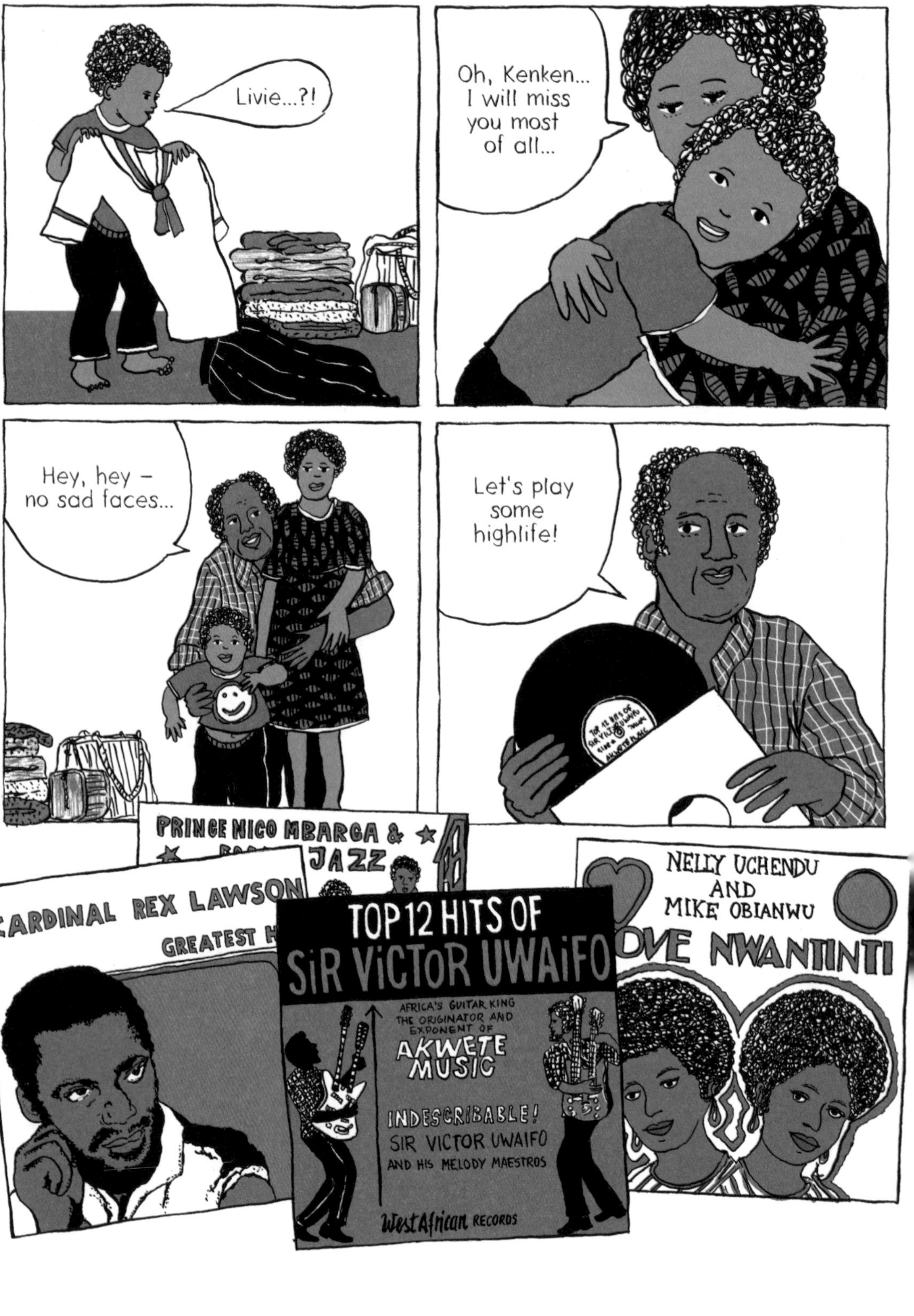
Livie...?!
Oh, Kenken... I will miss you most of all...
Hey, hey – no sad faces...
Let's play some highlife!
PRINCE NICO MBARGA &
JAZZ
CARDINAL REX LAWSON
GREATEST H
TOP 12 HITS OF SIR VICTOR UWAIFO
AFRICA'S GUITAR KING THE ORIGINATOR AND EXPONENT OF
AKWETE MUSIC
INDESCRIBABLE!
SIR VICTOR UWAIFO
AND HIS MELODY MAESTROS
West African RECORDS
NELLY UCHENDU AND MIKE OBIANWU
OVE NWANTINTI

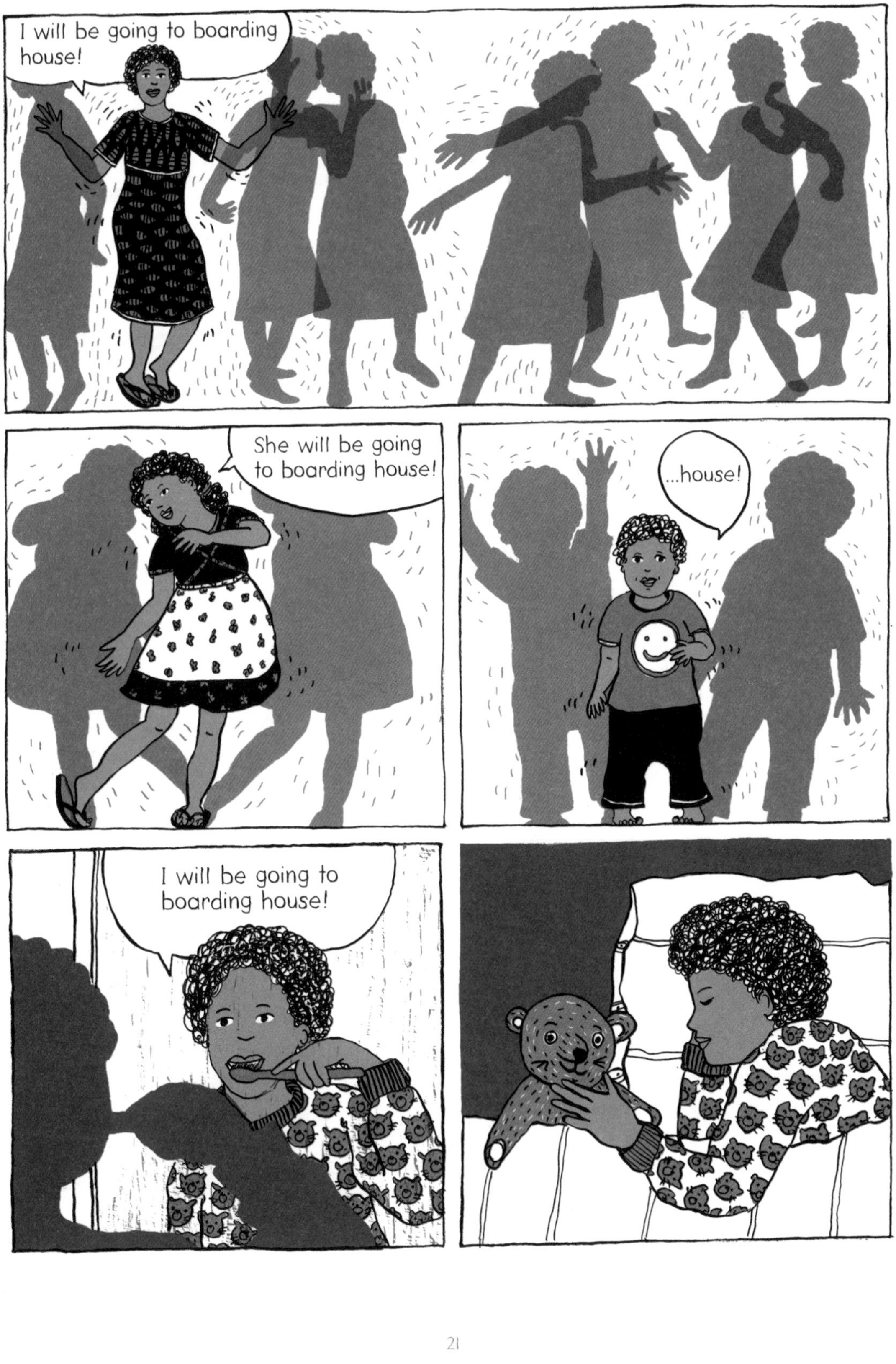

I will be going to boarding house!
She will be going to boarding house!
...house!
I will be going to boarding house!

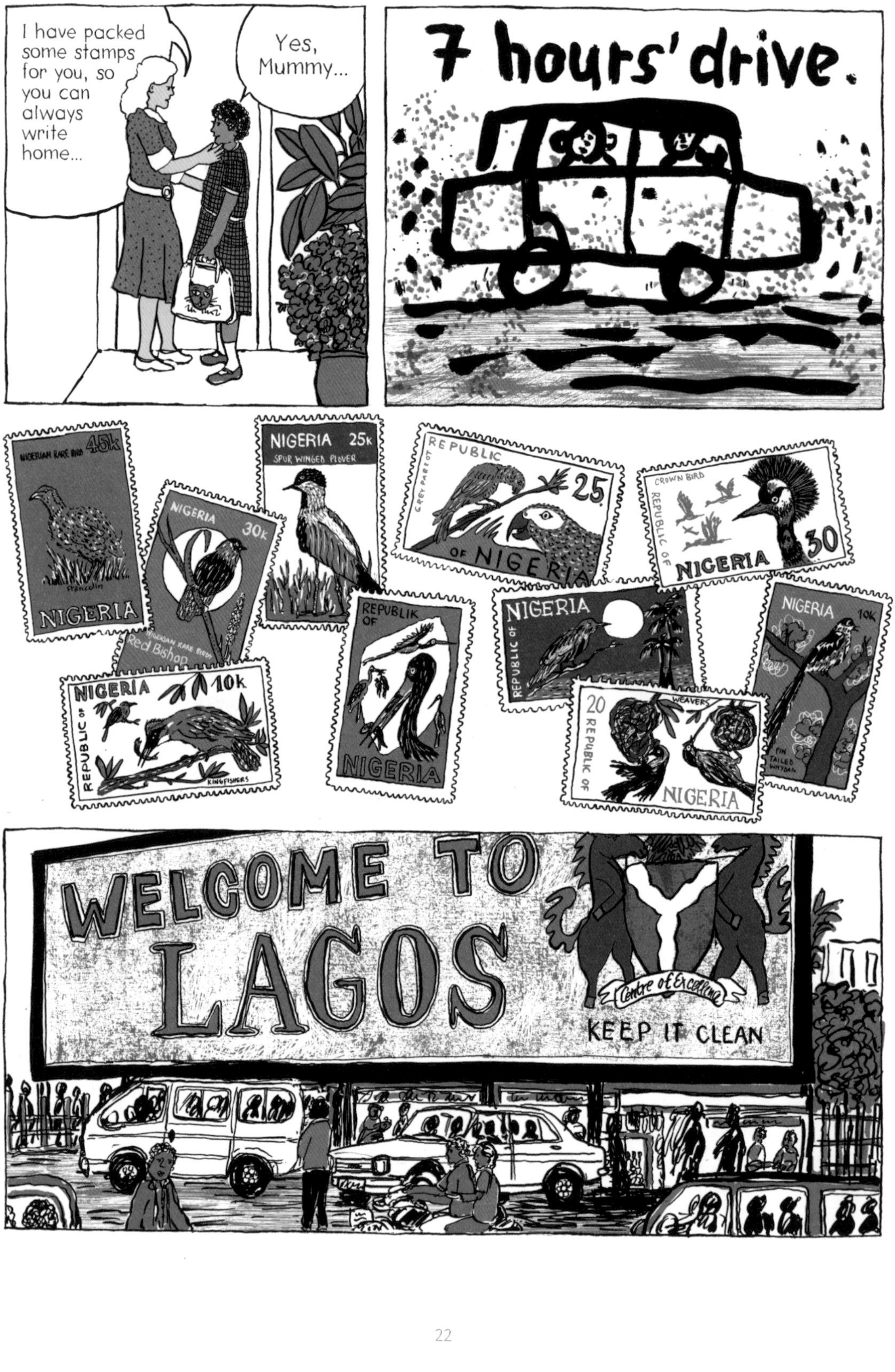
I have packed some stamps for you, so you can always write home...
Yes, Mummy...
7 hours' drive.
NIGERIAN RARE BIRD 45k
Francolin
NIGERIA
NIGERIA 30k
NIGERIAN RARE BIRDS
Red Bishop
NIGERIA 25k
SPUR WINGED PLOVER
REPUBLIC OF NIGERIA
GREY PARROT
25
CROWN BIRD
REPUBLIC OF NIGERIA 30
NIGERIA 10k
REPUBLIC OF
KINGFISHERS
REPUBLIK OF
NIGERIA
NIGERIA
REPUBLIC OF
NIGERIA 10k
PIN TAILED WHYDAH
20
WEAVERS
REPUBLIC OF
NIGERIA
WELCOME TO LAGOS
Centre of Excellence
KEEP IT CLEAN

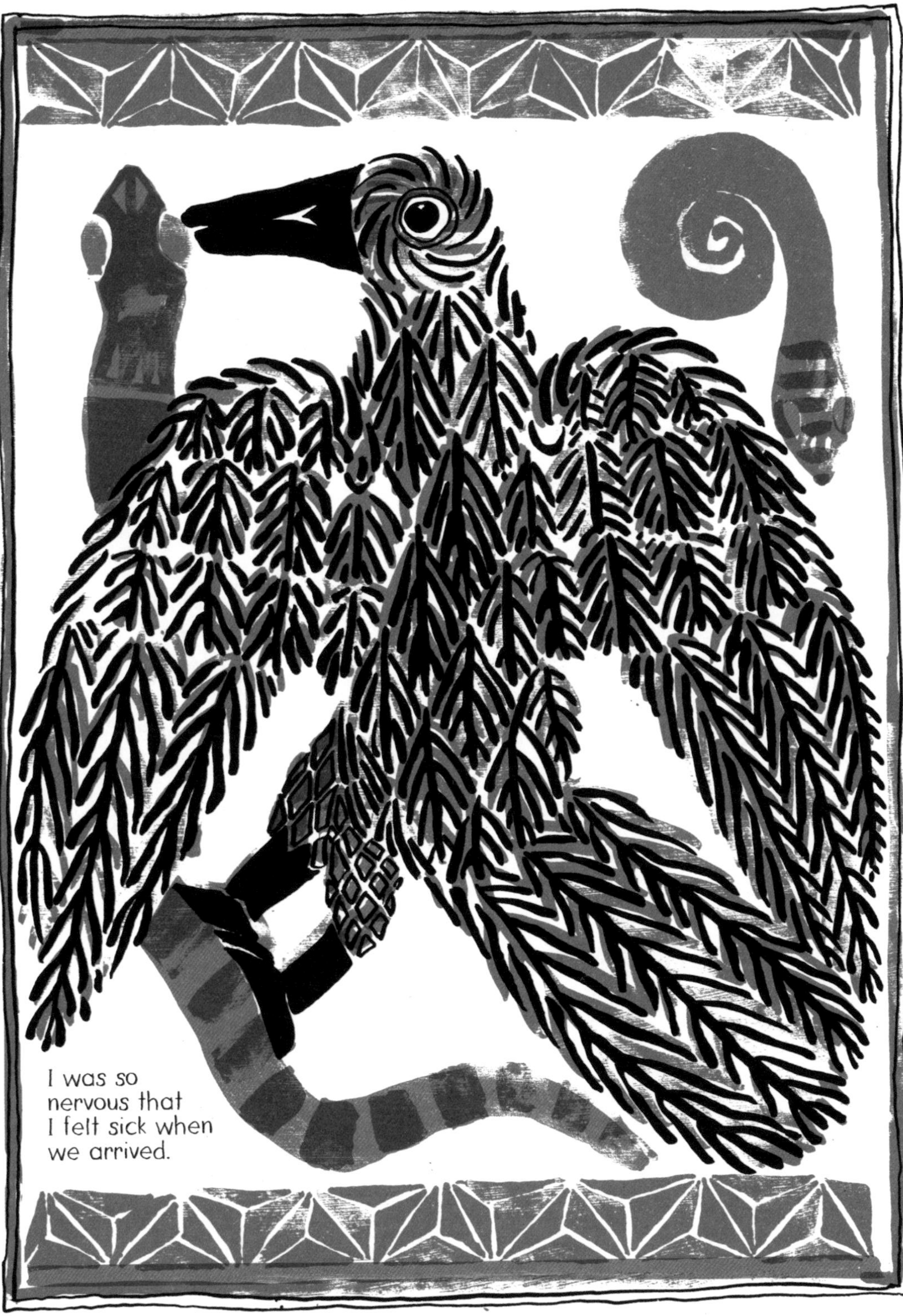
I was so nervous that I felt sick when we arrived.

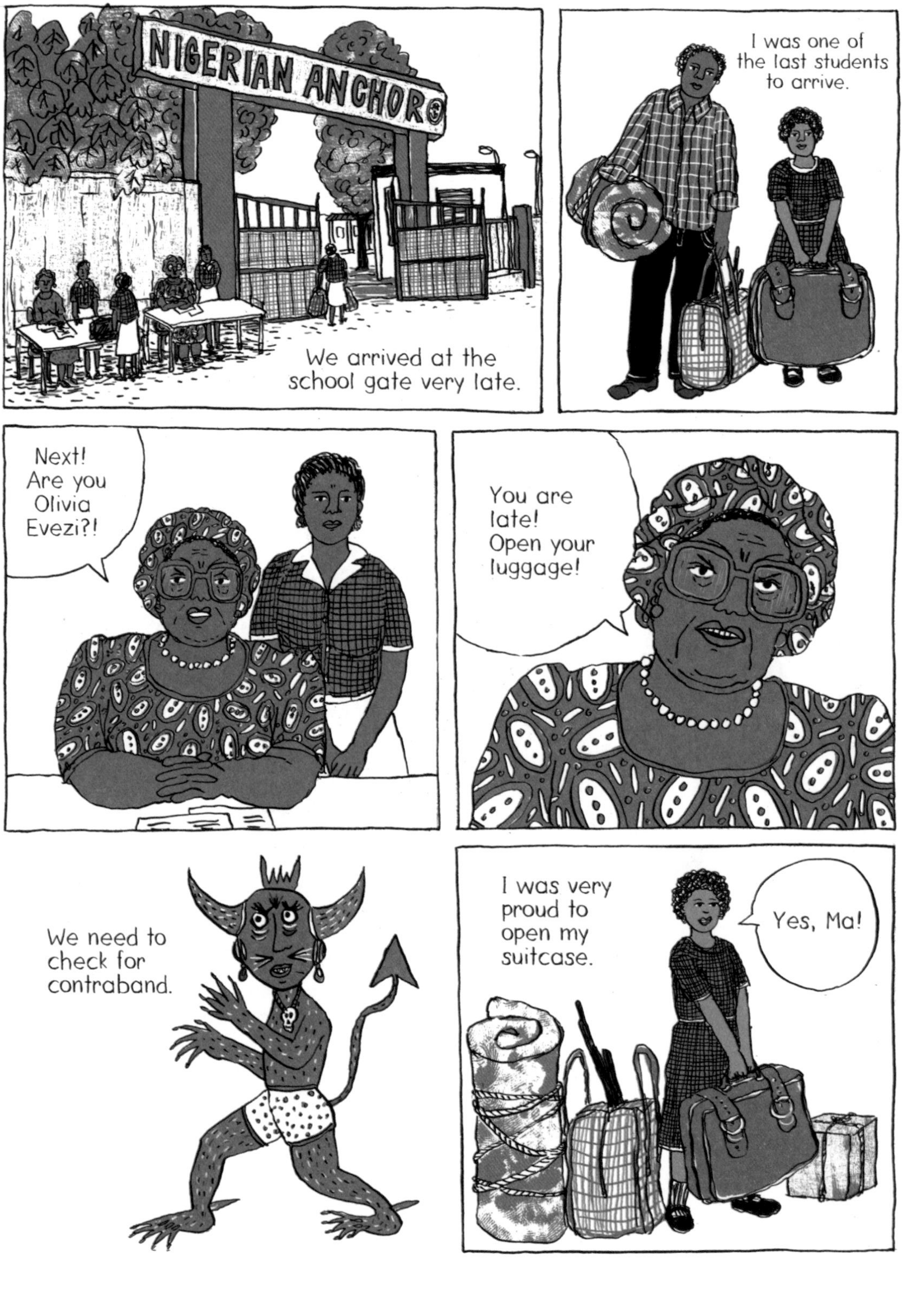
NIGERIAN ANCHOR
We arrived at the school gate very late.
I was one of the last students to arrive.
Next! Are you Olivia Evezi?!
You are late! Open your luggage!
We need to check for contraband.
I was very proud to open my suitcase.
Yes, Ma!

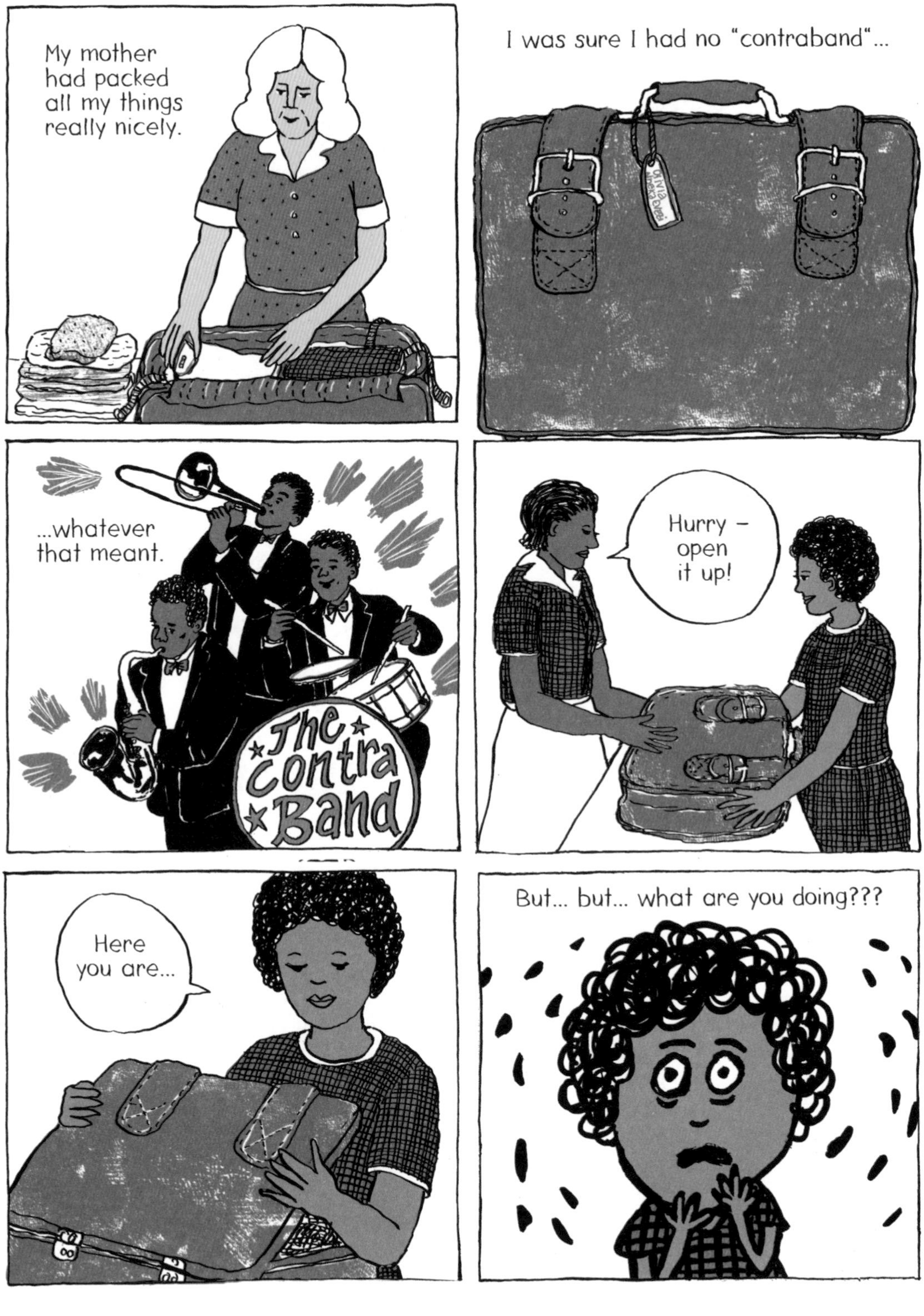
My mother had packed all my things really nicely.
I was sure I had no "contraband"...
...whatever that meant.
The Contra Band
Hurry – open it up!
Here you are...
But... but... what are you doing???

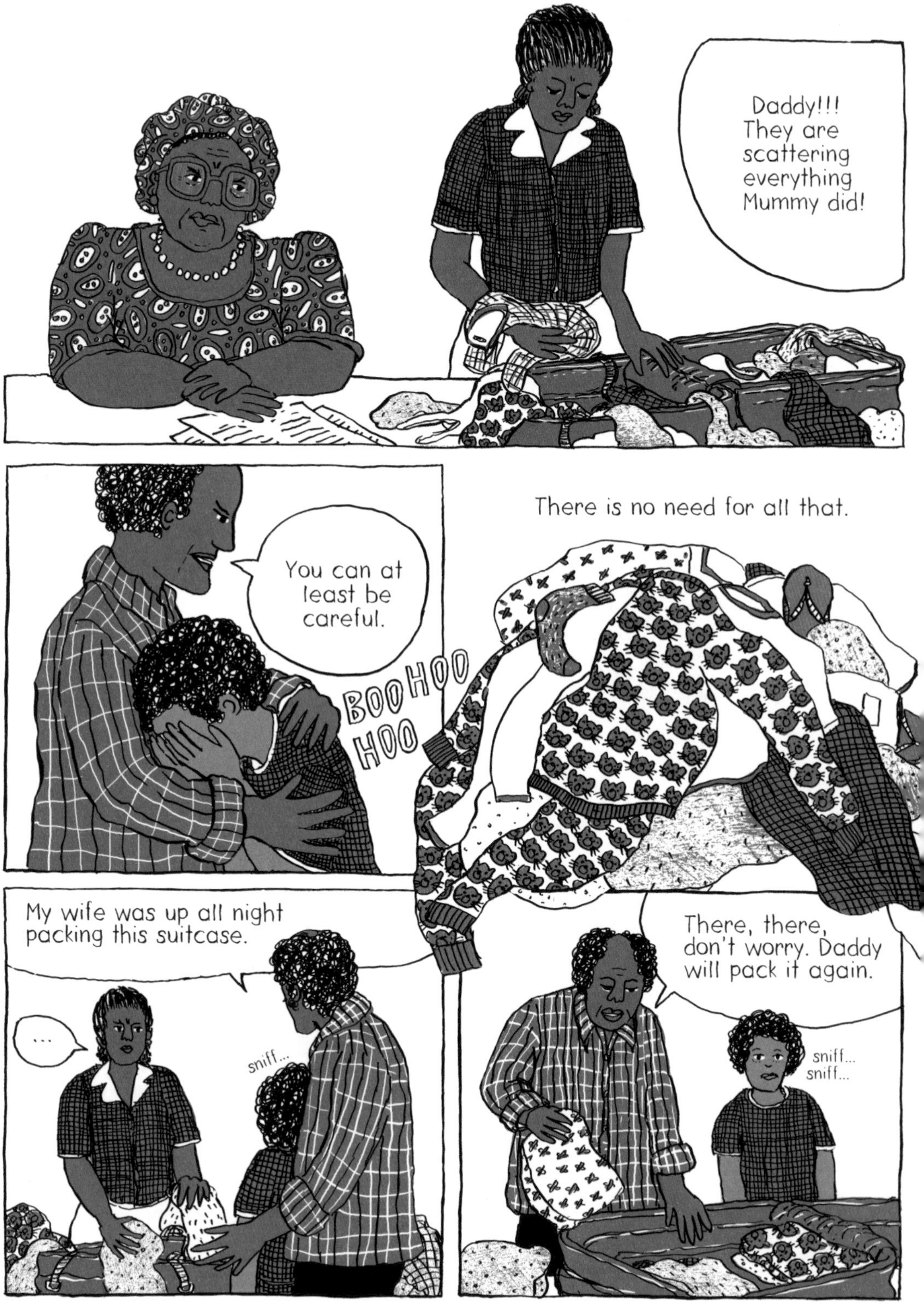
Daddy!!! They are scattering everything Mummy did!
You can at least be careful.
BOOHOO HOO
There is no need for all that.
My wife was up all night packing this suitcase.
...
sniff...
There, there, don't worry. Daddy will pack it again.
sniff... sniff...

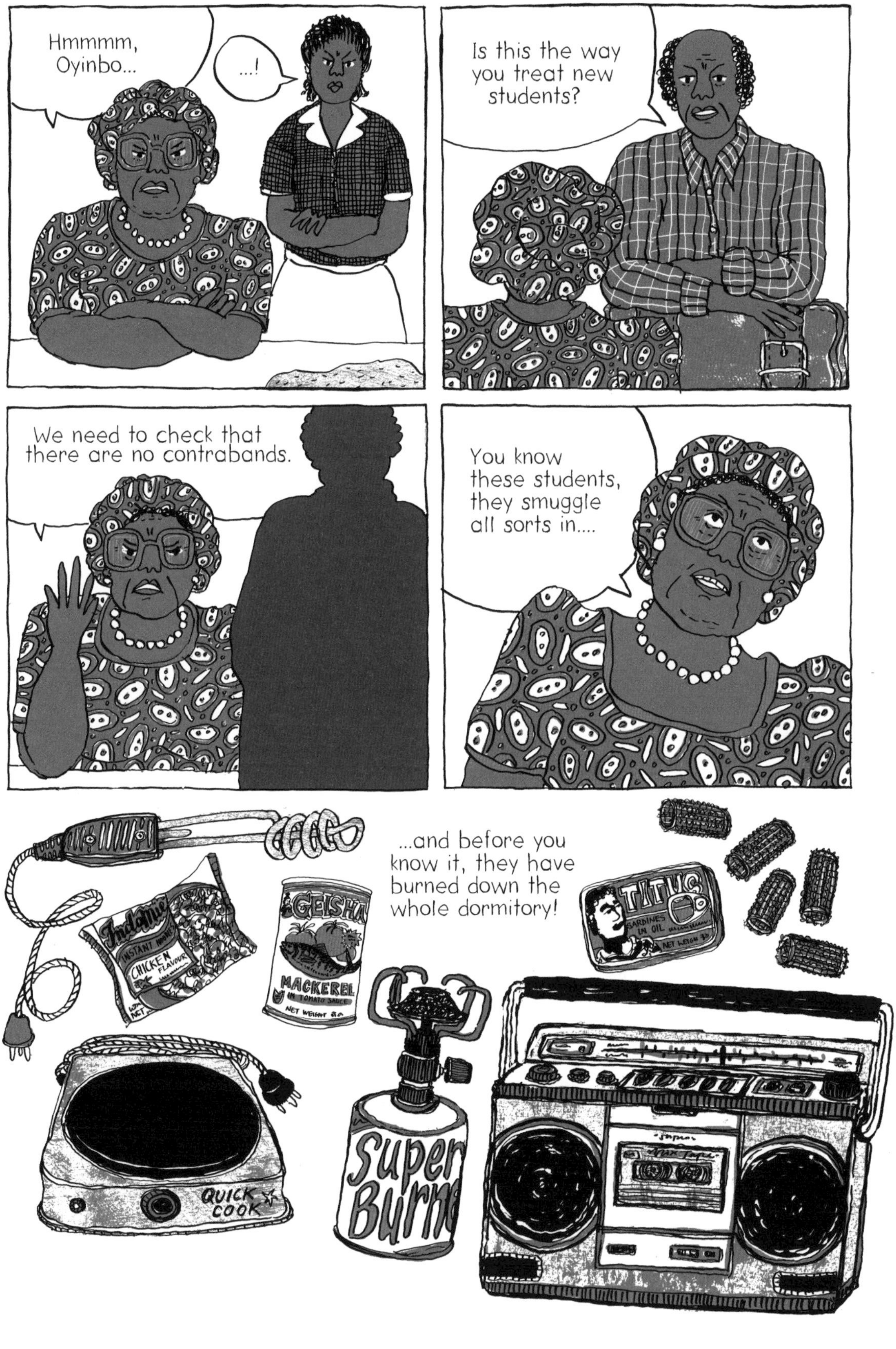
Hmmmm, Oyinbo...
...!
Is this the way you treat new students?
We need to check that there are no contrabands.
You know these students, they smuggle all sorts in....
...and before you know it, they have burned down the whole dormitory!
INSTANT NOODLES
CHICKEN FLAVOUR
GEISHA
MACKEREL
IN TOMATO SAUCE
NET WEIGHT
TITUS
SARDINES IN OIL
QUICK COOK
Super Burne

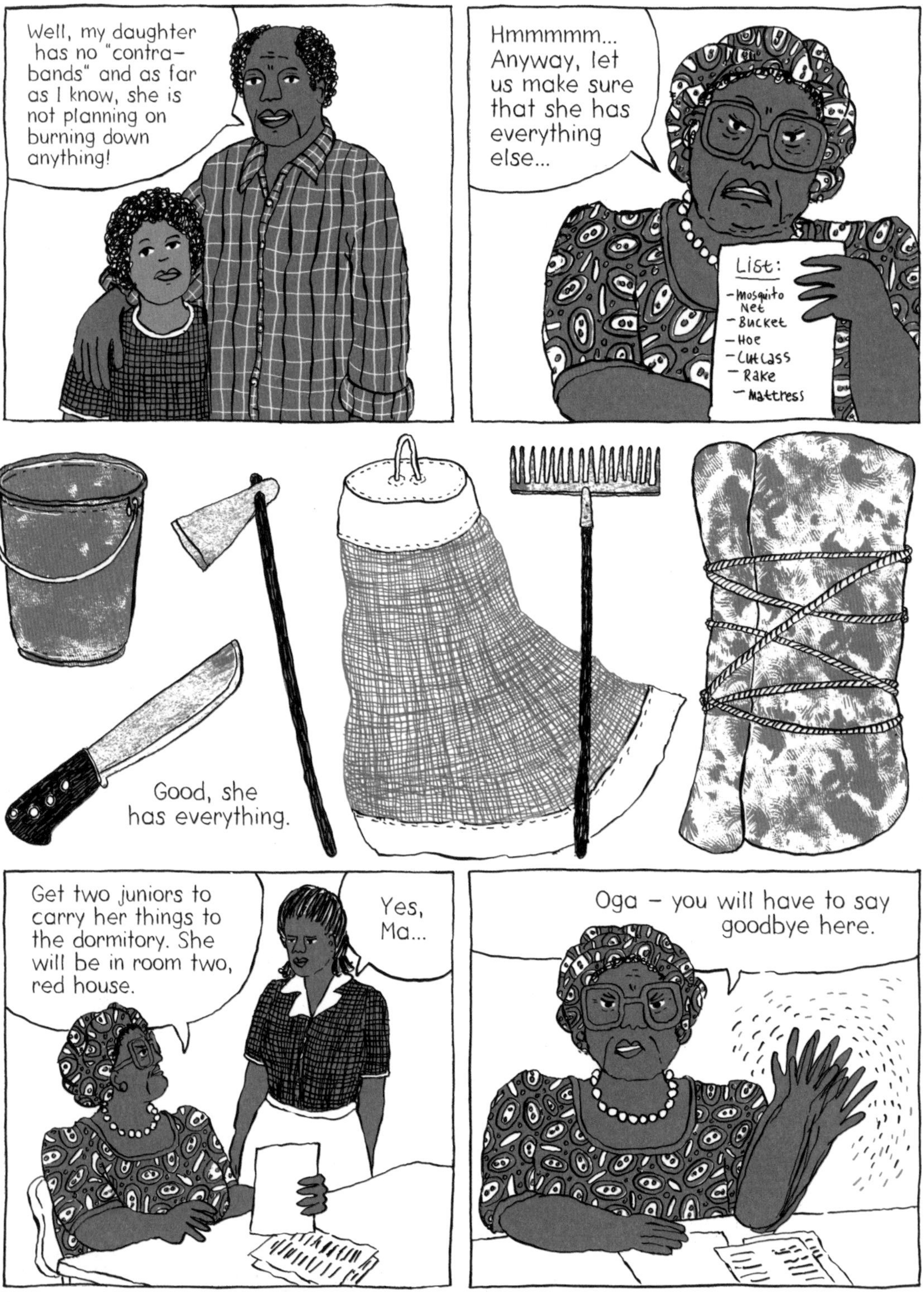
Well, my daughter has no "contra-bands" and as far as I know, she is not planning on burning down anything!
Hmmmmm... Anyway, let us make sure that she has everything else...
List:
-Mosquito Net
-Bucket
-Hoe
-Cutlass
-Rake
-Mattress
Good, she has everything.
Get two juniors to carry her things to the dormitory. She will be in room two, red house.
Yes, Ma...
Oga – you will have to say goodbye here.

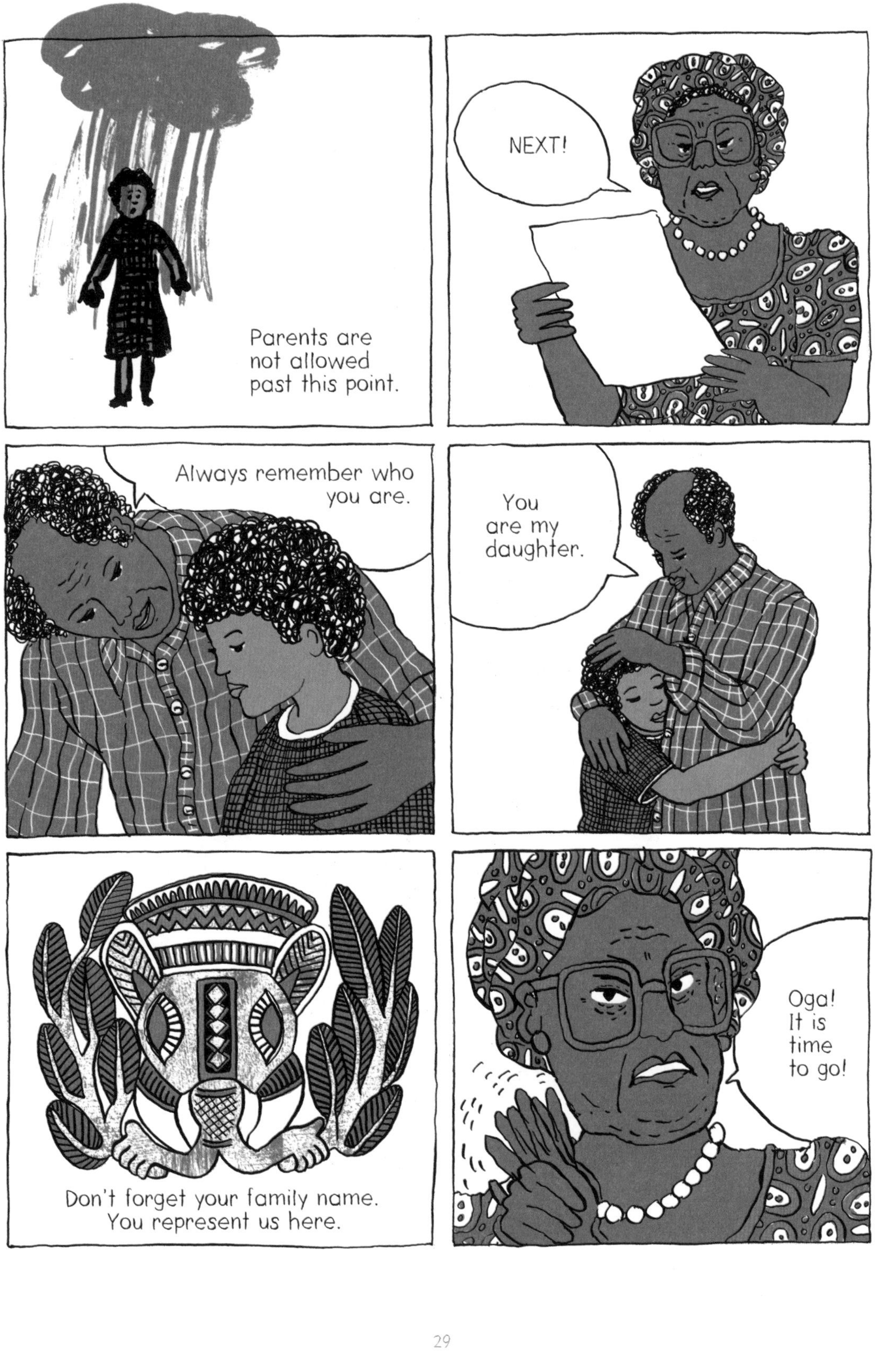
Parents are not allowed past this point.
NEXT!
Always remember who you are.
You are my daughter.
Don't forget your family name. You represent us here.
Oga! It is time to go!

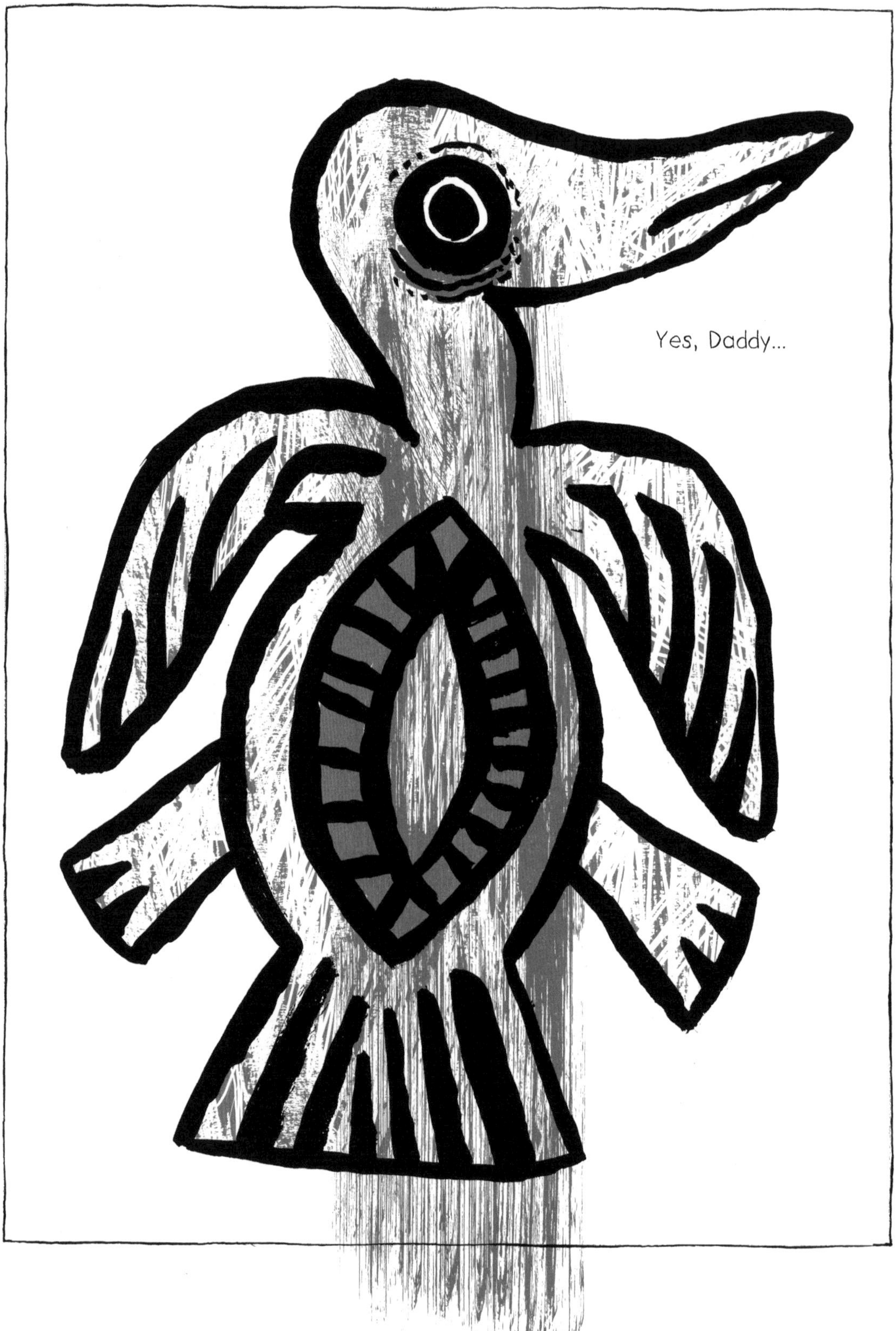
Yes, Daddy...

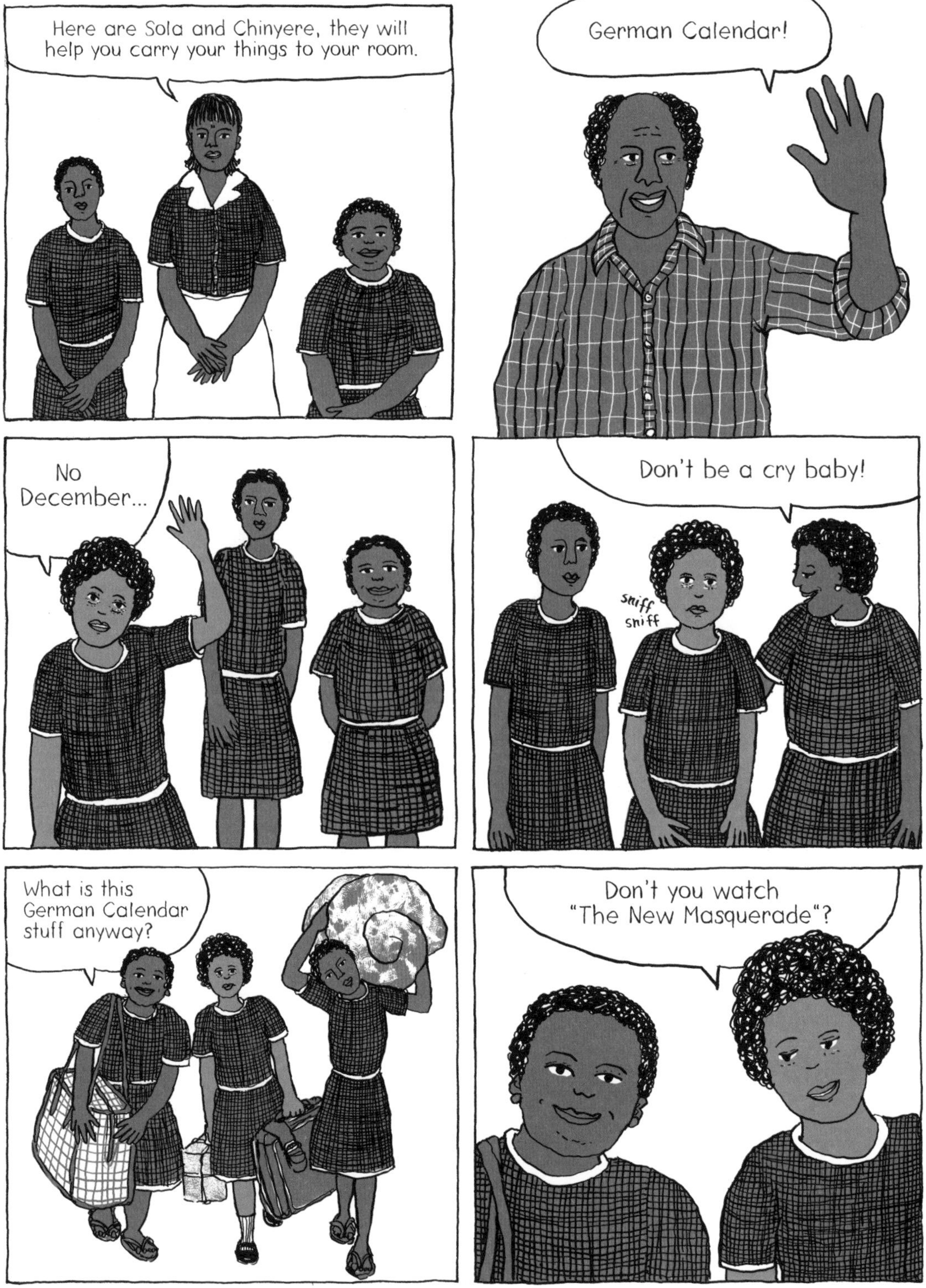
Here are Sola and Chinyere, they will help you carry your things to your room.
German Calendar!
No December...
Don't be a cry baby!
sniff sniff
What is this German Calendar stuff anyway?
Don't you watch "The New Masquerade"?

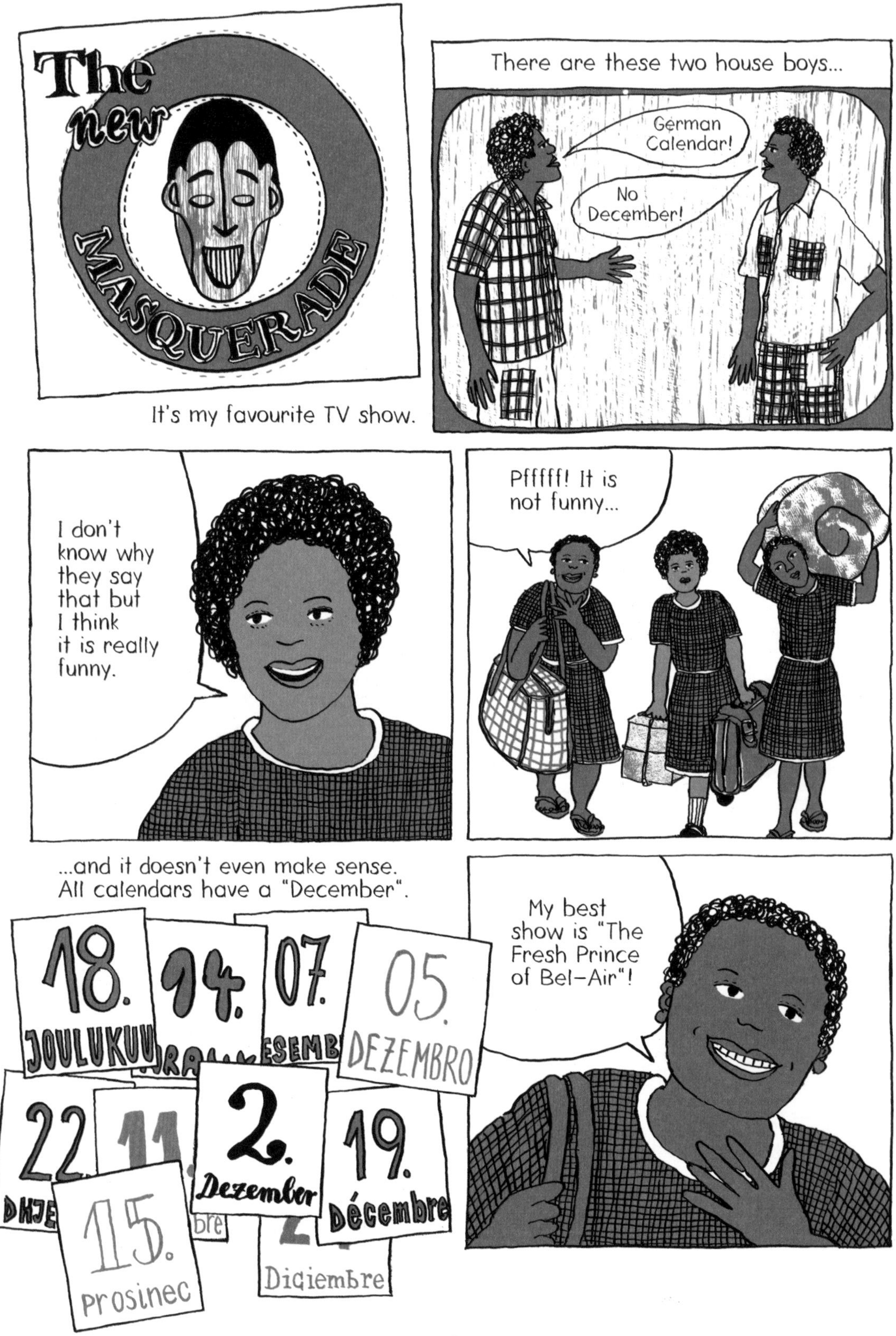
The new MASQUERADE
It's my favourite TV show.
There are these two house boys...
German Calendar!
No December!
I don't know why they say that but I think it is really funny.
Pffffff! It is not funny...
...and it doesn't even make sense. All calendars have a "December".
18. JOULUKUU
07.
05. DEZEMBRO
22.
2. Dezember
19. décembre
15. prosinec
Diciembre
My best show is "The Fresh Prince of Bel-Air"!

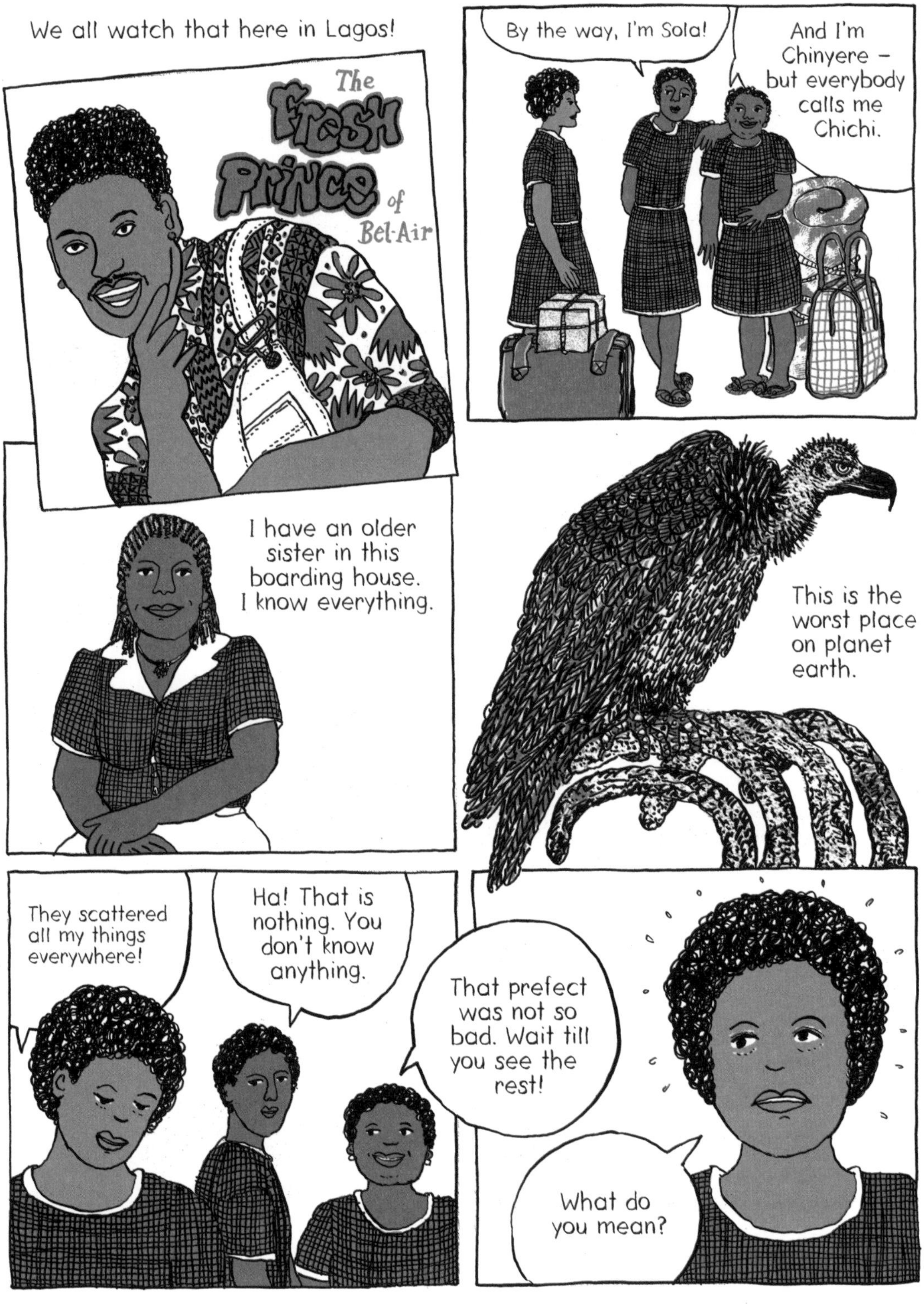
We all watch that here in Lagos!
The Fresh Prince of Bel-Air
By the way, I'm Sola!
And I'm Chinyere – but everybody calls me Chichi.
I have an older sister in this boarding house. I know everything.
This is the worst place on planet earth.
They scattered all my things everywhere!
Ha! That is nothing. You don't know anything.
That prefect was not so bad. Wait till you see the rest!
What do you mean?

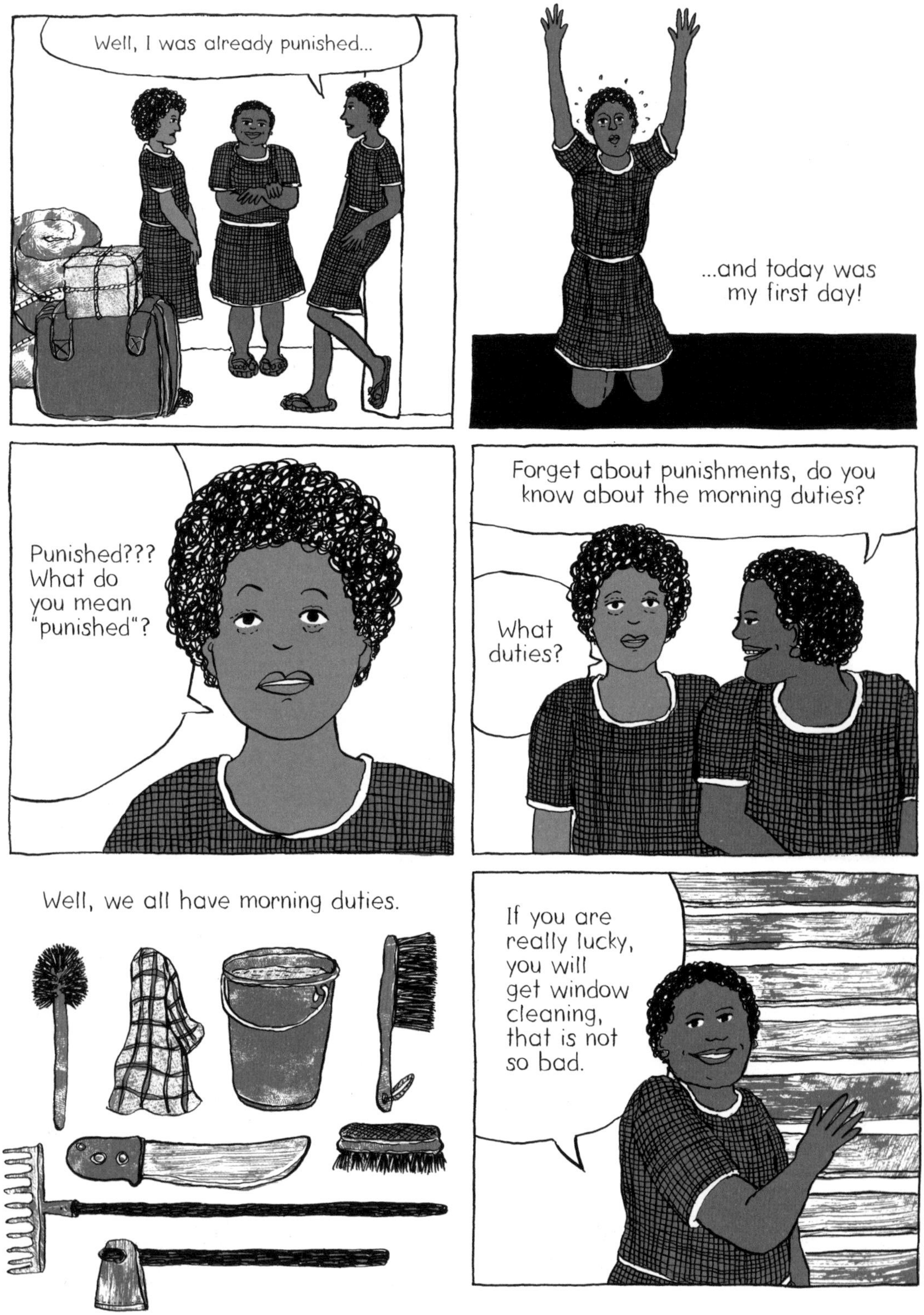
Well, I was already punished...
...and today was my first day!
Punished??? What do you mean "punished"?
Forget about punishments, do you know about the morning duties?
What duties?
Well, we all have morning duties.
If you are really lucky, you will get window cleaning, that is not so bad.

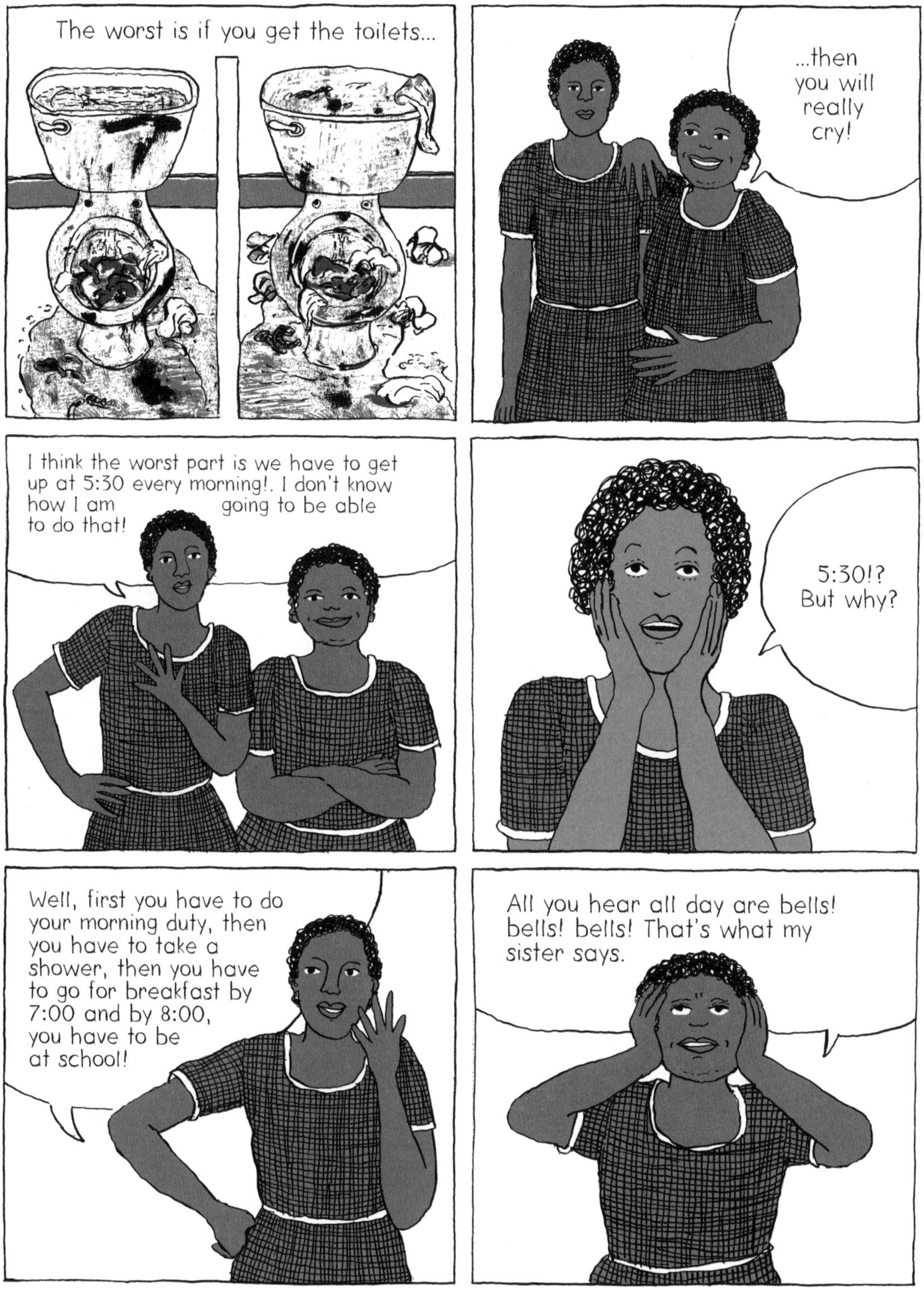
The worst is if you get the toilets...
...then you will really cry!
I think the worst part is we have to get up at 5:30 every morning!. I don't know how I am going to be able to do that!
5:30!? But why?
Well, first you have to do your morning duty, then you have to take a shower, then you have to go for breakfast by 7:00 and by 8:00, you have to be at school!
All you hear all day are bells! bells! bells! That's what my sister says.

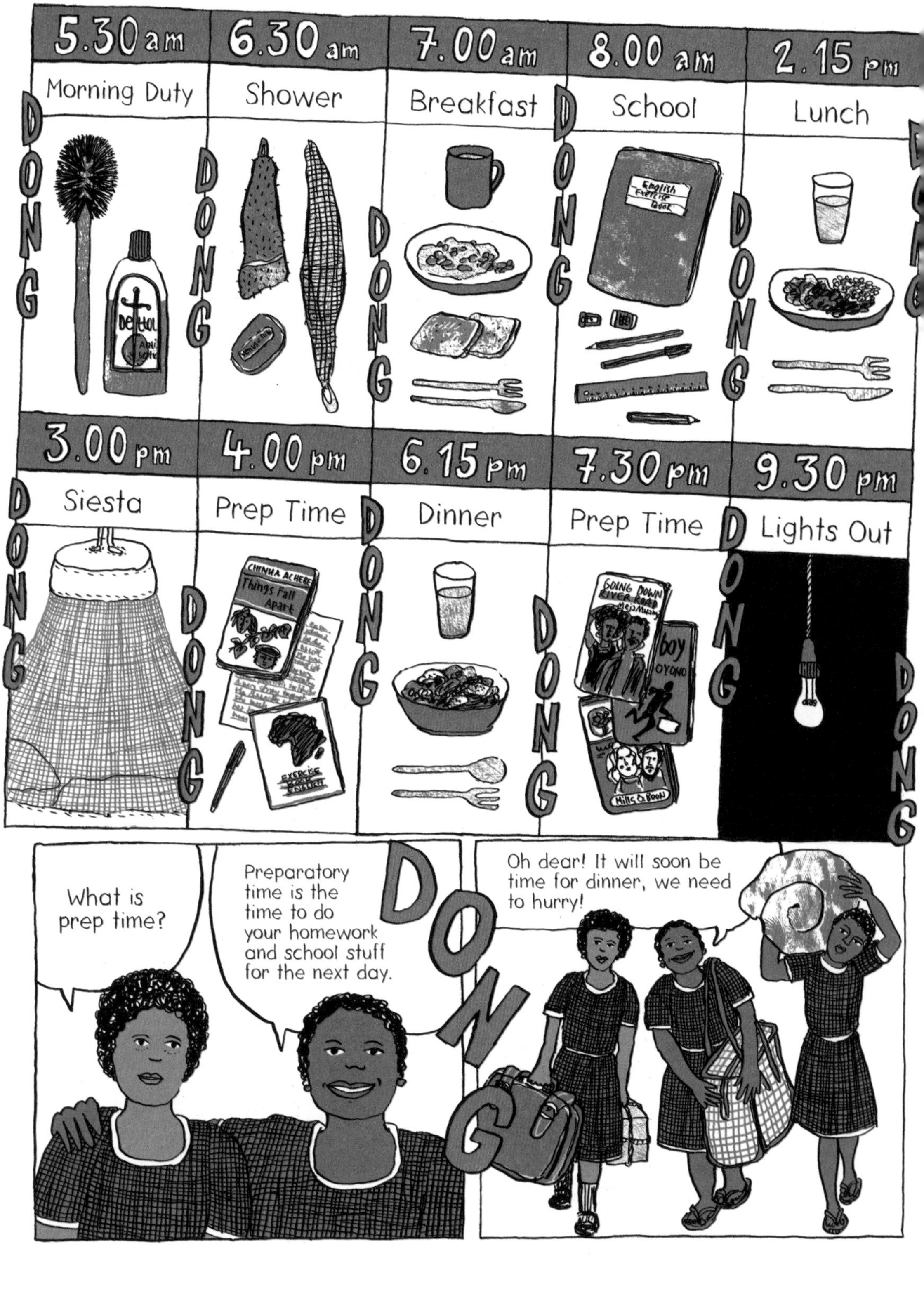

5.30 am
Morning Duty
DONG
6.30 am
Shower
DONG
7.00 am
Breakfast
DONG
8.00 am
School
English Exercise Book
DONG
2.15 pm
Lunch
DONG
3.00 pm
Siesta
DONG
4.00 pm
Prep Time
CHINUA ACHEBE
Things Fall Apart
Exercise Book English
DONG
6.15 pm
Dinner
DONG
7.30 pm
Prep Time
GOING DOWN RIVER ROAD
Meja Mwangi
boy
OYONO
Mills & Boon
DONG
9.30 pm
Lights Out
DONG
What is prep time?
Preparatory time is the time to do your homework and school stuff for the next day.
DONG
Oh dear! It will soon be time for dinner, we need to hurry!

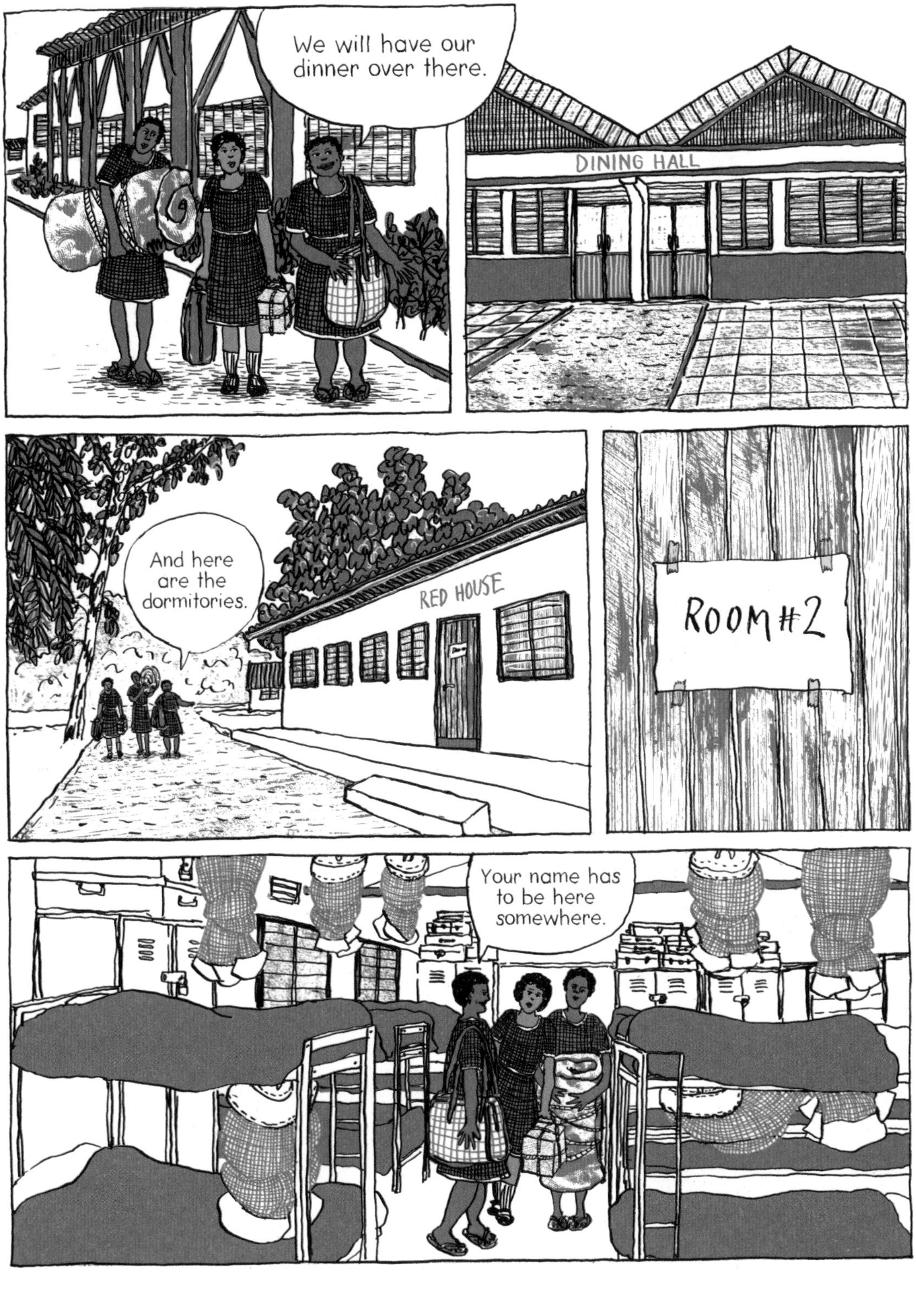

We will have our dinner over there.
DINING HALL
And here are the dormitories.
RED HOUSE
ROOM #2
Your name has to be here somewhere.

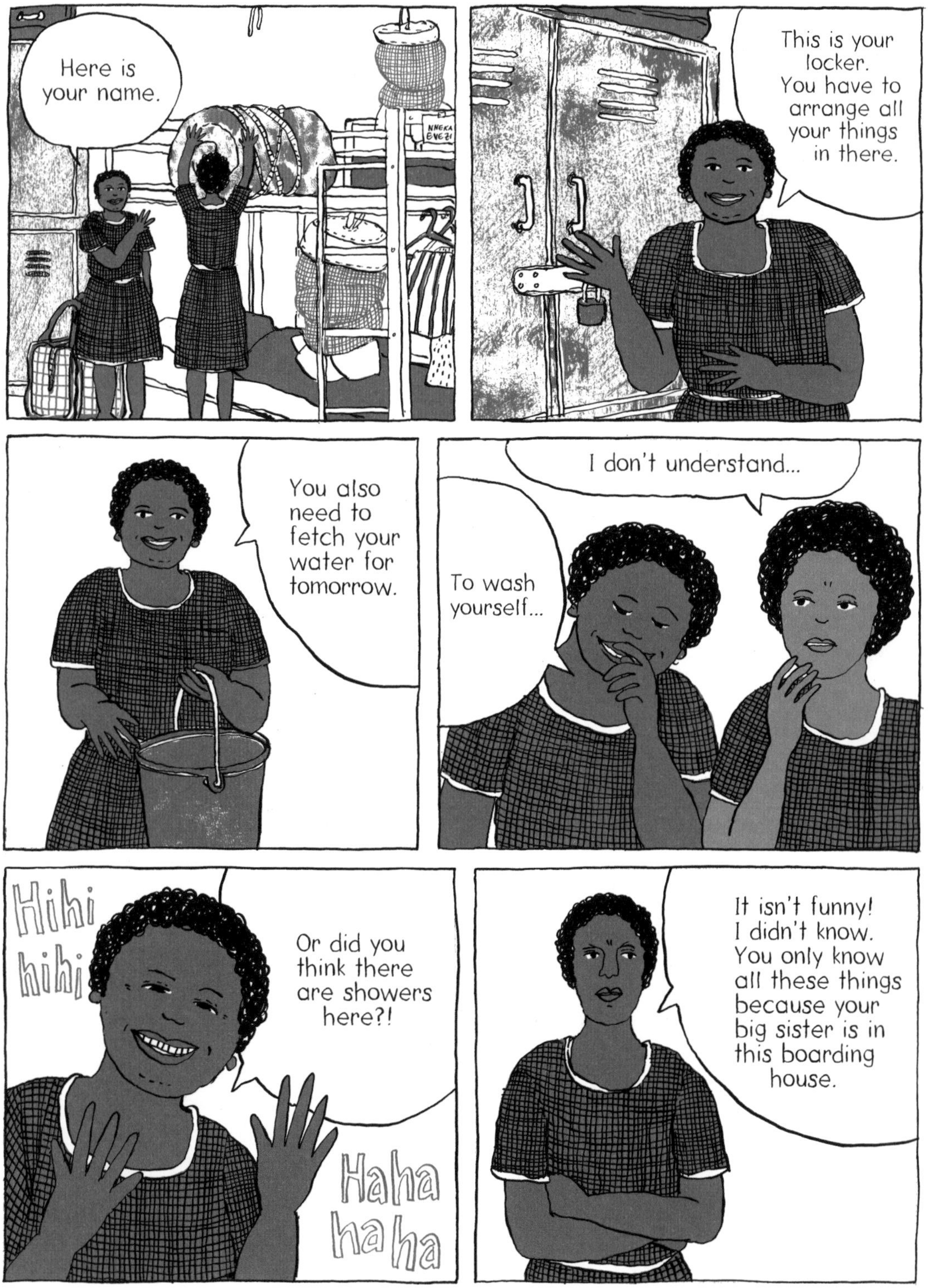
Here is your name.
NNEKA EVEZI
This is your locker. You have to arrange all your things in there.
You also need to fetch your water for tomorrow.
I don't understand...
To wash yourself...
Hihi hihi
Or did you think there are showers here?!
Haha haha
It isn't funny! I didn't know. You only know all these things because your big sister is in this boarding house.

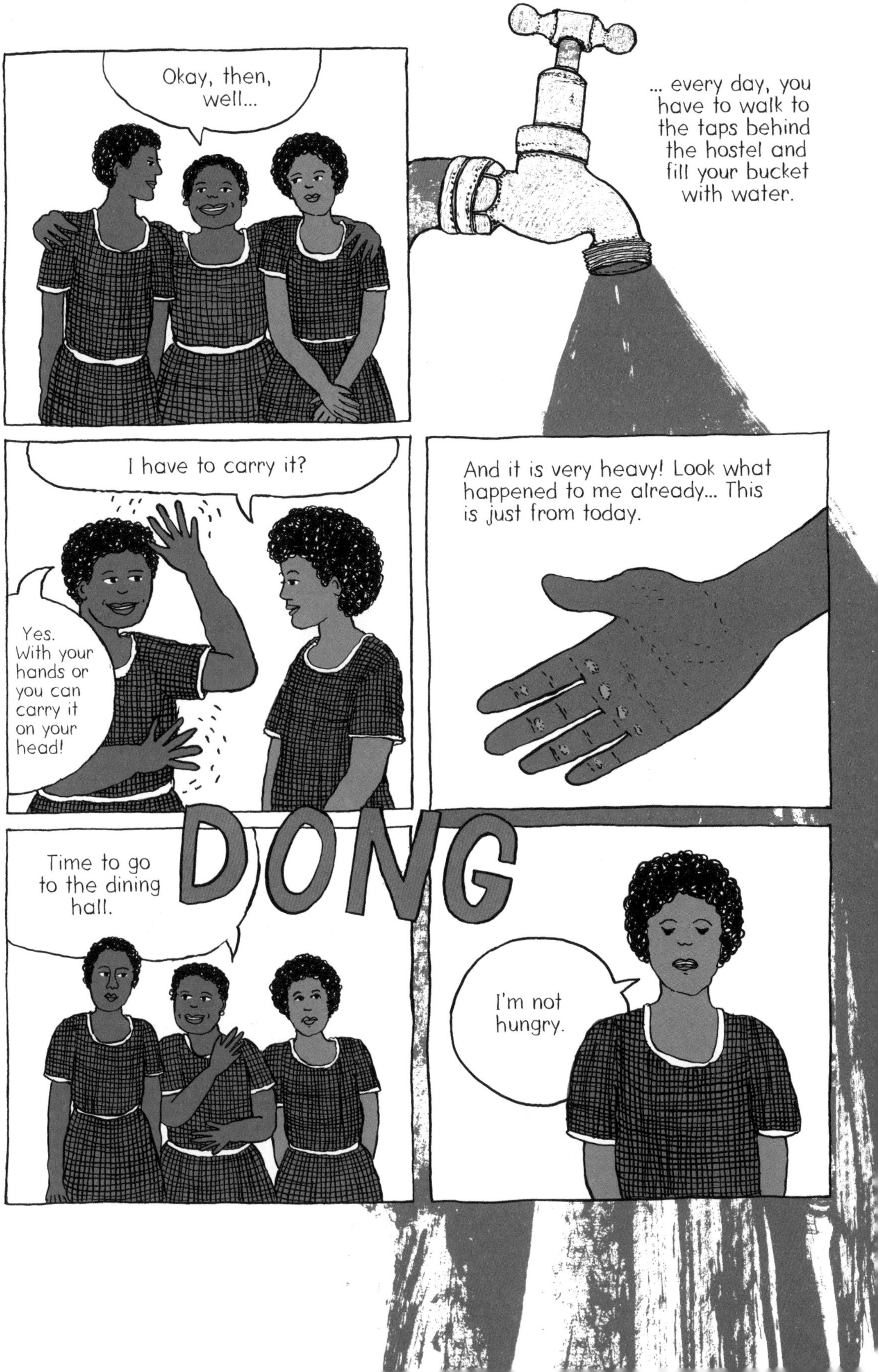
Okay, then, well...
... every day, you have to walk to the taps behind the hostel and fill your bucket with water.
I have to carry it?
Yes. With your hands or you can carry it on your head!
And it is very heavy! Look what happened to me already... This is just from today.
DONG
Time to go to the dining hall.
I'm not hungry.

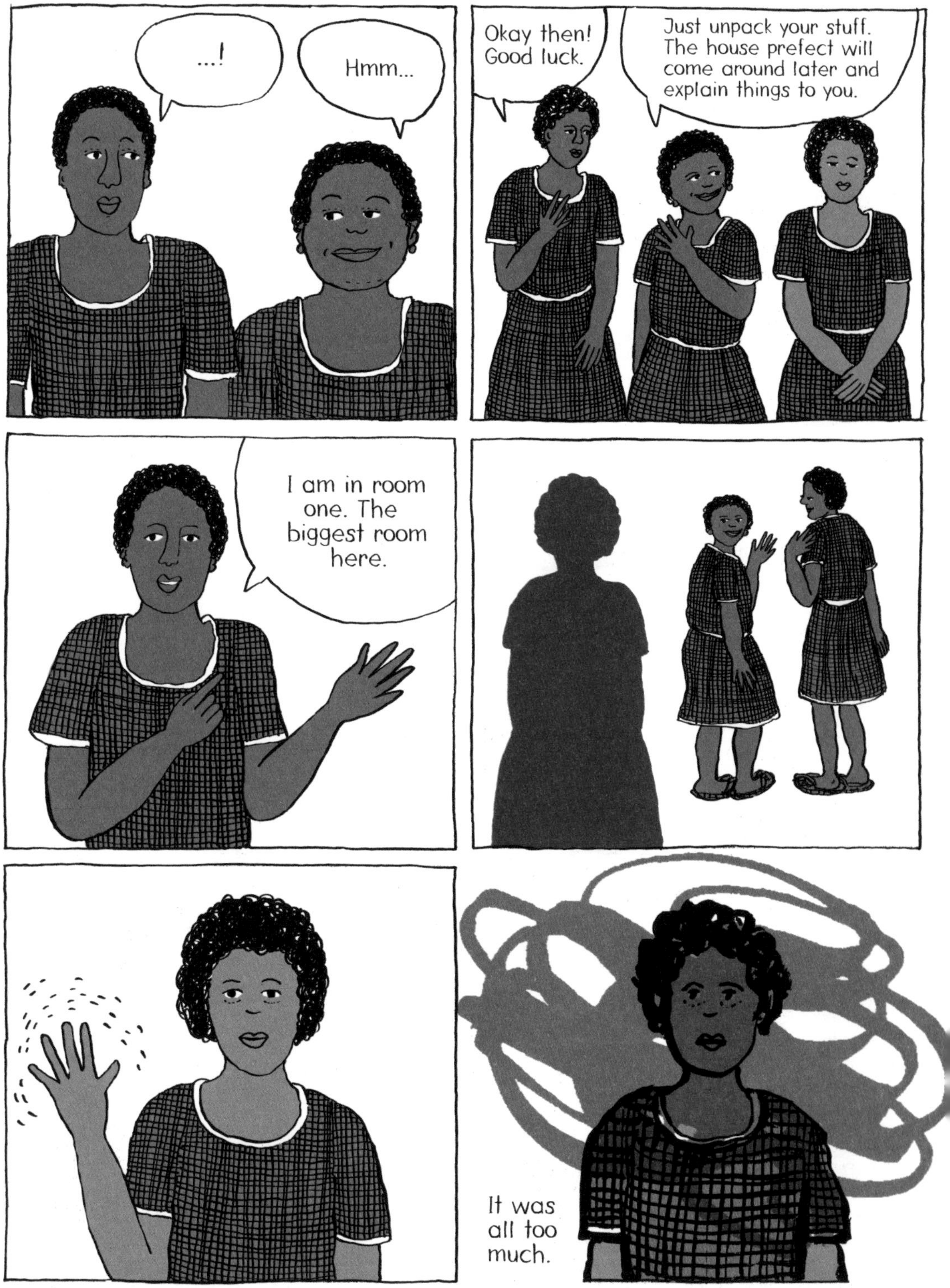

...!
Hmm...
Okay then! Good luck.
Just unpack your stuff. The house prefect will come around later and explain things to you.
I am in room one. The biggest room here.
It was all too much.

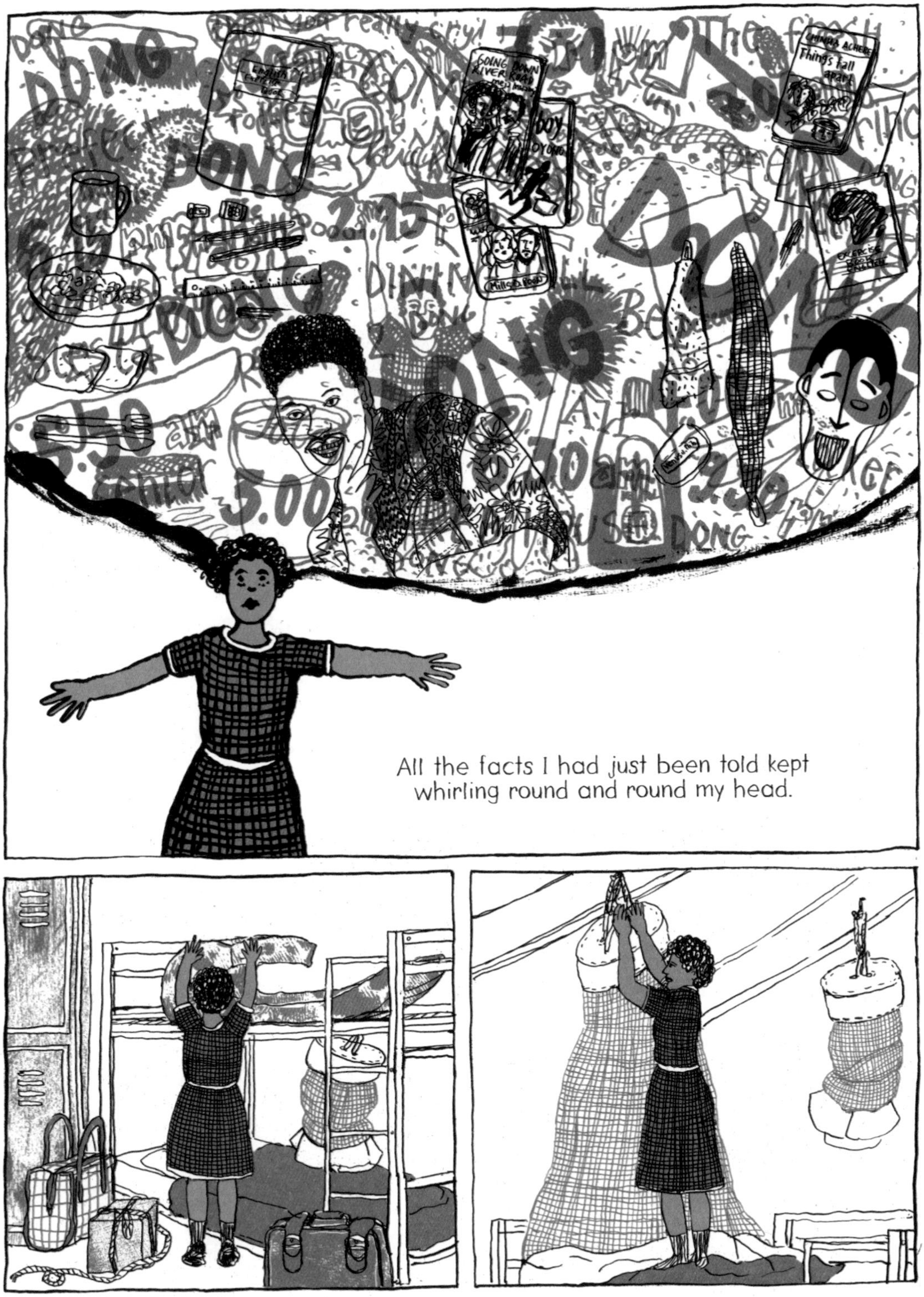
DONG
All the facts I had just been told kept whirling round and round my head.

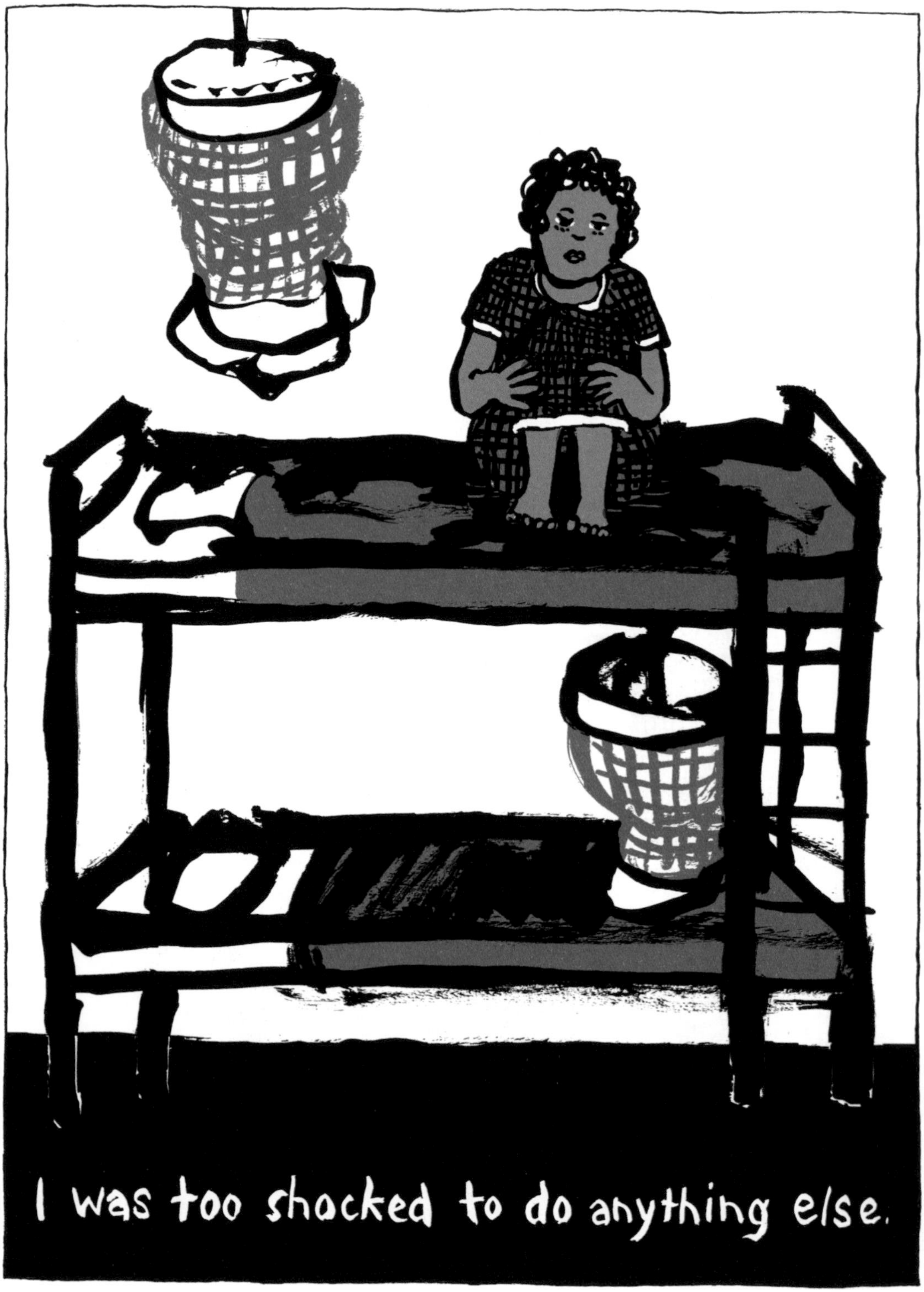
I was too shocked to do anything else.

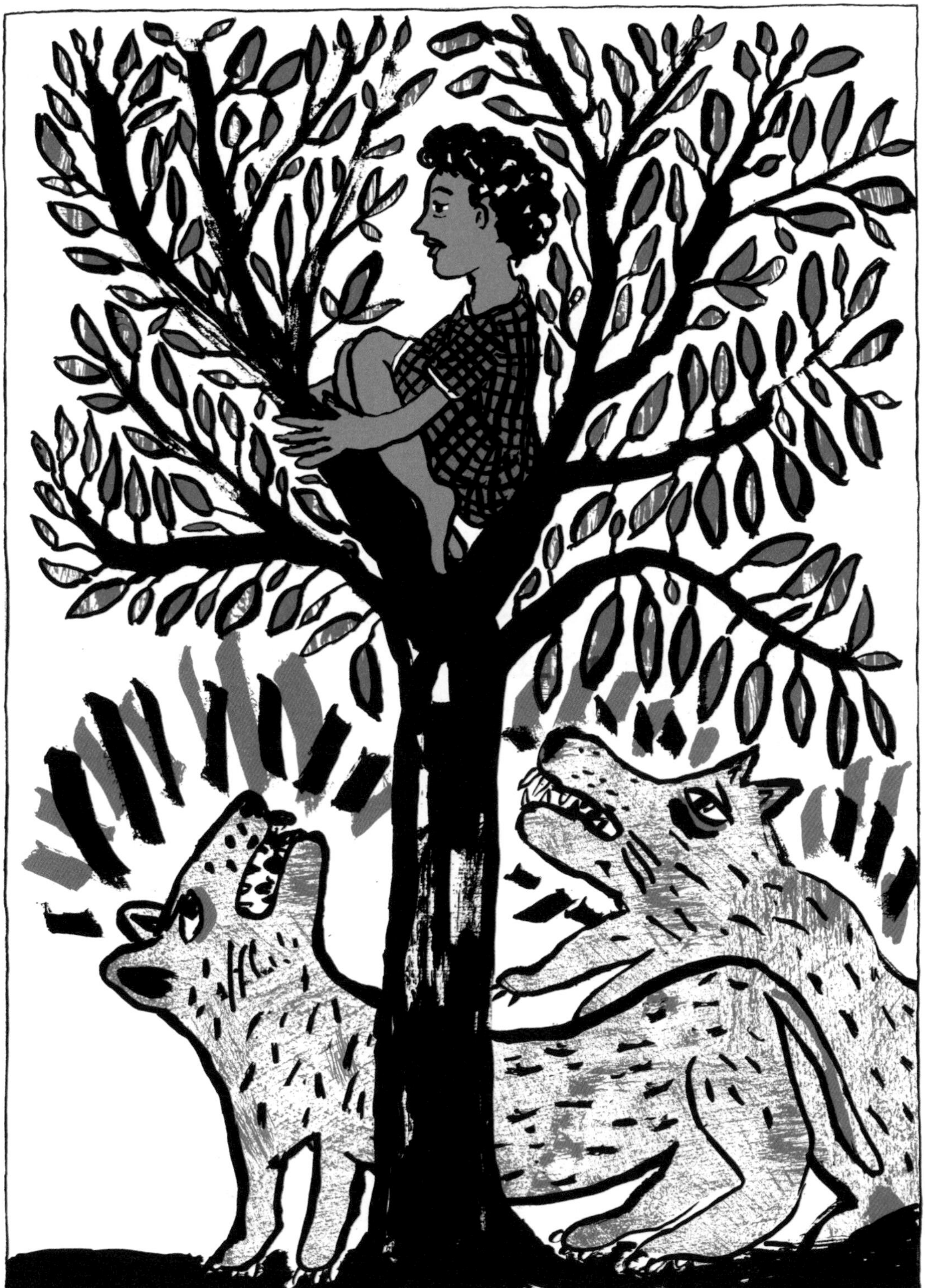

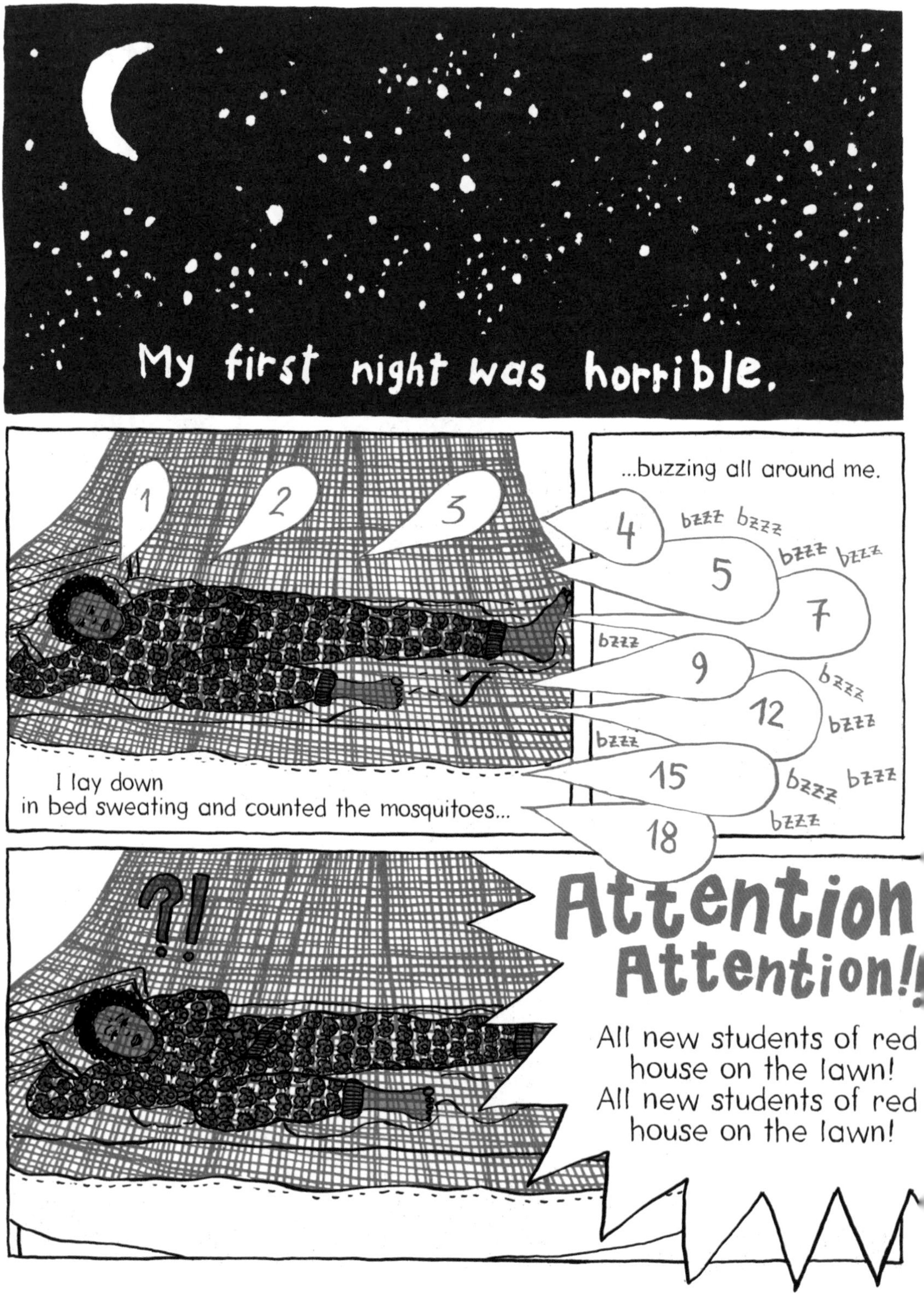

My first night was horrible.
I lay down in bed sweating and counted the mosquitoes...
1
2
3
...buzzing all around me.
4
bzzz bzzz
5
bzzz bzzz
7
bzzz
9
bzzz
12
bzzz
bzzz
15
bzzz bzzz
18
bzzz
?!
Attention Attention!!
All new students of red house on the lawn!
All new students of red house on the lawn!

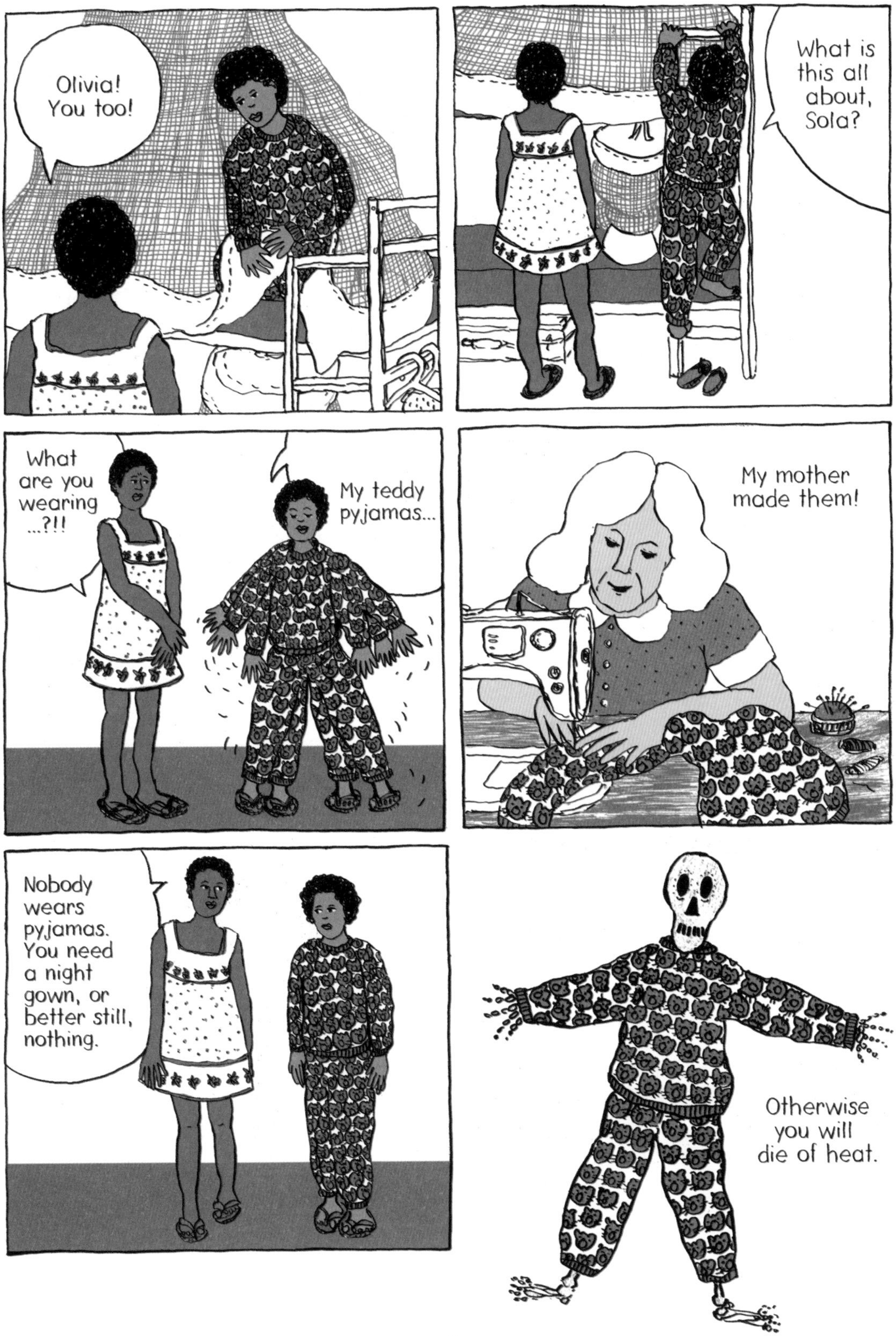
Olivia! You too!
What is this all about, Sola?
What are you wearing ...?!!
My teddy pyjamas...
My mother made them!
Nobody wears pyjamas. You need a night gown, or better still, nothing.
Otherwise you will die of heat.

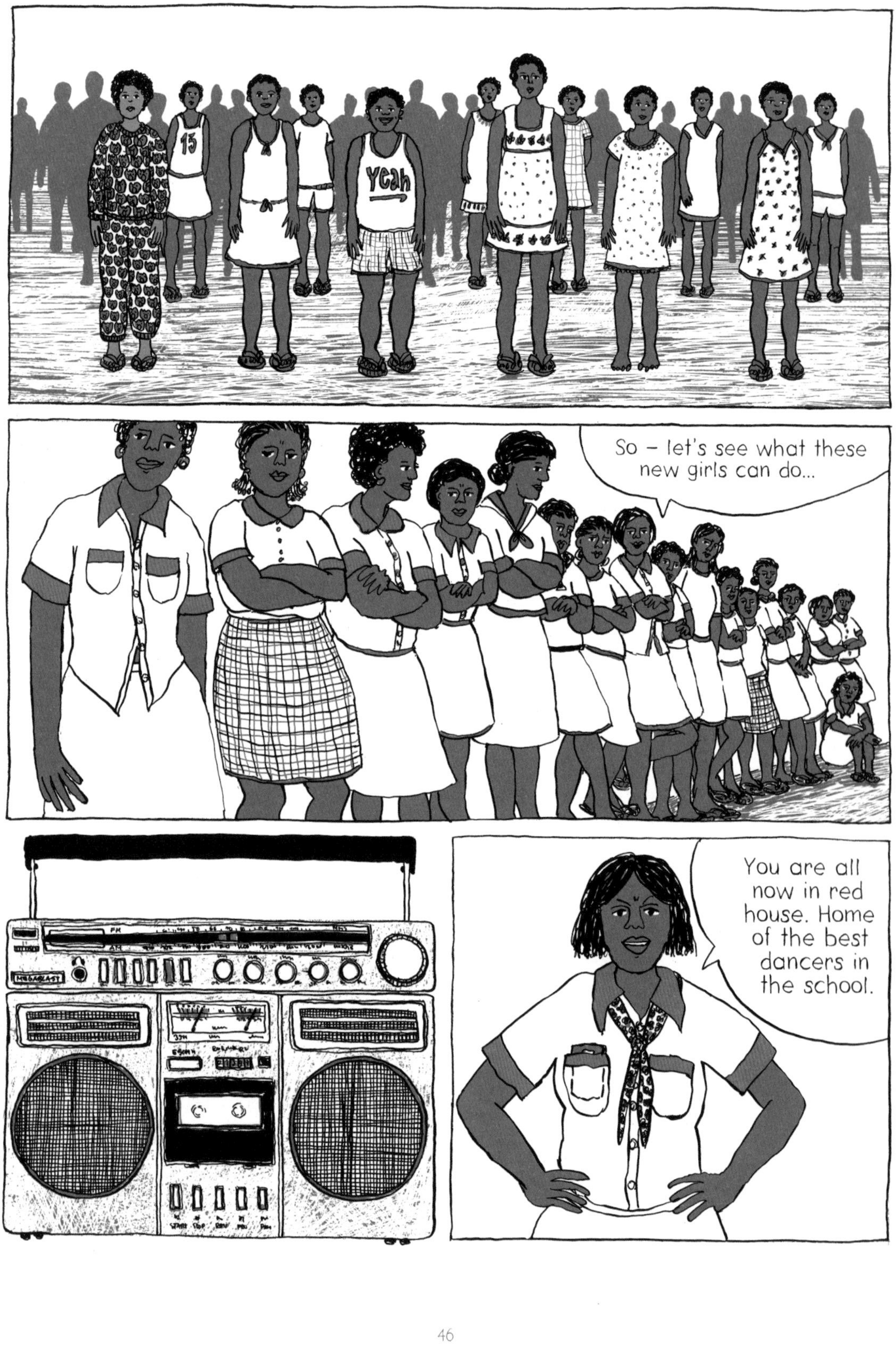
So – let's see what these new girls can do...
You are all now in red house. Home of the best dancers in the school.

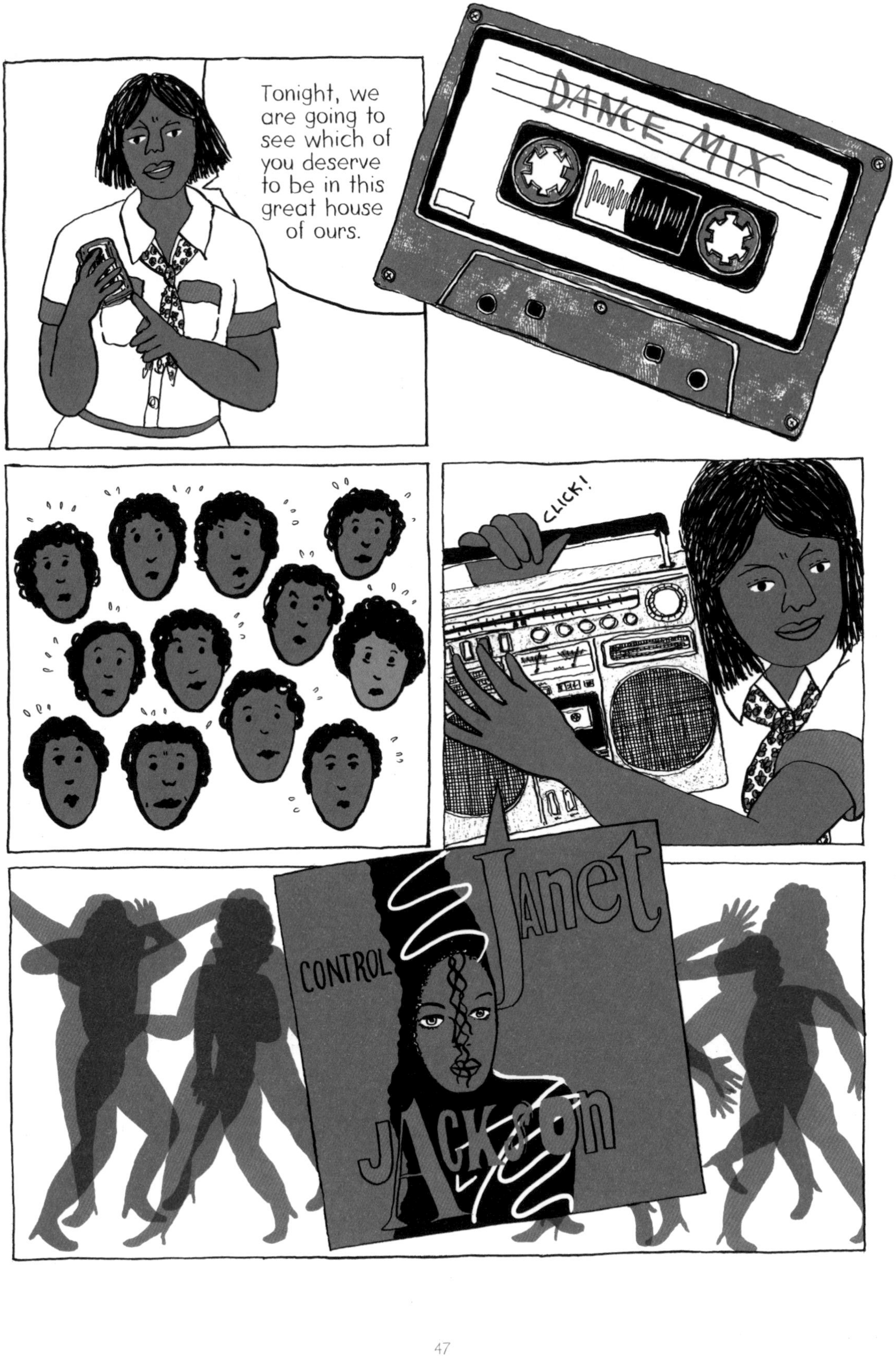
Tonight, we are going to see which of you deserve to be in this great house of ours.
DANCE MIX
CLICK!
CONTROL
Janet
JACKSON

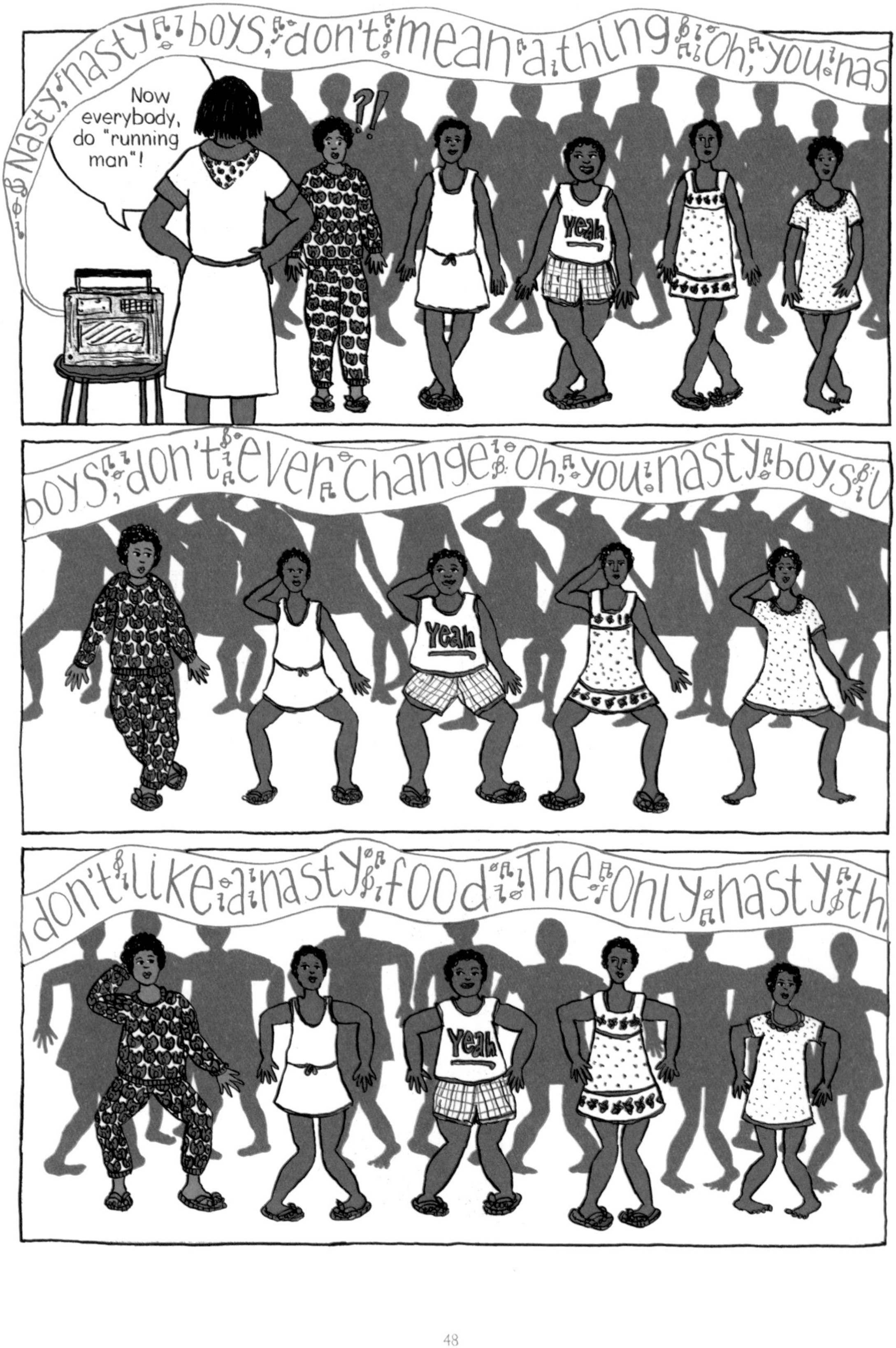

Nasty, nasty boys, don't mean a thing Oh, you nas
Now everybody, do "running man"!
?!
Yeah
boys, don't ever change Oh, you nasty boys
Yeah
don't like a nasty food The only nasty th
Yeah

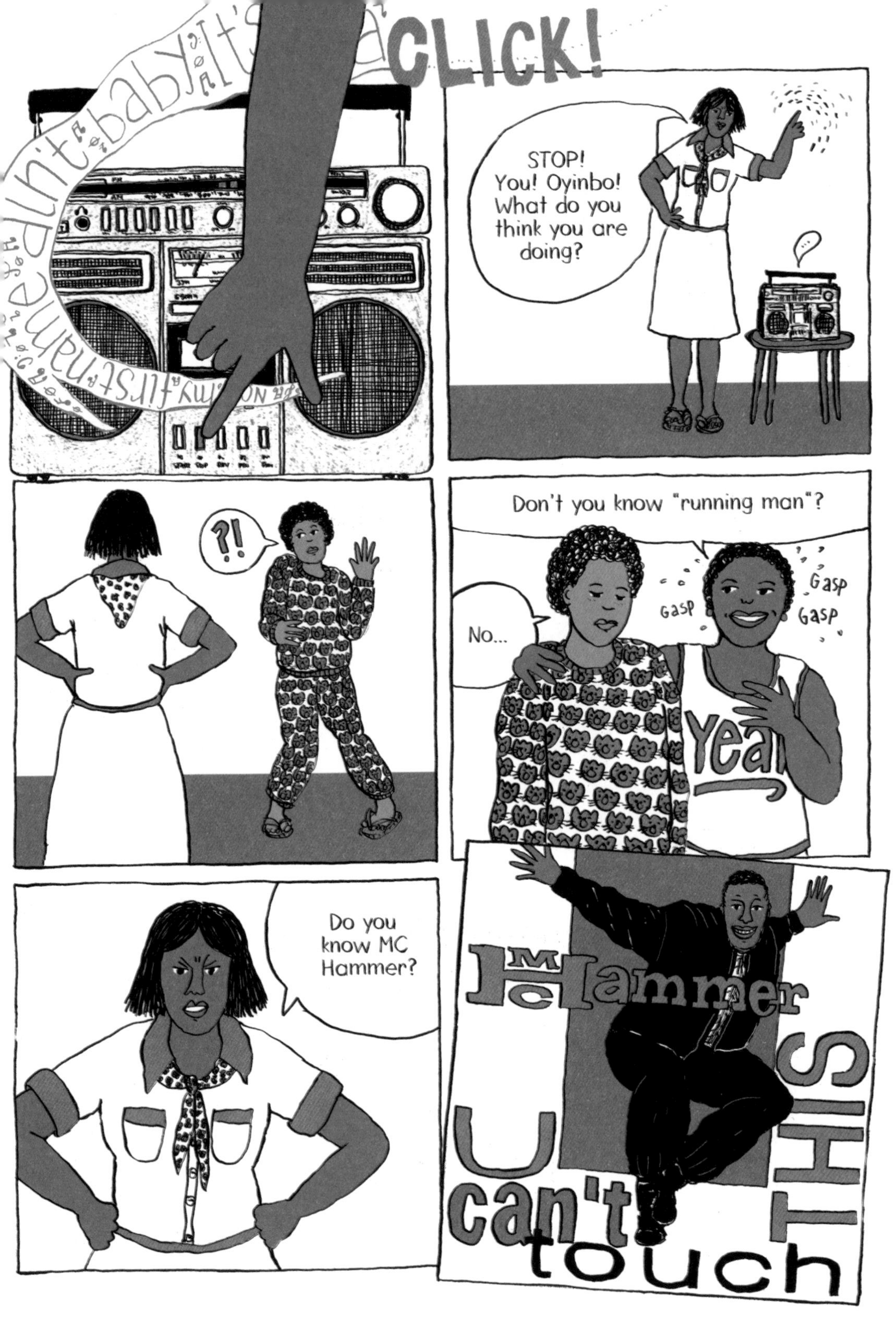
No my first name ain't baby It's
CLICK!
STOP! You! Oyinbo! What do you think you are doing?
?!
Don't you know "running man"?
No...
Gasp
Gasp
Gasp
Yea
Do you know MC Hammer?
MC Hammer
U can't touch THIS

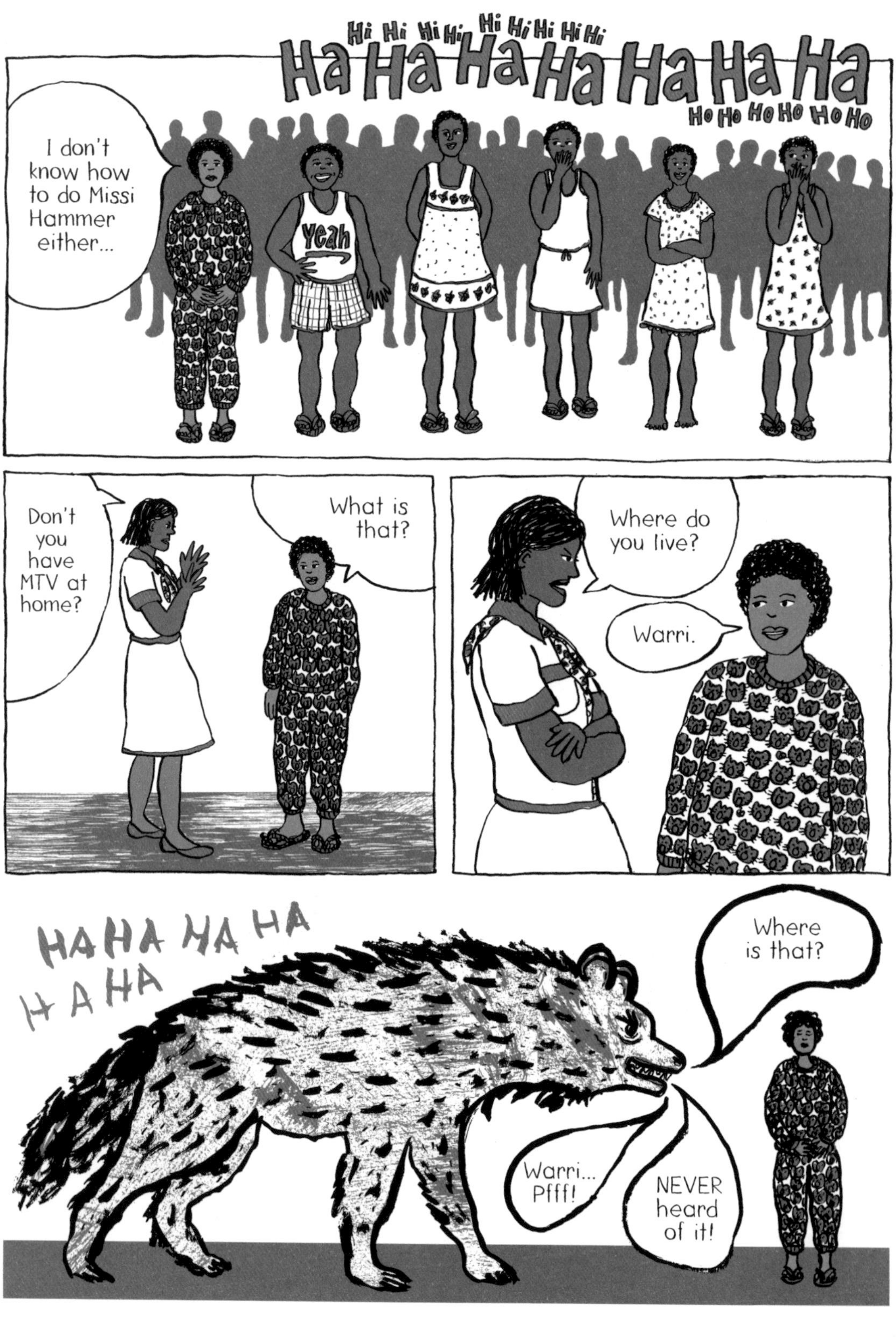
Hi Hi Hi Hi Hi Hi Hi Hi Hi Hi
Ha Ha Ha Ha Ha Ha Ha Ha Ha Ha
Ho Ho Ho Ho Ho Ho Ho
I don't know how to do Missi Hammer either...
Yeah
Don't you have MTV at home?
What is that?
Where do you live?
Warri.
HA HA HA HA HA
H A HA
Where is that?
Warri... Pfff!
NEVER heard of it!

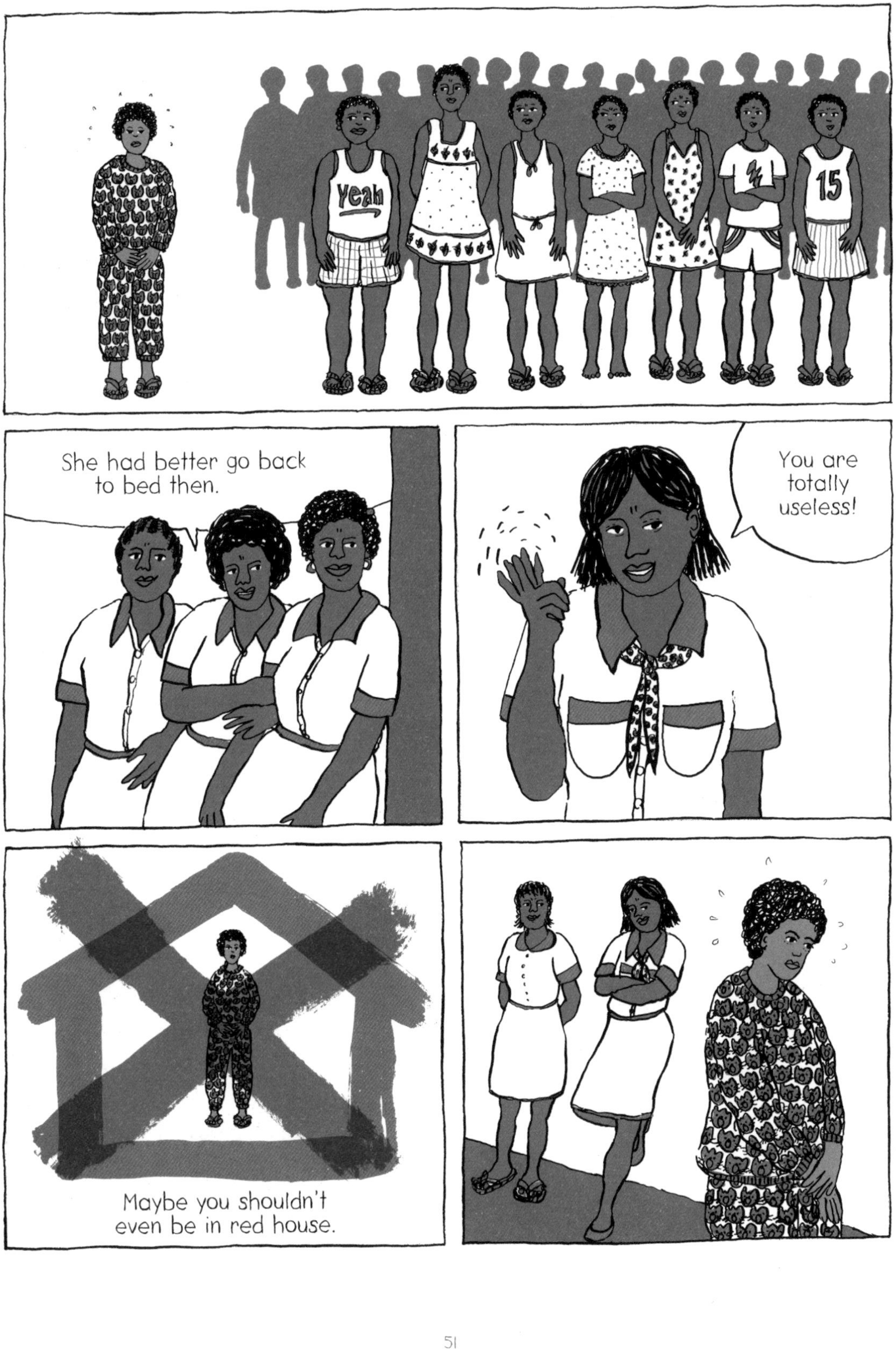
yeah
15
She had better go back to bed then.
You are totally useless!
Maybe you shouldn't even be in red house.

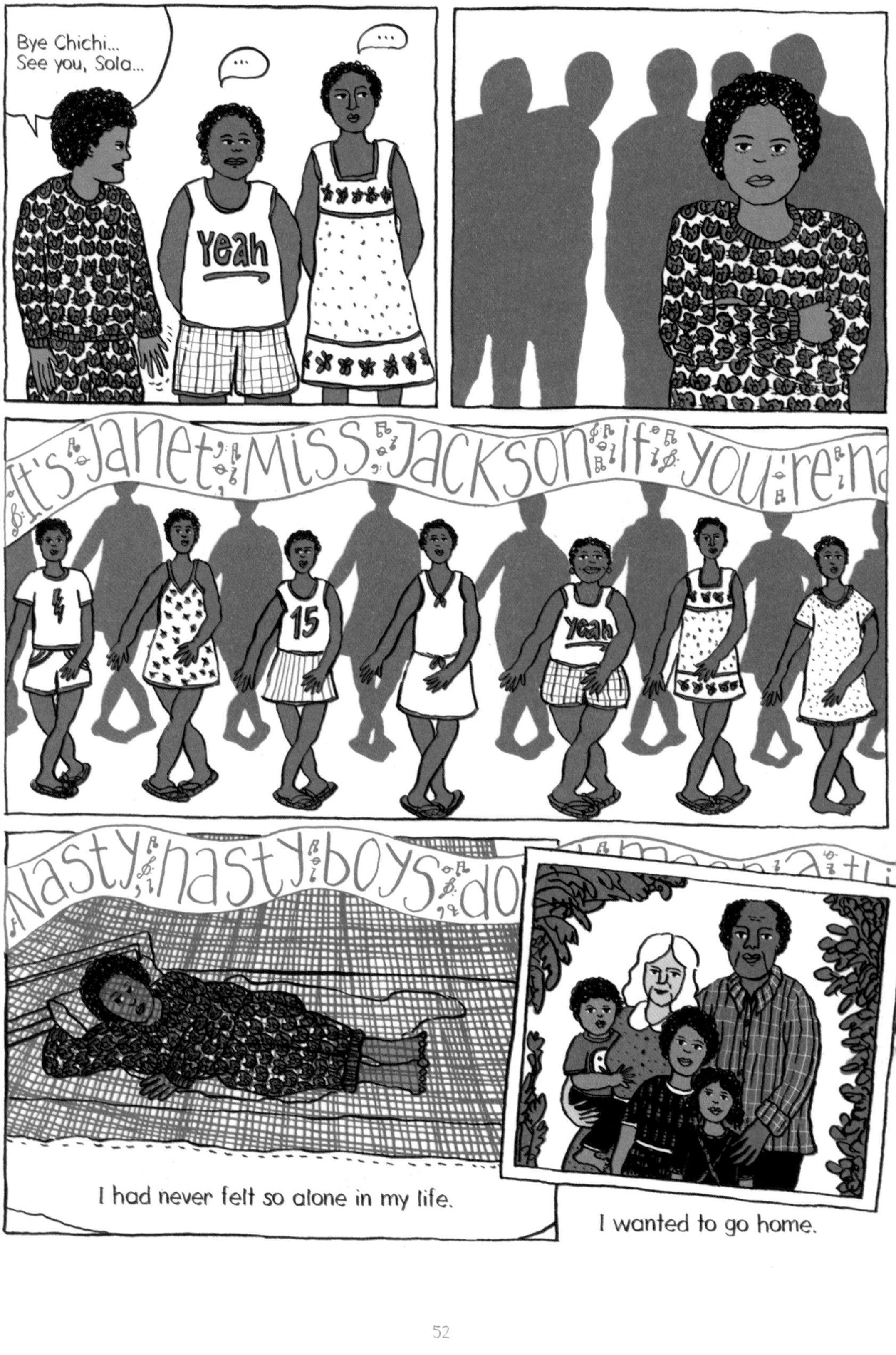
Bye Chichi...
See you, Sola...
...
...
Yeah
It's Janet Miss Jackson if you're
15
Yeah
Nasty nasty boys
I had never felt so alone in my life.
I wanted to go home.

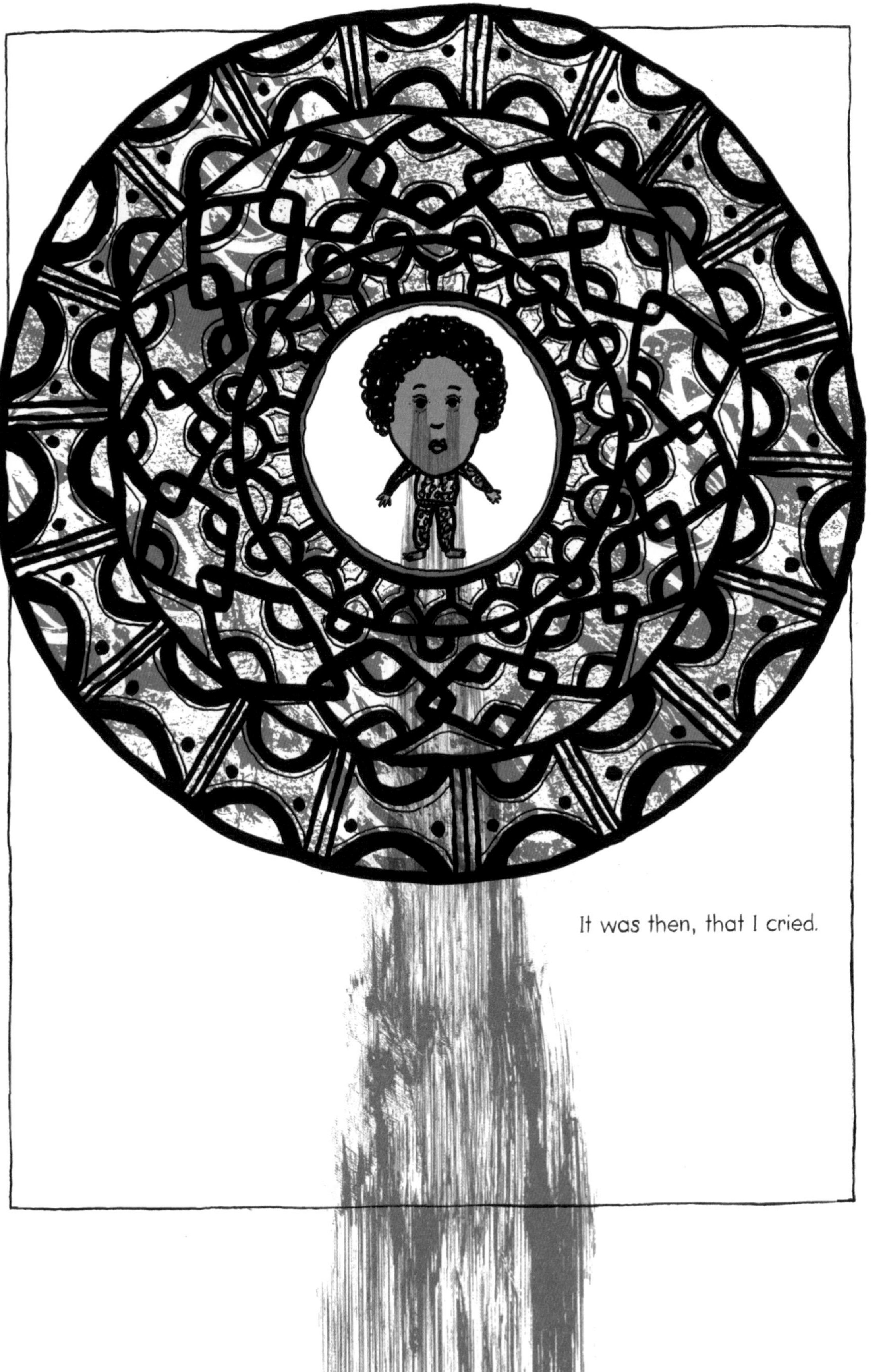
It was then, that I cried.

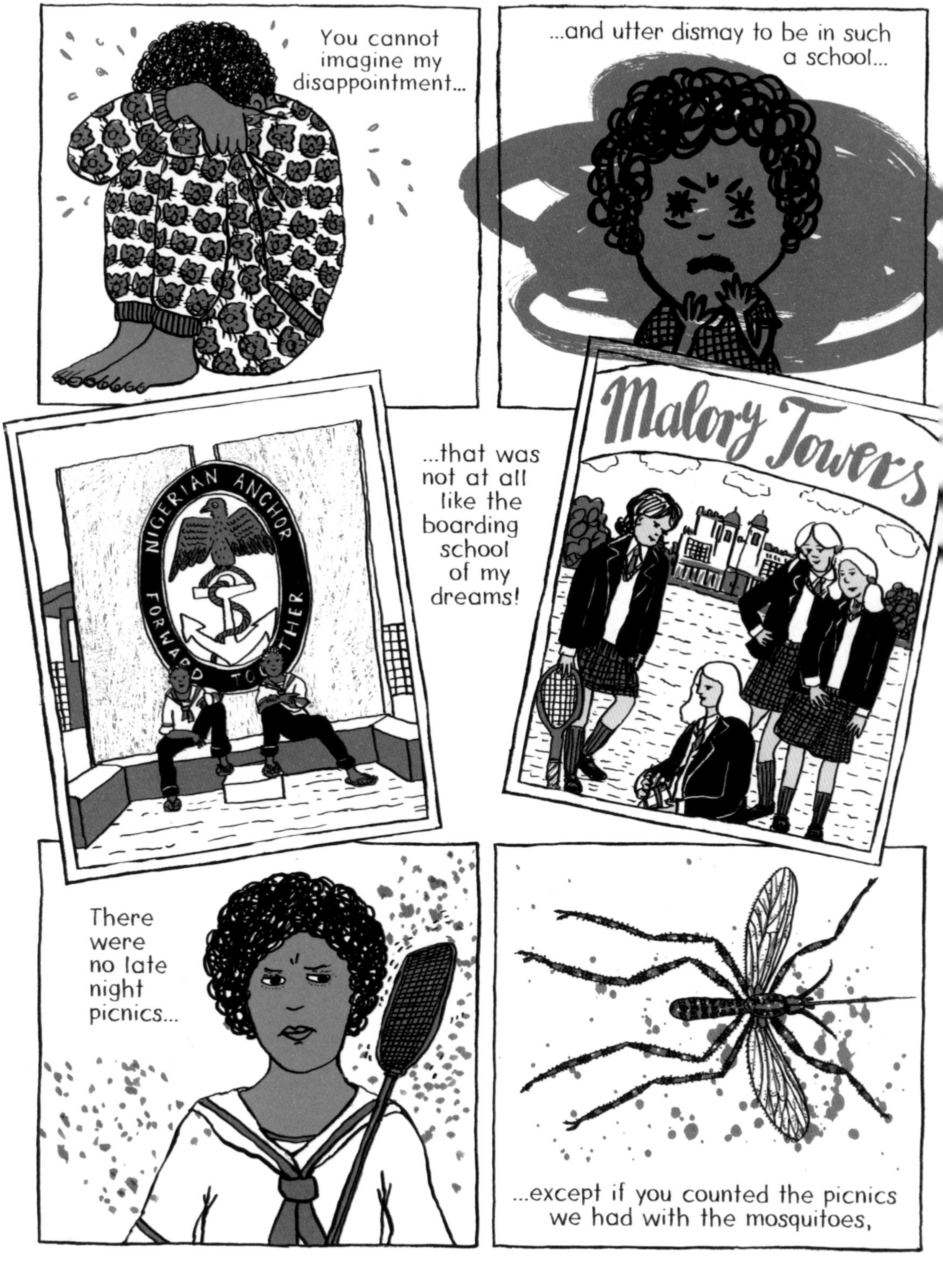
You cannot imagine my disappointment...
...and utter dismay to be in such a school...
NIGERIAN ANCHOR
FORWARD TOGETHER
...that was not at all like the boarding school of my dreams!
Malory Towers
There were no late night picnics...
...except if you counted the picnics we had with the mosquitoes,

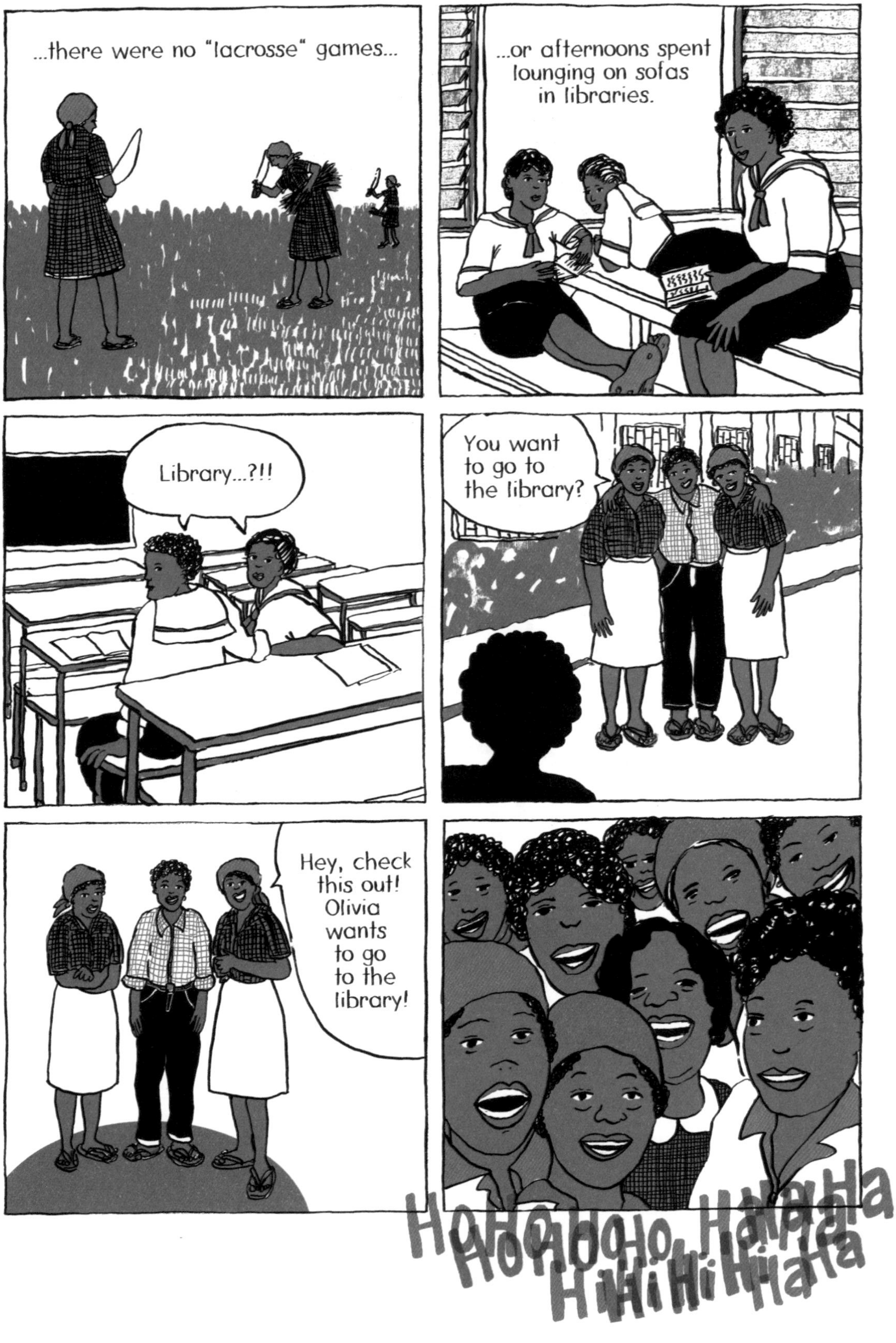
...there were no "lacrosse" games...
...or afternoons spent lounging on sofas in libraries.
Library...?!!
You want to go to the library?
Hey, check this out! Olivia wants to go to the library!
Ho Ho Ho Ho Ha Ha Ha Ha
Ho Ho Ho Ho Ha Ha Ha
Hi Hi Hi Hi Ha Ha

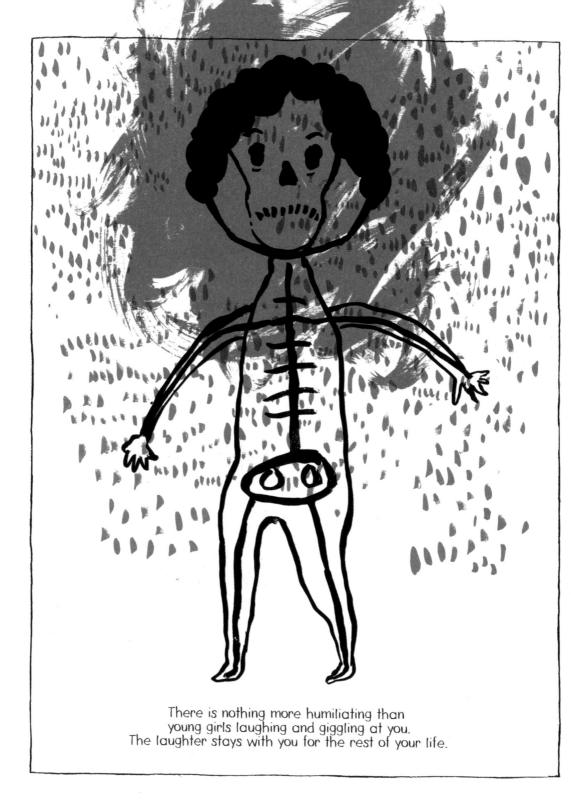

There is nothing more humiliating than
young girls laughing and giggling at you.
The laughter stays with you for the rest of your life.

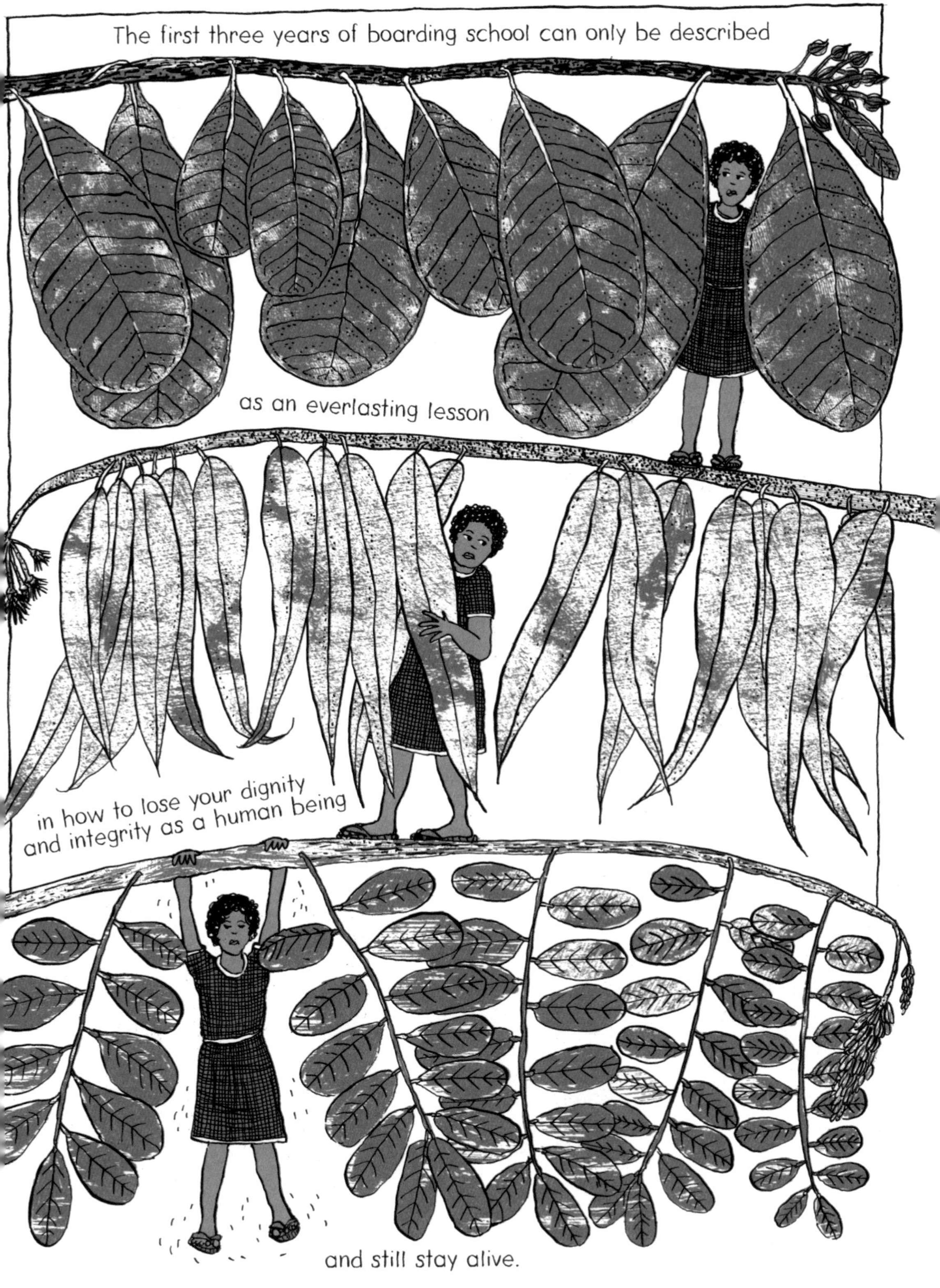
The first three years of boarding school can only be described
as an everlasting lesson
in how to lose your dignity and integrity as a human being
and still stay alive.

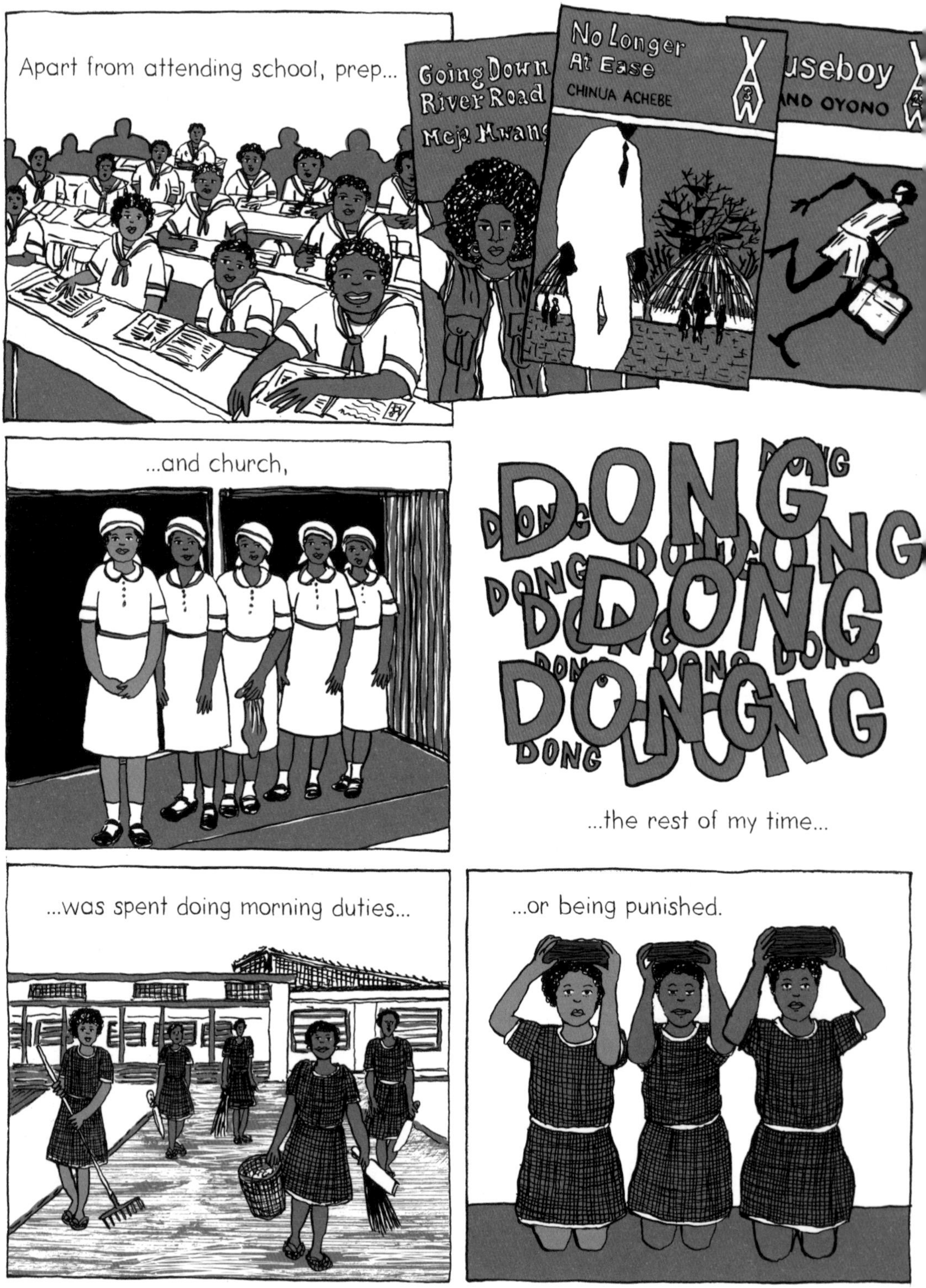
Apart from attending school, prep...
Going Down River Road
No Longer At Ease
CHINUA ACHEBE
...and church,
DONG
DONG
DONG
...the rest of my time...
...was spent doing morning duties...
...or being punished.

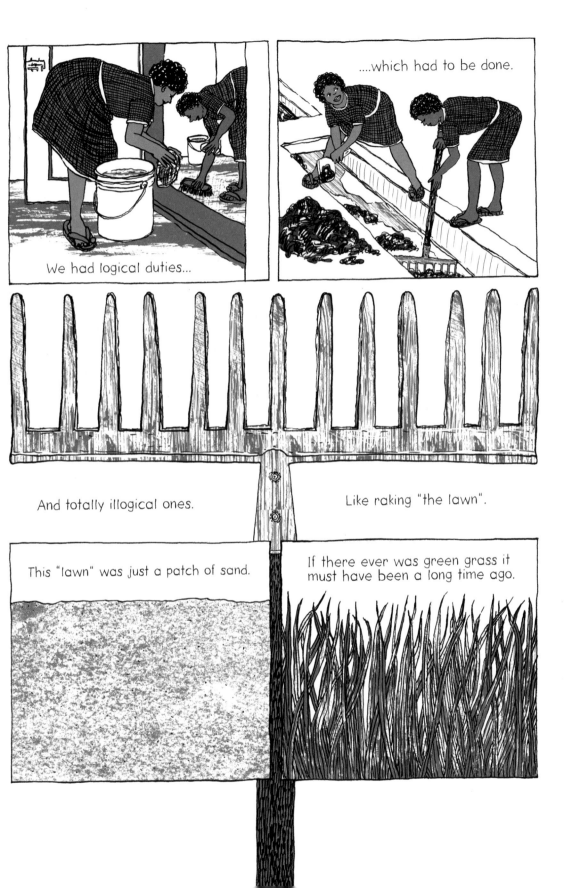

We had logical duties...

....which had to be done.

And totally illogical ones.

Like raking "the lawn".

This "lawn" was just a patch of sand.

If there ever was green grass it must have been a long time ago.

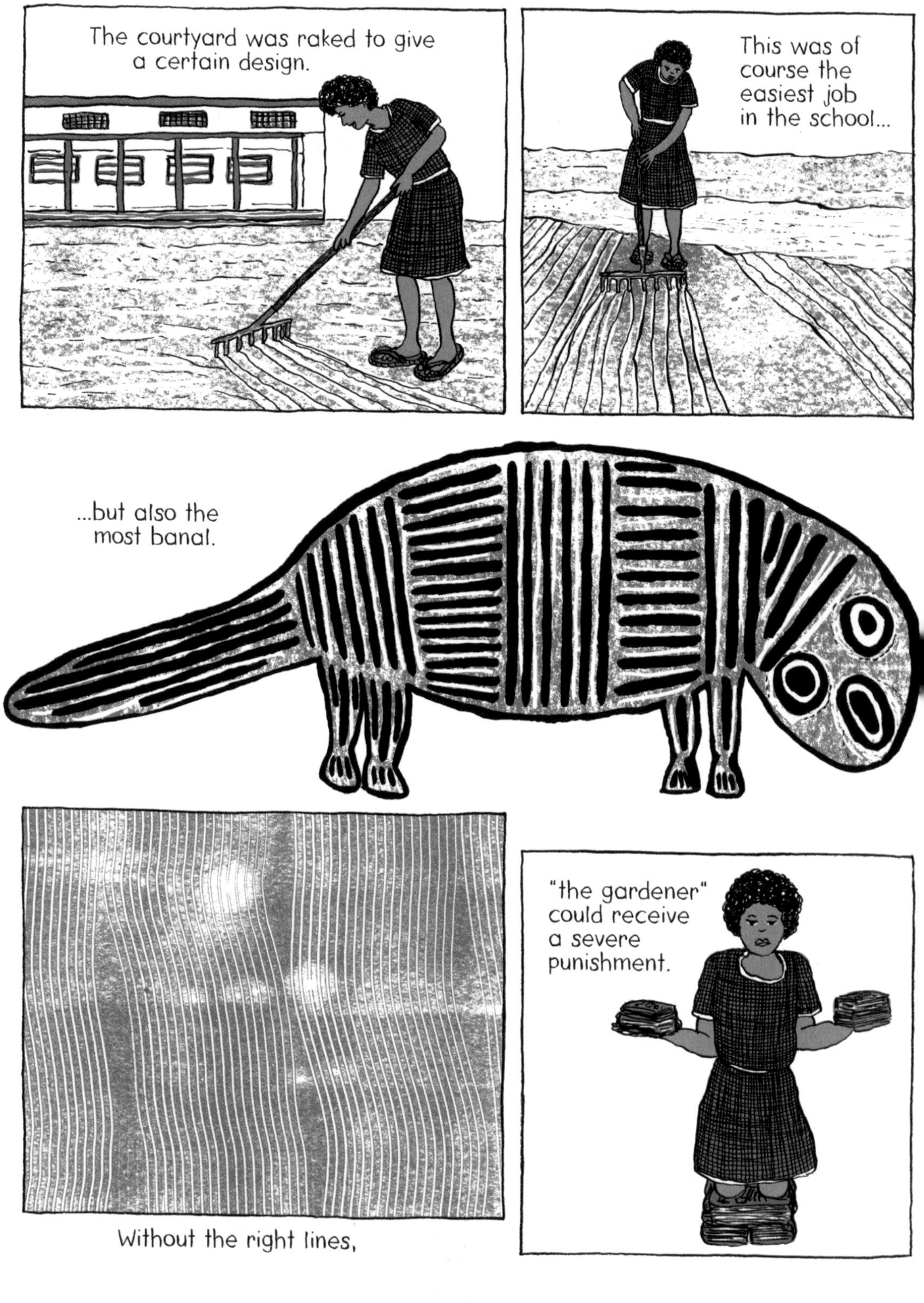
The courtyard was raked to give a certain design.
This was of course the easiest job in the school...
...but also the most banal.
Without the right lines,
"the gardener" could receive a severe punishment.

Sometimes if you were lucky,

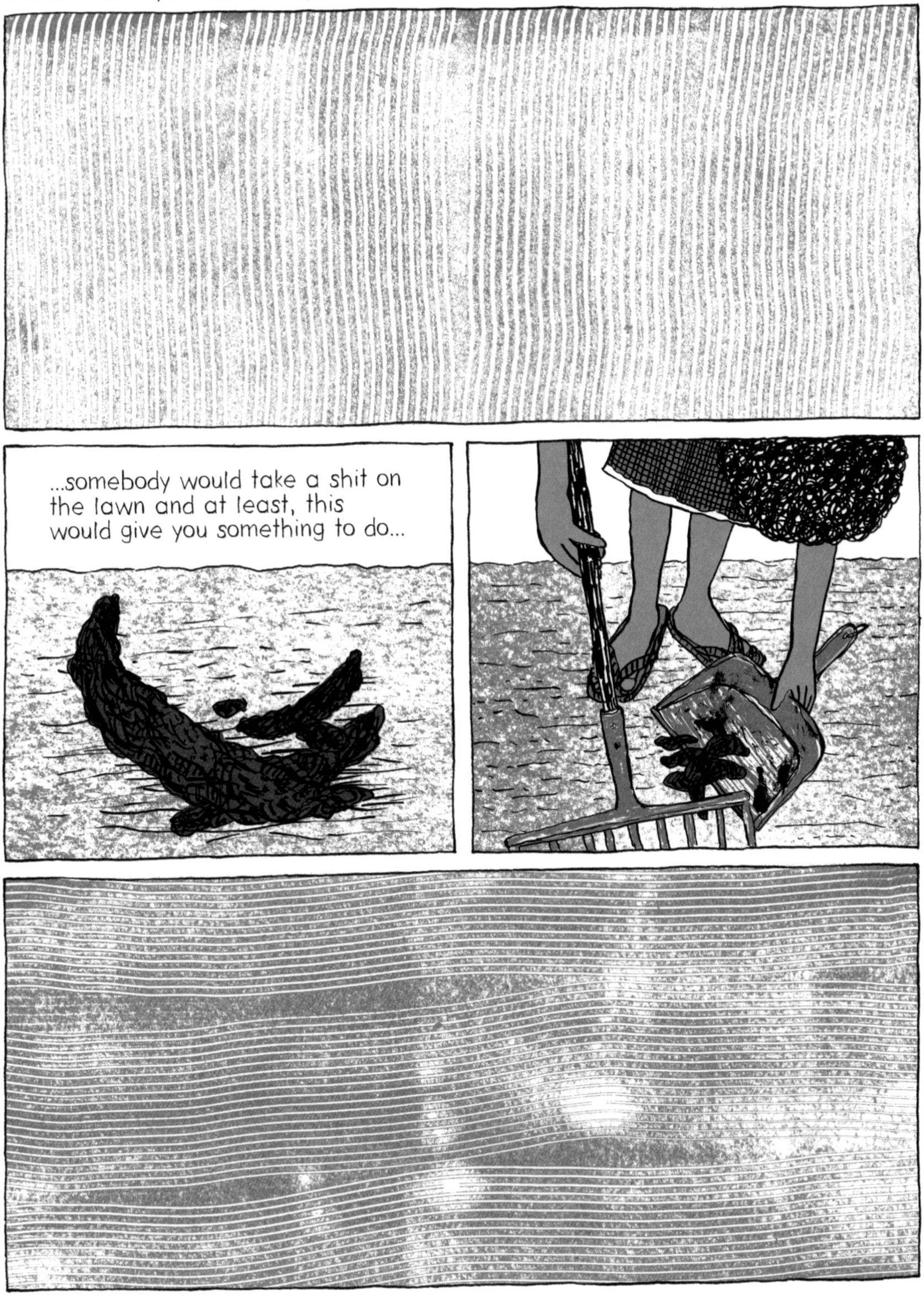
...somebody would take a shit on the lawn and at least, this would give you something to do...

...apart from trying to design lines across the sand.

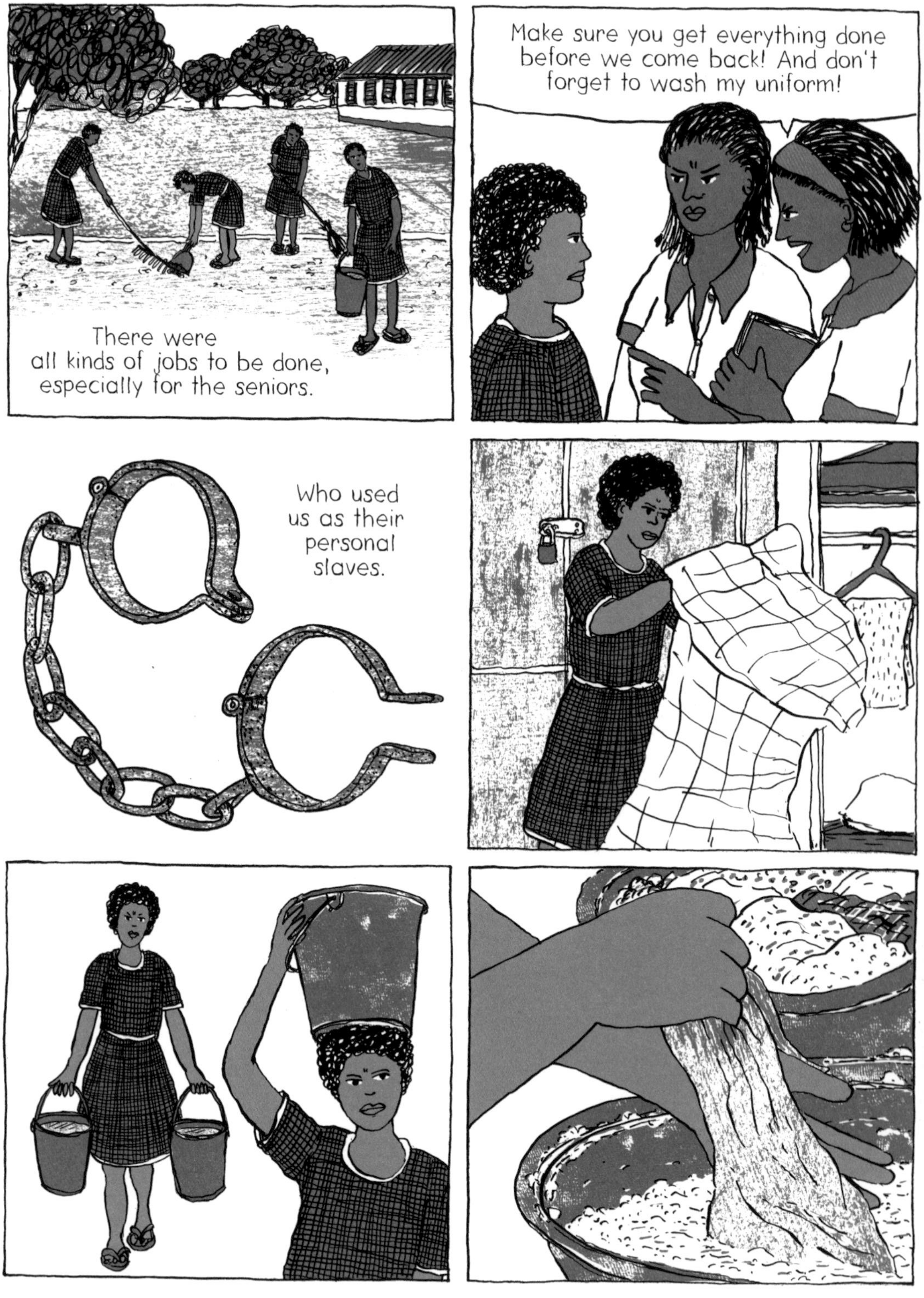
There were all kinds of jobs to be done, especially for the seniors.
Make sure you get everything done before we come back! And don't forget to wash my uniform!
Who used us as their personal slaves.

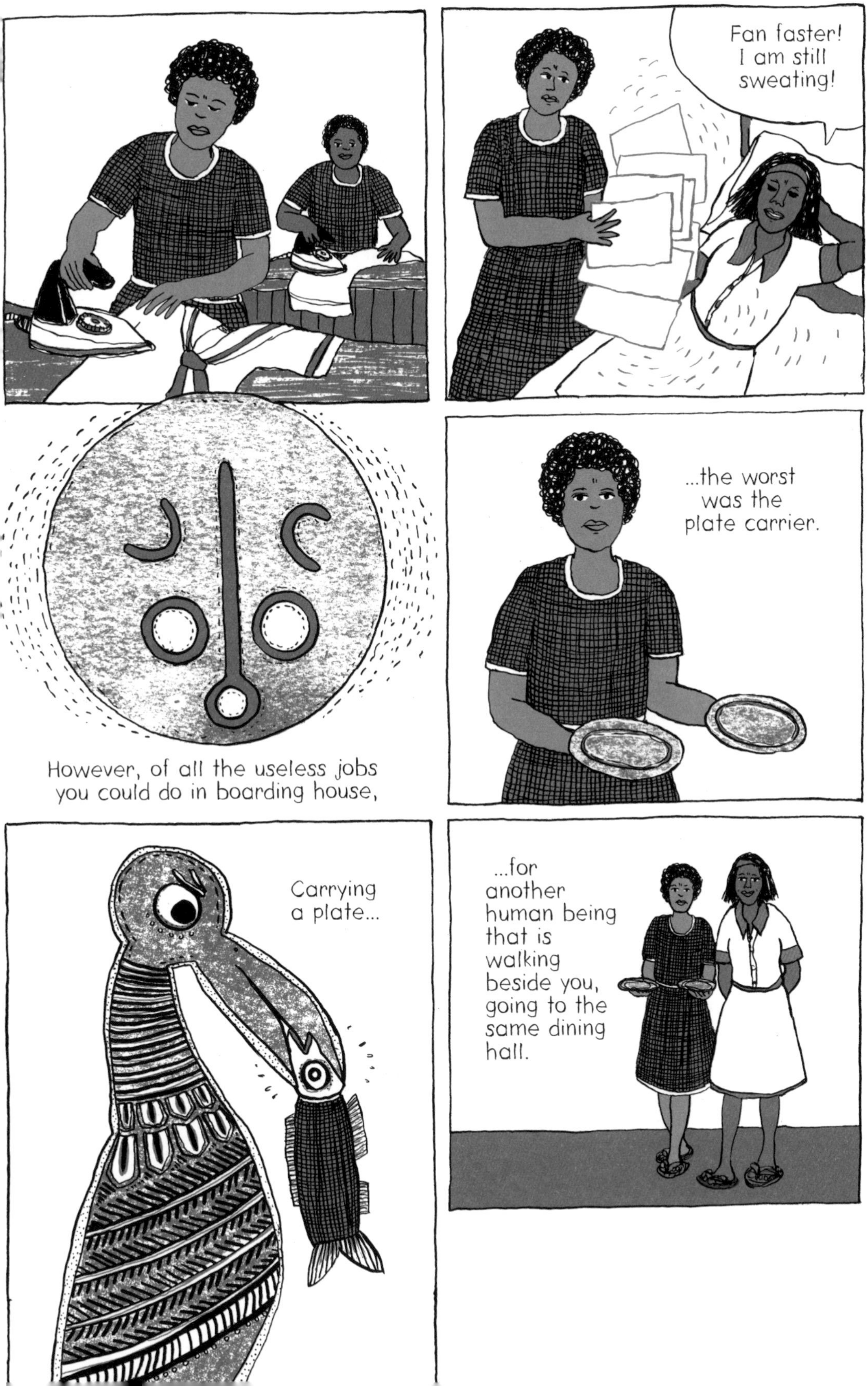
Fan faster! I am still sweating!
However, of all the useless jobs you could do in boarding house,
...the worst was the plate carrier.
Carrying a plate...
...for another human being that is walking beside you, going to the same dining hall.

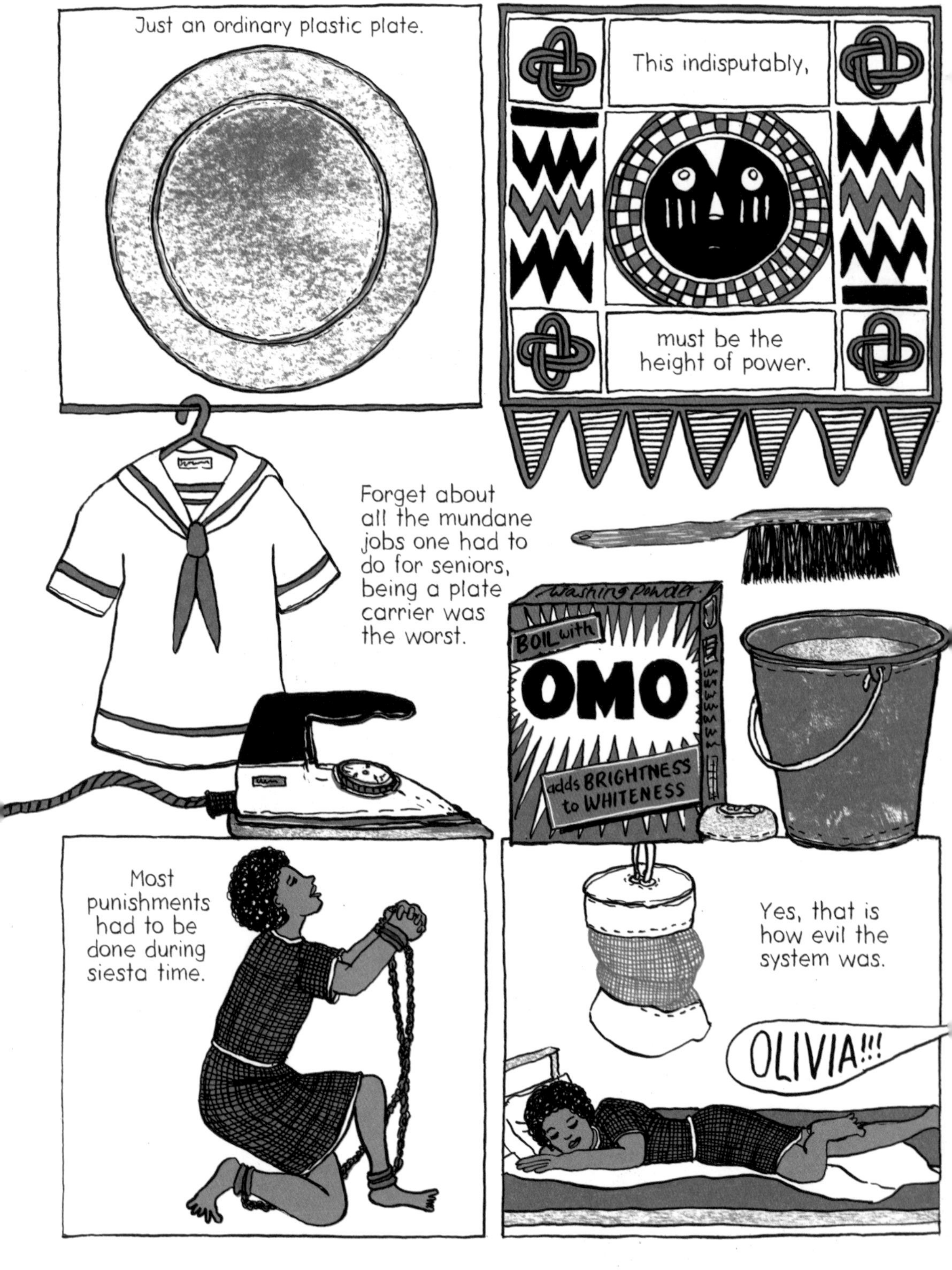
Just an ordinary plastic plate.
This indisputably,
must be the height of power.
Forget about all the mundane jobs one had to do for seniors, being a plate carrier was the worst.
washing powder
BOIL with
OMO
adds BRIGHTNESS to WHITENESS
Most punishments had to be done during siesta time.
Yes, that is how evil the system was.
OLIVIA!!!

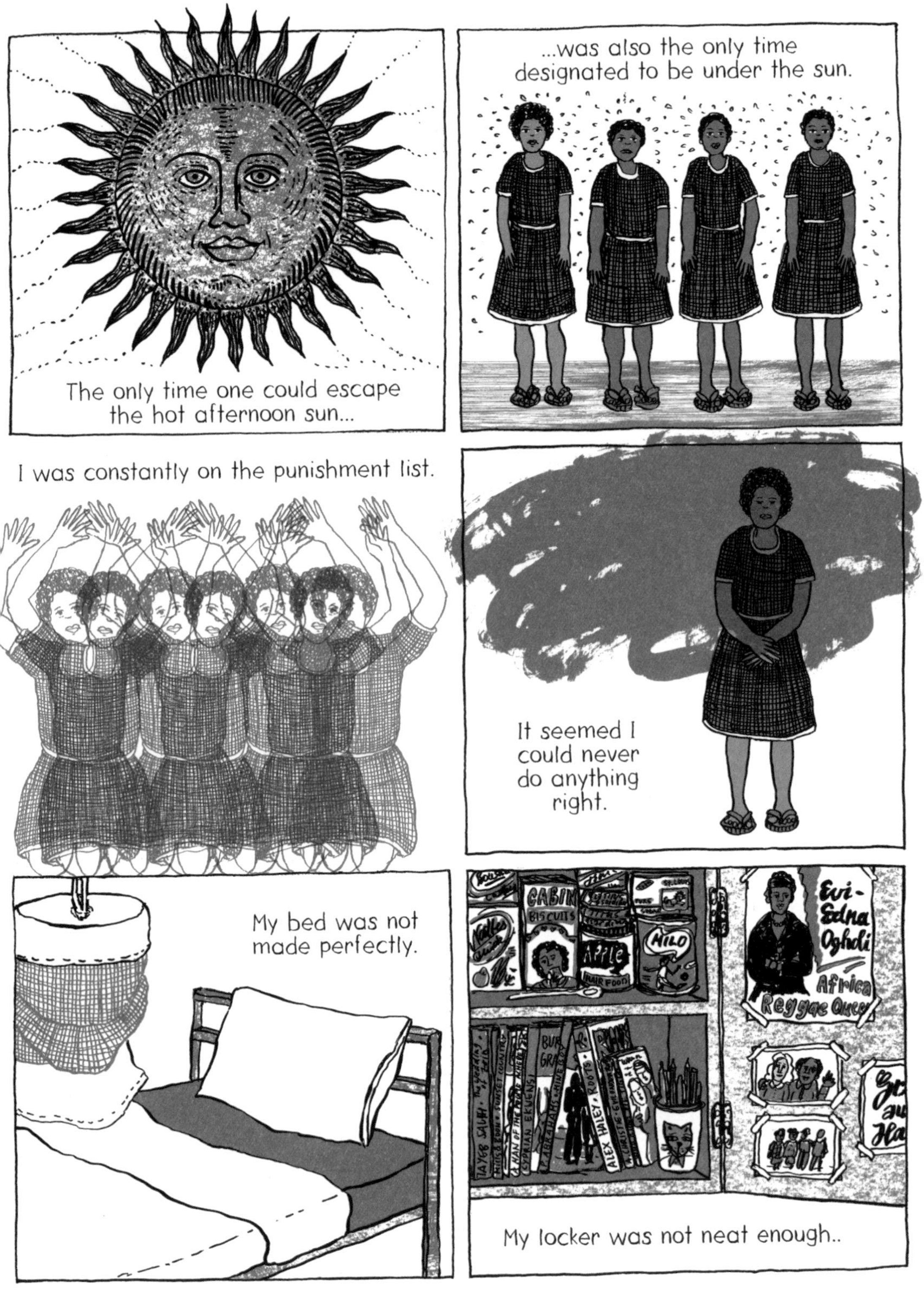
The only time one could escape the hot afternoon sun...
...was also the only time designated to be under the sun.
I was constantly on the punishment list.
It seemed I could never do anything right.
My bed was not made perfectly.
CABIN
BISCUITS
MILO
Evi-Edna Ogholi
My locker was not neat enough..

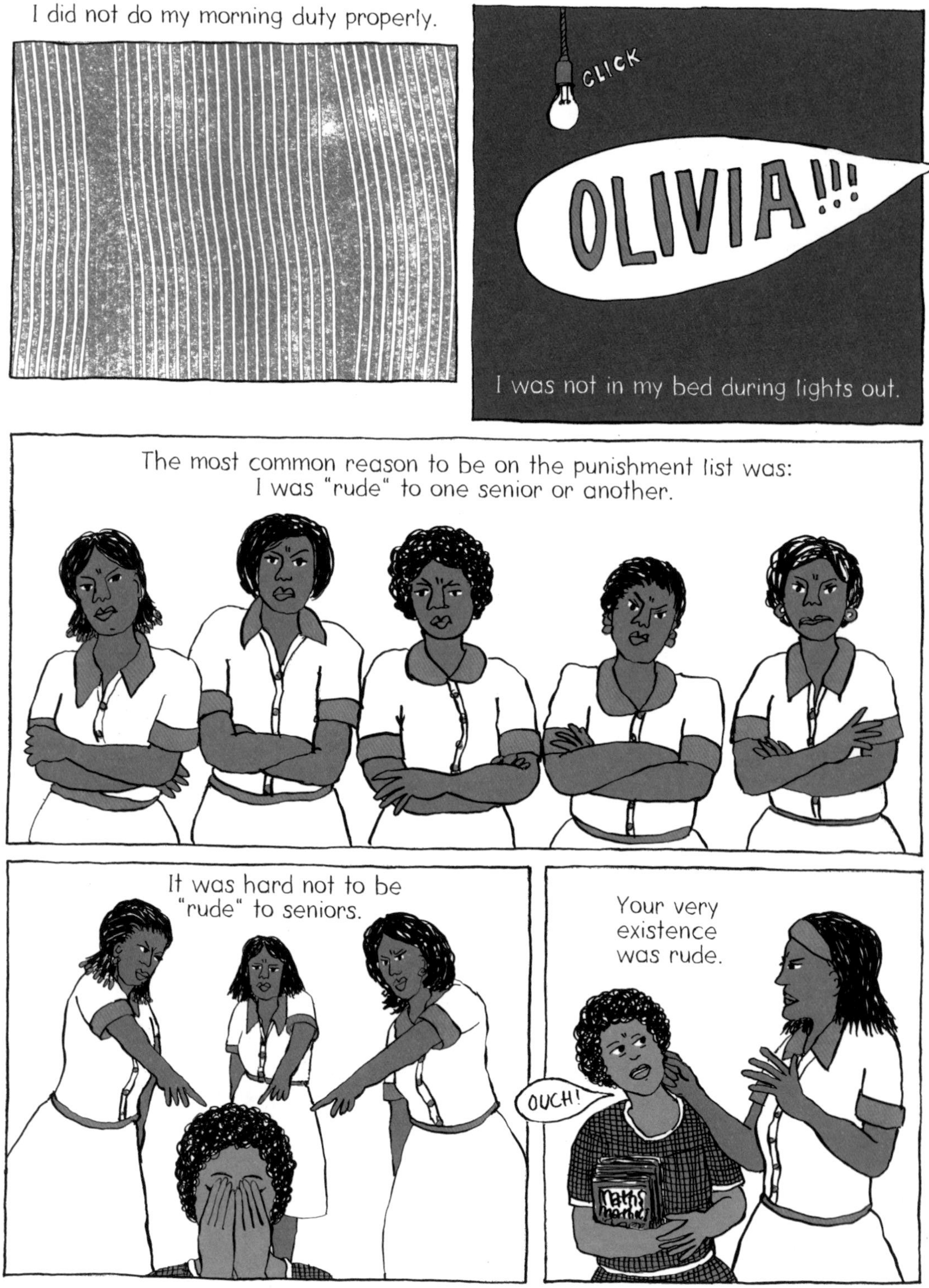
I did not do my morning duty properly.
CLICK
OLIVIA!!!
I was not in my bed during lights out.
The most common reason to be on the punishment list was:
I was "rude" to one senior or another.
It was hard not to be "rude" to seniors.
Your very existence was rude.
OUCH!

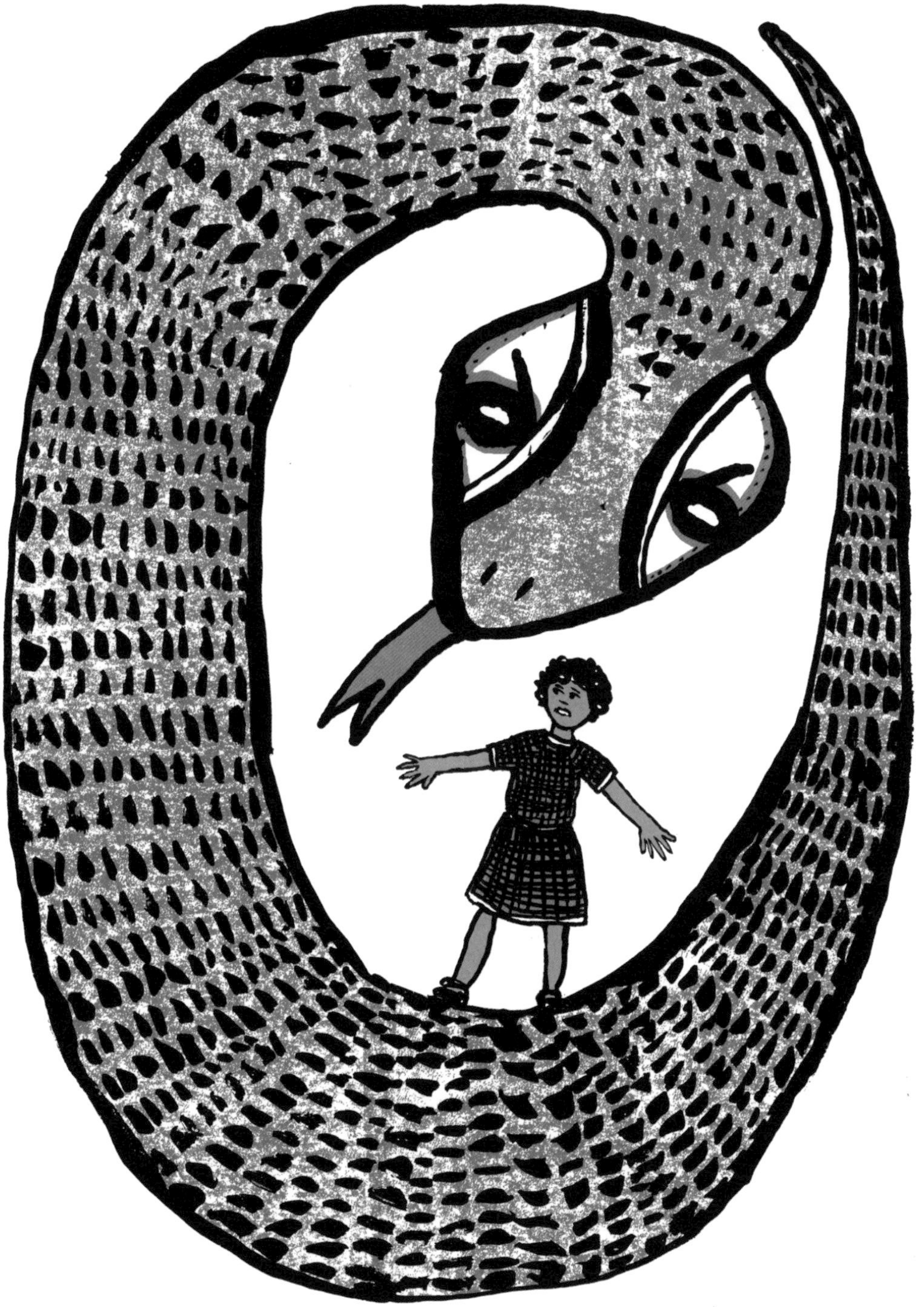

The most wicked, unforgiving and meanest senior ever, was Senior Elizabeth.

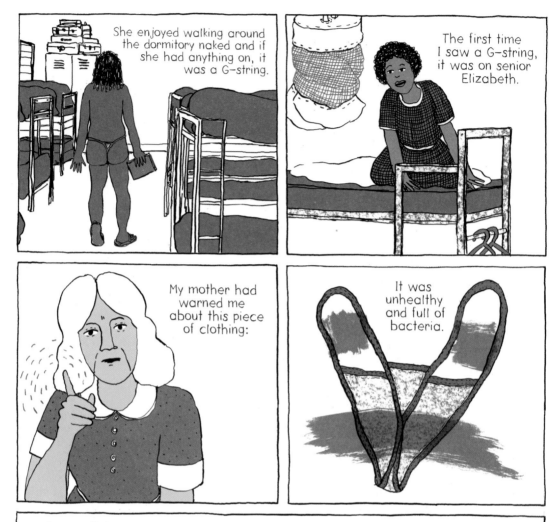

She enjoyed walking around the dormitory naked and if she had anything on, it was a G-string.

The first time I saw a G-string, it was on senior Elizabeth.

My mother had warned me about this piece of clothing:

It was unhealthy and full of bacteria.

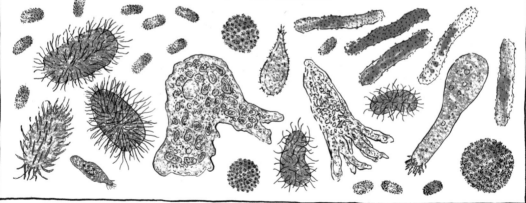

I was often worried about the kind of bacteria Senior Elizabeth was carrying around in her bum bum.

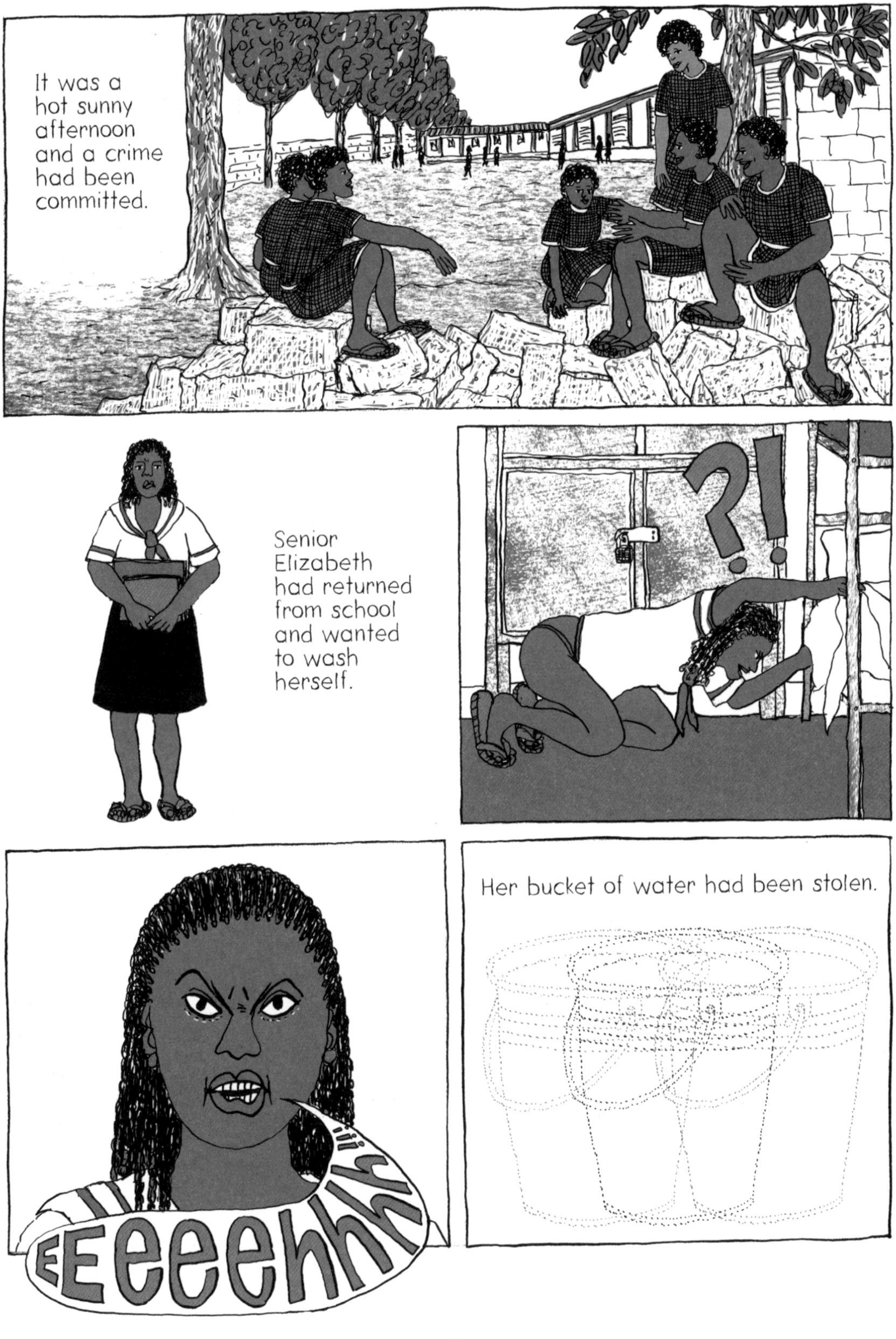

It was a hot sunny afternoon and a crime had been committed.
Senior Elizabeth had returned from school and wanted to wash herself.
?!
EEeeehhh!!!
Her bucket of water had been stolen.

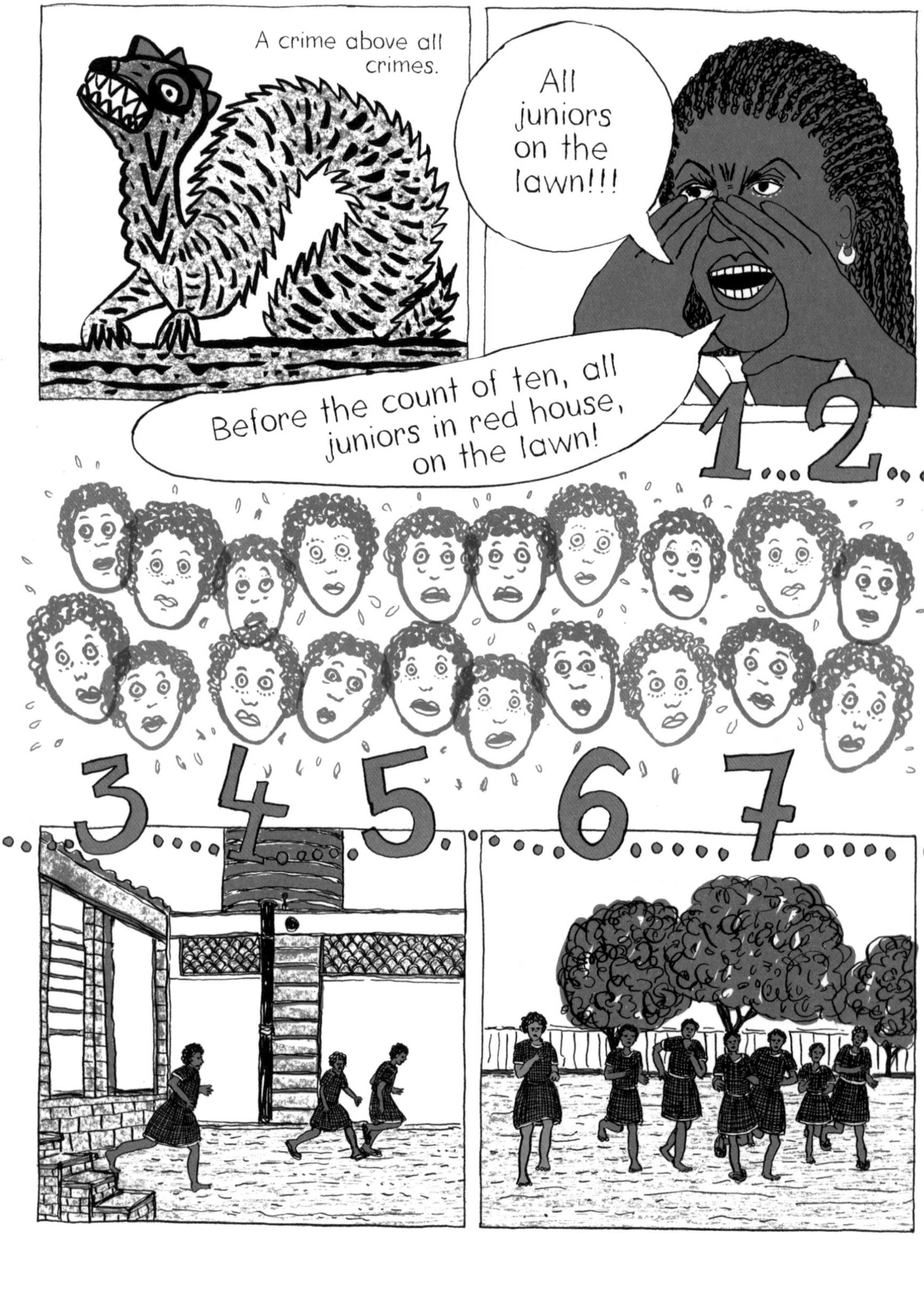
A crime above all crimes.
All juniors on the lawn!!!
Before the count of ten, all juniors in red house, on the lawn!
1...2...
3...4...5...6...7...

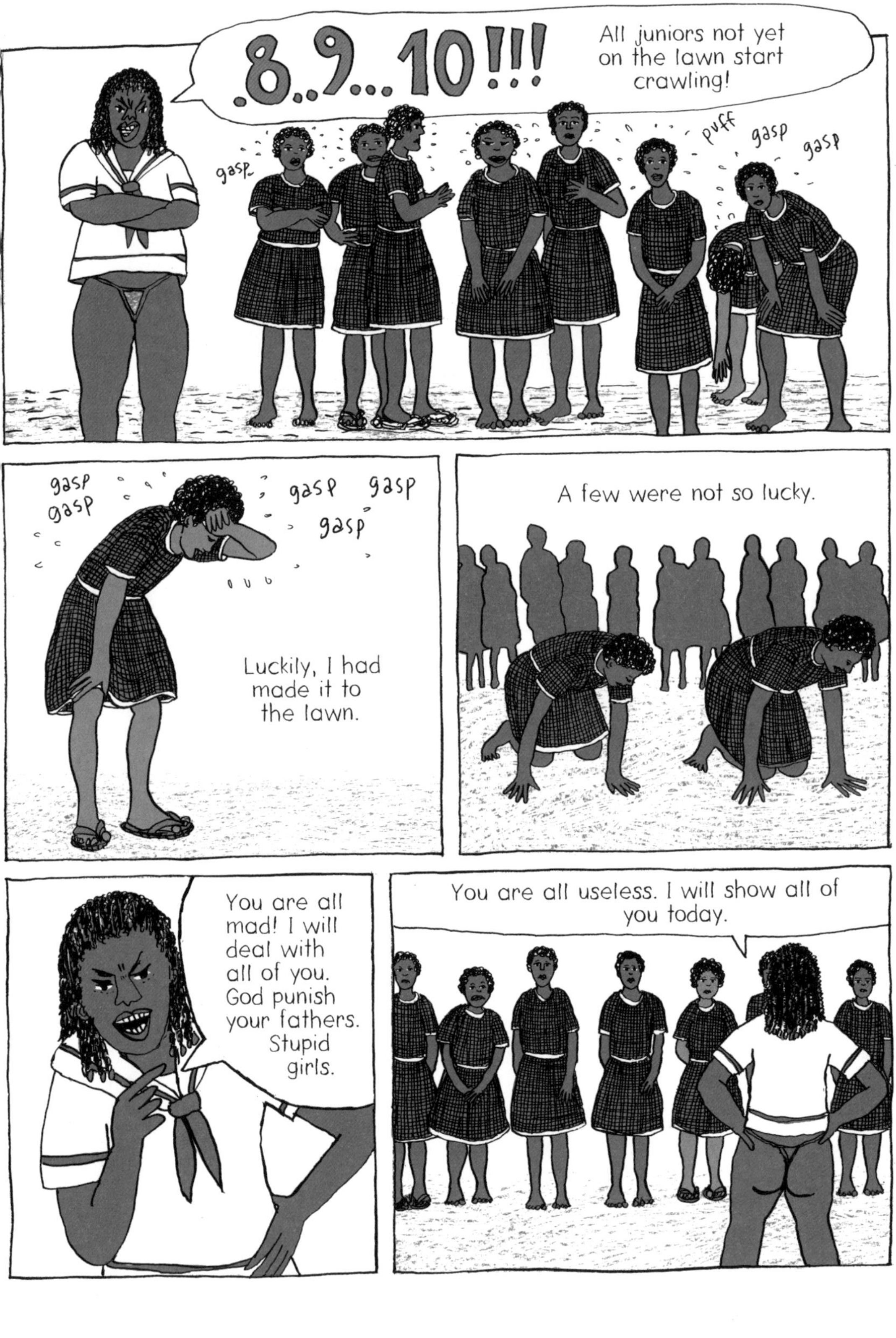
.8..9...10!!!
All juniors not yet on the lawn start crawling!
gasp
puff
gasp
gasp
gasp
gasp
gasp
gasp
gasp
Luckily, I had made it to the lawn.
A few were not so lucky.
You are all mad! I will deal with all of you. God punish your fathers. Stupid girls.
You are all useless. I will show all of you today.

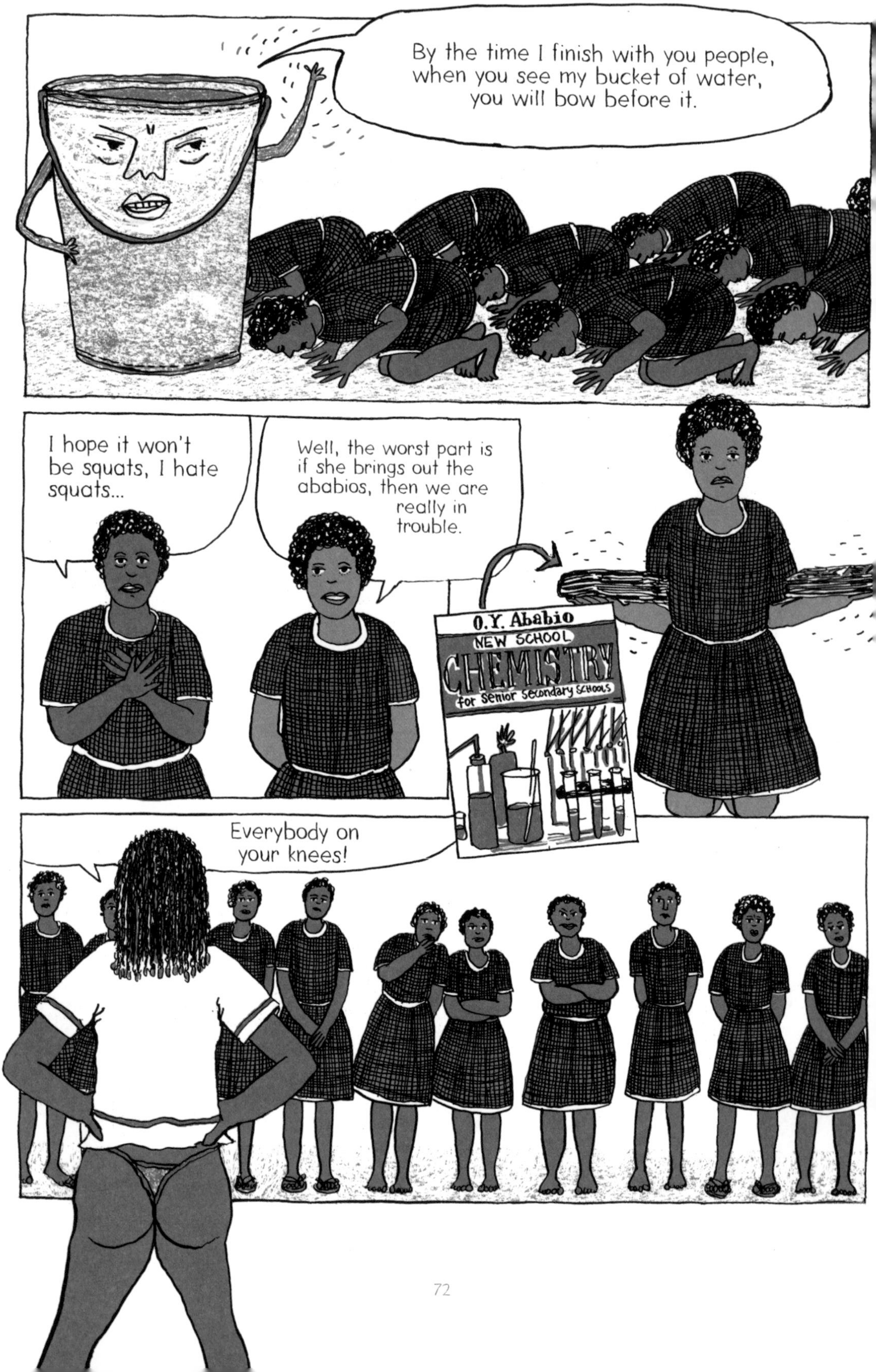

By the time I finish with you people, when you see my bucket of water, you will bow before it.
I hope it won't be squats, I hate squats...
Well, the worst part is if she brings out the ababios, then we are really in trouble.
O.Y. Ababio
NEW SCHOOL
CHEMISTRY
for Senior Secondary SCHOOLS
Everybody on your knees!

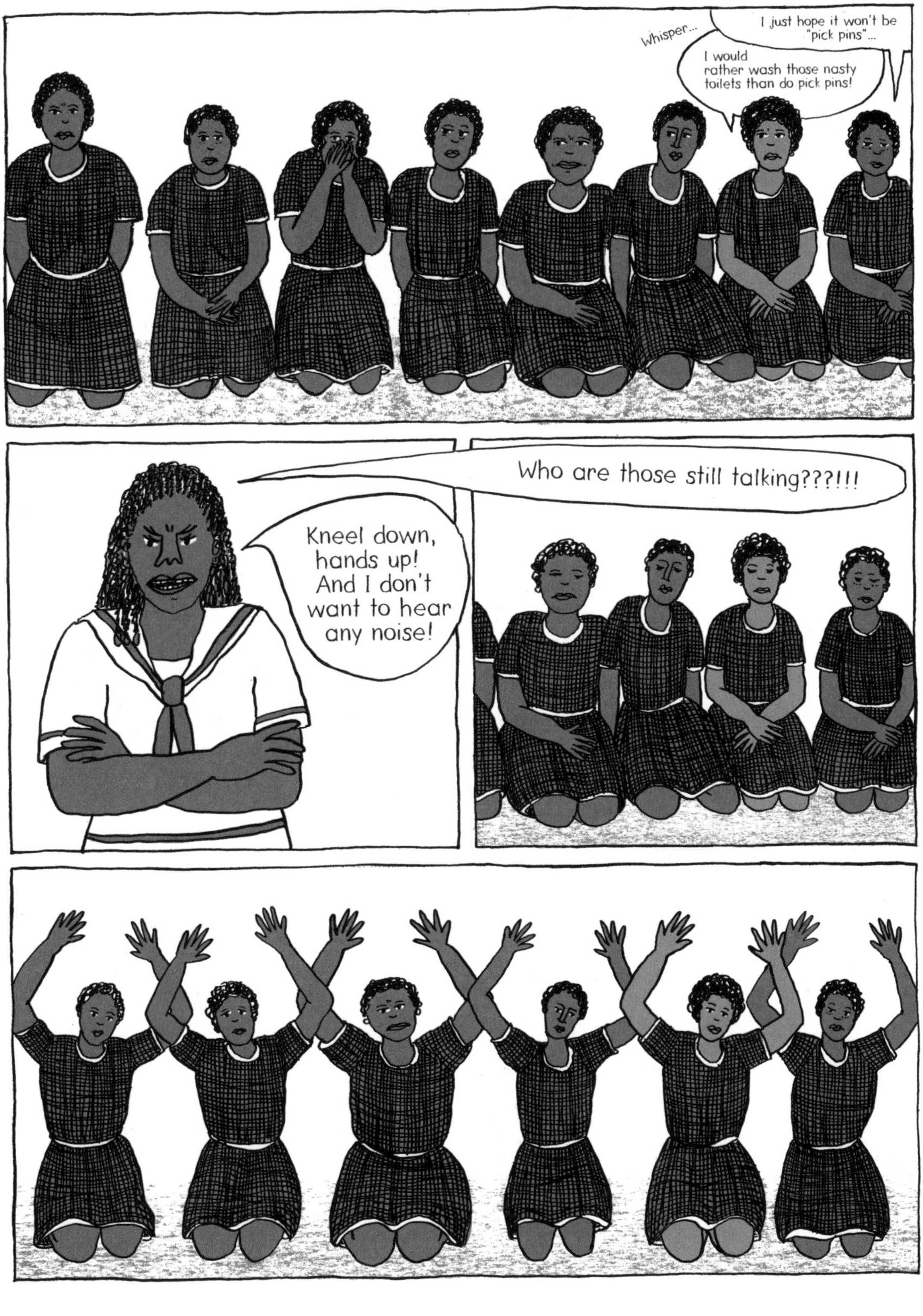
Whisper...
I just hope it won't be "pick pins"...
I would rather wash those nasty toilets than do pick pins!
Who are those still talking???!!!
Kneel down, hands up! And I don't want to hear any noise!

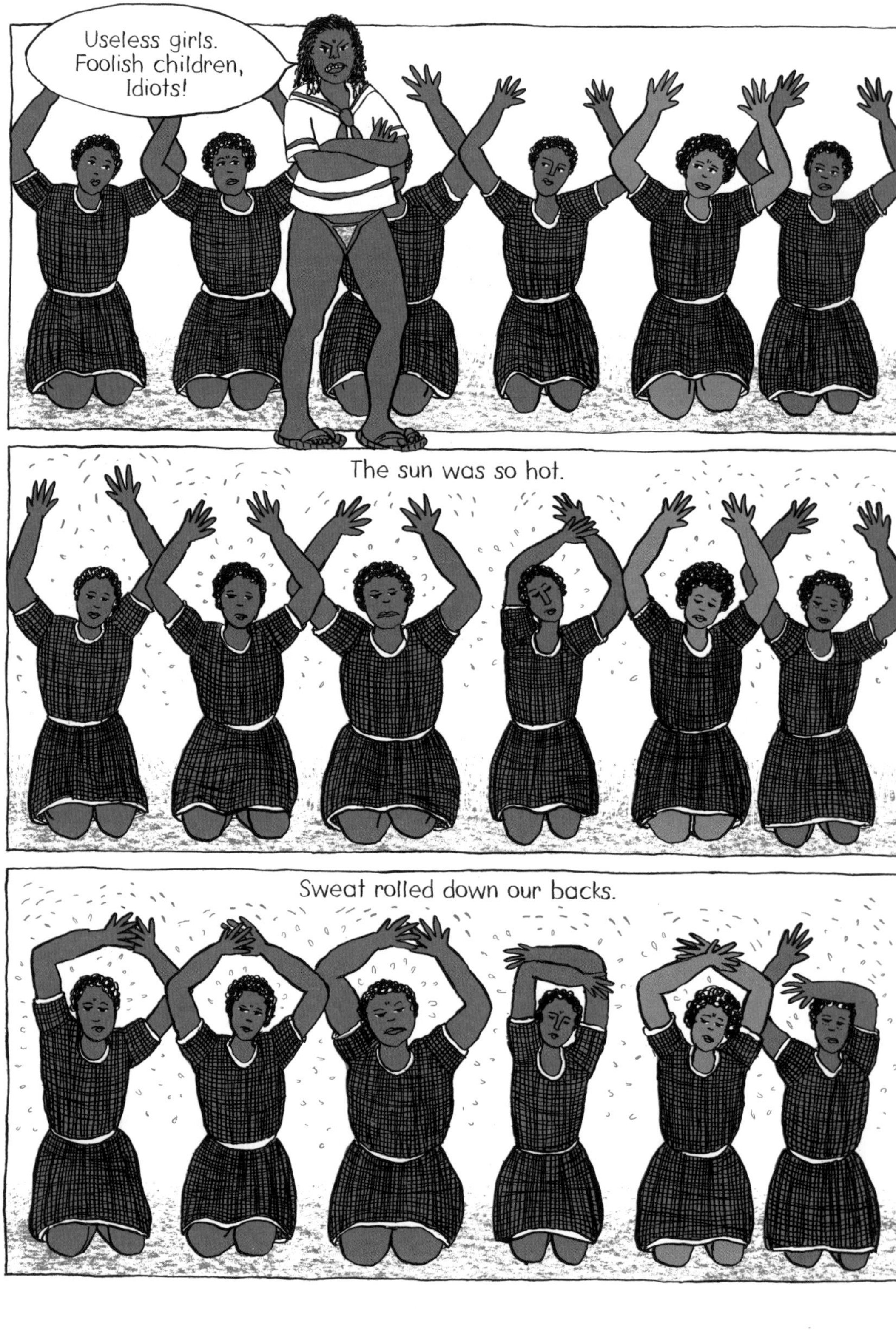
Useless girls. Foolish children, Idiots!
The sun was so hot.
Sweat rolled down our backs.

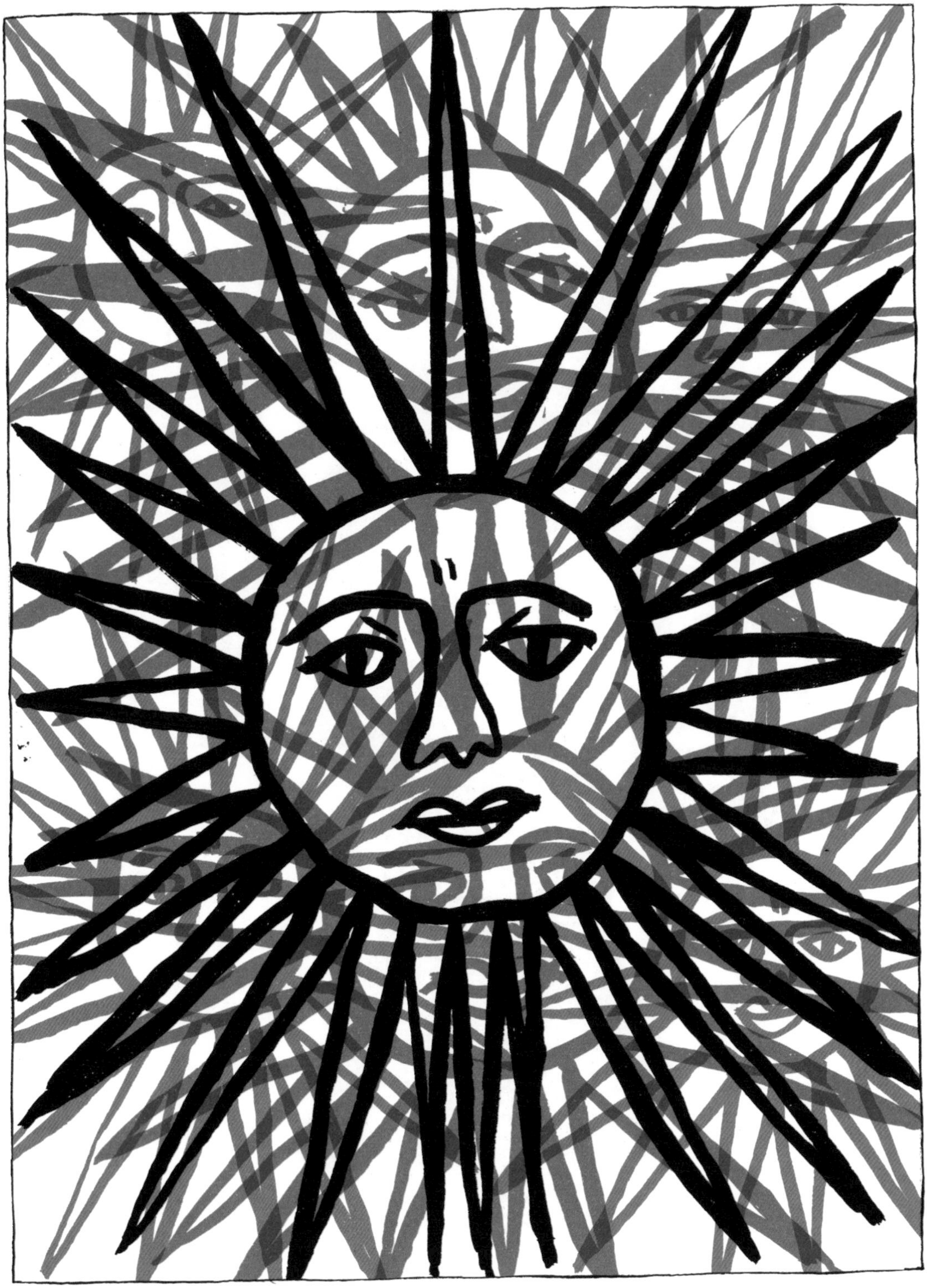

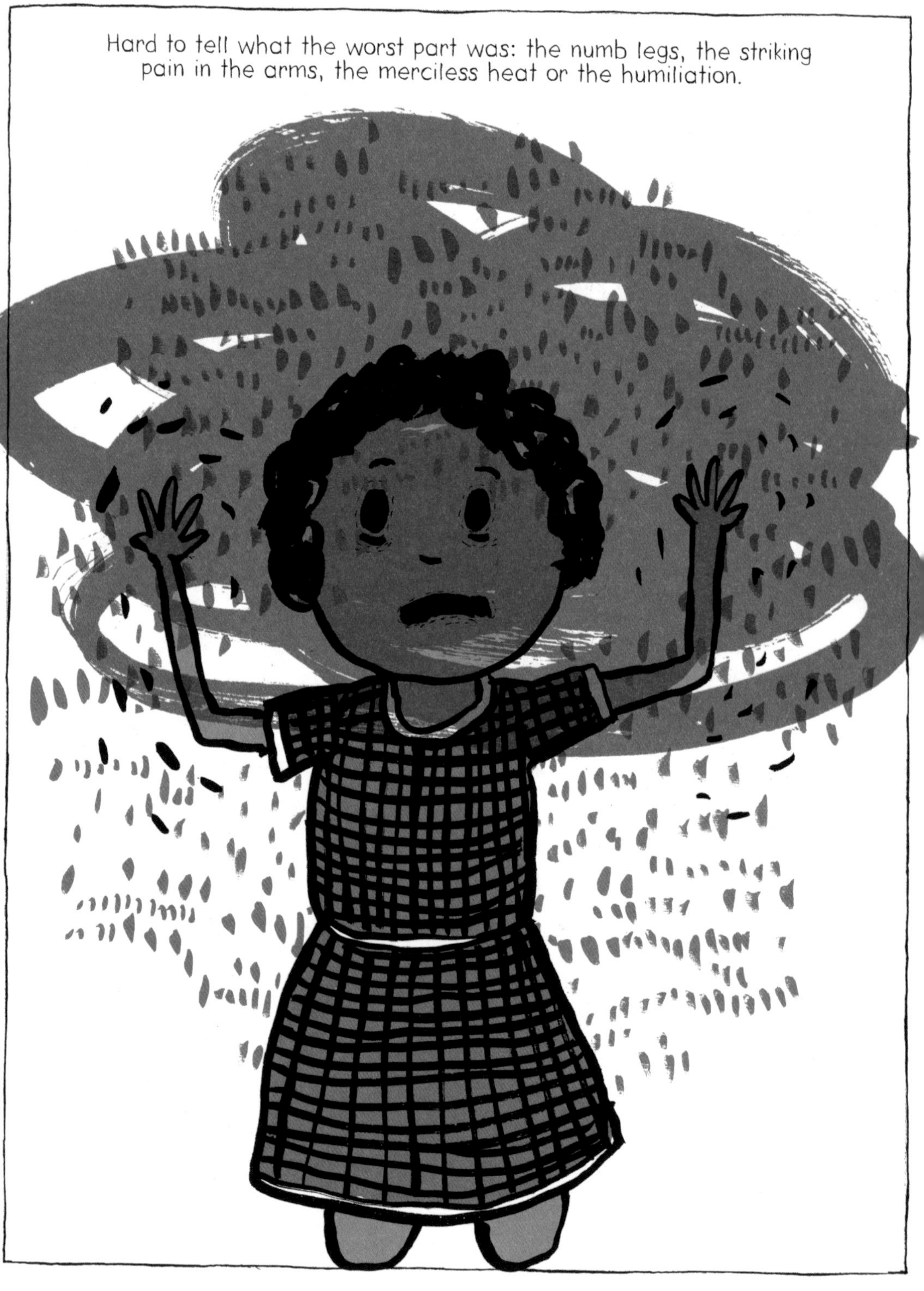
Hard to tell what the worst part was: the numb legs, the striking pain in the arms, the merciless heat or the humiliation.

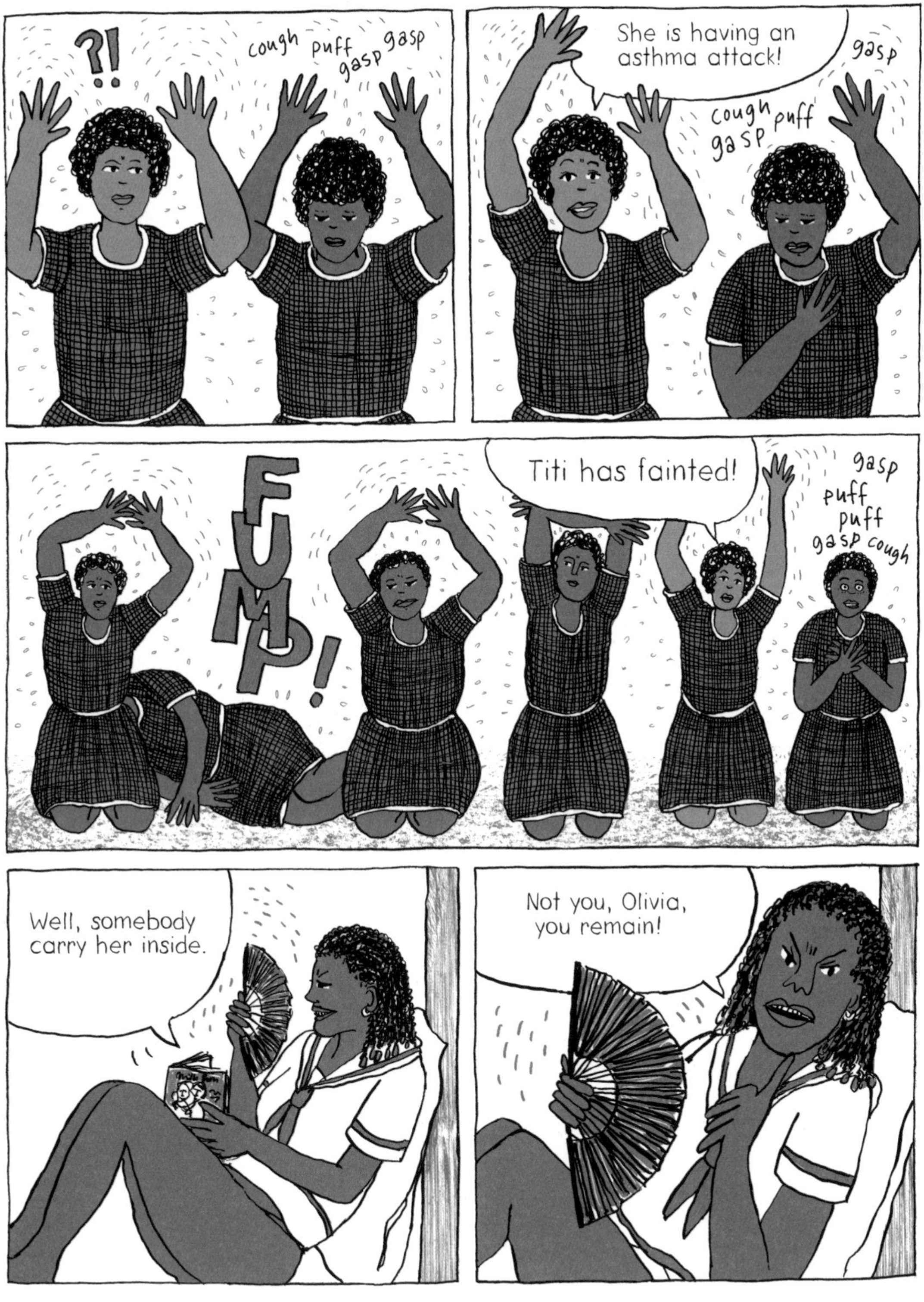
?!
cough puff gasp gasp
She is having an asthma attack!
gasp
cough puff gasp
FUMP!
Titi has fainted!
gasp puff puff gasp cough
Well, somebody carry her inside.
Not you, Olivia, you remain!

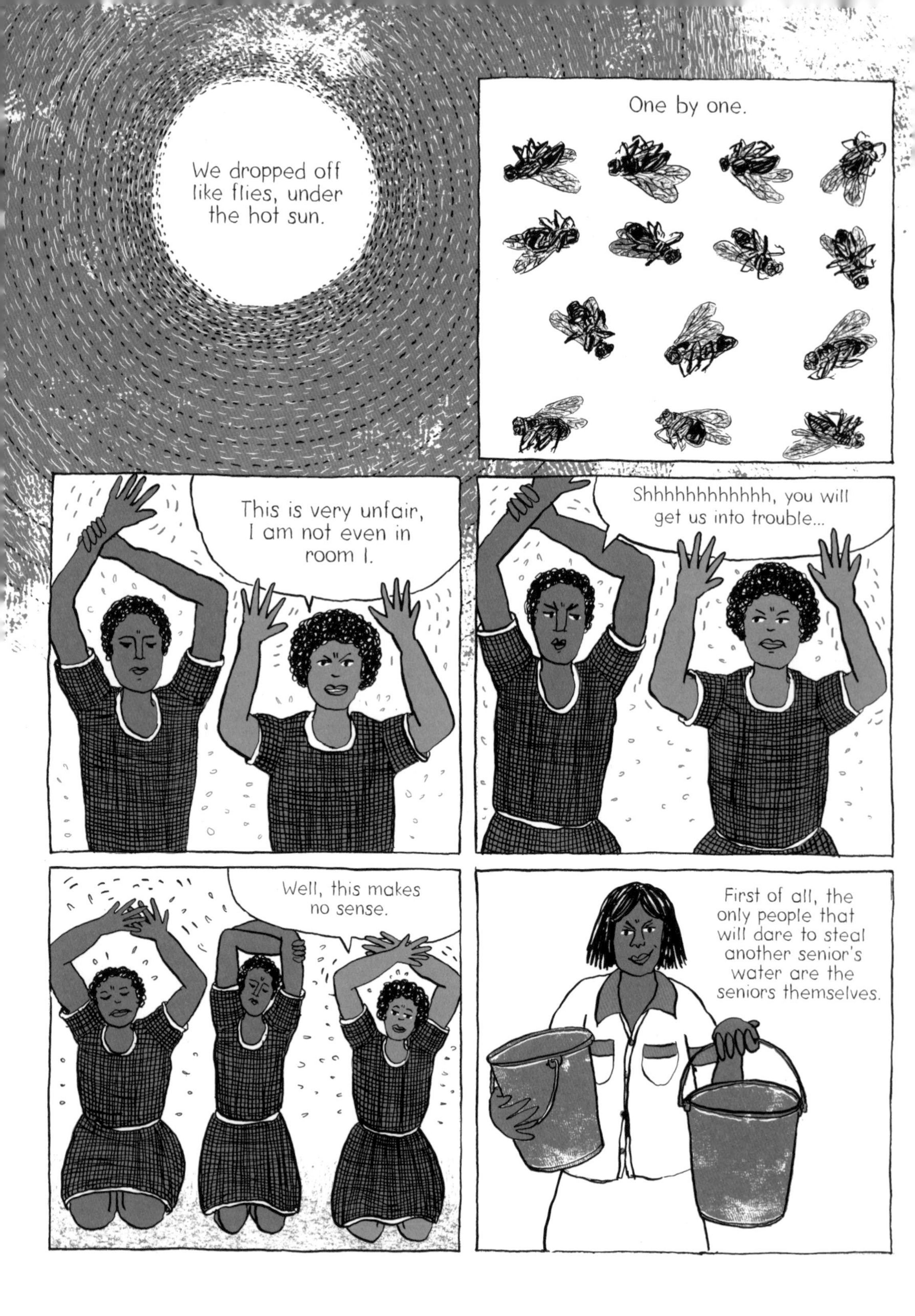
We dropped off like flies, under the hot sun.
One by one.
This is very unfair, I am not even in room 1.
Shhhhhhhhhhhh, you will get us into trouble...
Well, this makes no sense.
First of all, the only people that will dare to steal another senior's water are the seniors themselves.

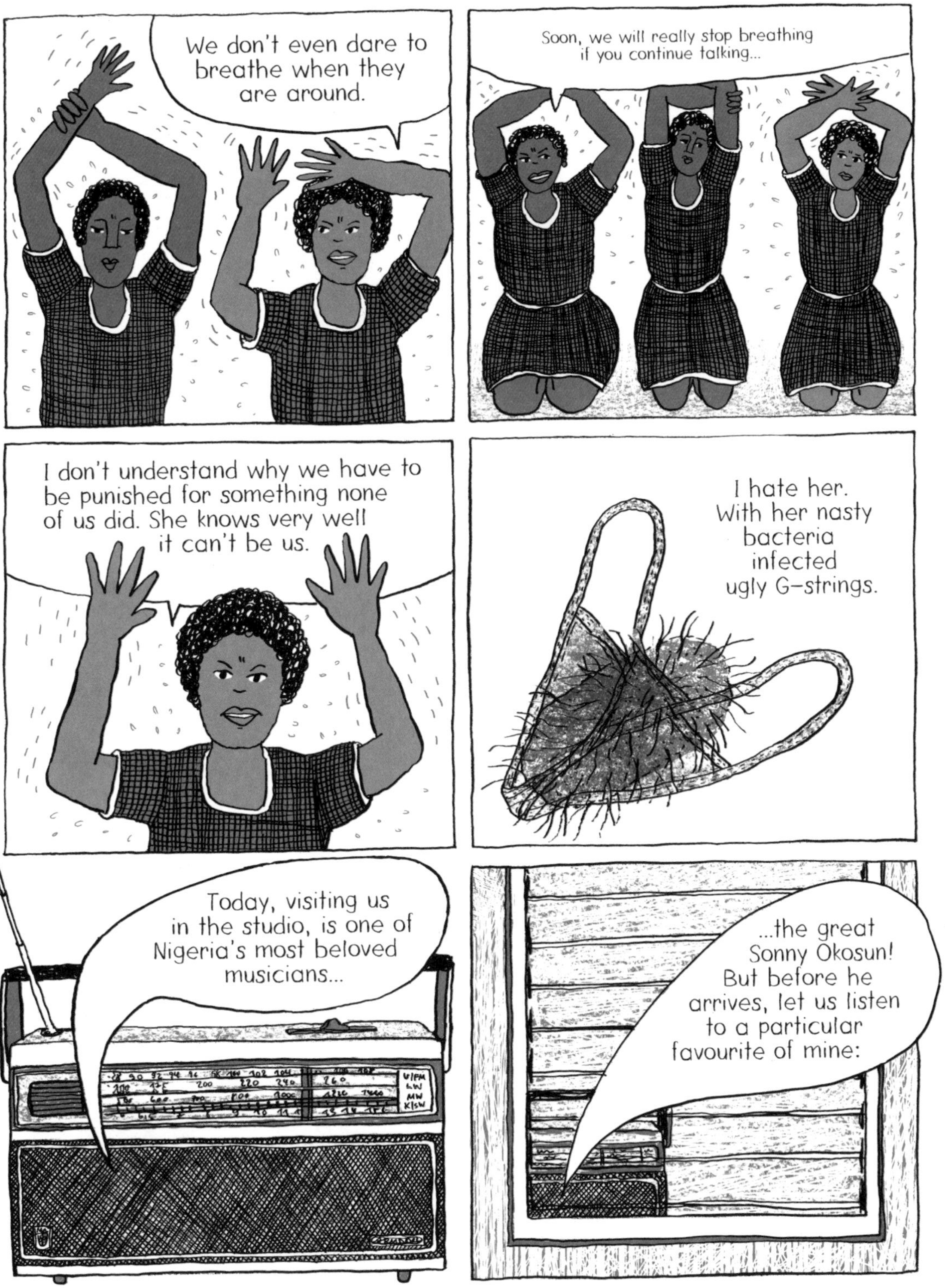

We don't even dare to breathe when they are around.
Soon, we will really stop breathing if you continue talking...
I don't understand why we have to be punished for something none of us did. She knows very well it can't be us.
I hate her. With her nasty bacteria infected ugly G-strings.
Today, visiting us in the studio, is one of Nigeria's most beloved musicians...
...the great Sonny Okosun! But before he arrives, let us listen to a particular favourite of mine:

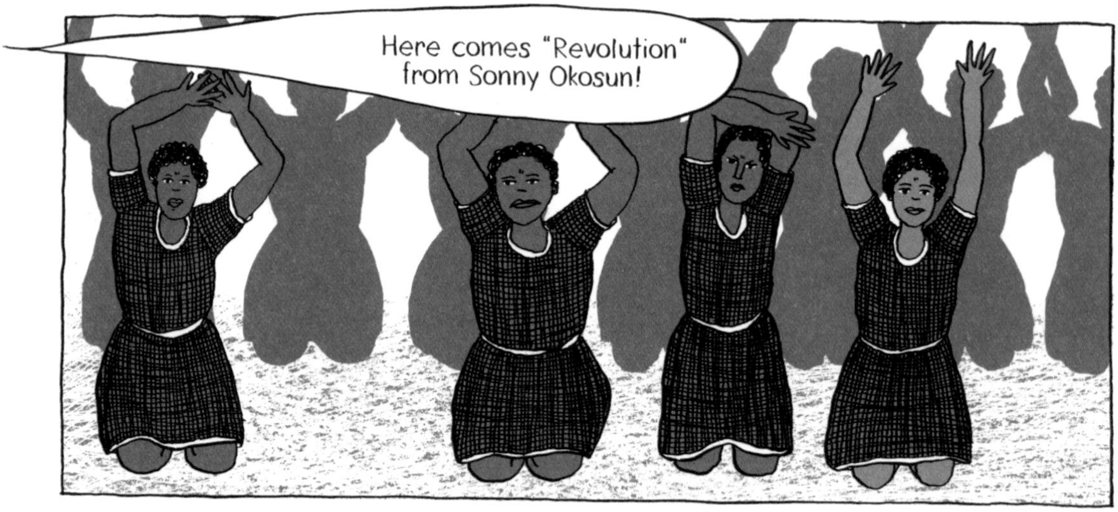
Here comes "Revolution" from Sonny Okosun!

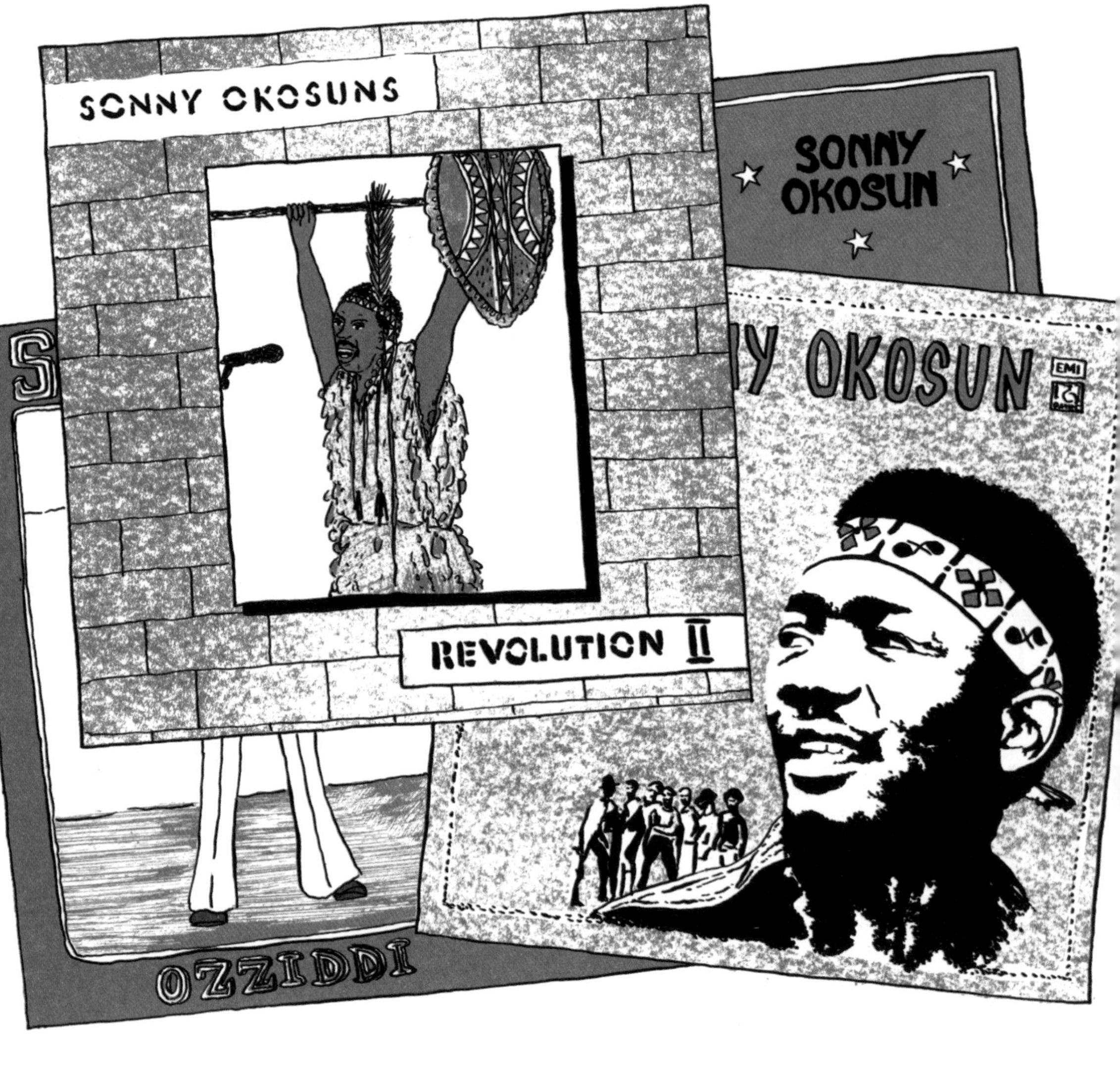
SONNY OKOSUNS
REVOLUTION II
SONNY OKOSUN
Y OKOSUN
EMI
OZZIDDI

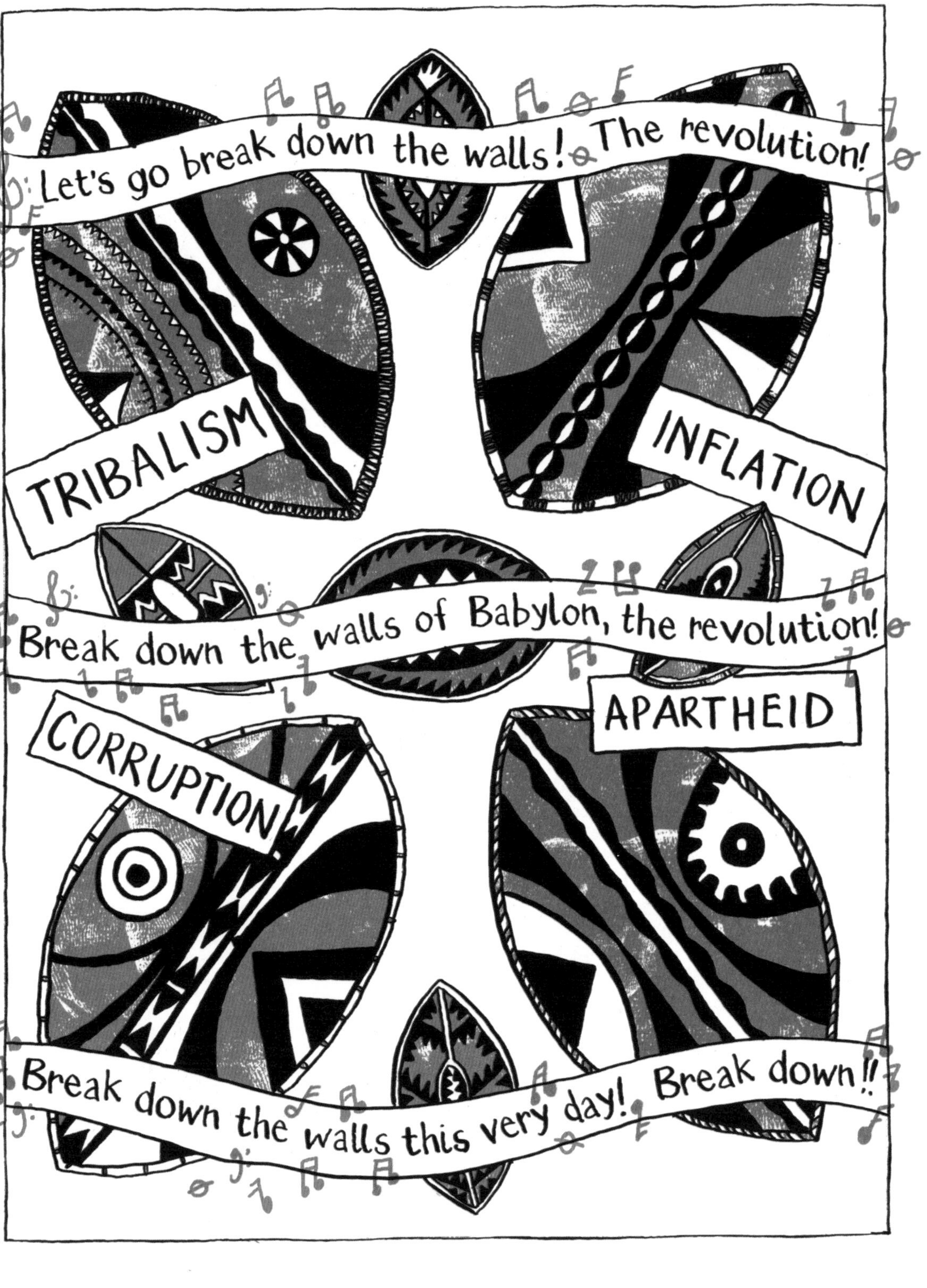
Let's go break down the walls! The revolution!
TRIBALISM
INFLATION
Break down the walls of Babylon, the revolution!
CORRUPTION
APARTHEID
Break down the walls this very day! Break down!!

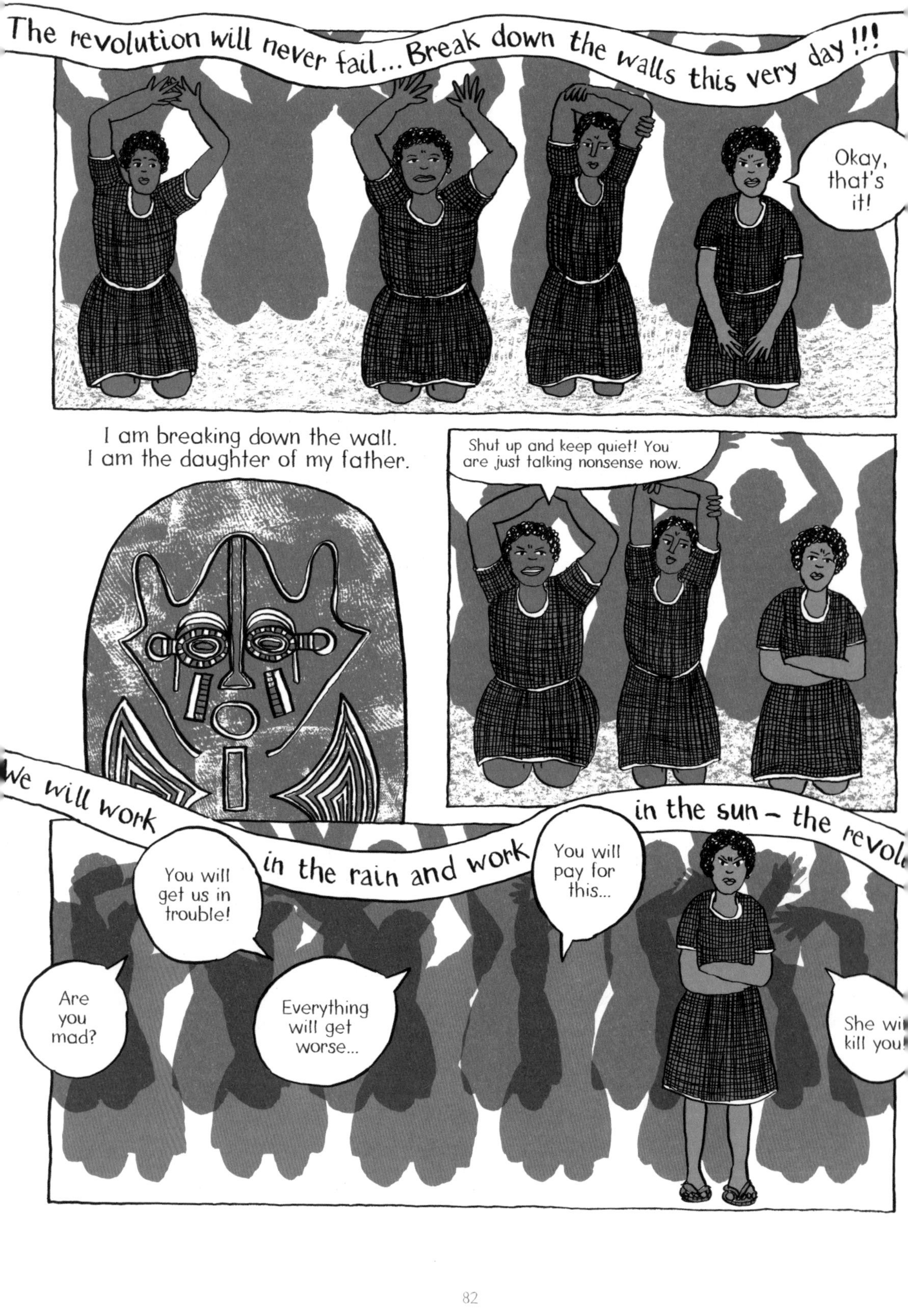
The revolution will never fail... Break down the walls this very day!!!
Okay, that's it!
I am breaking down the wall. I am the daughter of my father.
Shut up and keep quiet! You are just talking nonsense now.
We will work in the rain and work in the sun – the revol
You will get us in trouble!
Are you mad?
Everything will get worse...
You will pay for this...
She wi
kill you!

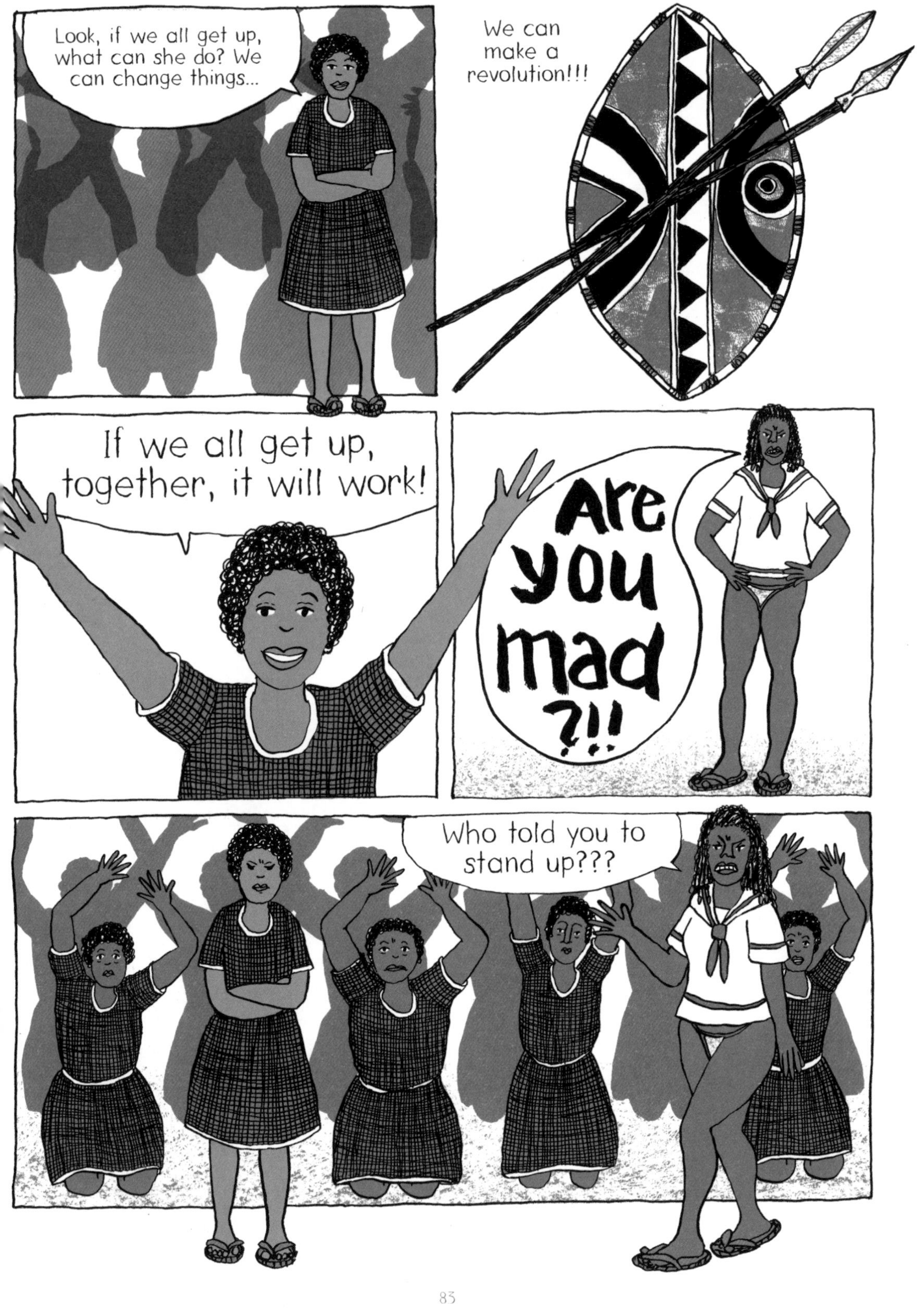
Look, if we all get up, what can she do? We can change things...
We can make a revolution!!!
If we all get up, together, it will work!
Are you mad ?!!
Who told you to stand up???

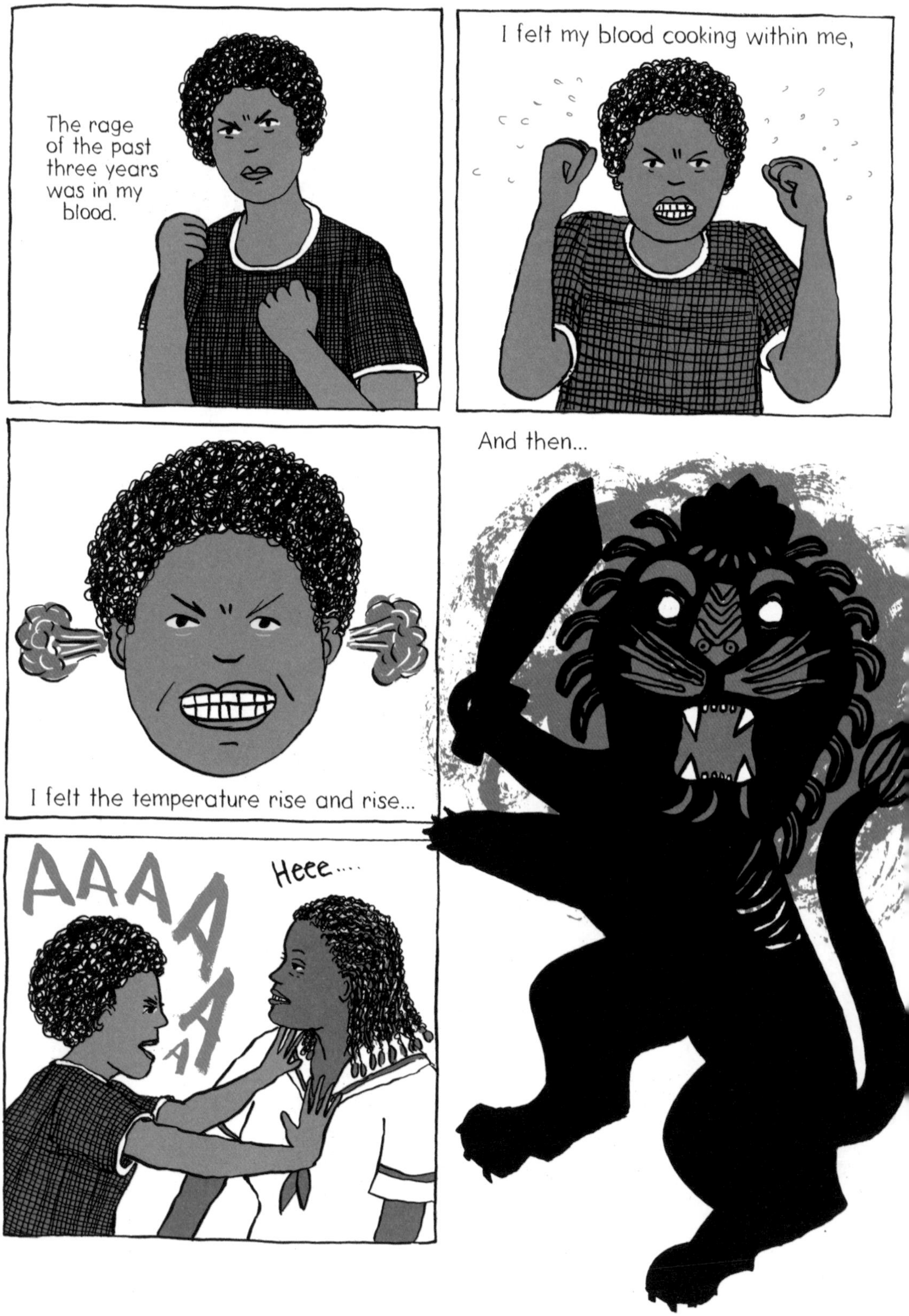
The rage of the past three years was in my blood.
I felt my blood cooking within me,
I felt the temperature rise and rise...
And then...
AAAAAAA
Heee....

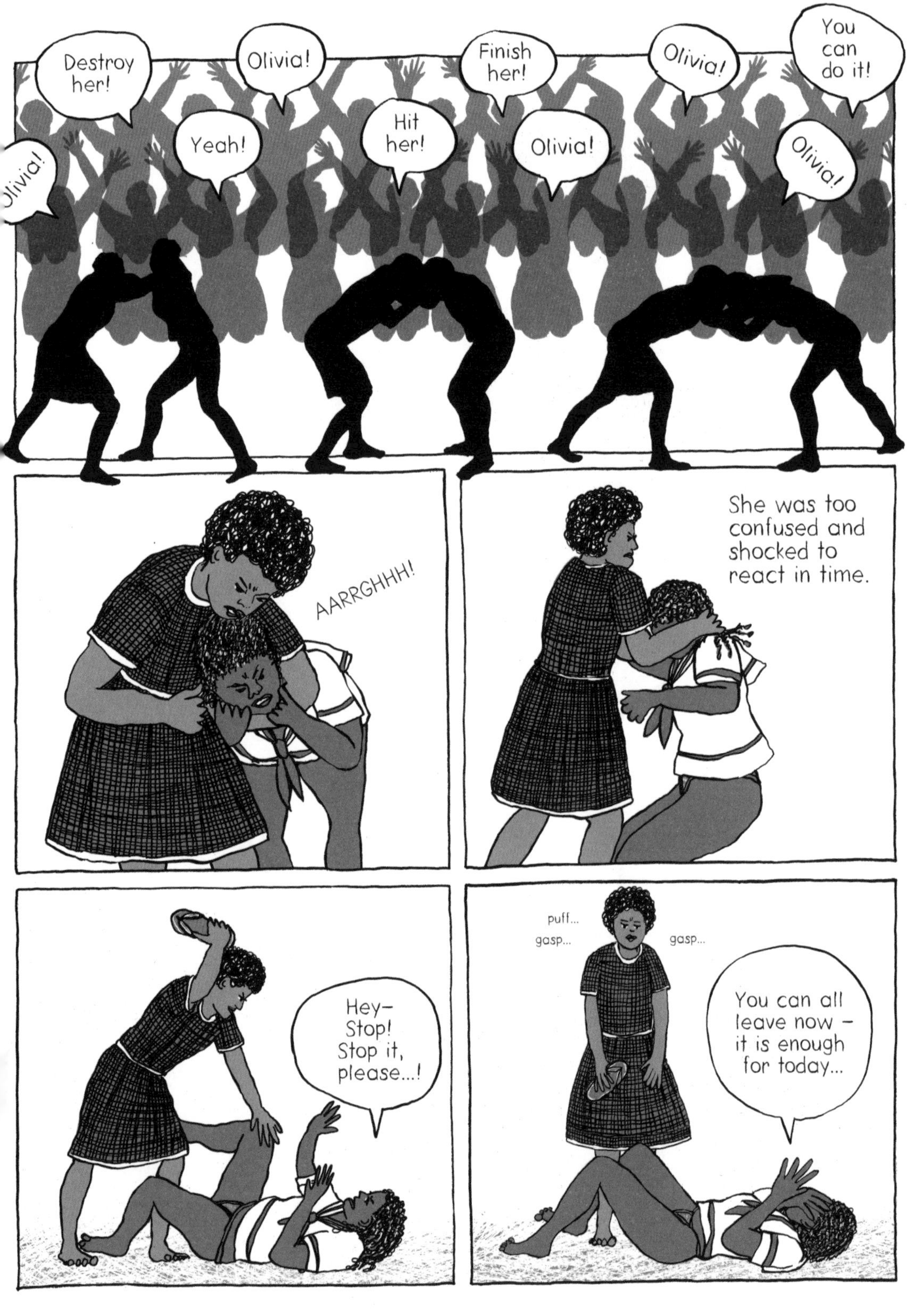
Olivia!
Destroy her!
Yeah!
Olivia!
Hit her!
Finish her!
Olivia!
Olivia!
You can do it!
Olivia!
AARRGHHH!
She was too confused and shocked to react in time.
Hey– Stop! Stop it, please...!
puff...
gasp...
gasp...
You can all leave now – it is enough for today...

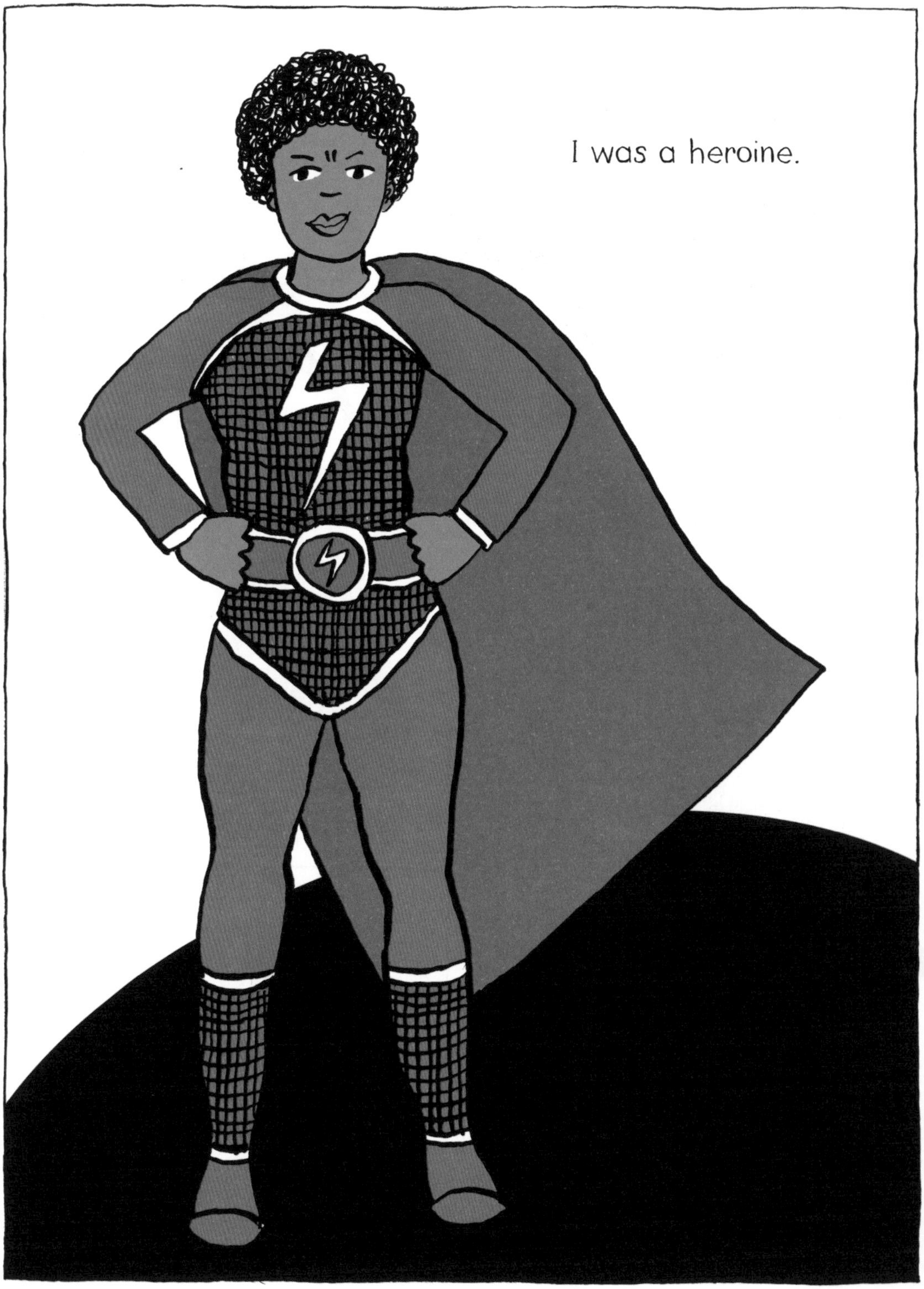
I was a heroine.

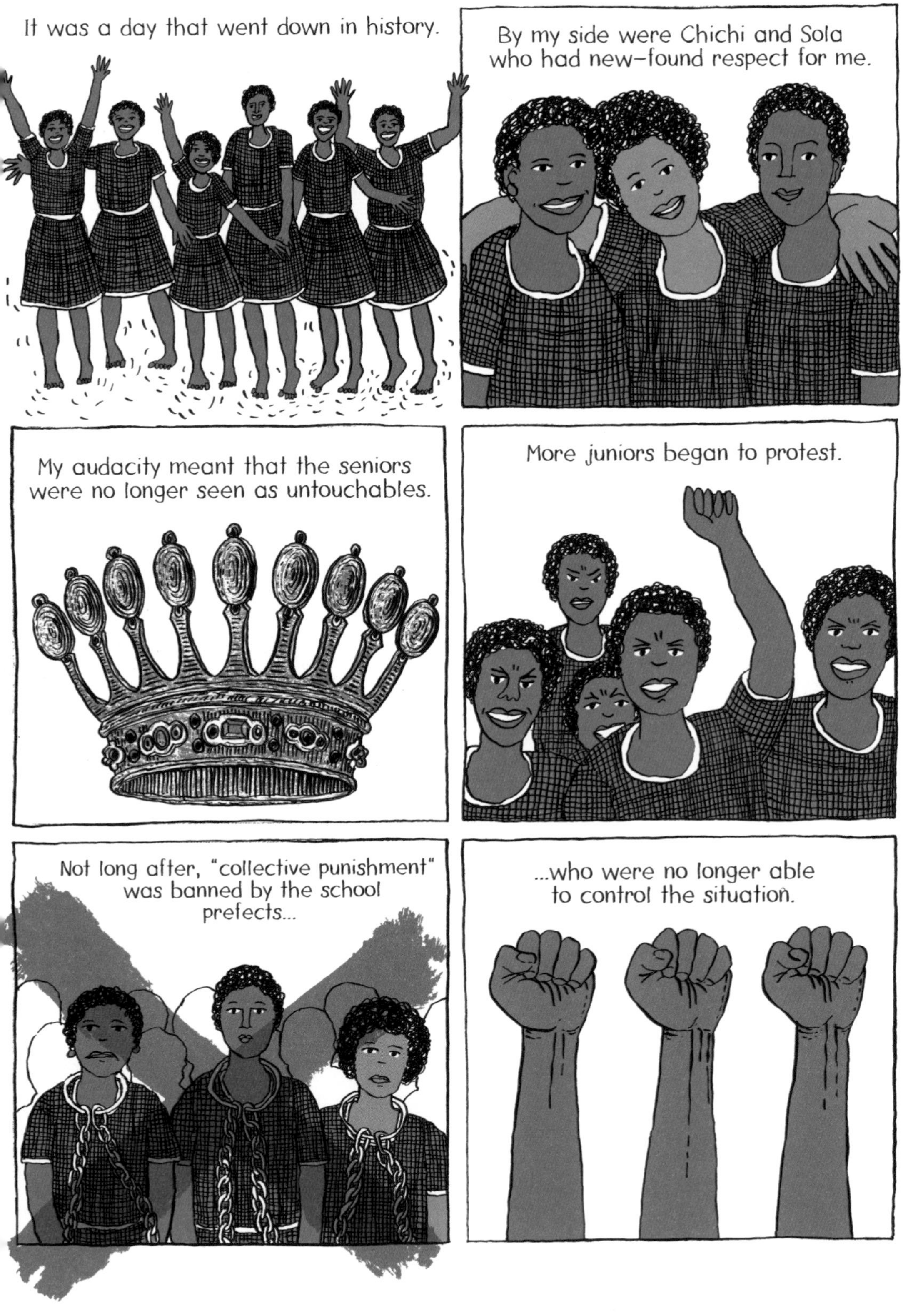

It was a day that went down in history.
By my side were Chichi and Sola who had new-found respect for me.
My audacity meant that the seniors were no longer seen as untouchables.
More juniors began to protest.
Not long after, "collective punishment" was banned by the school prefects...
...who were no longer able to control the situation.

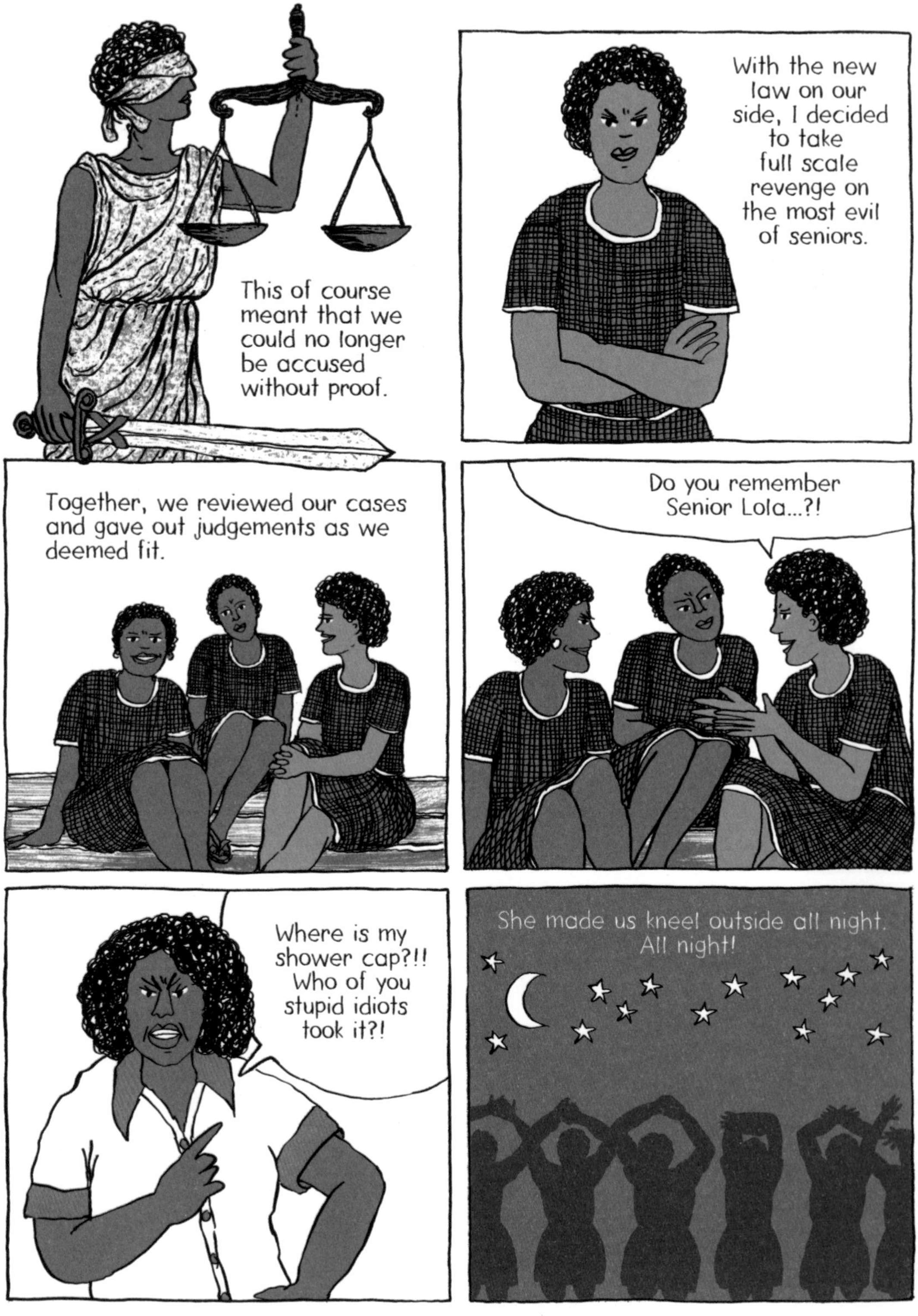
This of course meant that we could no longer be accused without proof.
With the new law on our side, I decided to take full scale revenge on the most evil of seniors.
Together, we reviewed our cases and gave out judgements as we deemed fit.
Do you remember Senior Lola...?!
Where is my shower cap?!! Who of you stupid idiots took it?!
She made us kneel outside all night. All night!

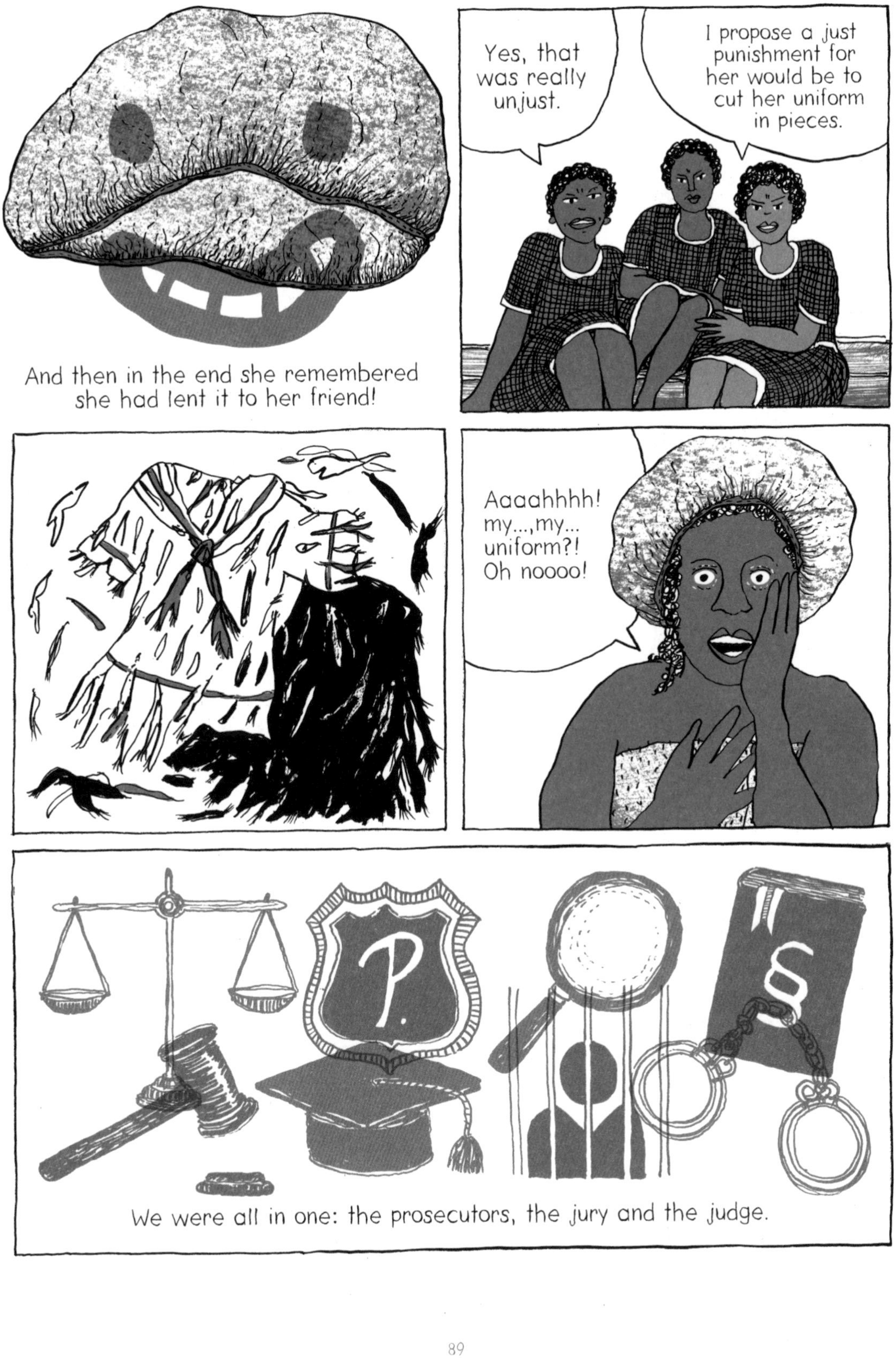
And then in the end she remembered she had lent it to her friend!
Yes, that was really unjust.
I propose a just punishment for her would be to cut her uniform in pieces.
Aaaahhhh! my...,my... uniform?! Oh noooo!
P.
§
We were all in one: the prosecutors, the jury and the judge.

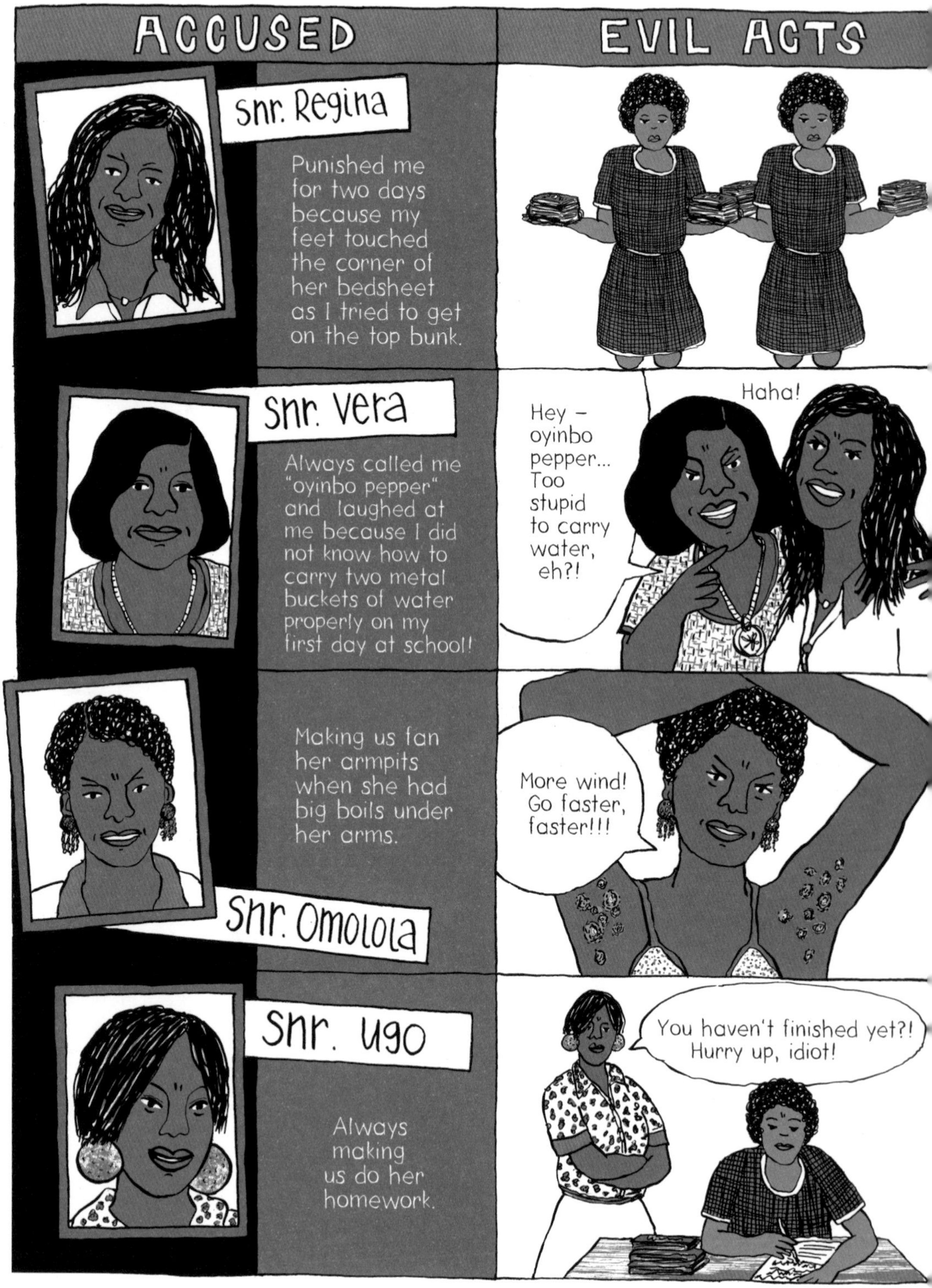
ACCUSED
EVIL ACTS
Snr. Regina
Punished me for two days because my feet touched the corner of her bedsheet as I tried to get on the top bunk.
Snr. Vera
Always called me "oyinbo pepper" and laughed at me because I did not know how to carry two metal buckets of water properly on my first day at school!
Hey – oyinbo pepper... Too stupid to carry water, eh?!
Haha!
Making us fan her armpits when she had big boils under her arms.
Snr. Omolola
More wind! Go faster, faster!!!
Snr. Ugo
Always making us do her homework.
You haven't finished yet?! Hurry up, idiot!

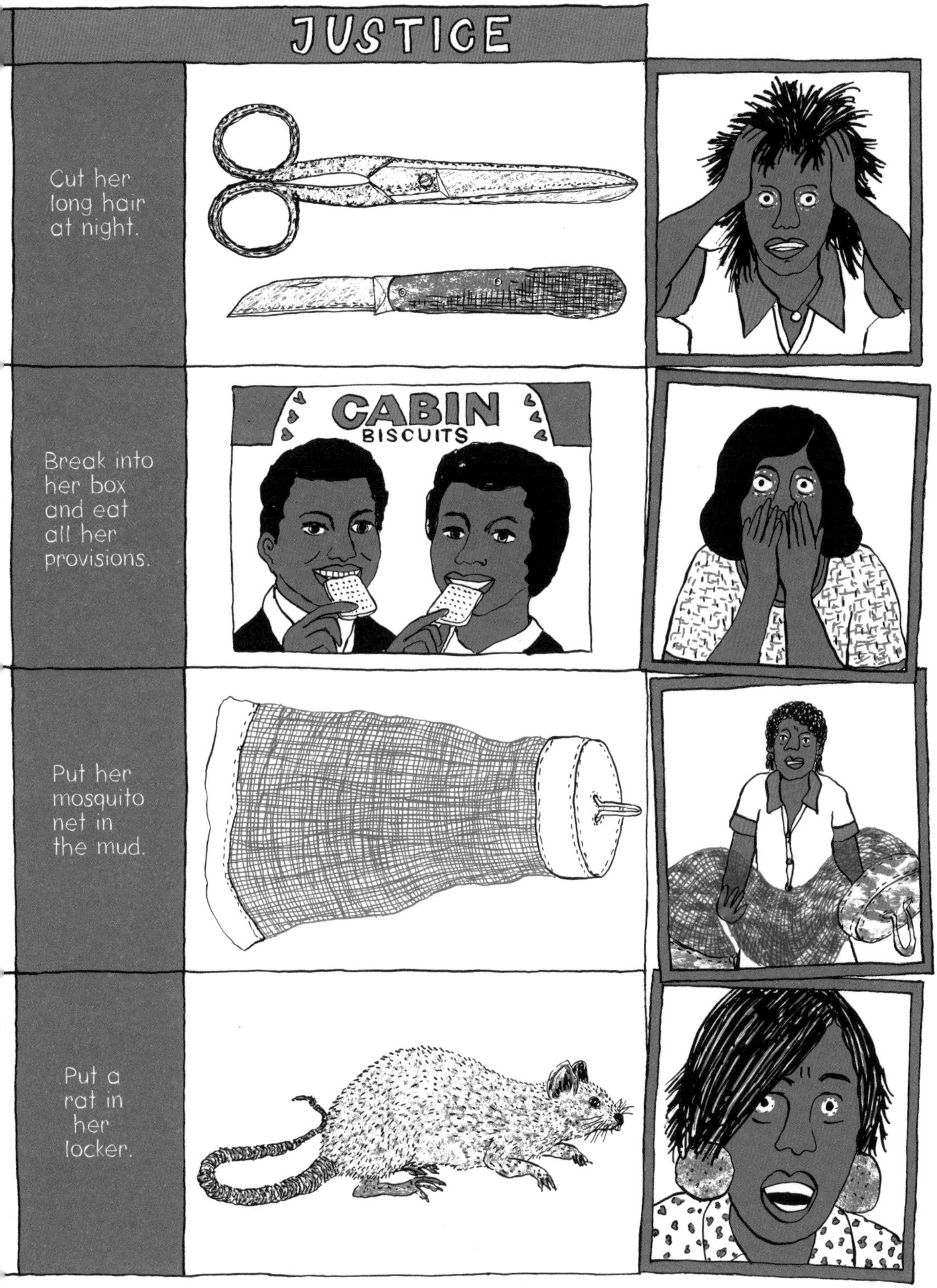
JUSTICE
Cut her long hair at night.
Break into her box and eat all her provisions.
CABIN BISCUITS
Put her mosquito net in the mud.
Put a rat in her locker.

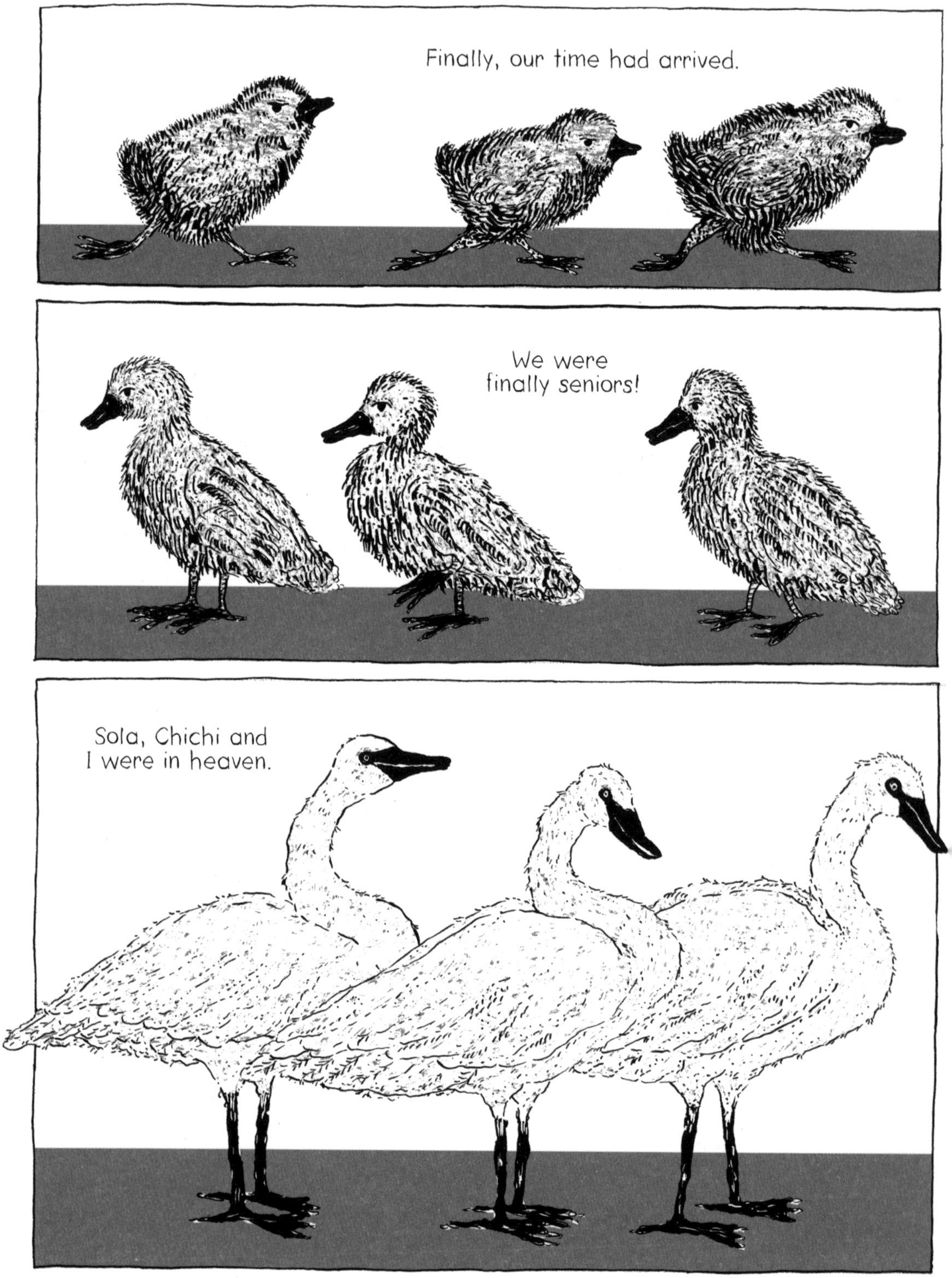
Finally, our time had arrived.
We were finally seniors!
Sola, Chichi and I were in heaven.

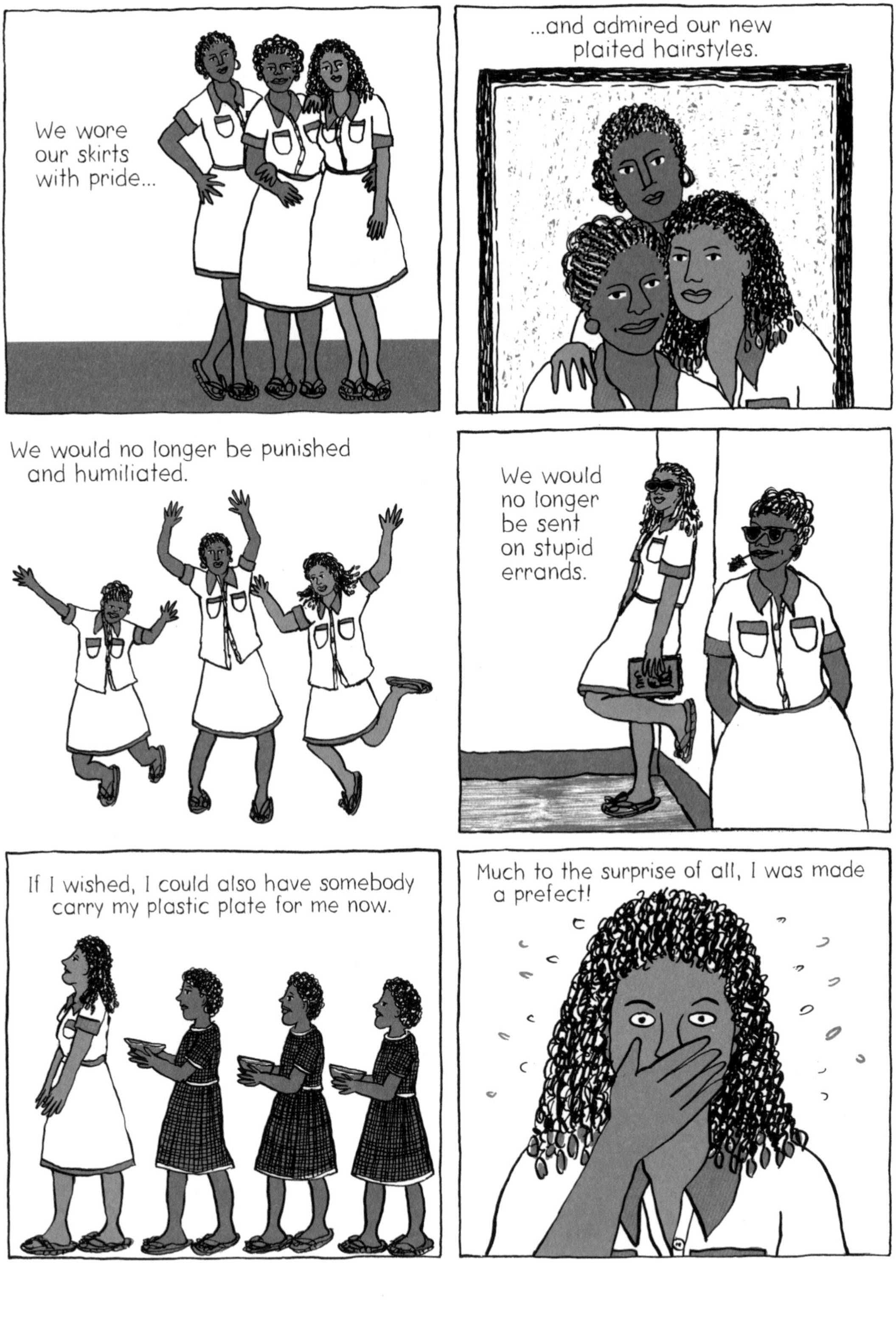
We wore our skirts with pride...
...and admired our new plaited hairstyles.
We would no longer be punished and humiliated.
We would no longer be sent on stupid errands.
If I wished, I could also have somebody carry my plastic plate for me now.
Much to the surprise of all, I was made a prefect!

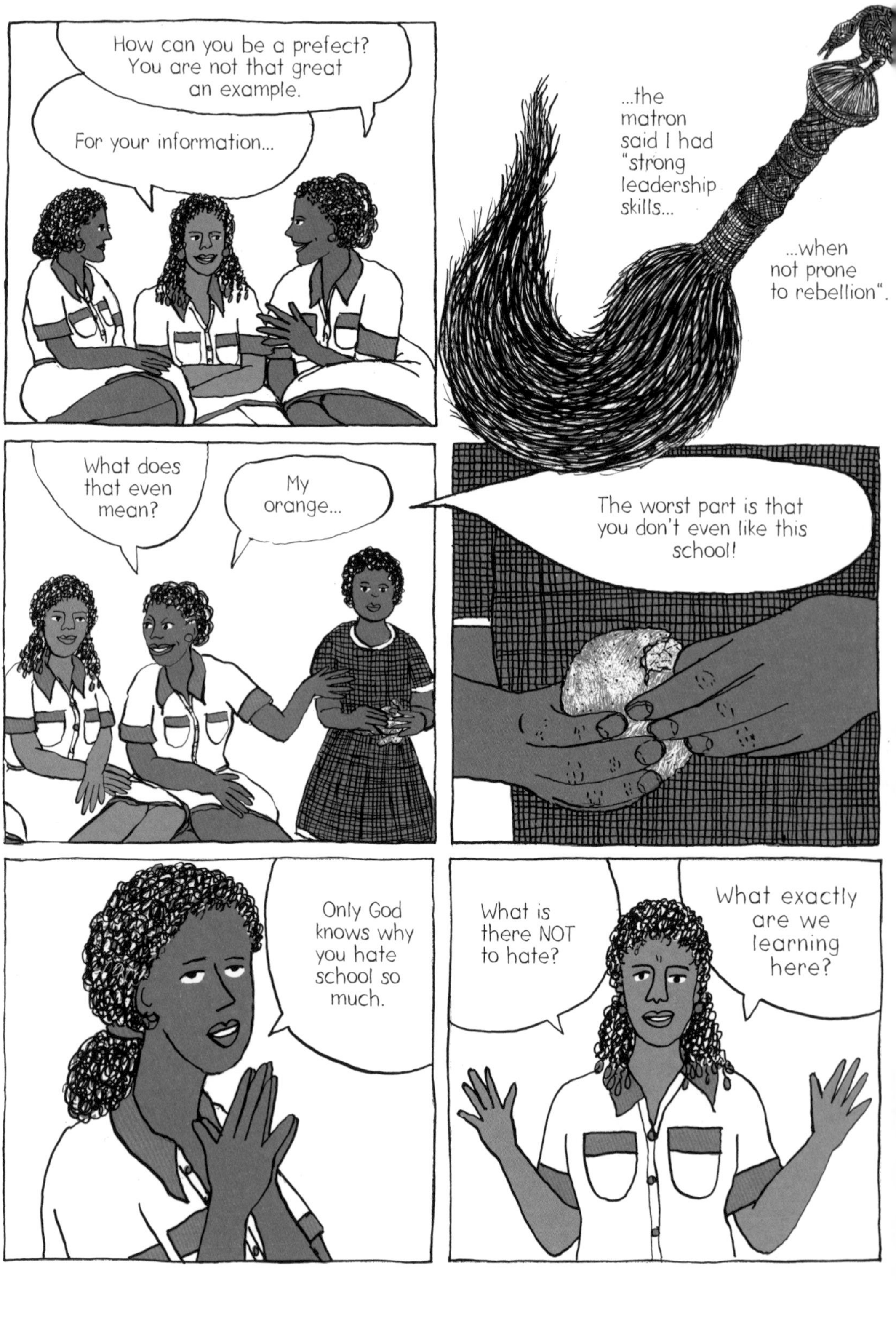
How can you be a prefect? You are not that great an example.
For your information...
...the matron said I had "strong leadership skills...
...when not prone to rebellion".
What does that even mean?
My orange...
The worst part is that you don't even like this school!
Only God knows why you hate school so much.
What is there NOT to hate?
What exactly are we learning here?

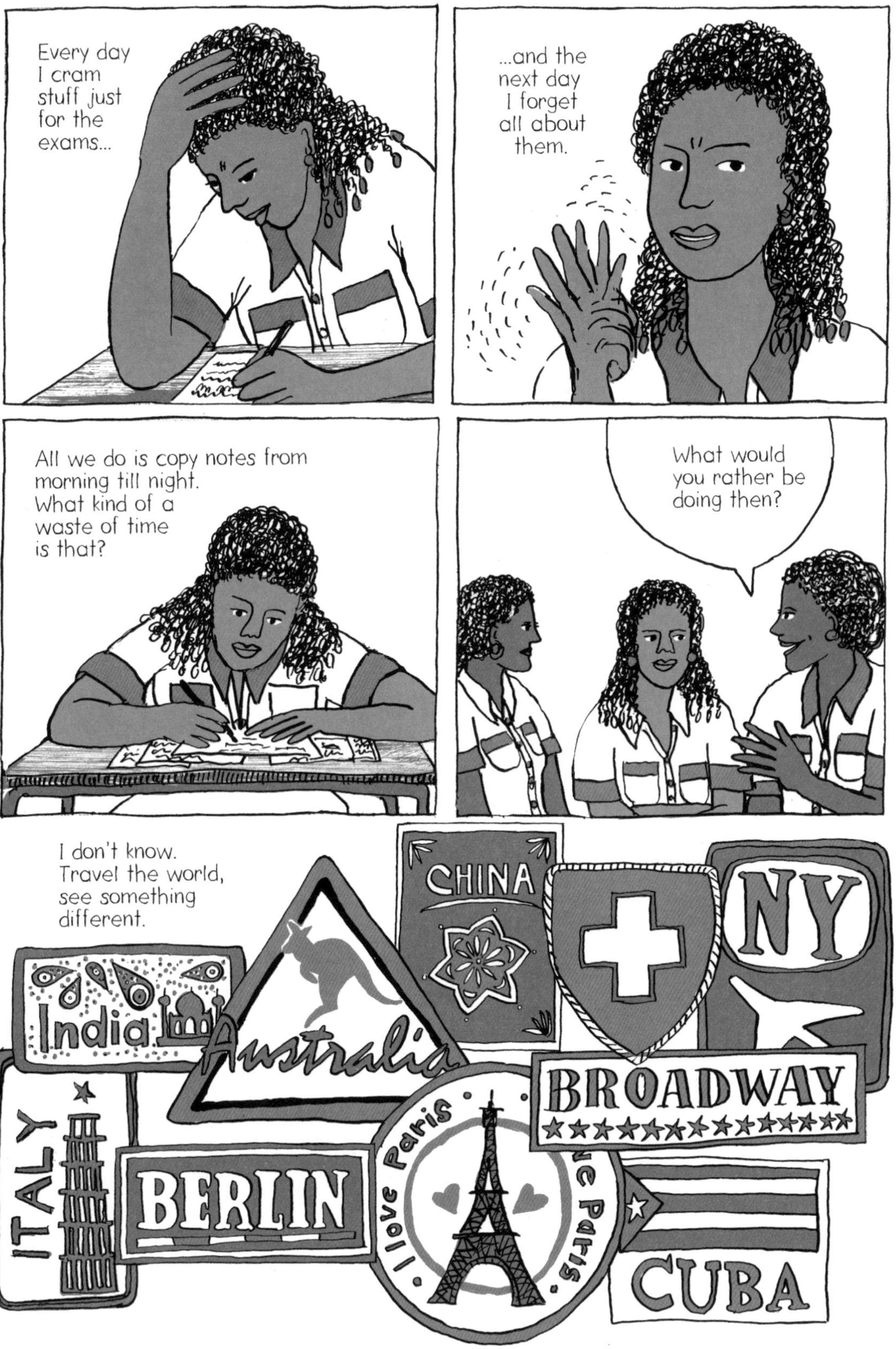
Every day I cram stuff just for the exams...
...and the next day I forget all about them.
All we do is copy notes from morning till night. What kind of a waste of time is that?
What would you rather be doing then?
I don't know. Travel the world, see something different.
CHINA
NY
India
Australia
BROADWAY
ITALY
BERLIN
I love Paris
I love Paris
CUBA

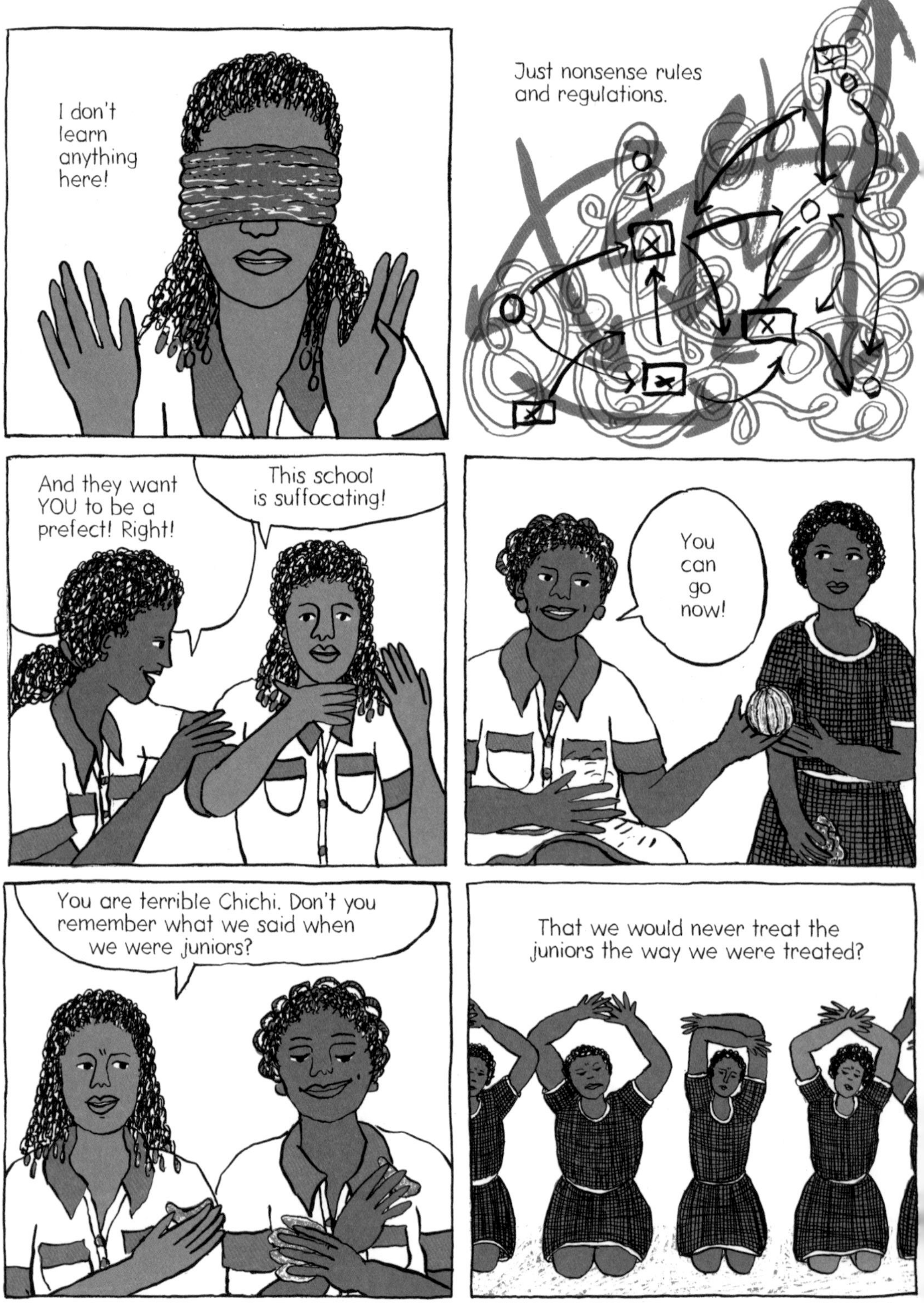
I don't learn anything here!
Just nonsense rules and regulations.
And they want YOU to be a prefect! Right!
This school is suffocating!
You can go now!
You are terrible Chichi. Don't you remember what we said when we were juniors?
That we would never treat the juniors the way we were treated?

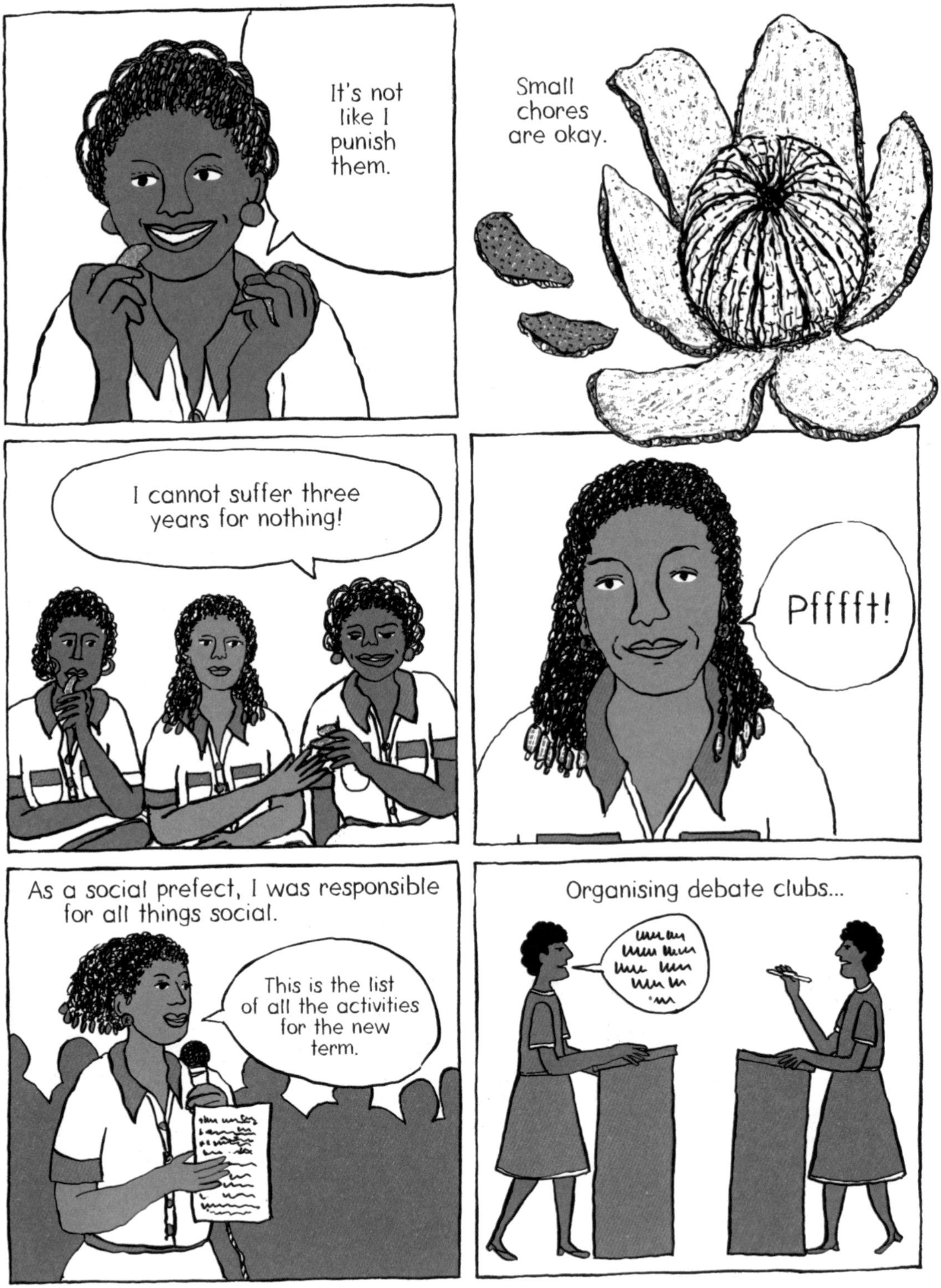

It's not like I punish them.
Small chores are okay.
I cannot suffer three years for nothing!
Pfffft!
As a social prefect, I was responsible for all things social.
This is the list of all the activities for the new term.
Organising debate clubs...

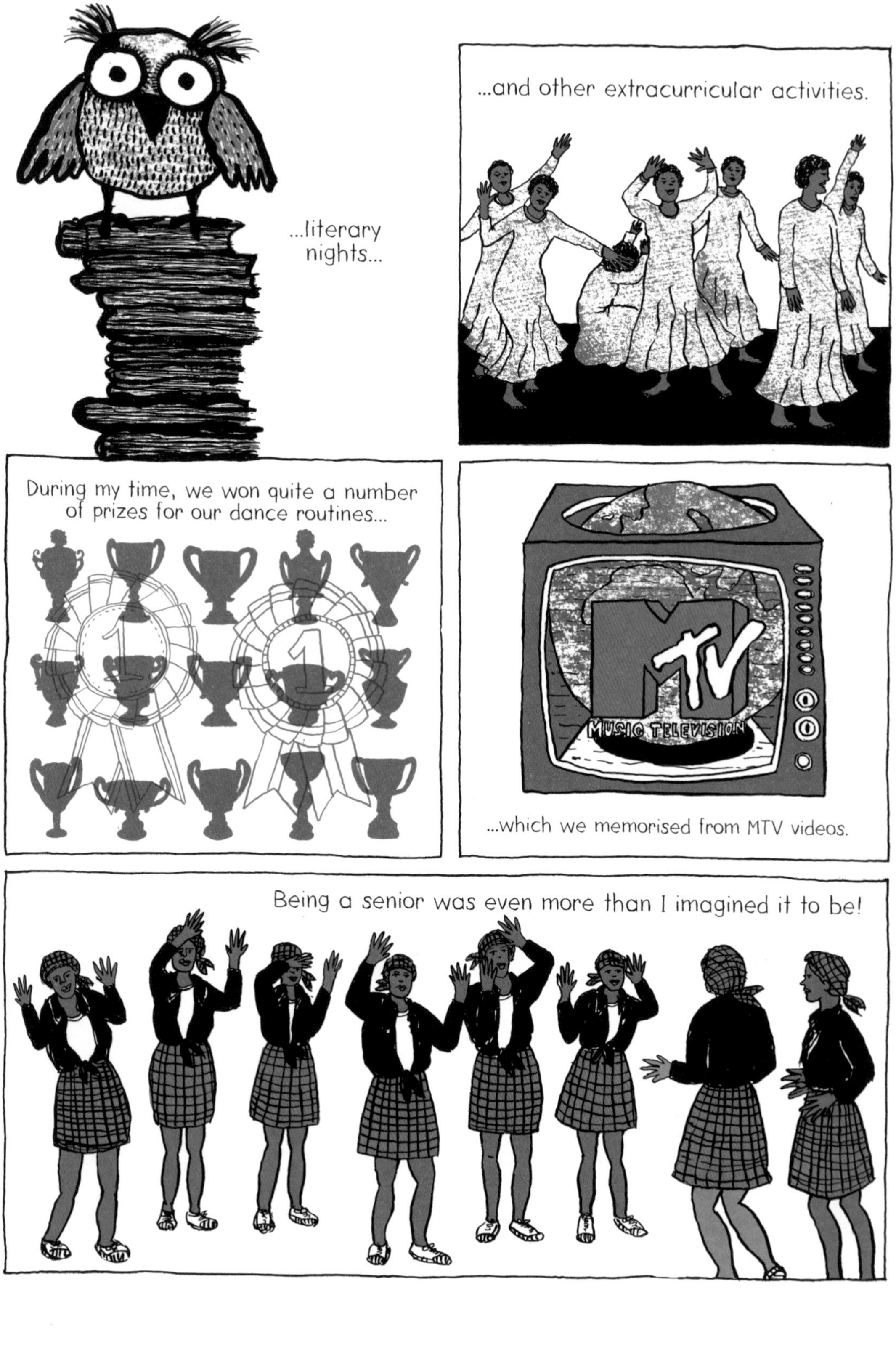
...literary nights...
...and other extracurricular activities.
During my time, we won quite a number of prizes for our dance routines...
MTV
MUSIC TELEVISION
...which we memorised from MTV videos.
Being a senior was even more than I imagined it to be!

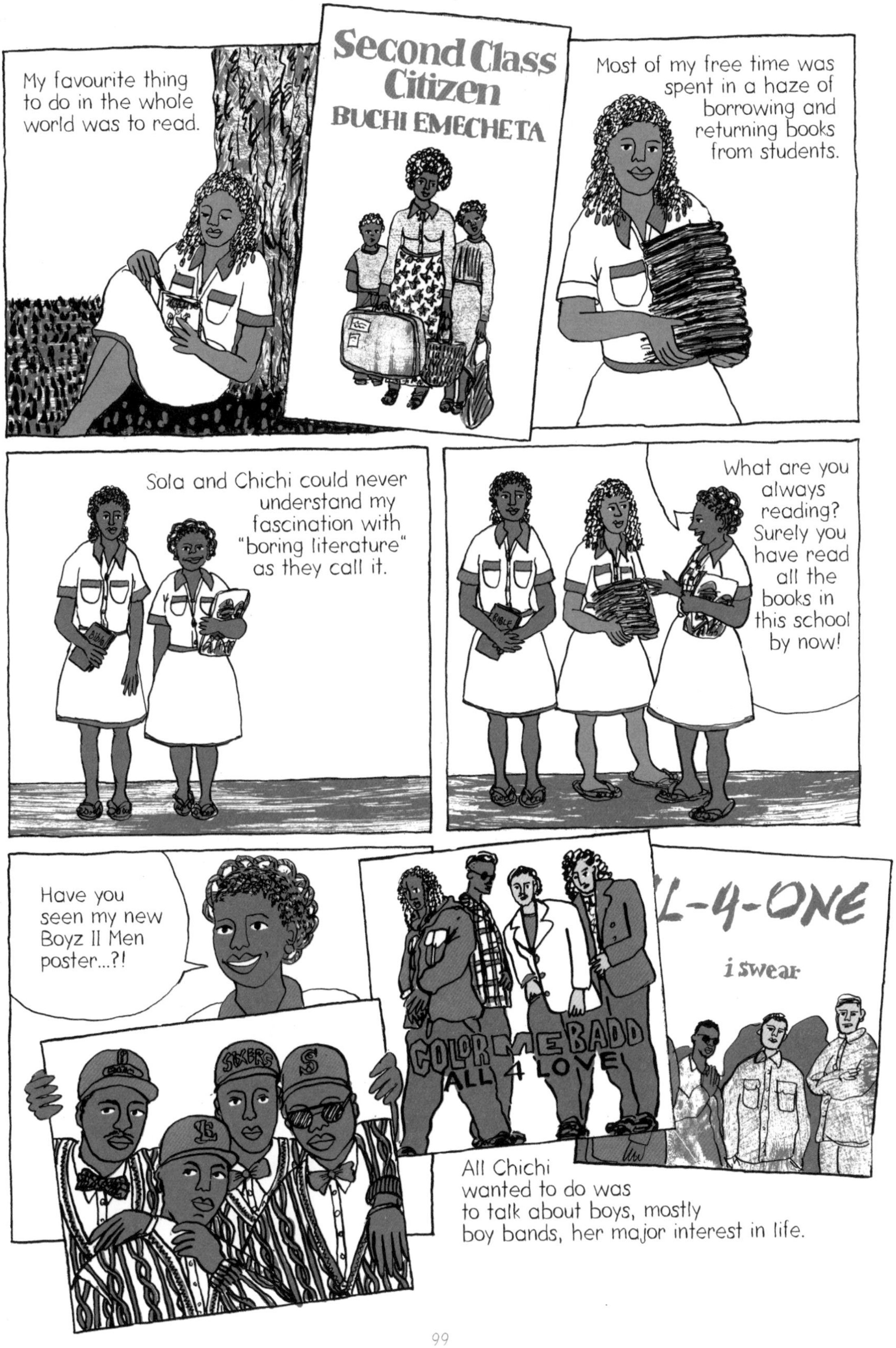
My favourite thing to do in the whole world was to read.
Second Class Citizen
BUCHI EMECHETA
Most of my free time was spent in a haze of borrowing and returning books from students.
Sola and Chichi could never understand my fascination with "boring literature" as they call it.
What are you always reading? Surely you have read all the books in this school by now!
Have you seen my new Boyz II Men poster...?!
COLOR ME BADD
ALL 4 LOVE
L-4-ONE
i swear
All Chichi wanted to do was to talk about boys, mostly boy bands, her major interest in life.

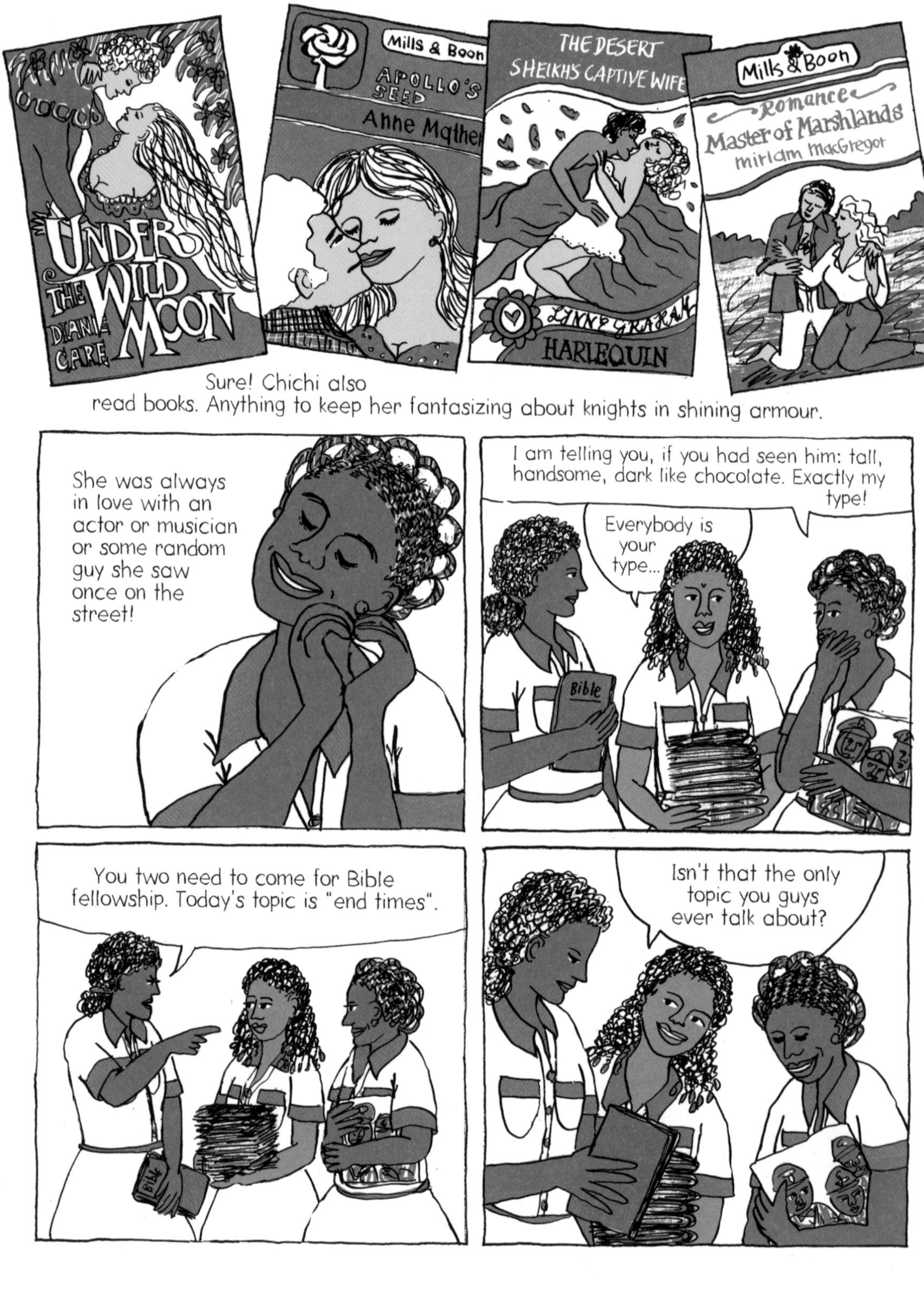
UNDER THE WILD MOON
DIANA CARE
Mills & Boon
APOLLO'S SEED
Anne Mather
THE DESERT SHEIKH'S CAPTIVE WIFE
HARLEQUIN
Mills & Boon
Romance
Master of Marshlands
Miriam MacGregor
Sure! Chichi also read books. Anything to keep her fantasizing about knights in shining armour.
She was always in love with an actor or musician or some random guy she saw once on the street!
I am telling you, if you had seen him: tall, handsome, dark like chocolate. Exactly my type!
Everybody is your type...
Bible
You two need to come for Bible fellowship. Today's topic is "end times".
Bible
Isn't that the only topic you guys ever talk about?

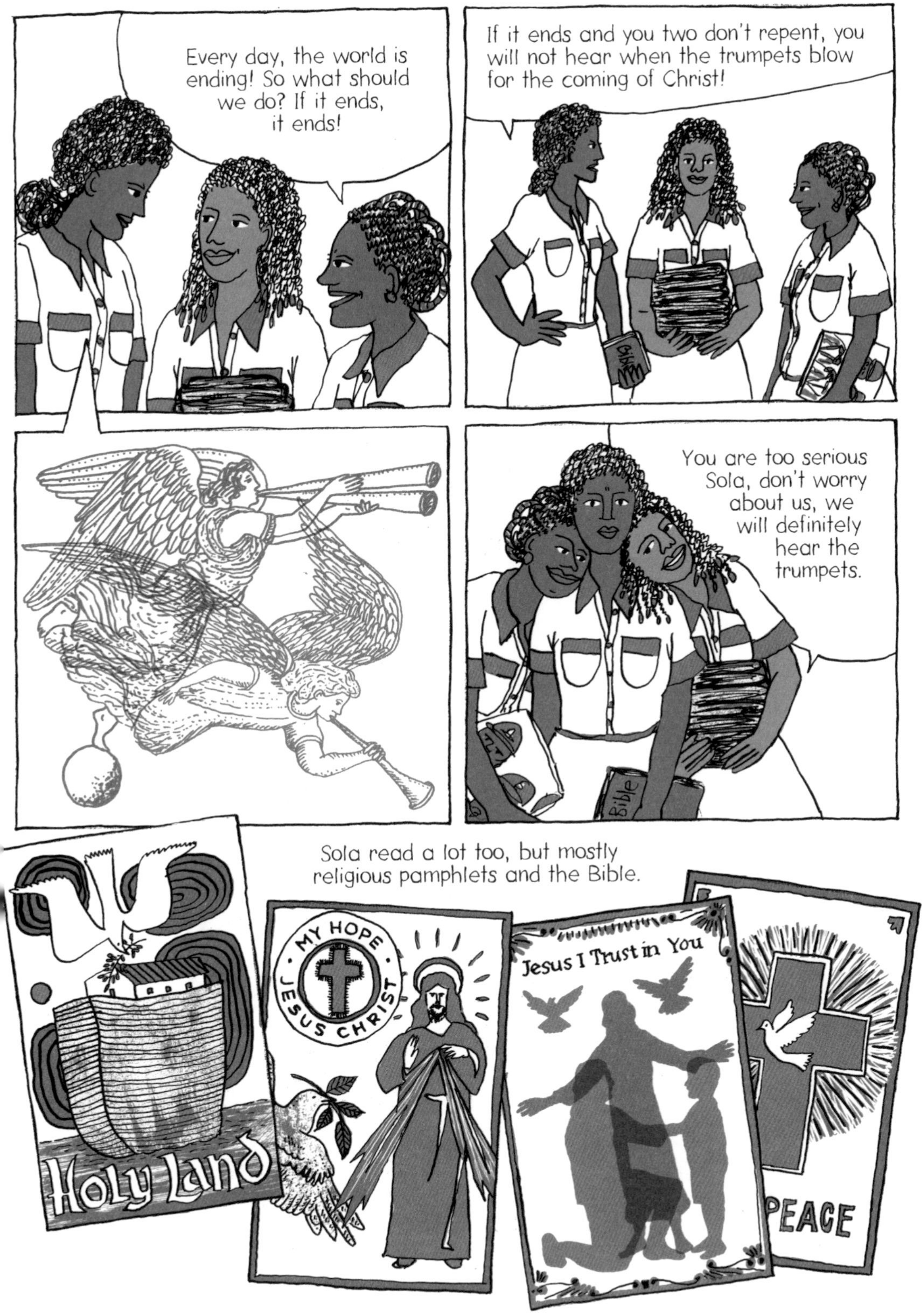
Every day, the world is ending! So what should we do? If it ends, it ends!
If it ends and you two don't repent, you will not hear when the trumpets blow for the coming of Christ!
Bible
You are too serious Sola, don't worry about us, we will definitely hear the trumpets.
Bible
Sola read a lot too, but mostly religious pamphlets and the Bible.
Holy Land
MY HOPE JESUS CHRIST
Jesus I Trust in You
PEACE

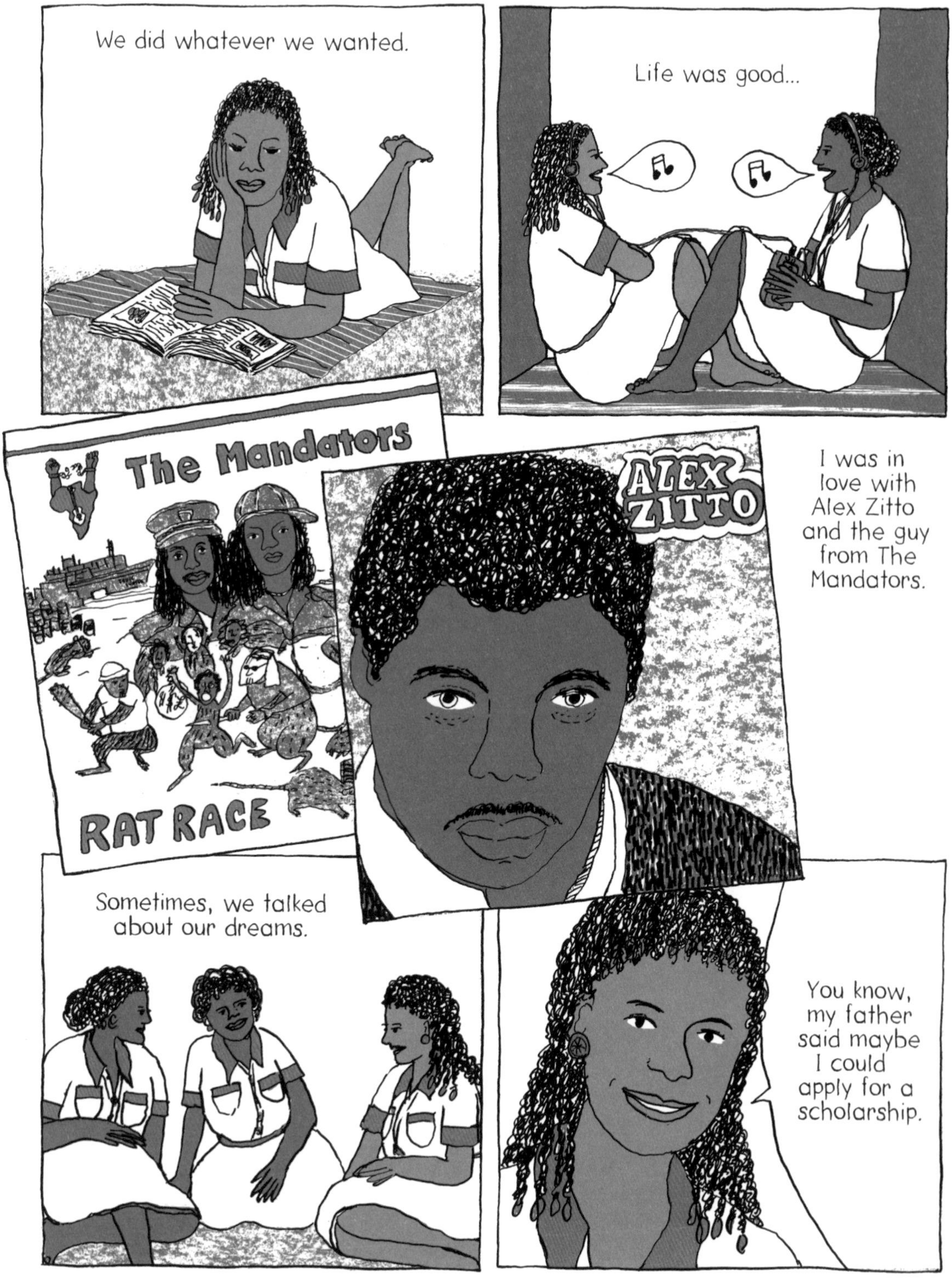

We did whatever we wanted.
Life was good...
The Mandators
RAT RACE
ALEX ZITTO
I was in love with Alex Zitto and the guy from The Mandators.
Sometimes, we talked about our dreams.
You know, my father said maybe I could apply for a scholarship.

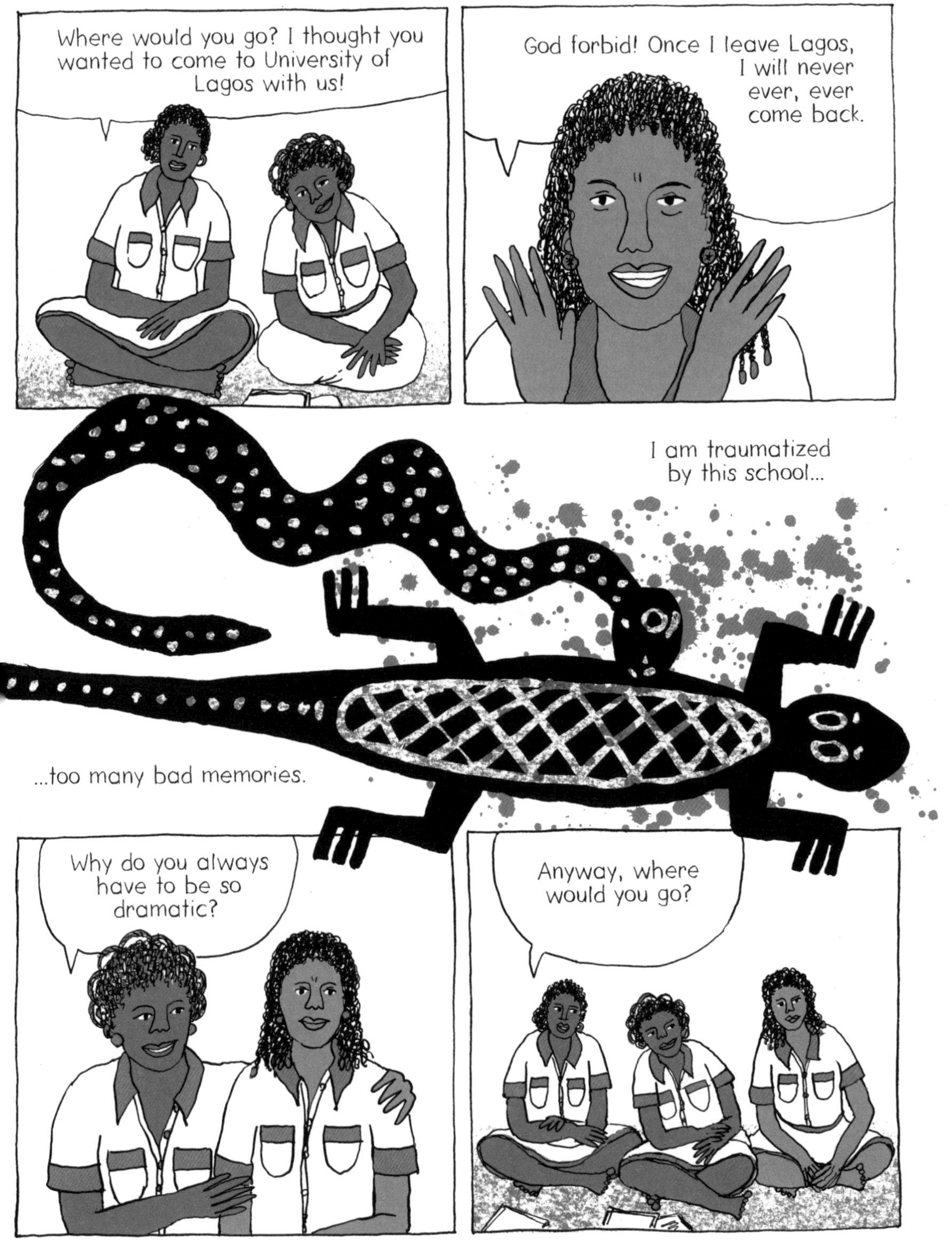
Where would you go? I thought you wanted to come to University of Lagos with us!
God forbid! Once I leave Lagos, I will never ever, ever come back.
I am traumatized by this school...
...too many bad memories.
Why do you always have to be so dramatic?
Anyway, where would you go?

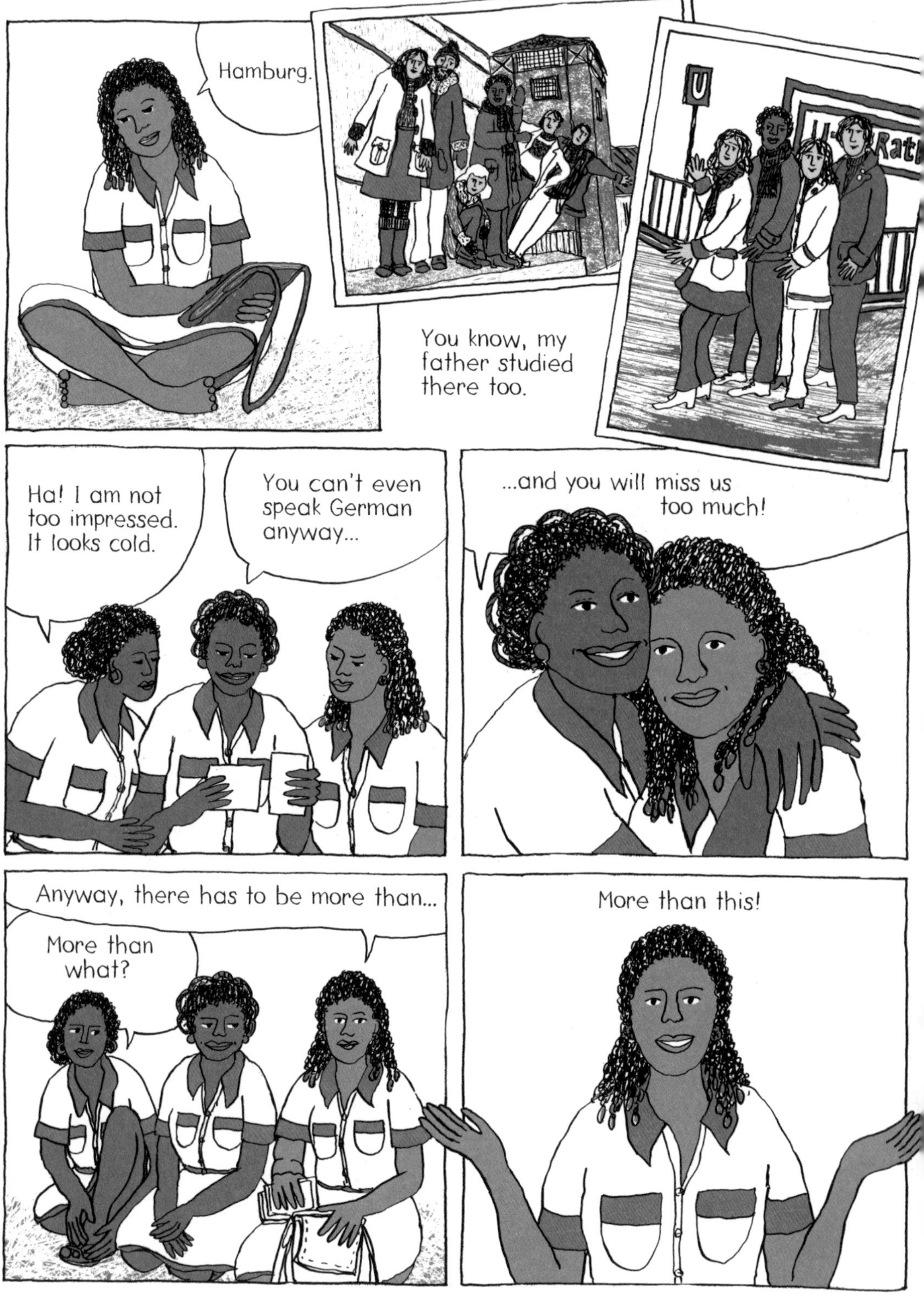
Hamburg.
You know, my father studied there too.
U
Ha! I am not too impressed. It looks cold.
You can't even speak German anyway...
...and you will miss us too much!
Anyway, there has to be more than...
More than what?
More than this!

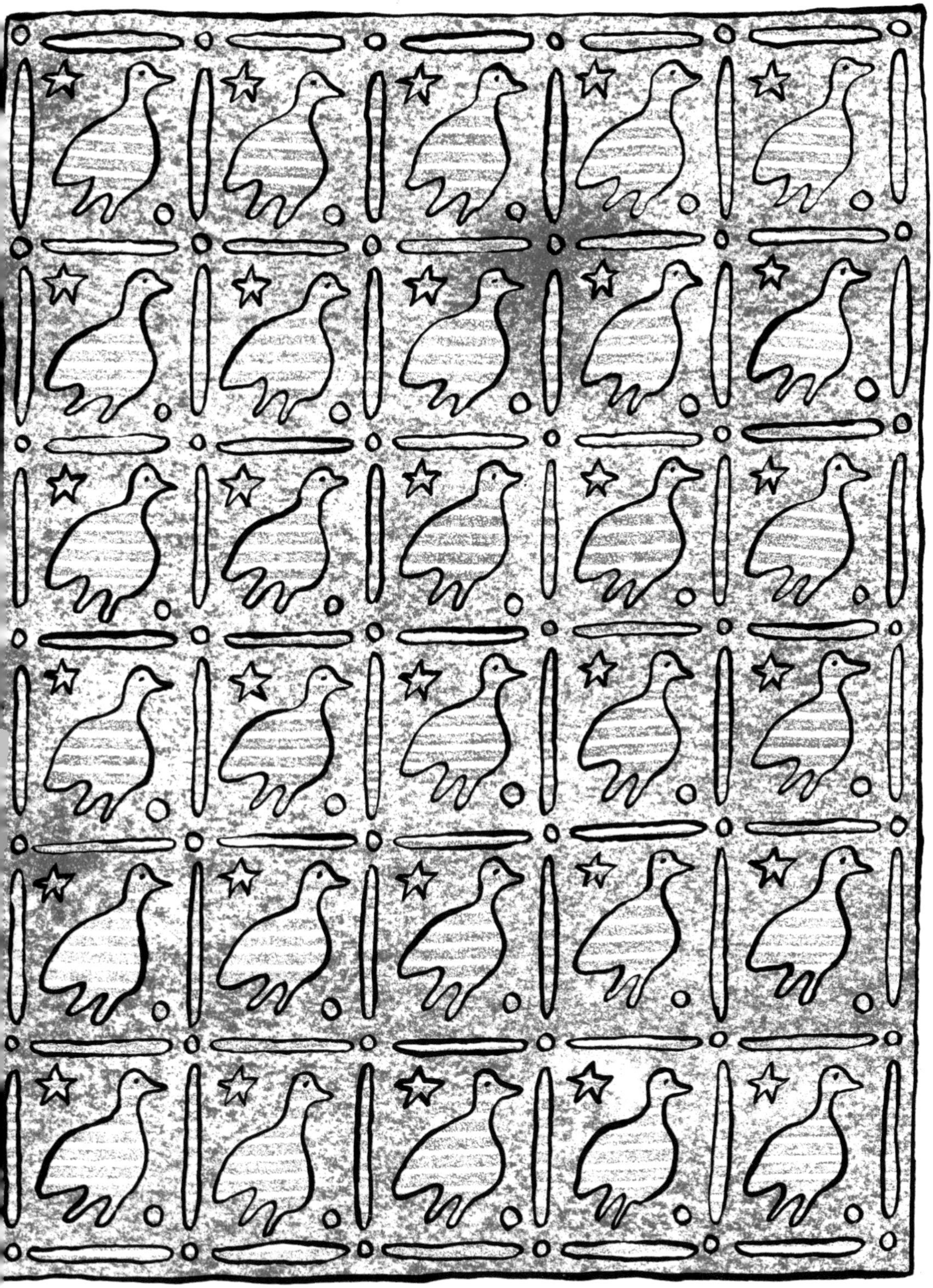

My time as a senior was flying by.

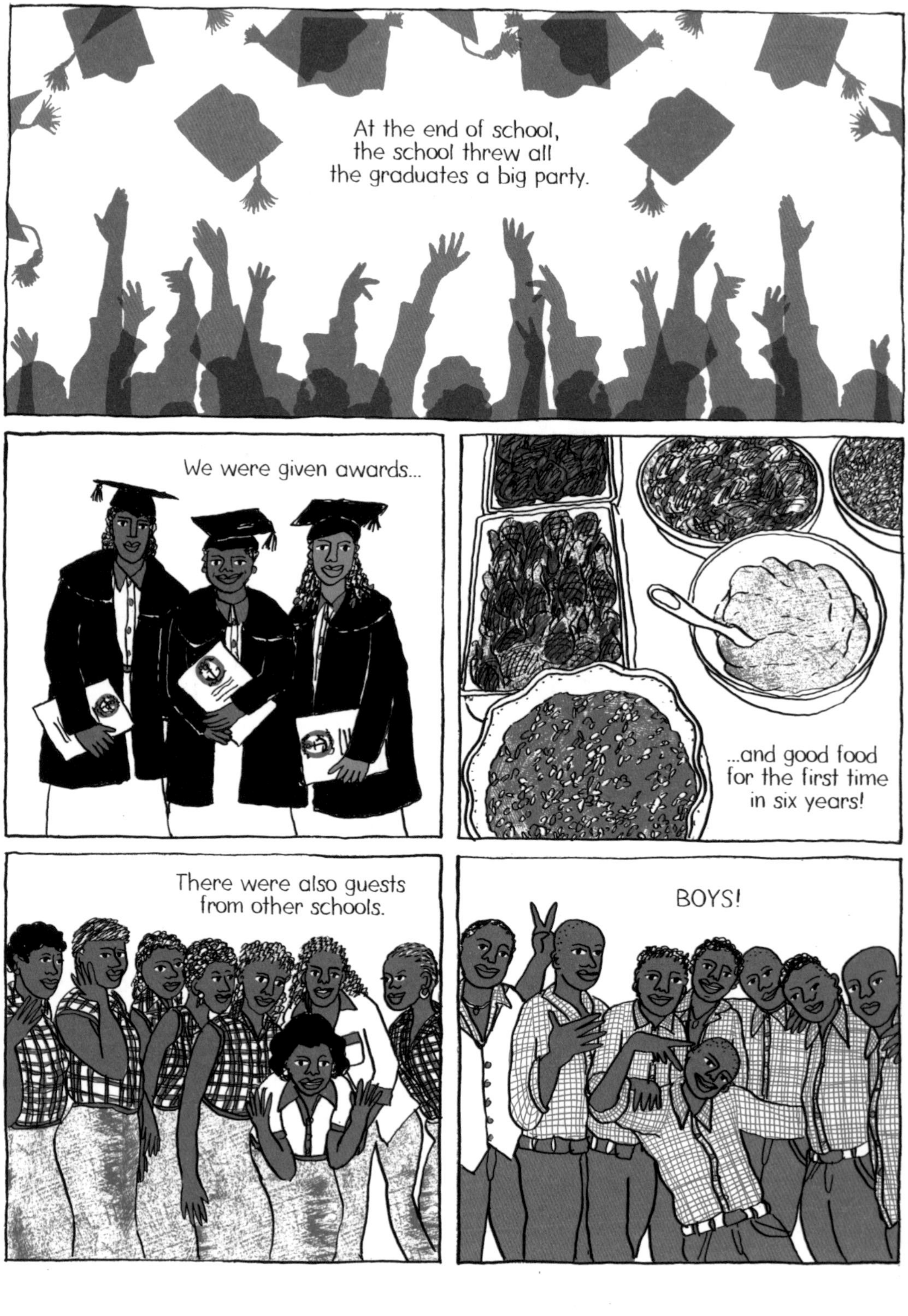
At the end of school, the school threw all the graduates a big party.
We were given awards...
...and good food for the first time in six years!
There were also guests from other schools.
BOYS!

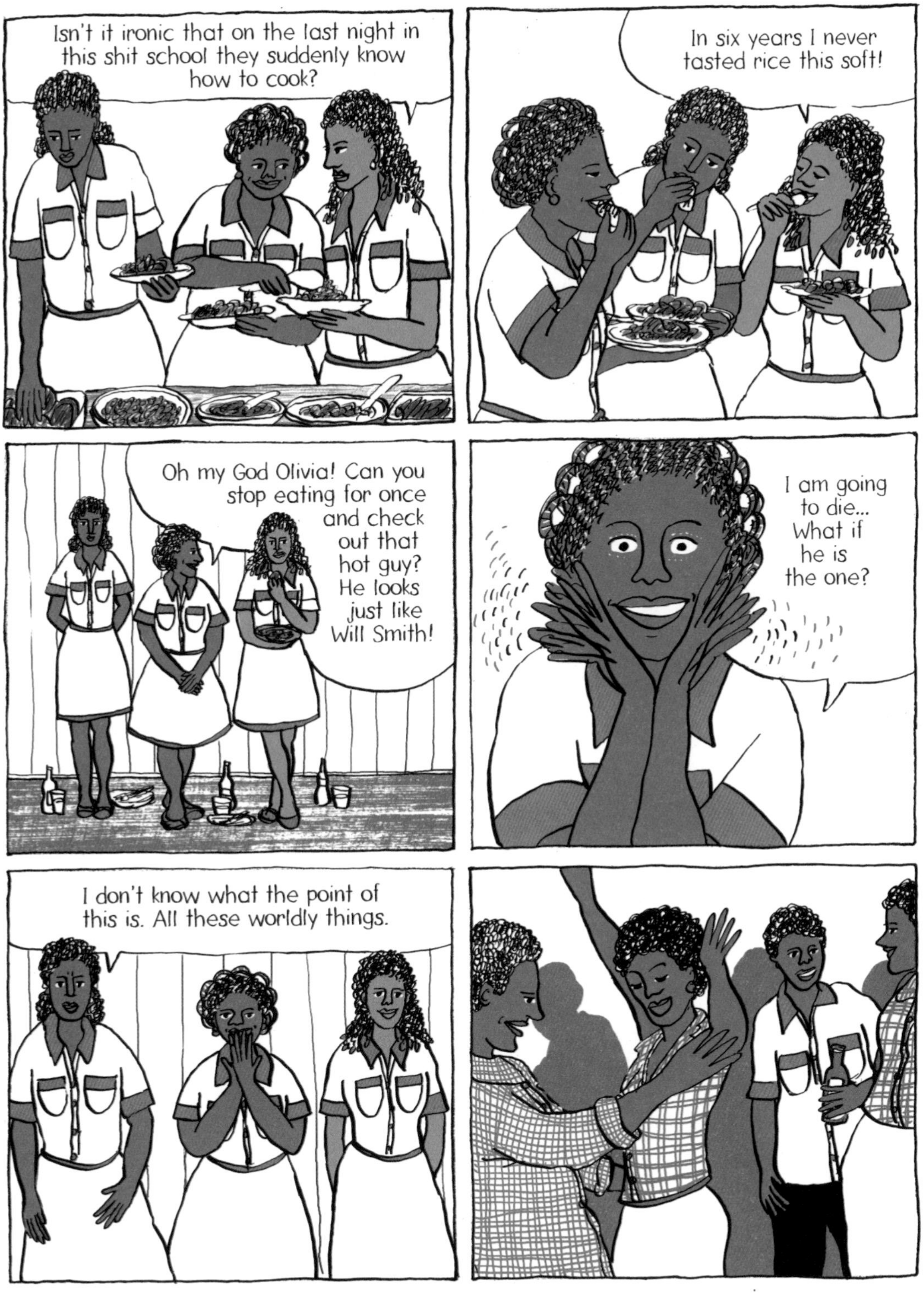

Isn't it ironic that on the last night in this shit school they suddenly know how to cook?
In six years I never tasted rice this soft!
Oh my God Olivia! Can you stop eating for once and check out that hot guy? He looks just like Will Smith!
I am going to die... What if he is the one?
I don't know what the point of this is. All these worldly things.

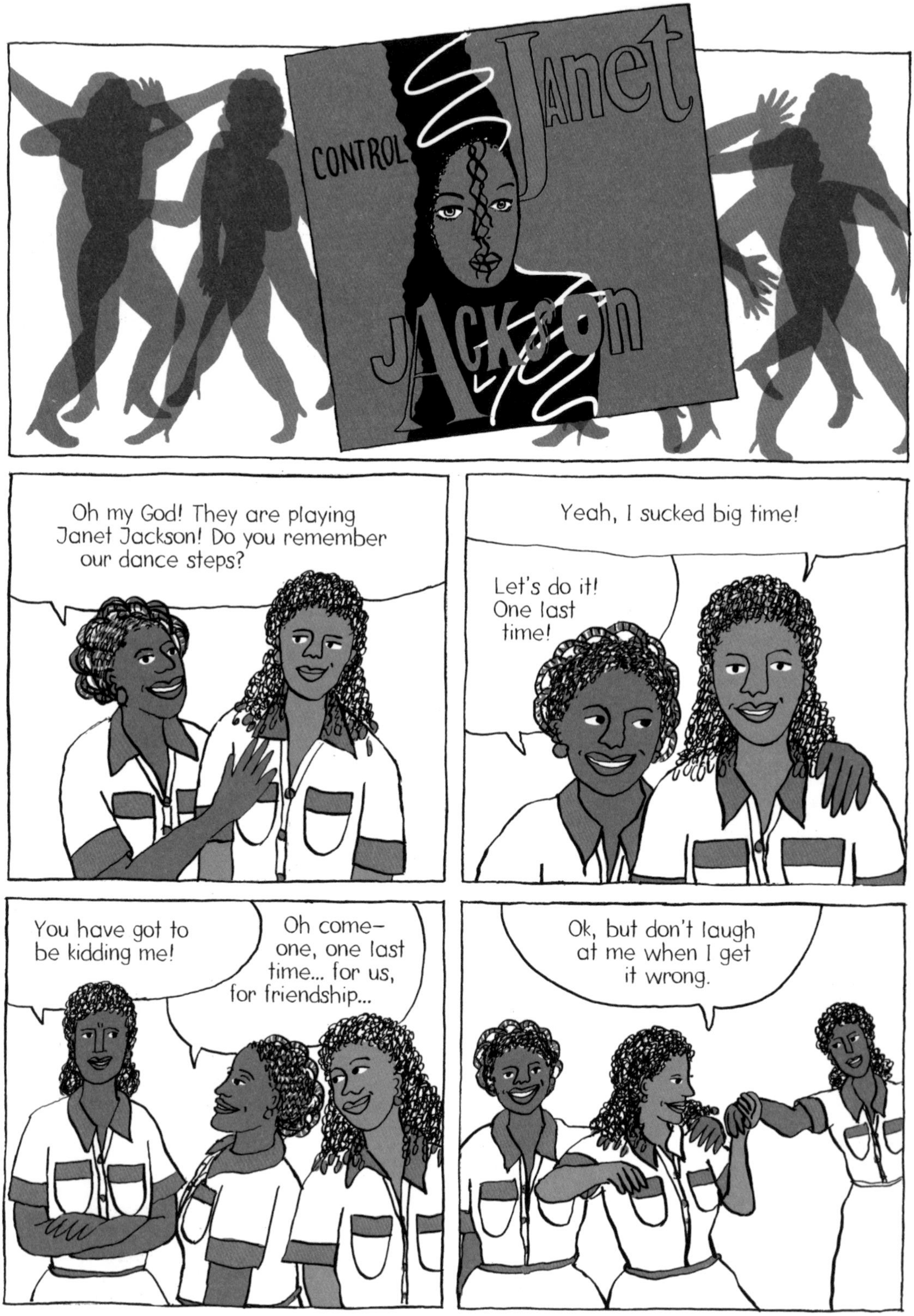
CONTROL
Janet
Jackson
Oh my God! They are playing Janet Jackson! Do you remember our dance steps?
Yeah, I sucked big time!
Let's do it! One last time!
You have got to be kidding me!
Oh come-one, one last time... for us, for friendship...
Ok, but don't laugh at me when I get it wrong.

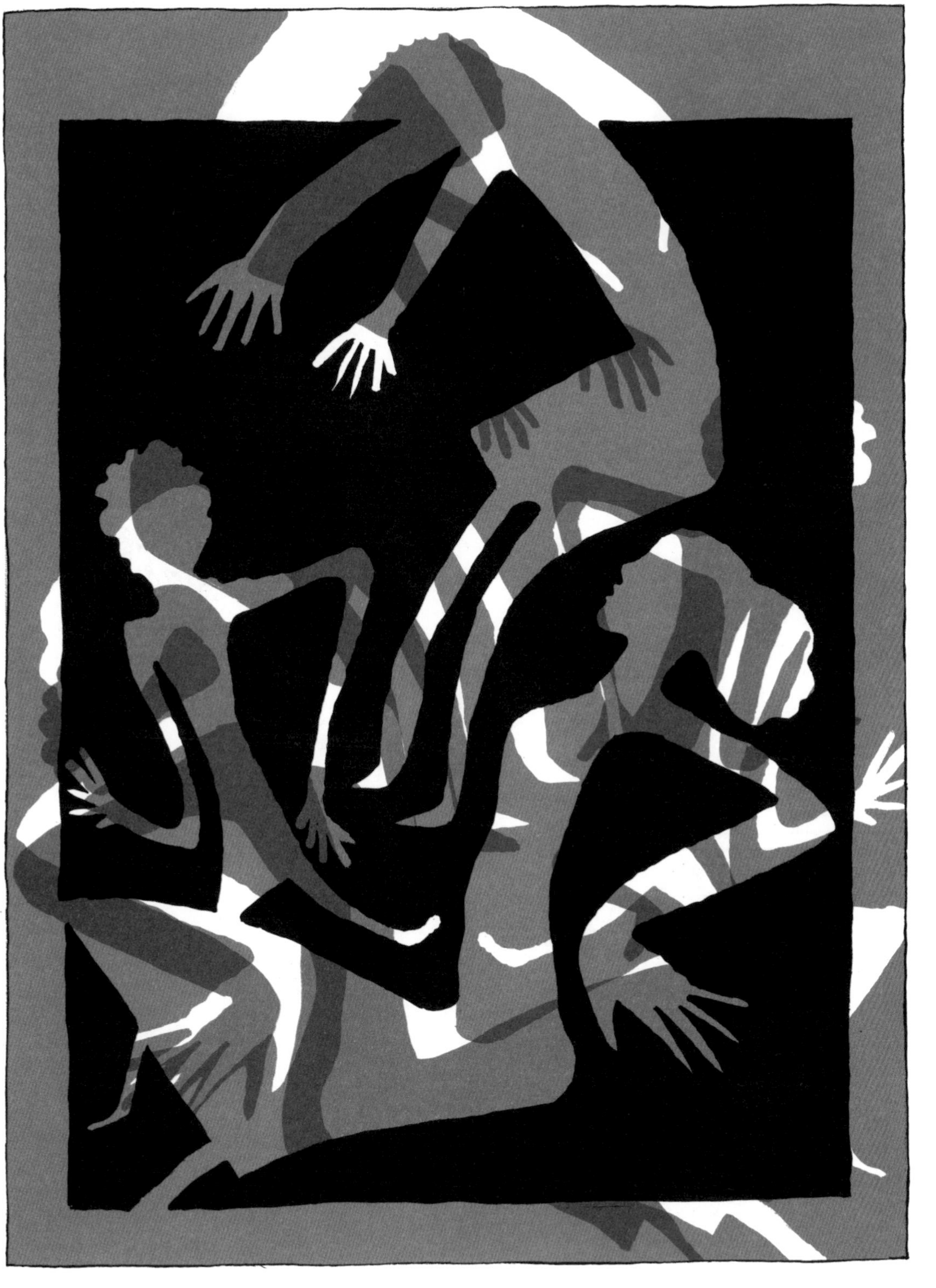

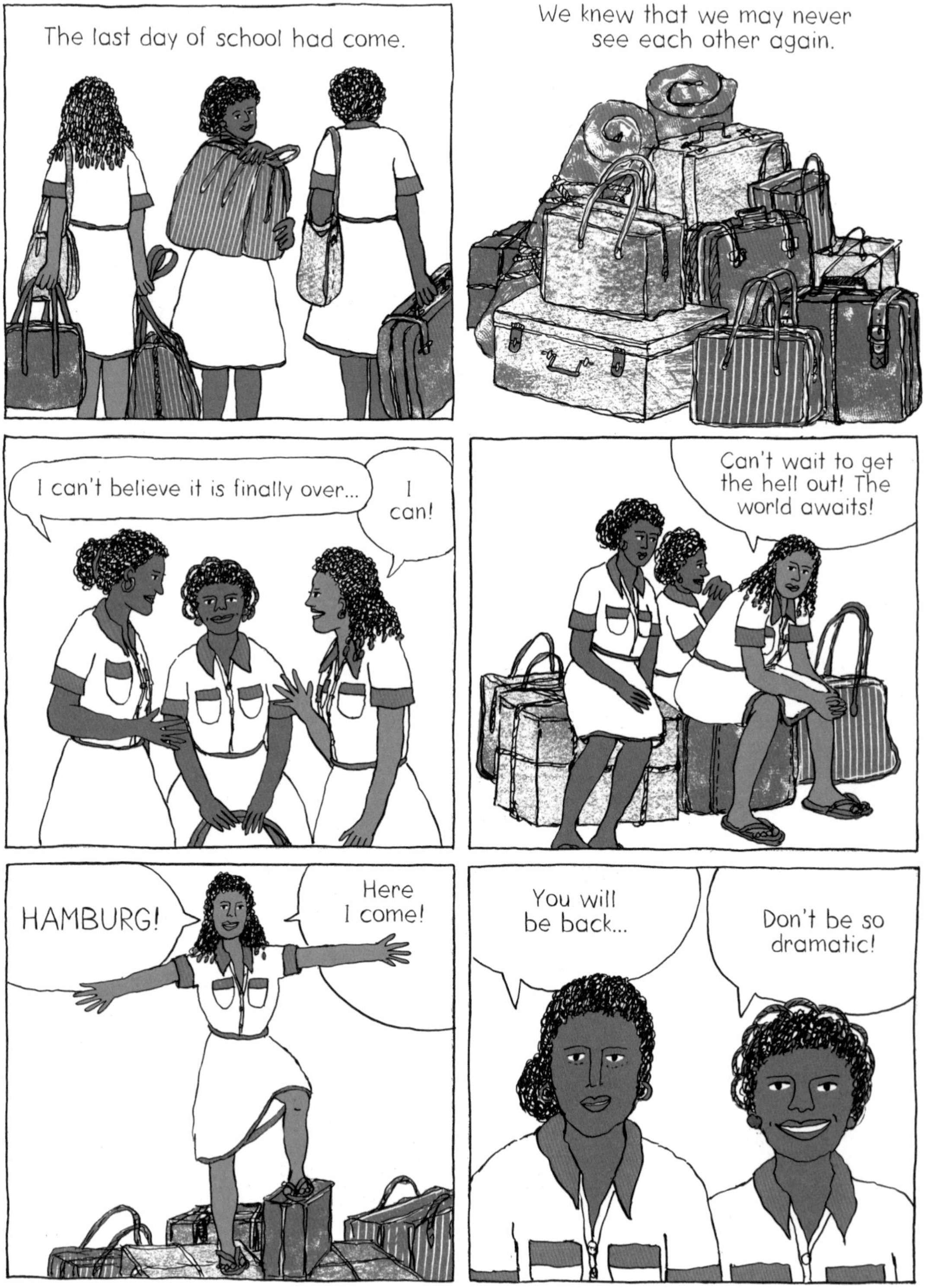
The last day of school had come.
We knew that we may never see each other again.
I can't believe it is finally over...
I can!
Can't wait to get the hell out! The world awaits!
HAMBURG!
Here I come!
You will be back...
Don't be so dramatic!

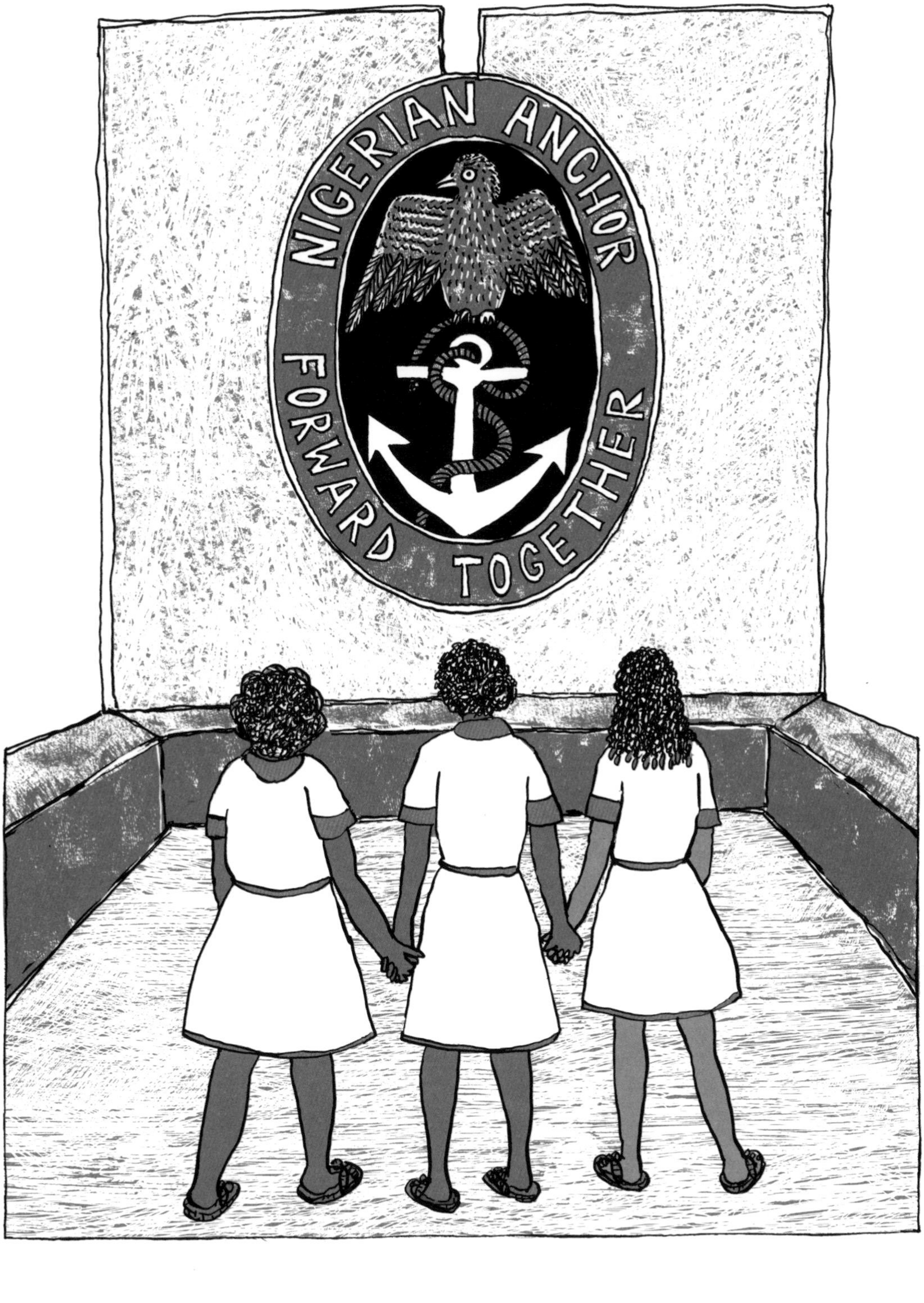
NIGERIAN ANCHOR
FORWARD TOGETHER

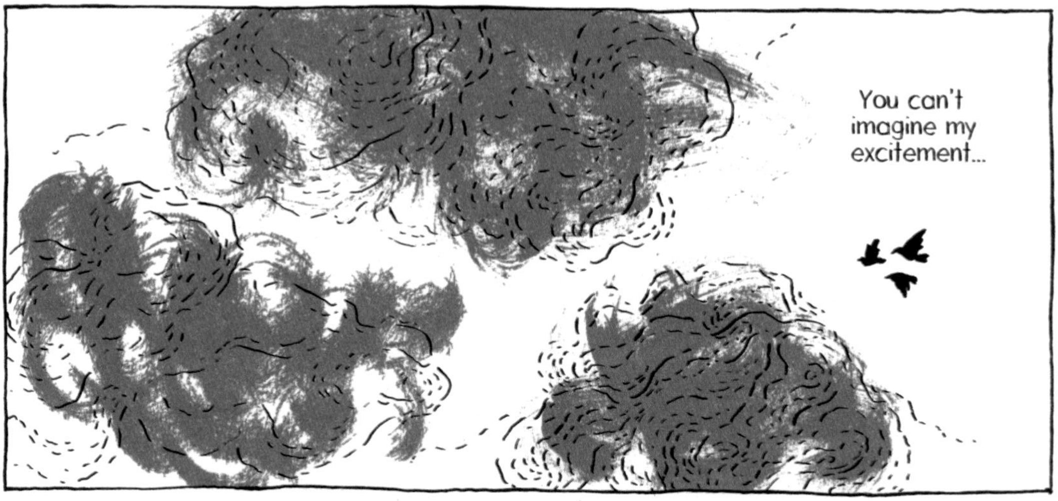
You can't imagine my excitement...

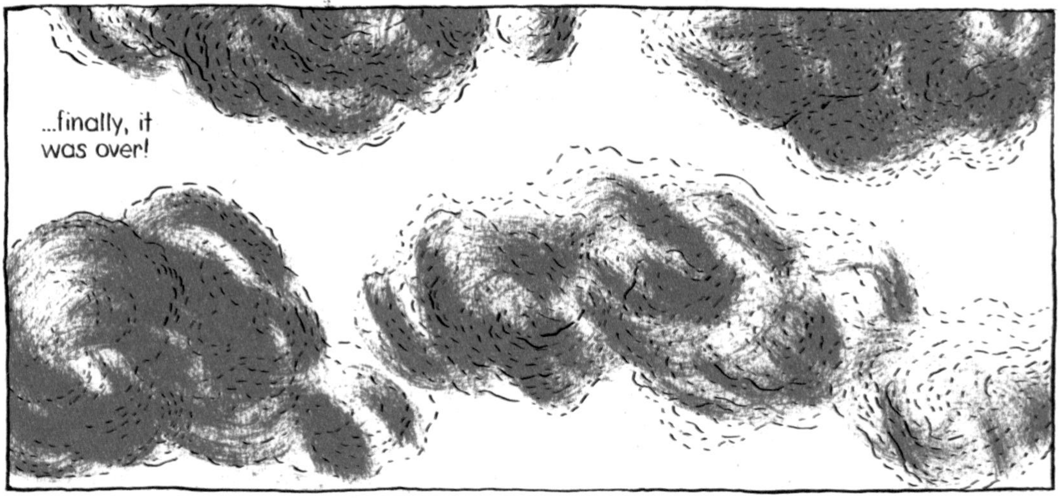
...finally, it was over!

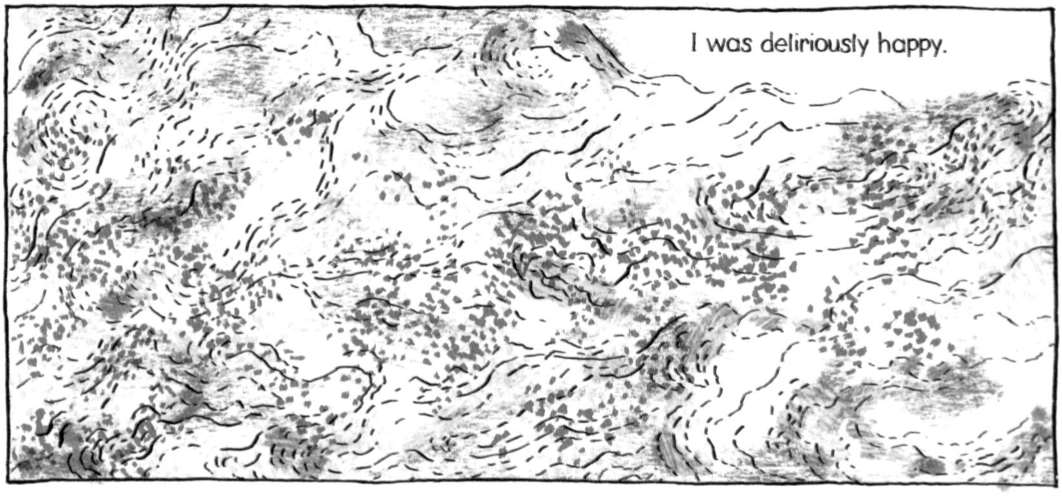
I was deliriously happy.

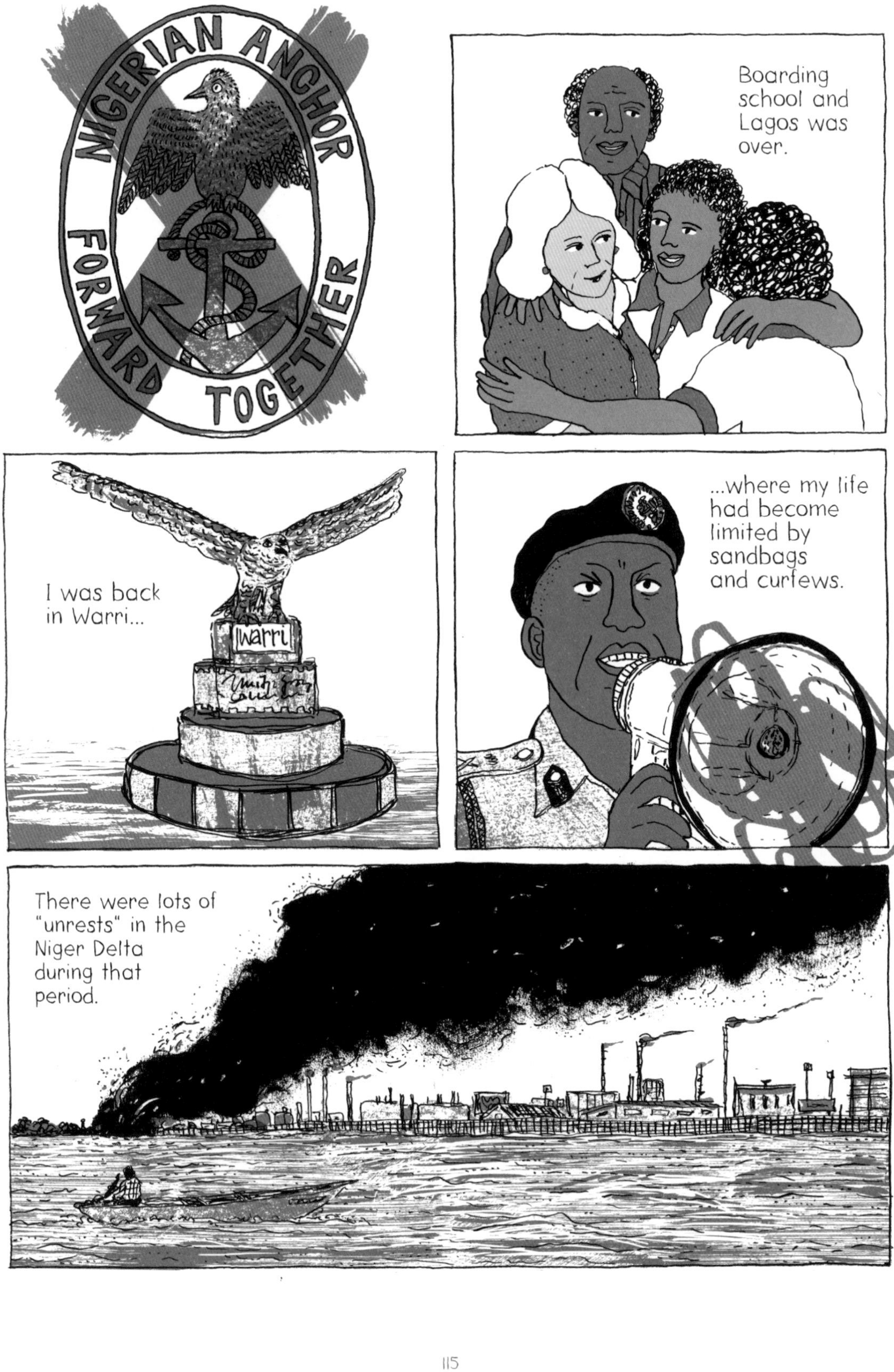
NIGERIAN ANCHOR
FORWARD TOGETHER
Boarding school and Lagos was over.
I was back in Warri...
Warri
...where my life had become limited by sandbags and curfews.
There were lots of "unrests" in the Niger Delta during that period.

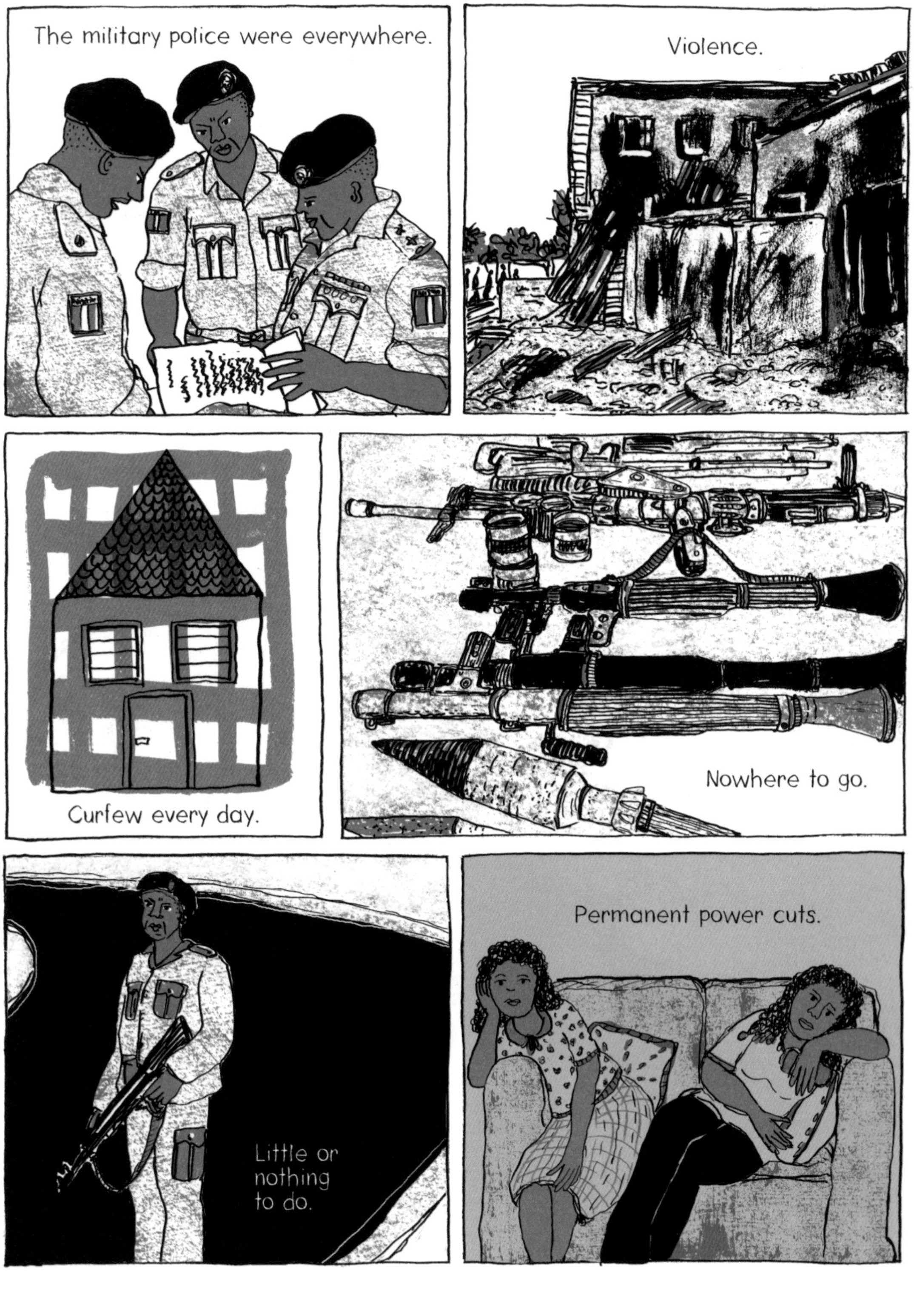
The military police were everywhere.
Violence.
Curfew every day.
Nowhere to go.
Little or nothing to do.
Permanent power cuts.

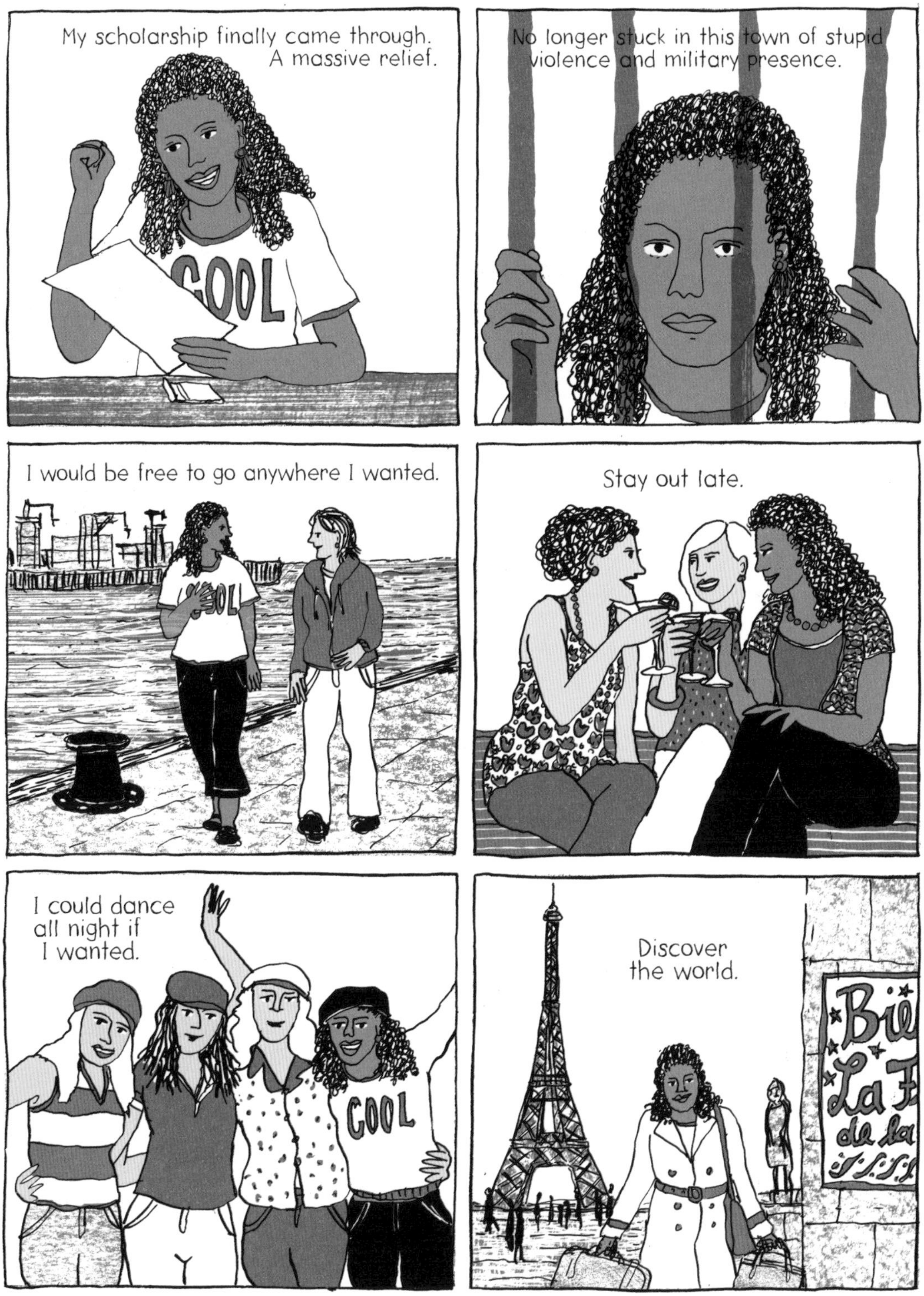
My scholarship finally came through. A massive relief.
COOL
No longer stuck in this town of stupid violence and military presence.
I would be free to go anywhere I wanted.
Stay out late.
I could dance all night if I wanted.
COOL
Discover the world.

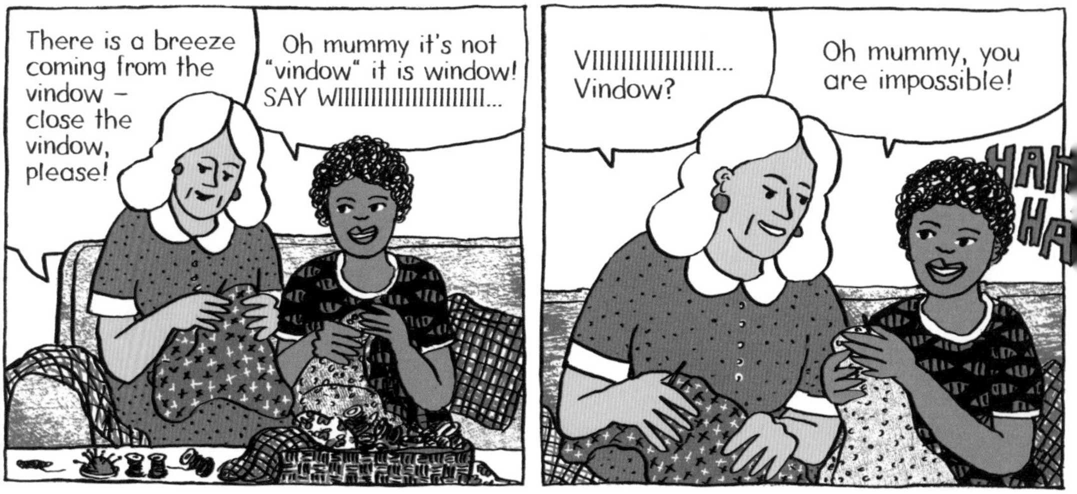
There is a breeze coming from the vindow – close the vindow, please!
Oh mummy it's not "vindow" it is window! SAY WIIIIIIIIIIIIIIIIIII...
VIIIIIIIIIIIIIII... Vindow?
Oh mummy, you are impossible!
HAH HA

My mother never spoke German with us, instead she learned English through us.

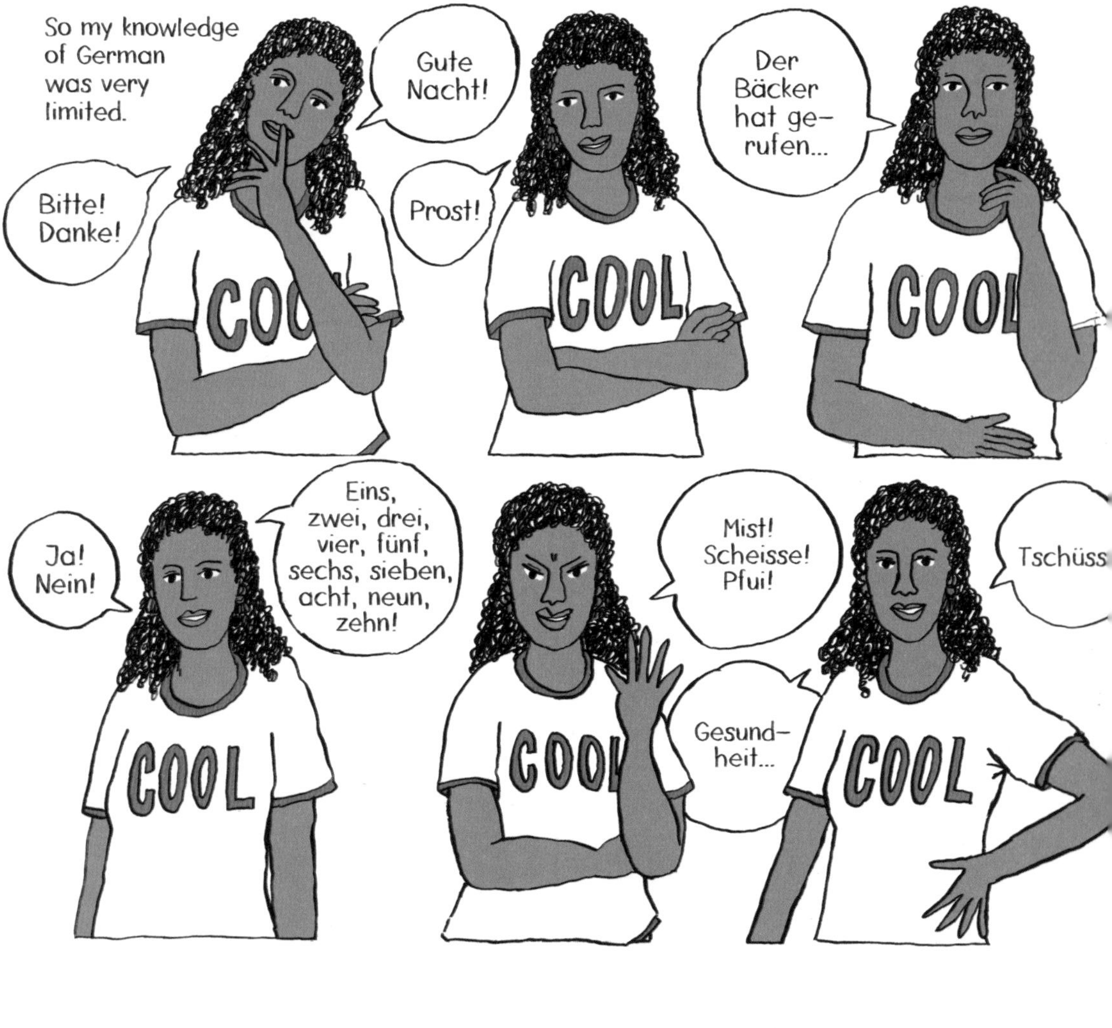
So my knowledge of German was very limited.
Bitte! Danke!
Gute Nacht!
COOL
Prost!
COOL
Der Bäcker hat gerufen...
COOL
Ja! Nein!
Eins, zwei, drei, vier, fünf, sechs, sieben, acht, neun, zehn!
COOL
Mist! Scheisse! Pfui!
COOL
Gesundheit...
Tschüss
COOL

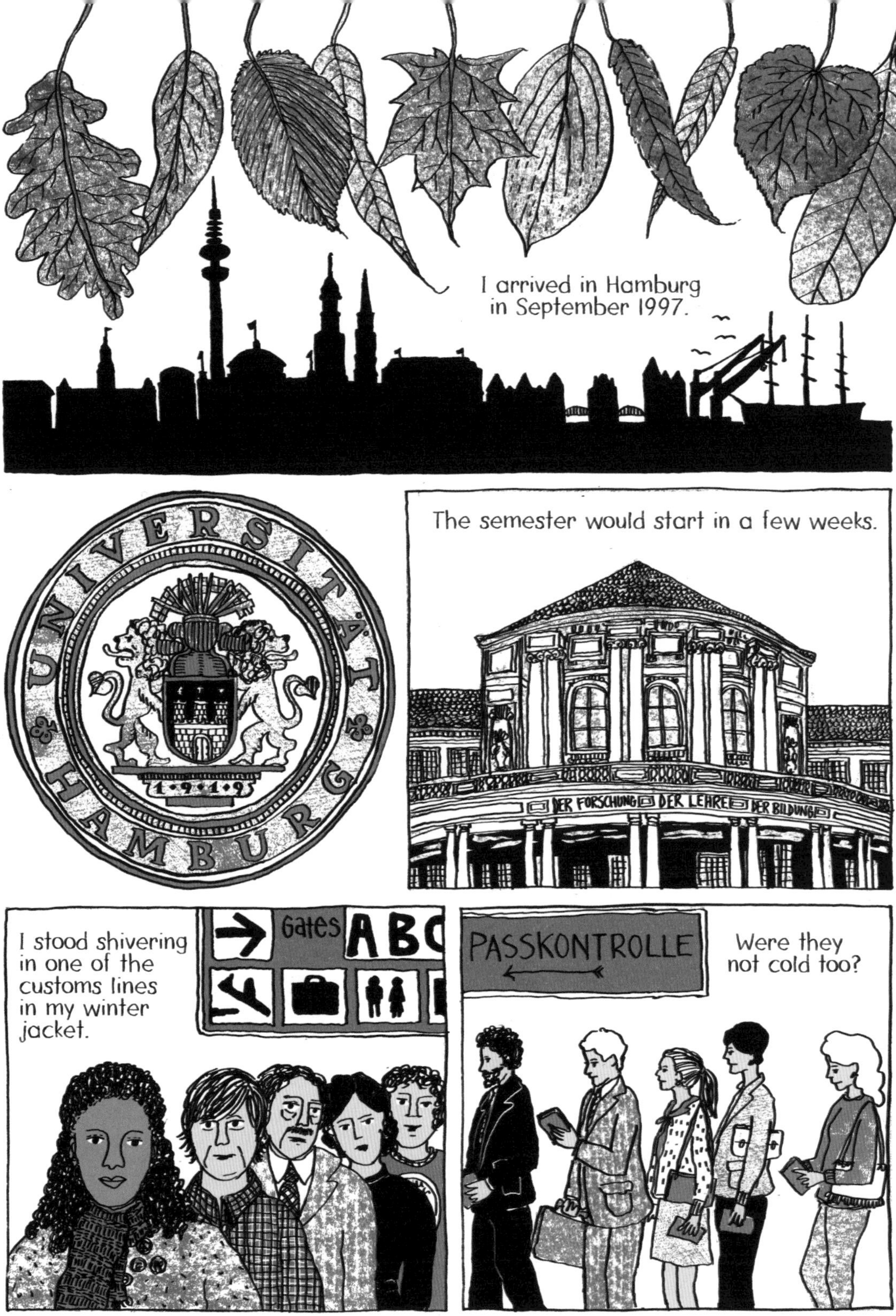
I arrived in Hamburg in September 1997.
UNIVERSITÄT HAMBURG
1919
The semester would start in a few weeks.
DER FORSCHUNG DER LEHRE DER BILDUNG
I stood shivering in one of the customs lines in my winter jacket.
Gates ABC
PASSKONTROLLE
Were they not cold too?

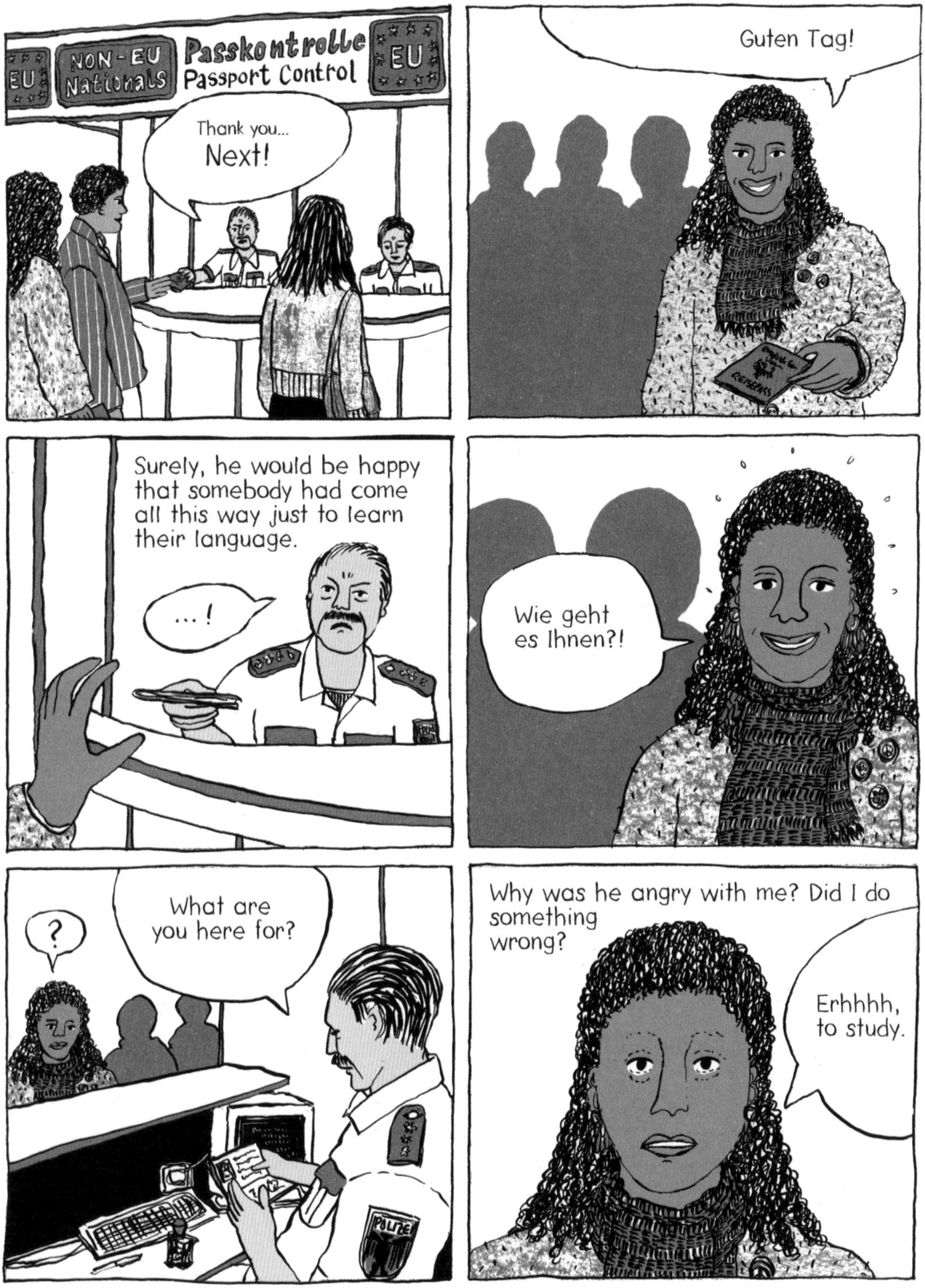
NON-EU Nationals
Passkontrolle
Passport Control
EU
EU
Thank you...
Next!
Guten Tag!
Surely, he would be happy that somebody had come all this way just to learn their language.
... !
Wie geht es Ihnen?!
?
What are you here for?
POLIZEI
Why was he angry with me? Did I do something wrong?
Erhhhh, to study.

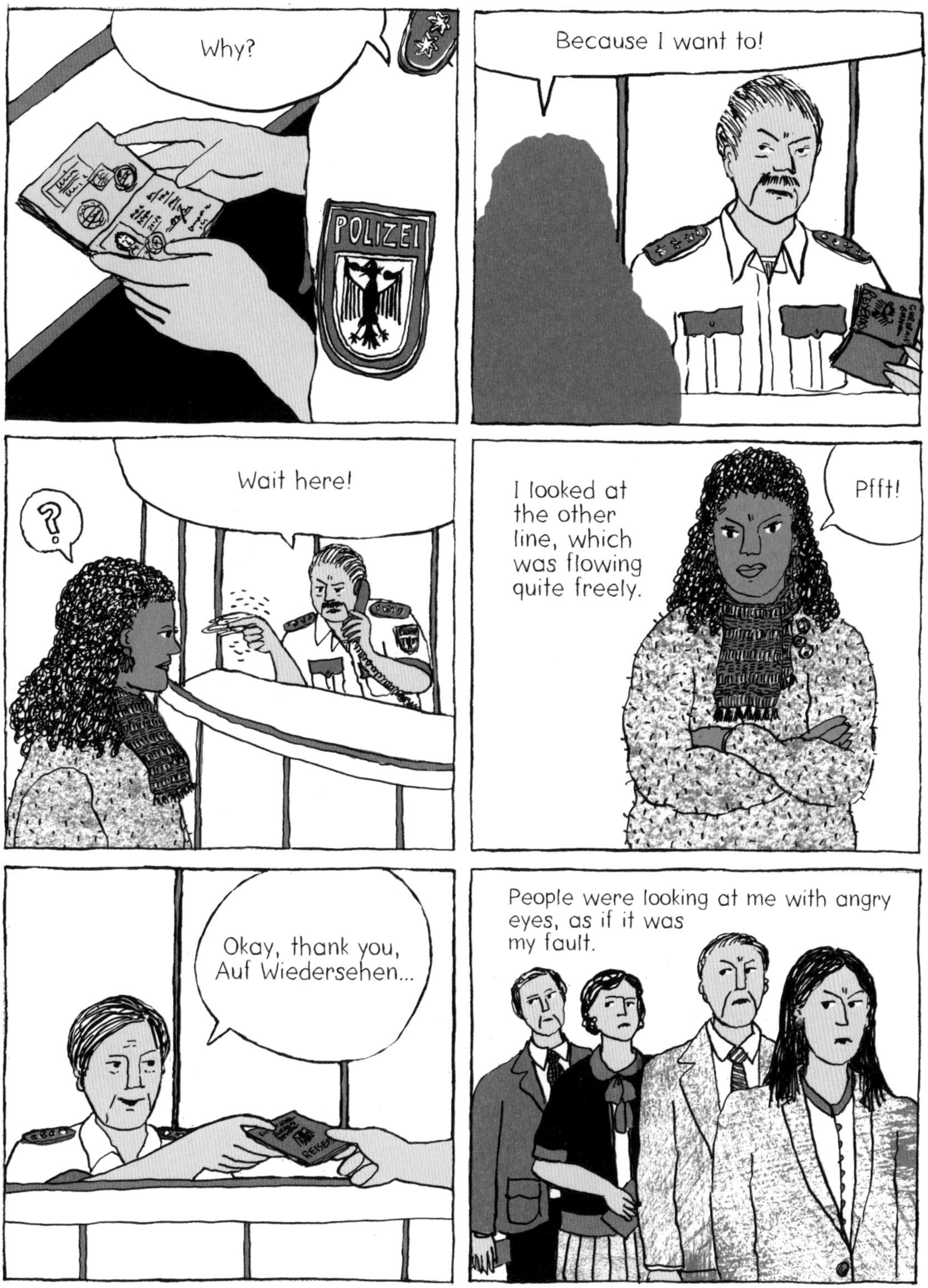
Why?
POLIZEI
Because I want to!
Wait here!
?
I looked at the other line, which was flowing quite freely.
Pfft!
Okay, thank you, Auf Wiedersehen...
REISEP
People were looking at me with angry eyes, as if it was my fault.

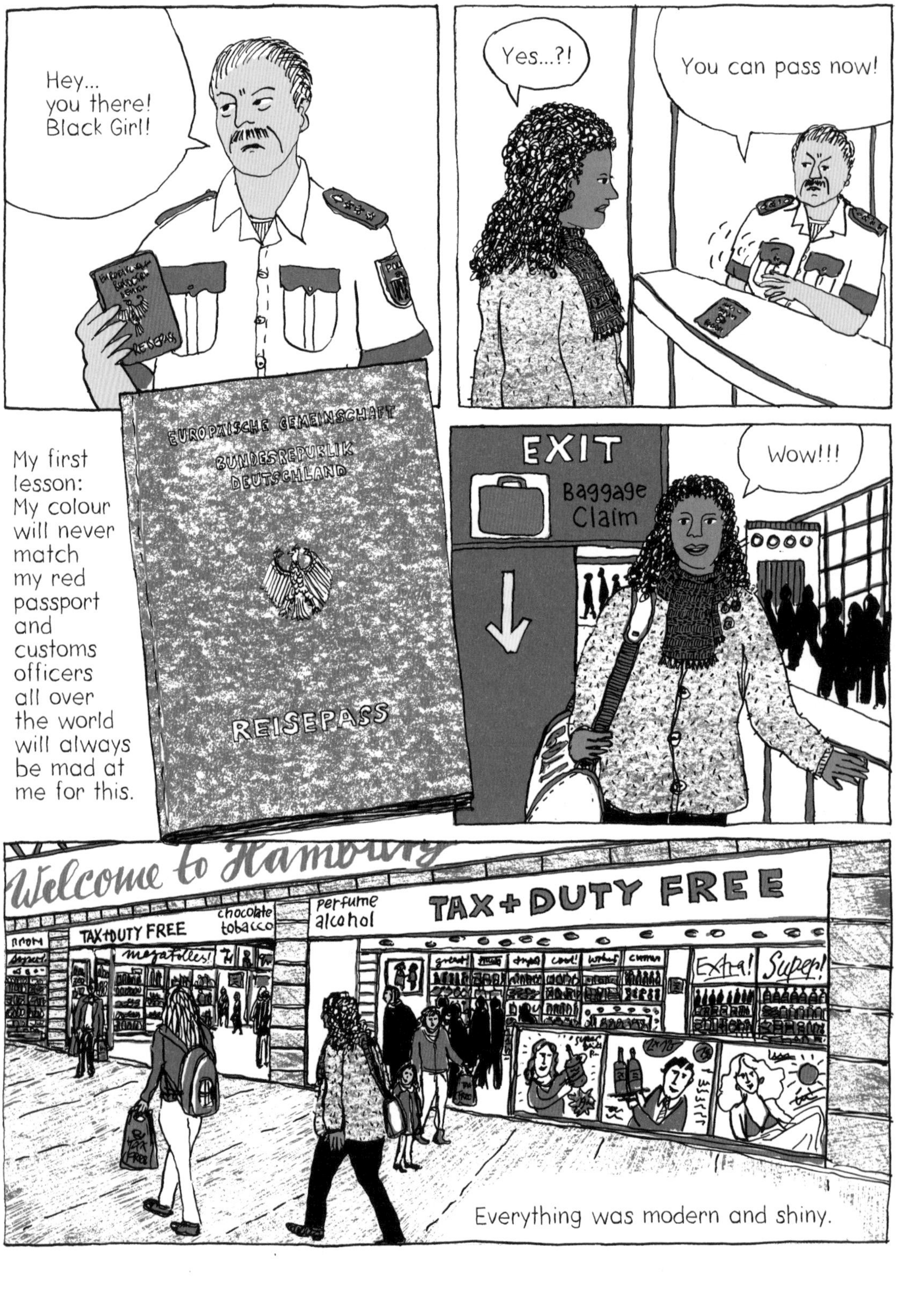
Hey... you there! Black Girl!
EUROPÄISCHE GEMEINSCHAFT
BUNDESREPUBLIK DEUTSCHLAND
REISEPASS
Yes...?!
You can pass now!
My first lesson: My colour will never match my red passport and customs officers all over the world will always be mad at me for this.
EXIT
Baggage Claim
Wow!!!
Welcome to Hamburg
TAX+DUTY FREE
chocolate tobacco
perfume alcohol
TAX+DUTY FREE
Extra!
Super!
Everything was modern and shiny.

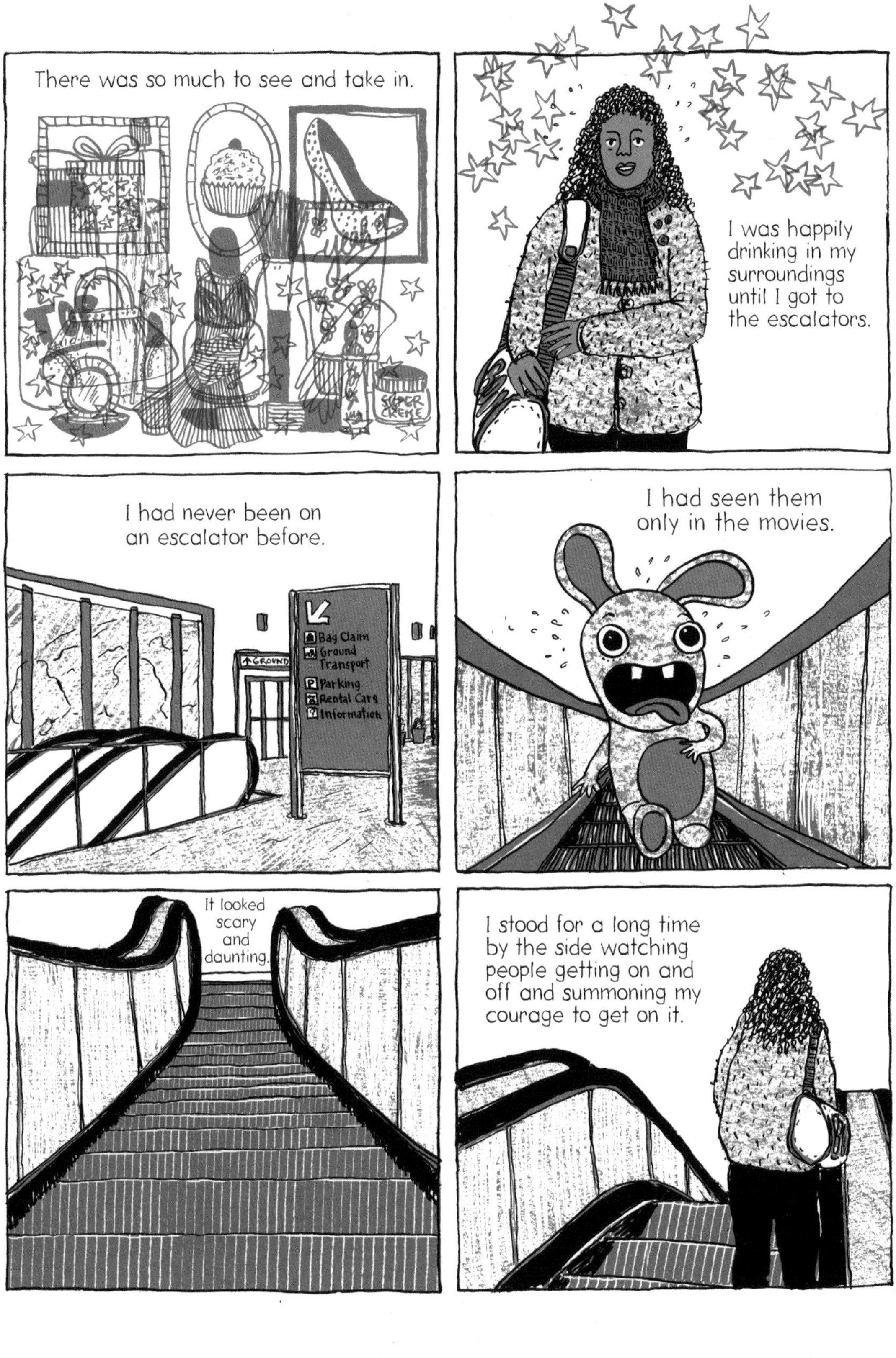

There was so much to see and take in.
SUPER CREME
I was happily drinking in my surroundings until I got to the escalators.
I had never been on an escalator before.
GROUND
Bag Claim
Ground Transport
Parking
Rental Cars
Information
I had seen them only in the movies.
It looked scary and daunting.
I stood for a long time by the side watching people getting on and off and summoning my courage to get on it.

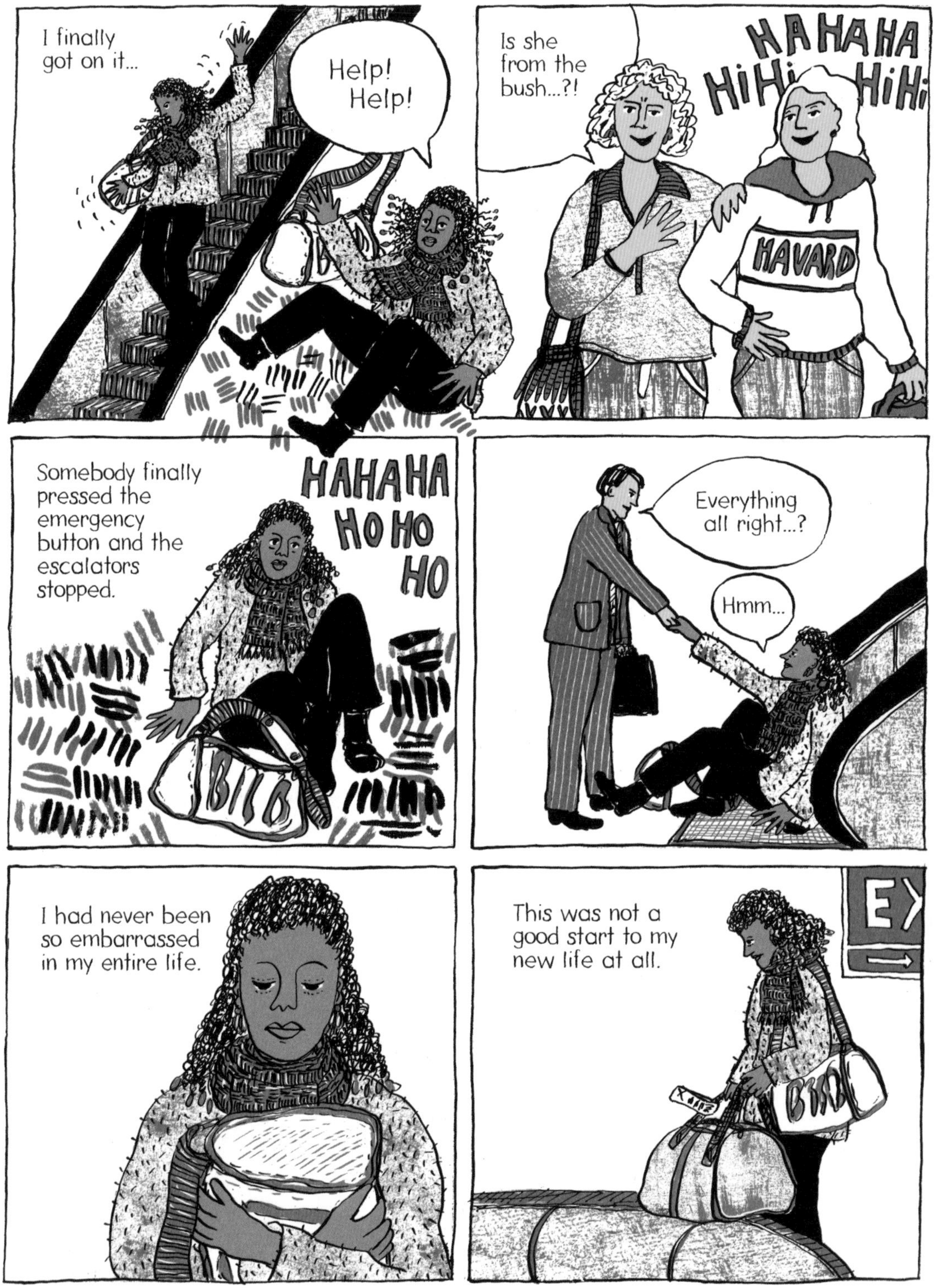
I finally got on it...
Help! Help!
Is she from the bush...?!
HAHAHA
HiHi HiHi
HAVARD
Somebody finally pressed the emergency button and the escalators stopped.
HAHAHA
HO HO HO
Everything all right...?
Hmm...
I had never been so embarrassed in my entire life.
This was not a good start to my new life at all.

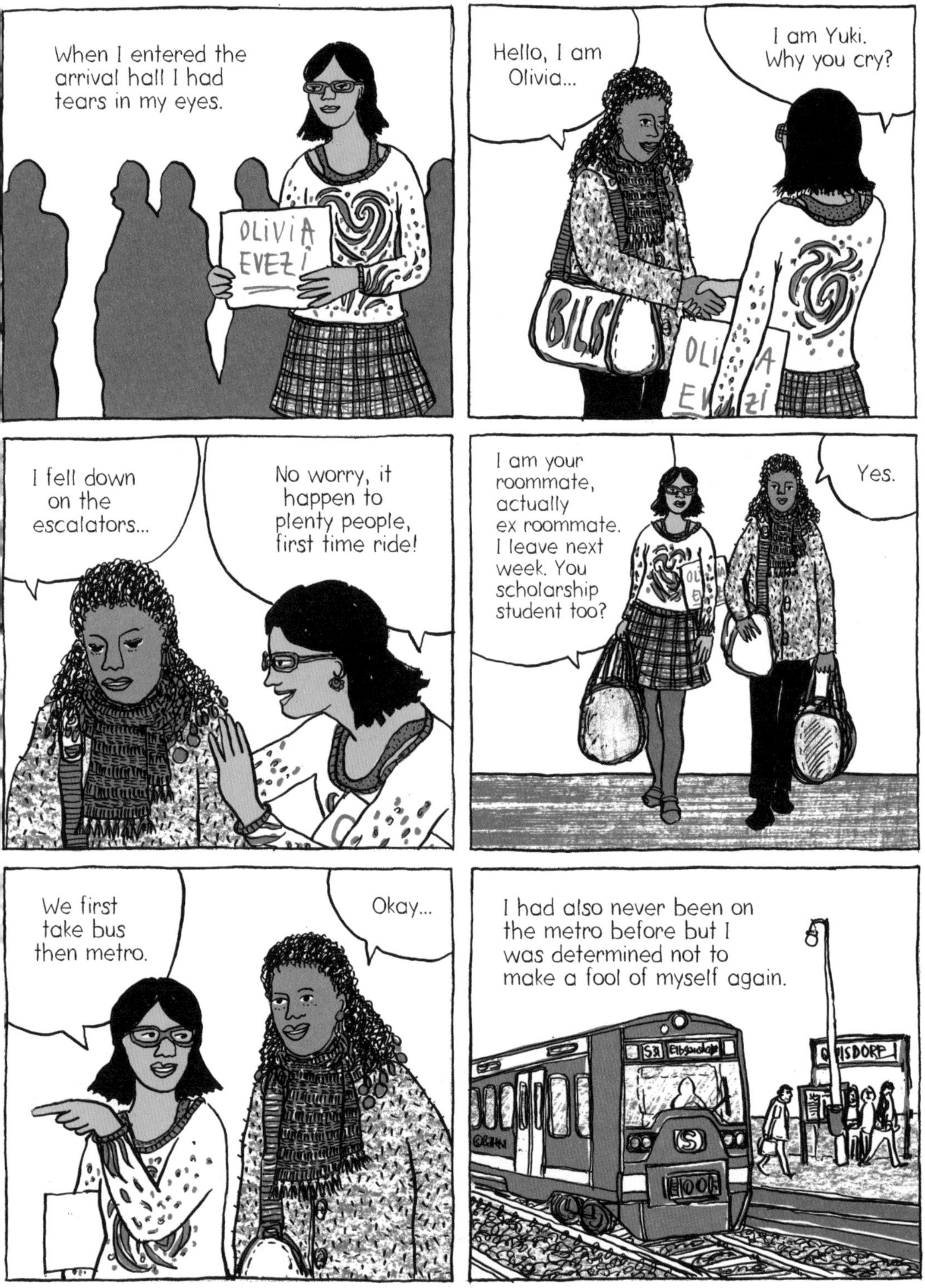
When I entered the arrival hall I had tears in my eyes.
OLIVIA EVEZI
Hello, I am Olivia...
I am Yuki. Why you cry?
I fell down on the escalators...
No worry, it happen to plenty people, first time ride!
I am your roommate, actually ex roommate. I leave next week. You scholarship student too?
Yes.
We first take bus then metro.
Okay...
I had also never been on the metro before but I was determined not to make a fool of myself again.

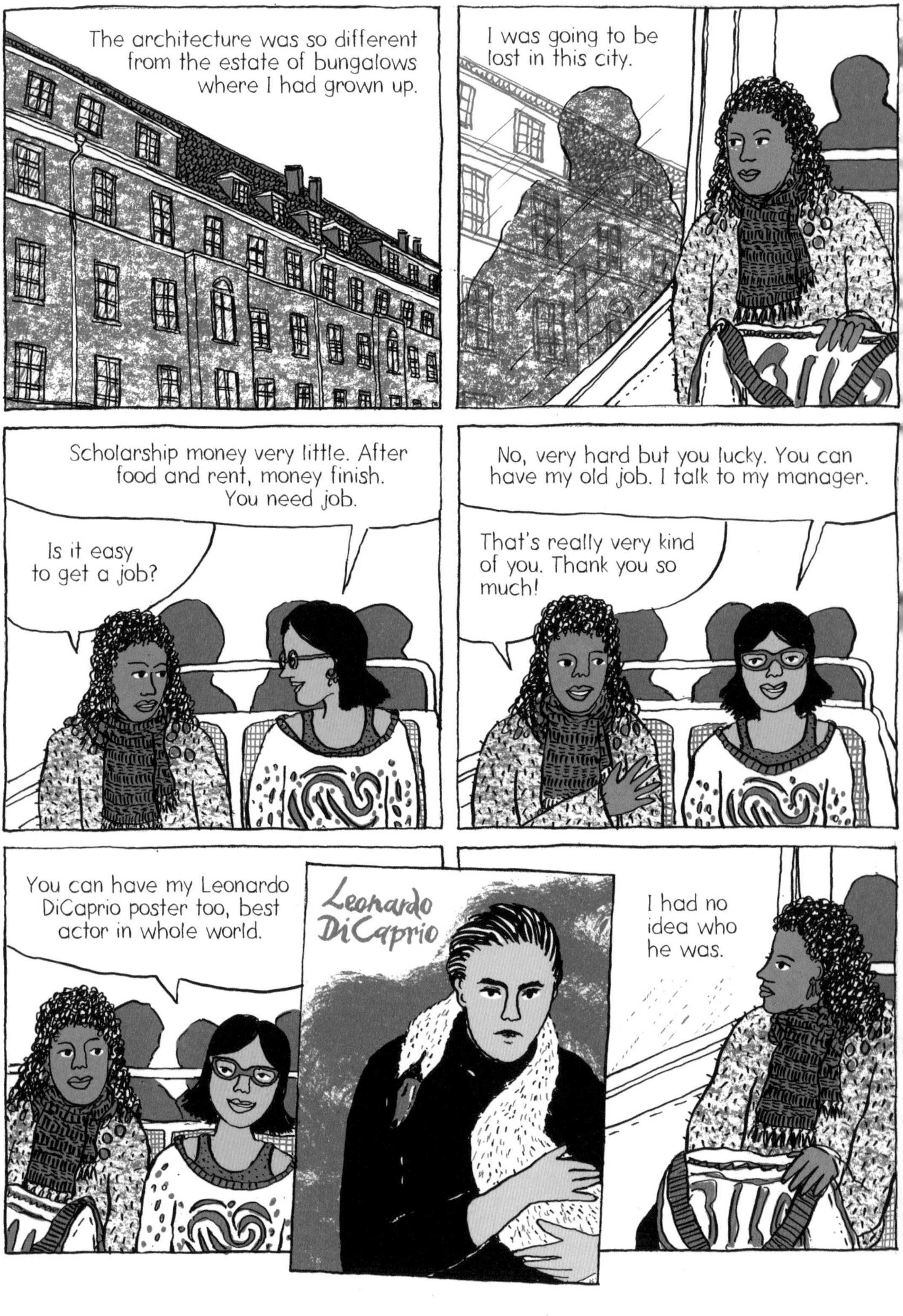
The architecture was so different from the estate of bungalows where I had grown up.
I was going to be lost in this city.
Scholarship money very little. After food and rent, money finish. You need job.
Is it easy to get a job?
No, very hard but you lucky. You can have my old job. I talk to my manager.
That's really very kind of you. Thank you so much!
You can have my Leonardo DiCaprio poster too, best actor in whole world.
Leonardo DiCaprio
I had no idea who he was.

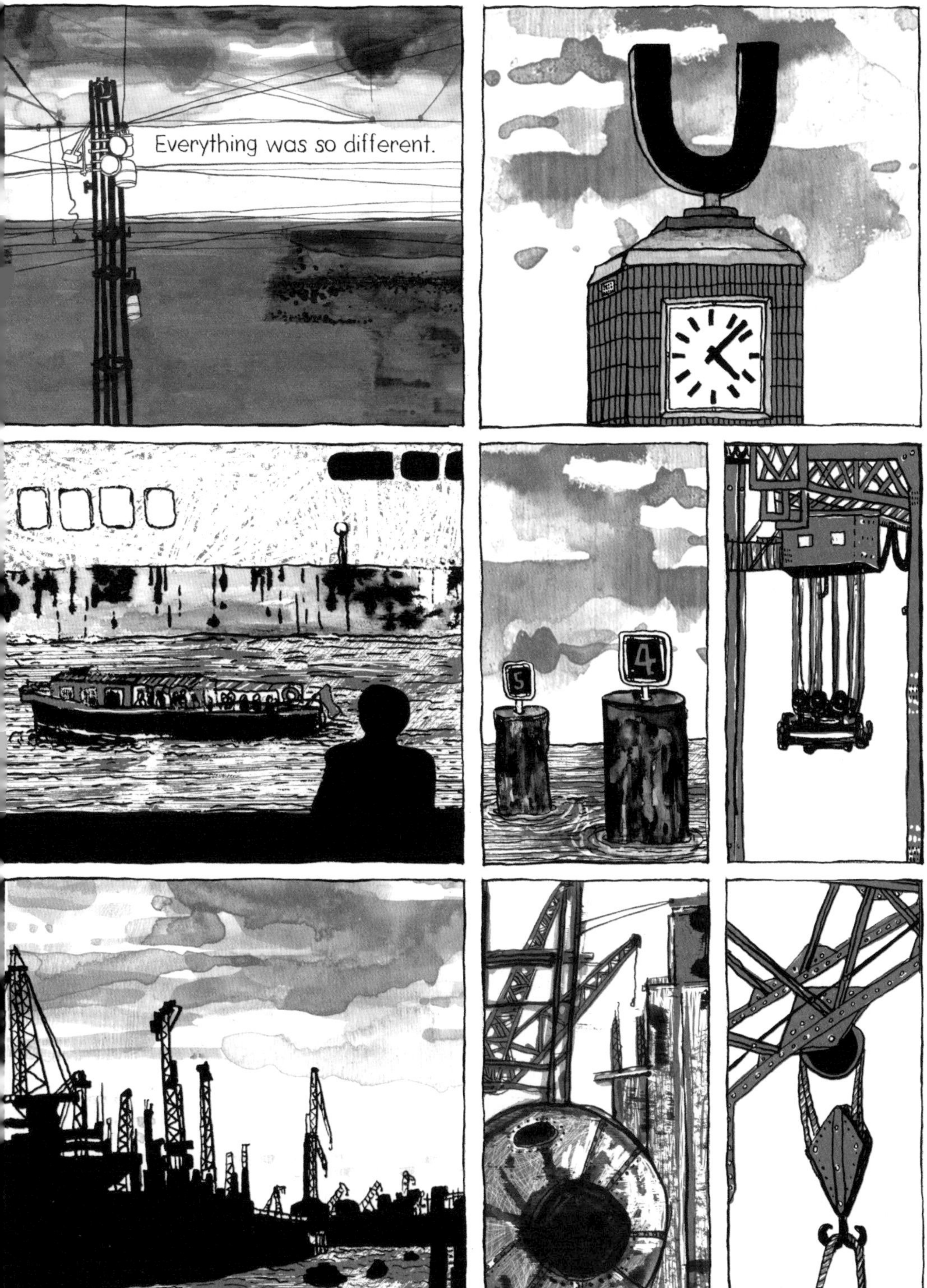
Everything was so different.
5
4

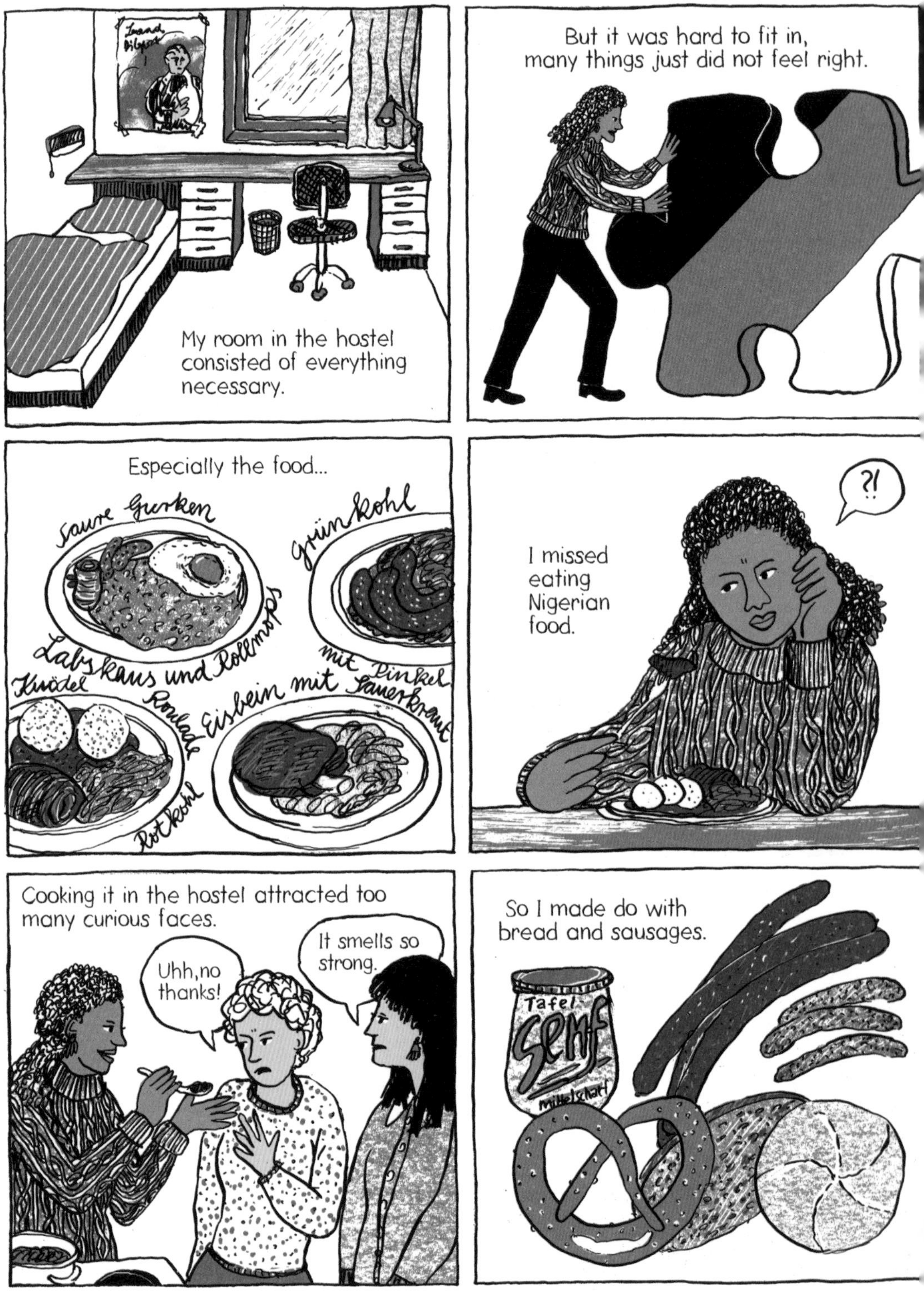
My room in the hostel consisted of everything necessary.
But it was hard to fit in, many things just did not feel right.
Especially the food...
Saure Gurken
grünkohl
Labskaus und Rollmops
mit Pinkel
Knödel
Roulade
Eisbein mit Sauerkraut
Rotkohl
I missed eating Nigerian food.
?!
Cooking it in the hostel attracted too many curious faces.
Uhh,no thanks!
It smells so strong.
So I made do with bread and sausages.
Tafel Senf mittelscharf

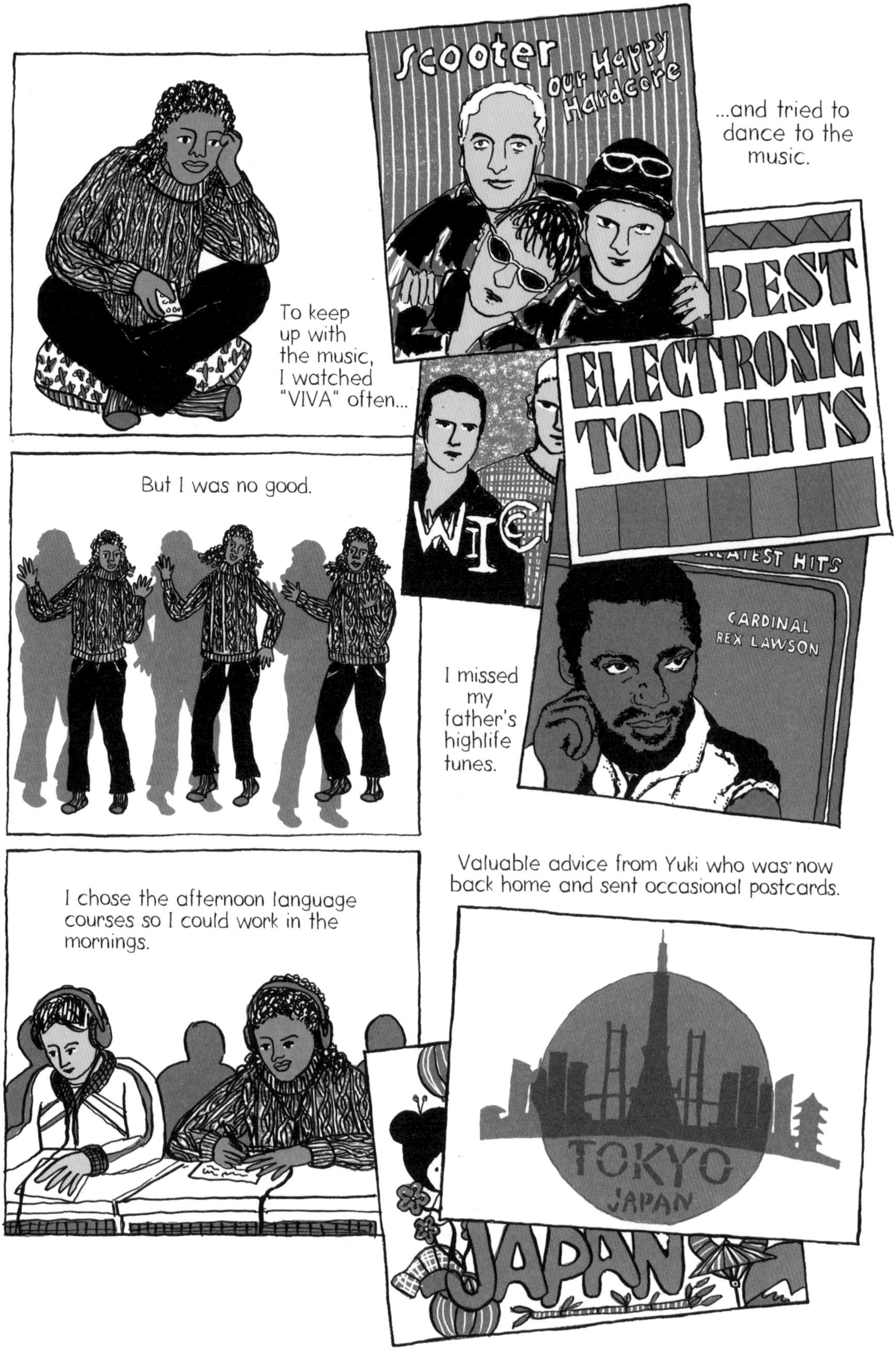
To keep up with the music, I watched "VIVA" often...
Scooter
Our Happy Hardcore
...and tried to dance to the music.
BEST ELECTRONIC TOP HITS
But I was no good.
GREATEST HITS
CARDINAL REX LAWSON
I missed my father's highlife tunes.
I chose the afternoon language courses so I could work in the mornings.
Valuable advice from Yuki who was now back home and sent occasional postcards.
TOKYO
JAPAN
JAPAN

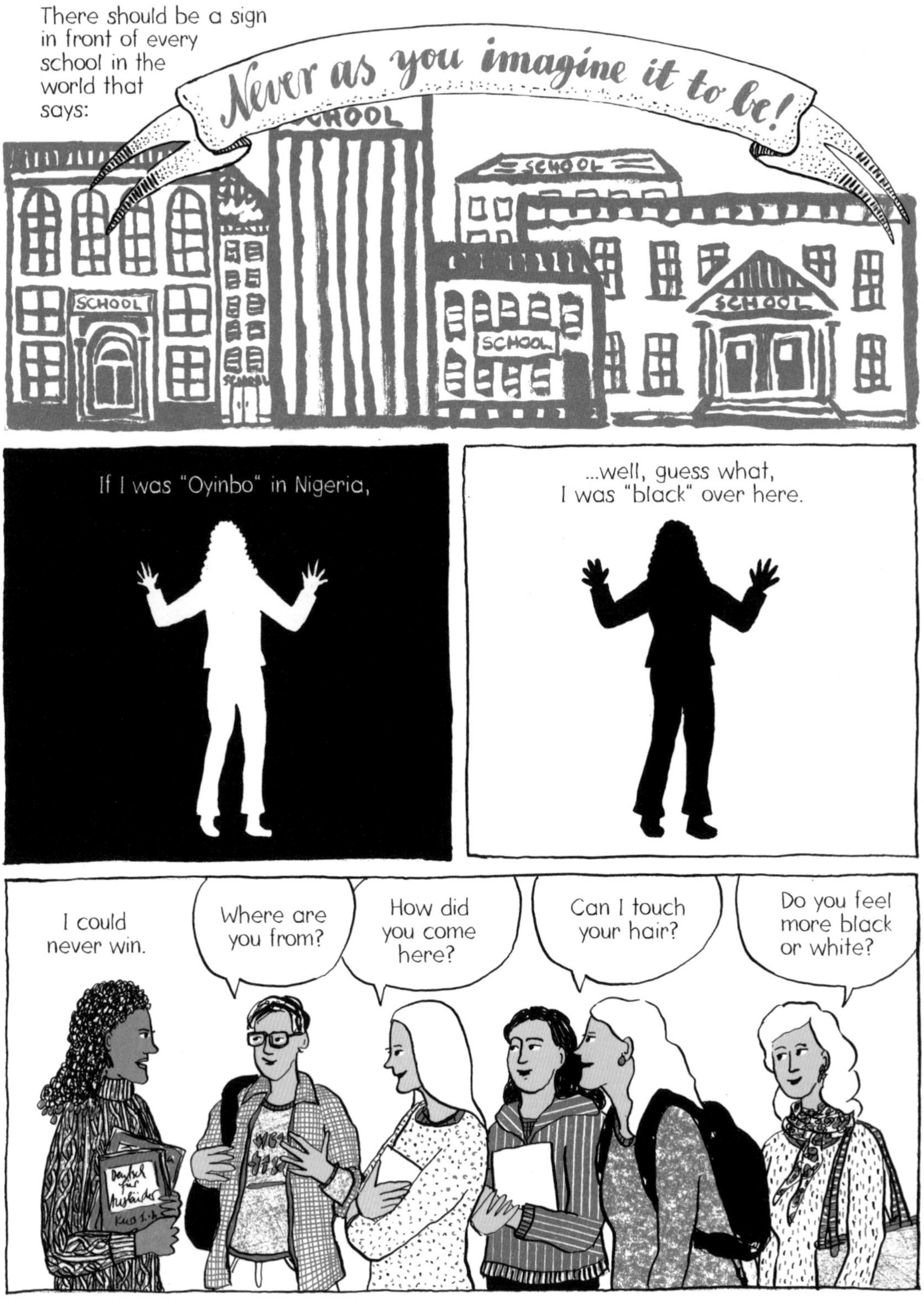
There should be a sign in front of every school in the world that says:
Never as you imagine it to be!
If I was "Oyinbo" in Nigeria,
...well, guess what, I was "black" over here.
I could never win.
Where are you from?
How did you come here?
Can I touch your hair?
Do you feel more black or white?

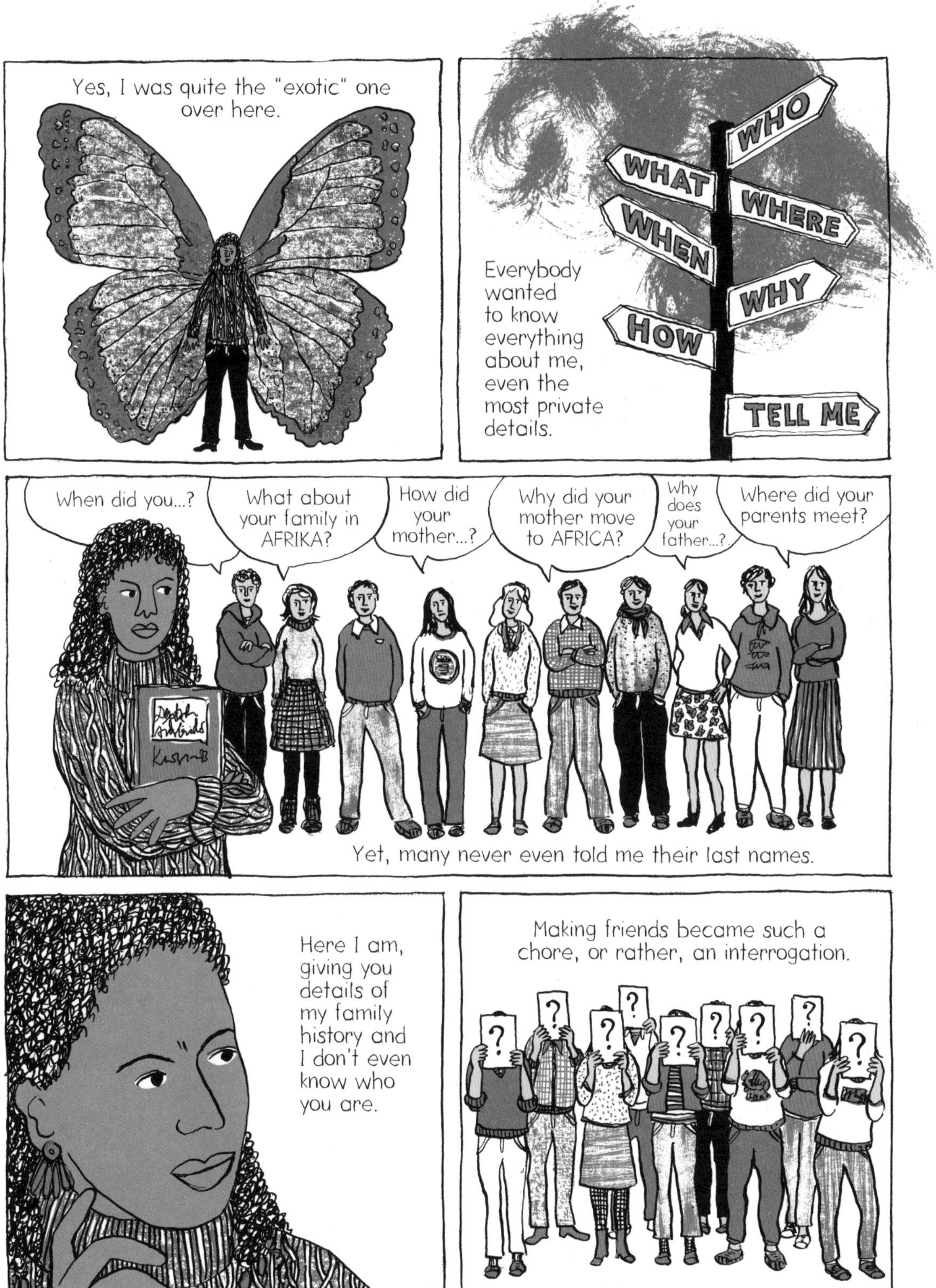
Yes, I was quite the "exotic" one over here.
WHO
WHAT
WHERE
WHEN
WHY
HOW
TELL ME
Everybody wanted to know everything about me, even the most private details.
When did you...?
What about your family in AFRIKA?
How did your mother...?
Why did your mother move to AFRICA?
Why does your father...?
Where did your parents meet?
Yet, many never even told me their last names.
Here I am, giving you details of my family history and I don't even know who you are.
Making friends became such a chore, or rather, an interrogation.
?
?
?
?
?
?
?
?
?

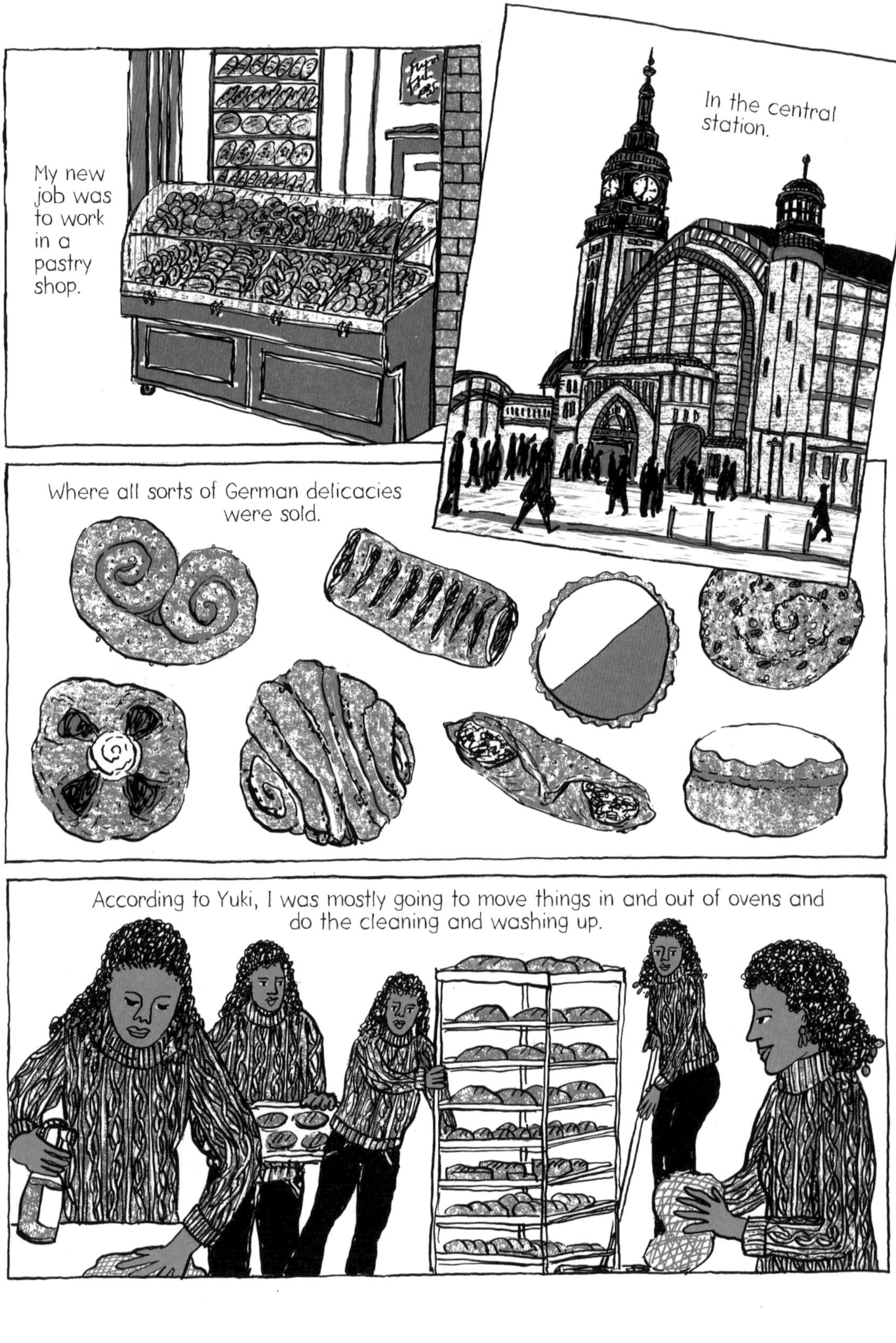
My new job was to work in a pastry shop.
In the central station.
Where all sorts of German delicacies were sold.
According to Yuki, I was mostly going to move things in and out of ovens and do the cleaning and washing up.

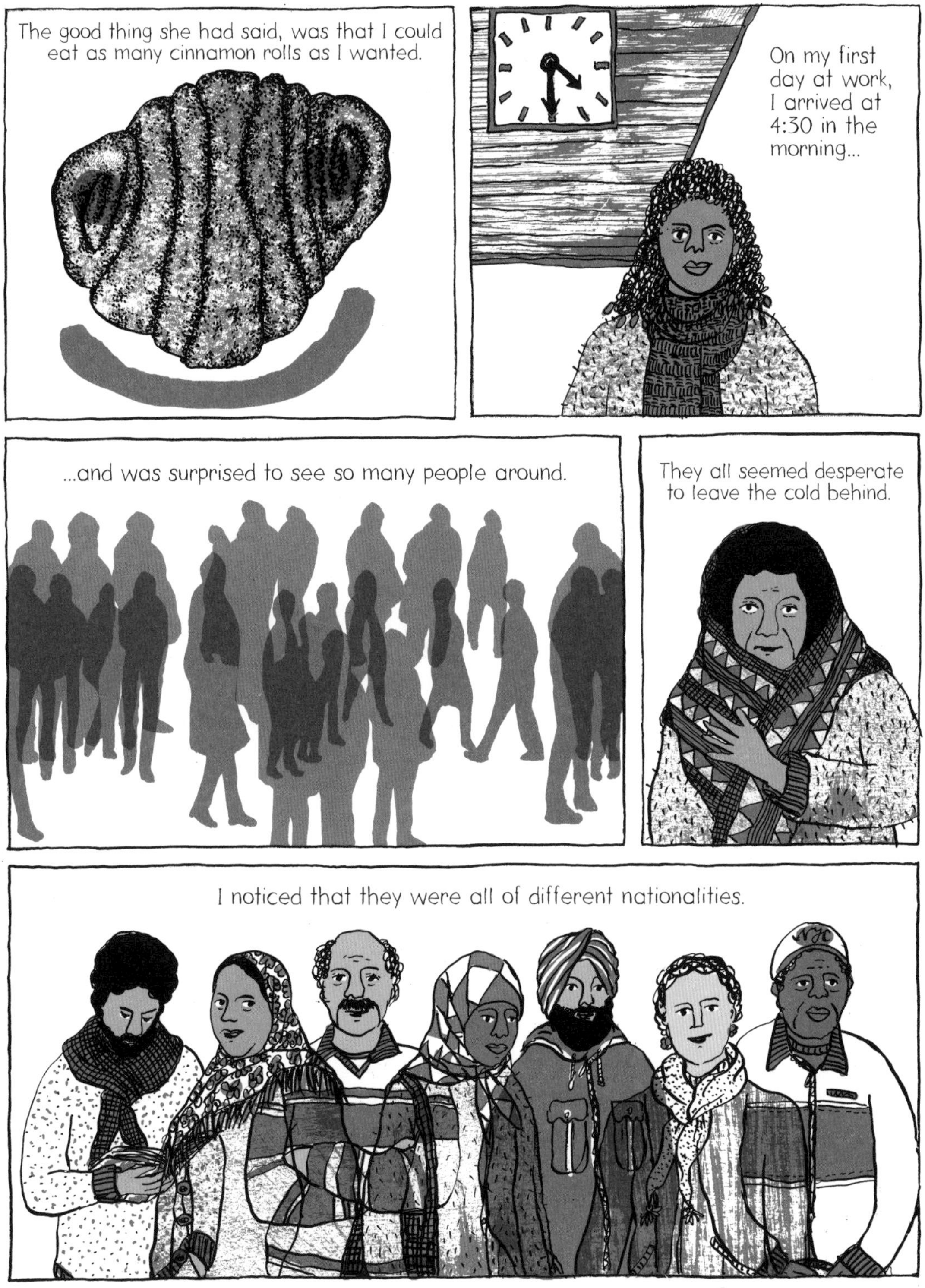
The good thing she had said, was that I could eat as many cinnamon rolls as I wanted.
On my first day at work, I arrived at 4:30 in the morning...
...and was surprised to see so many people around.
They all seemed desperate to leave the cold behind.
I noticed that they were all of different nationalities.
NYC

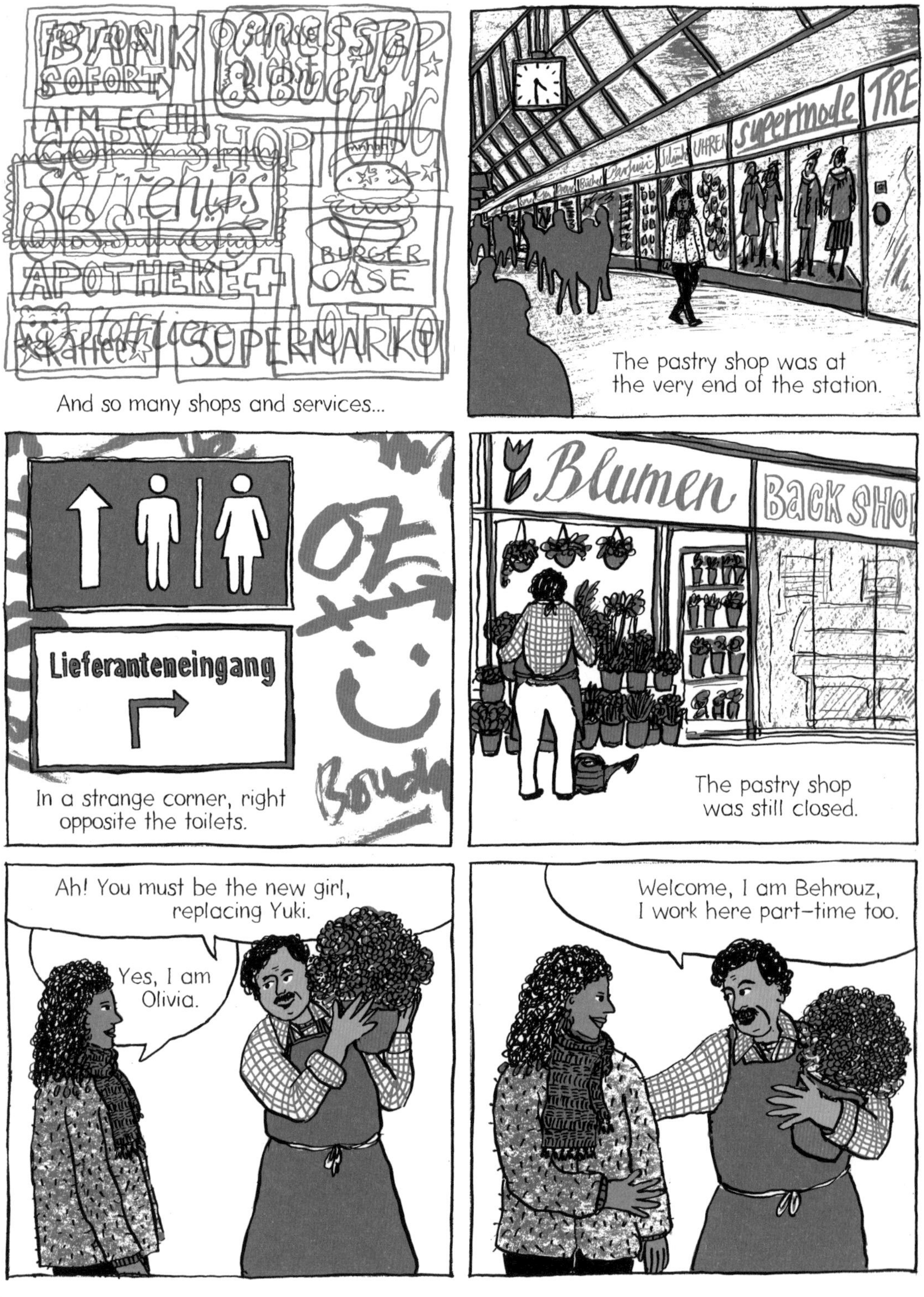
BANK
SOFORT
ATM EC
COPY SHOP
Souvenirs
OBST
APOTHEKE
BURGER
OASE
LOTTO
Kaffee
SUPERMARKT
And so many shops and services...
supermode
UHREN
The pastry shop was at the very end of the station.
Lieferanteneingang
In a strange corner, right opposite the toilets.
Blumen
The pastry shop was still closed.
Ah! You must be the new girl, replacing Yuki.
Yes, I am Olivia.
Welcome, I am Behrouz, I work here part-time too.

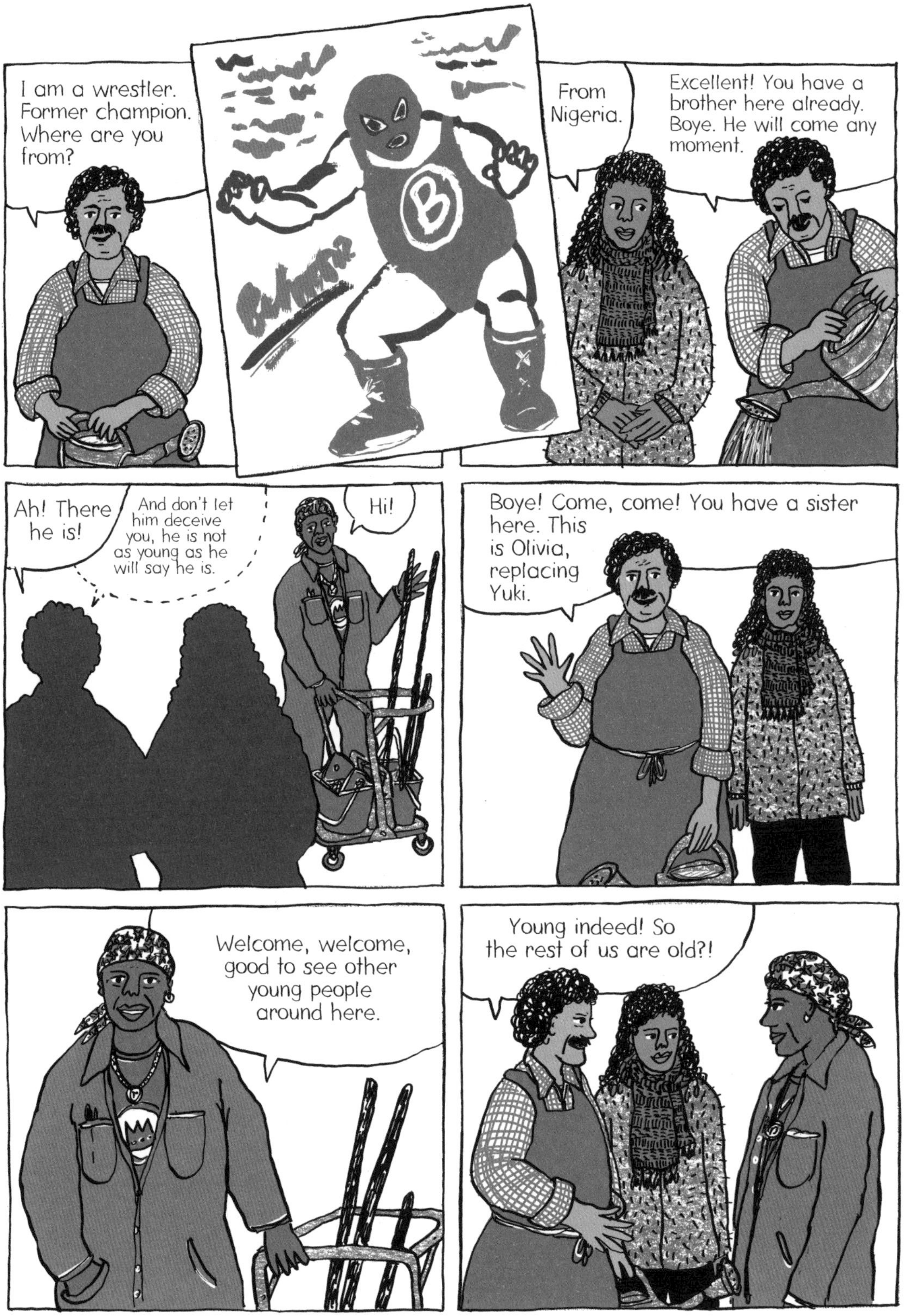
I am a wrestler. Former champion. Where are you from?
From Nigeria.
Excellent! You have a brother here already. Boye. He will come any moment.
Ah! There he is!
And don't let him deceive you, he is not as young as he will say he is.
Hi!
Boye! Come, come! You have a sister here. This is Olivia, replacing Yuki.
Welcome, welcome, good to see other young people around here.
Young indeed! So the rest of us are old?!

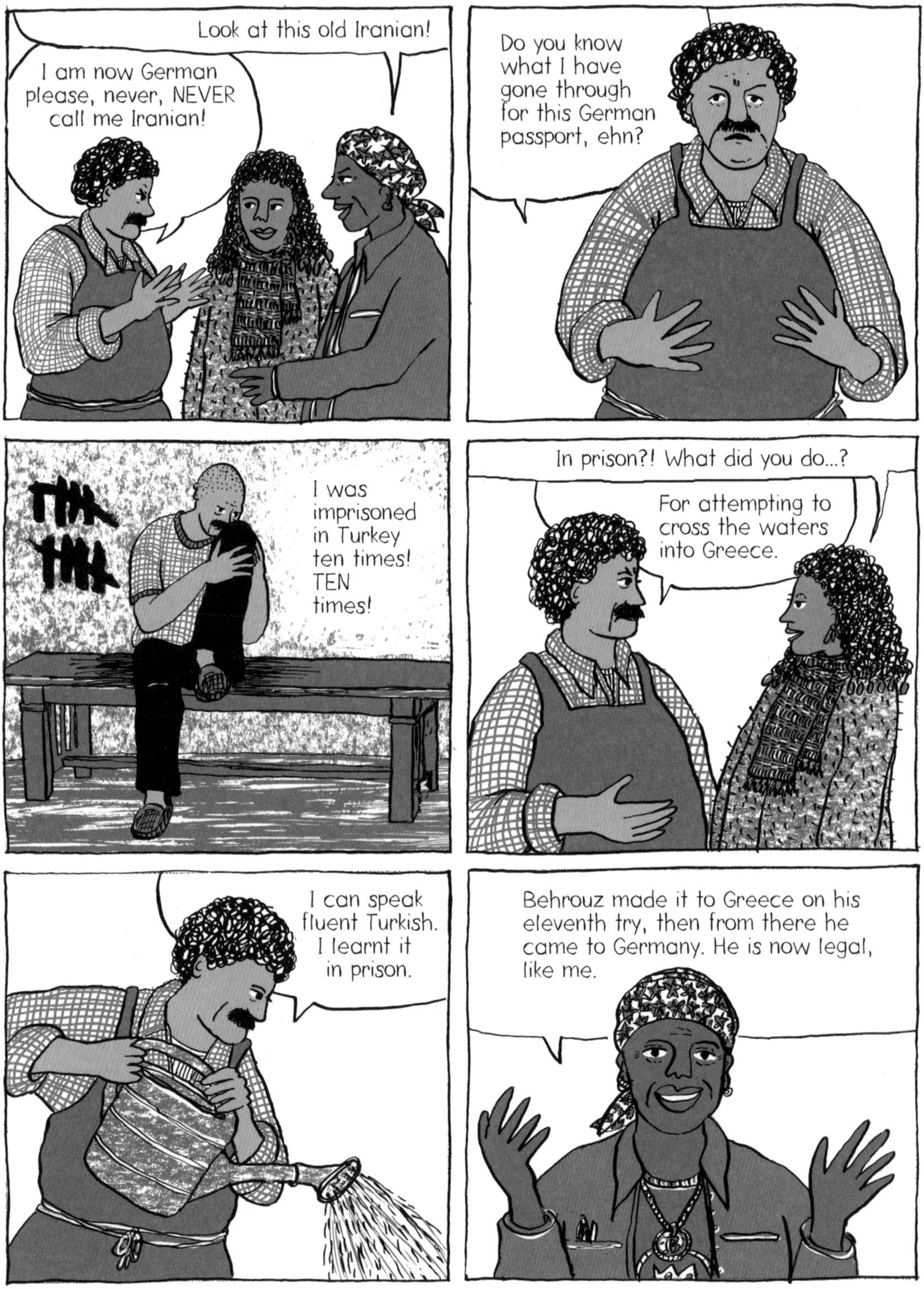
Look at this old Iranian!
I am now German please, never, NEVER call me Iranian!
Do you know what I have gone through for this German passport, ehn?
I was imprisoned in Turkey ten times! TEN times!
In prison?! What did you do...?
For attempting to cross the waters into Greece.
I can speak fluent Turkish. I learnt it in prison.
Behrouz made it to Greece on his eleventh try, then from there he came to Germany. He is now legal, like me.

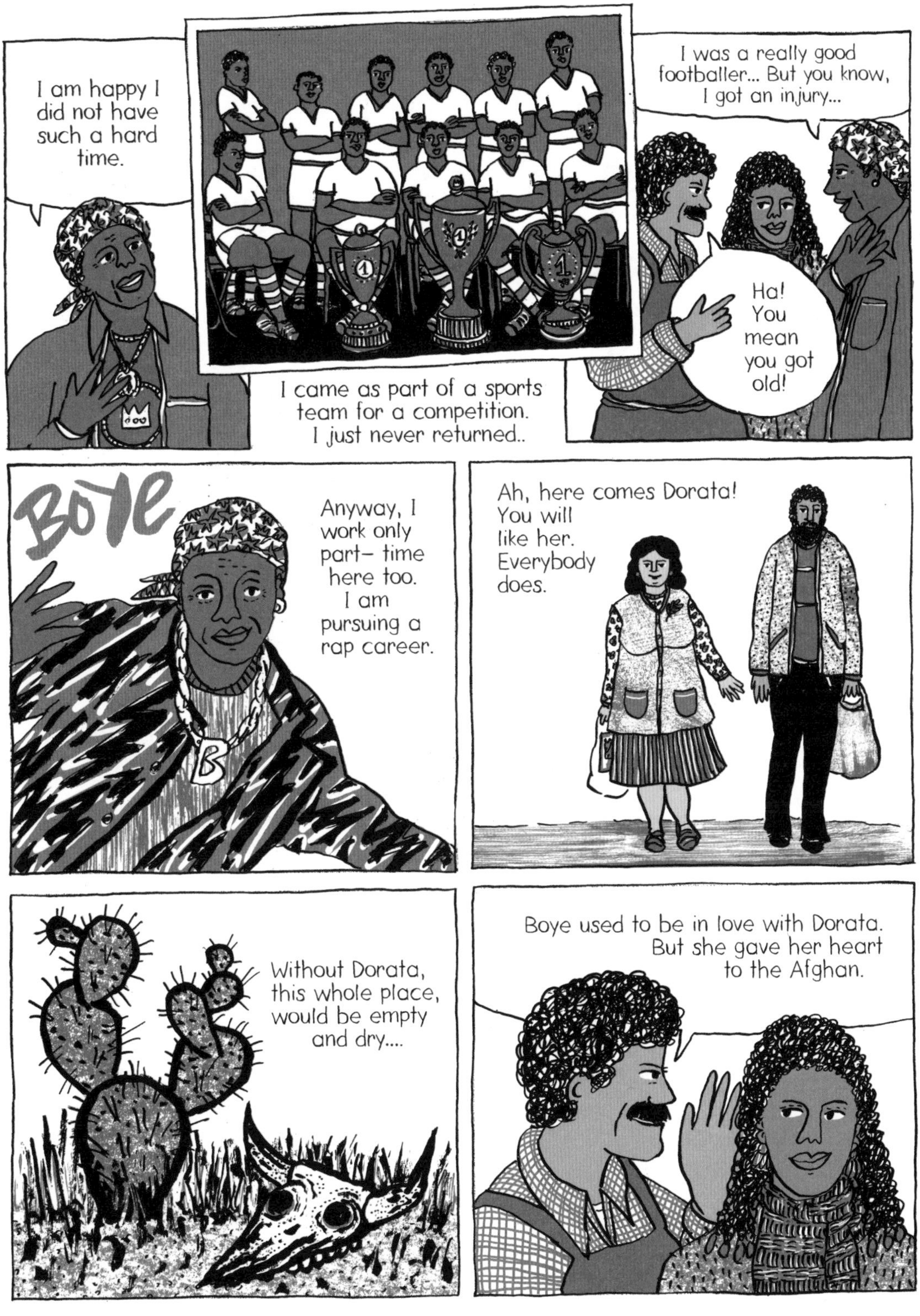
I am happy I did not have such a hard time.
I came as part of a sports team for a competition. I just never returned..
I was a really good footballer... But you know, I got an injury...
Ha! You mean you got old!
BOYE
Anyway, I work only part- time here too. I am pursuing a rap career.
Ah, here comes Dorata! You will like her. Everybody does.
Without Dorata, this whole place, would be empty and dry....
Boye used to be in love with Dorata. But she gave her heart to the Afghan.

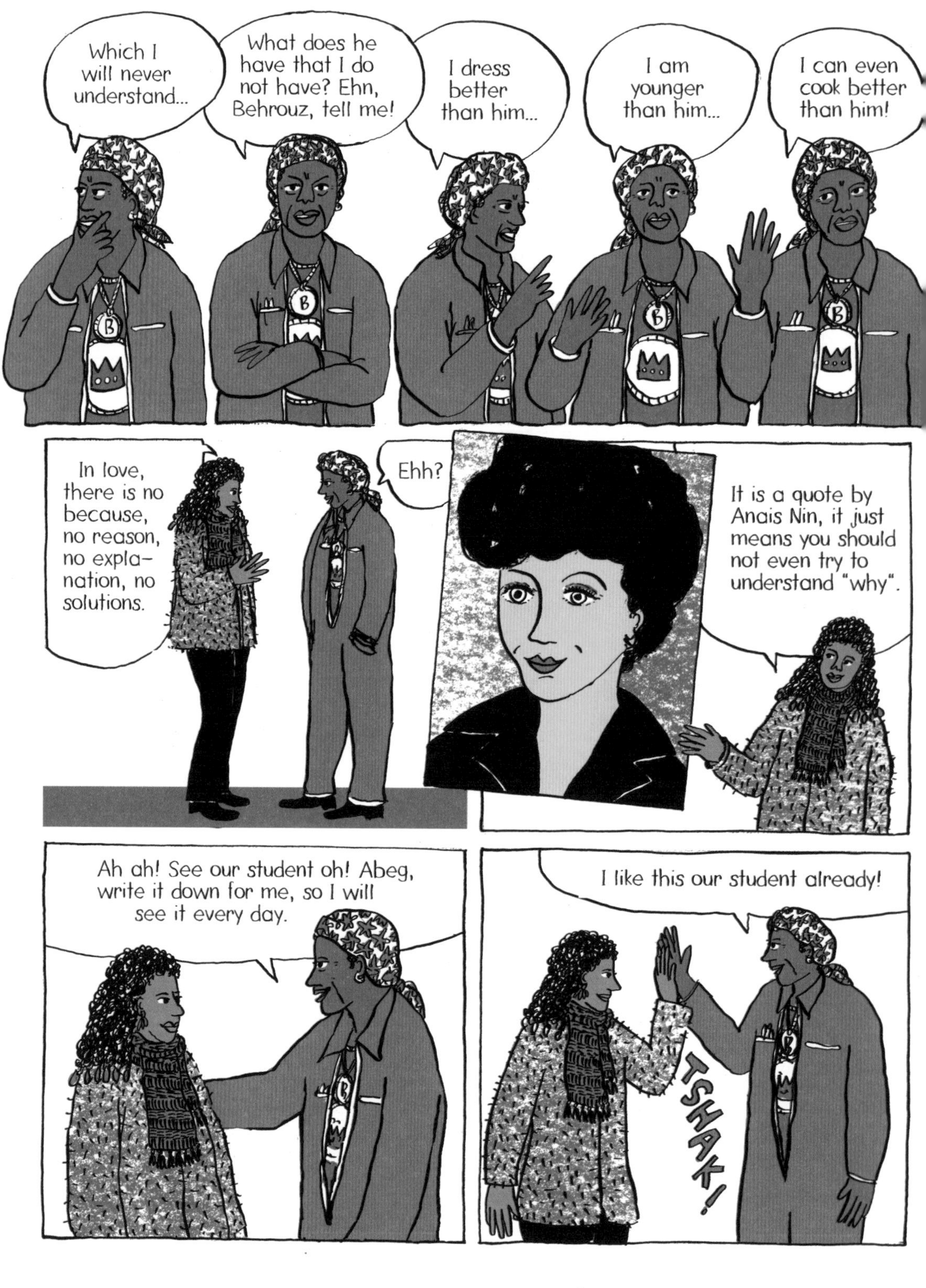
Which I will never understand...
What does he have that I do not have? Ehn, Behrouz, tell me!
I dress better than him...
I am younger than him...
I can even cook better than him!
In love, there is no because, no reason, no expla-nation, no solutions.
Ehh?
It is a quote by Anais Nin, it just means you should not even try to understand "why".
Ah ah! See our student oh! Abeg, write it down for me, so I will see it every day.
I like this our student already!
TSHAK!

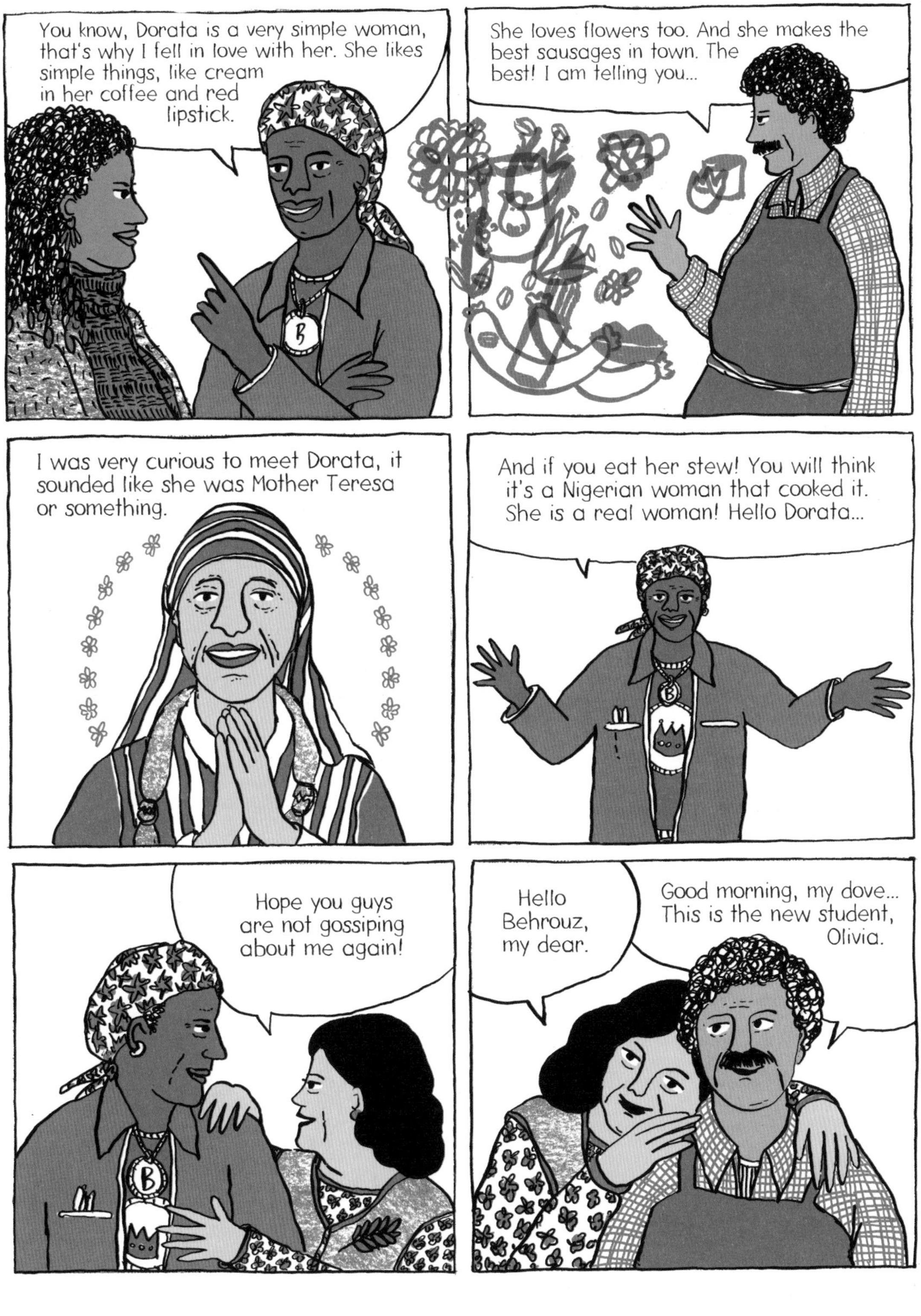
You know, Dorata is a very simple woman, that's why I fell in love with her. She likes simple things, like cream in her coffee and red lipstick.
She loves flowers too. And she makes the best sausages in town. The best! I am telling you...
I was very curious to meet Dorata, it sounded like she was Mother Teresa or something.
And if you eat her stew! You will think it's a Nigerian woman that cooked it. She is a real woman! Hello Dorata...
Hope you guys are not gossiping about me again!
Hello Behrouz, my dear.
Good morning, my dove... This is the new student, Olivia.

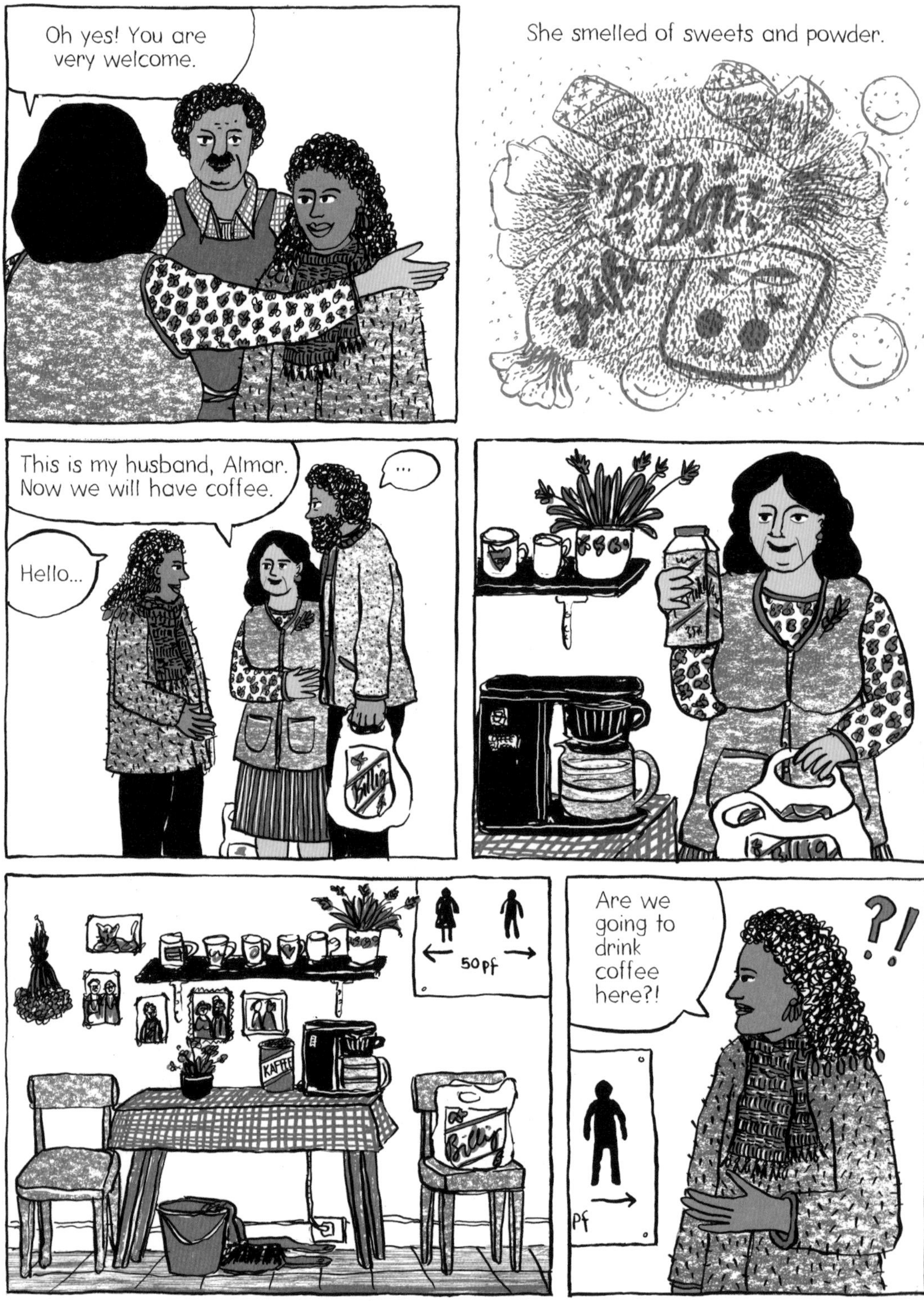
Oh yes! You are very welcome.
She smelled of sweets and powder.
This is my husband, Almar. Now we will have coffee.
...
Hello...
KAFFEE
50 pf
Are we going to drink coffee here?!
?!
pf

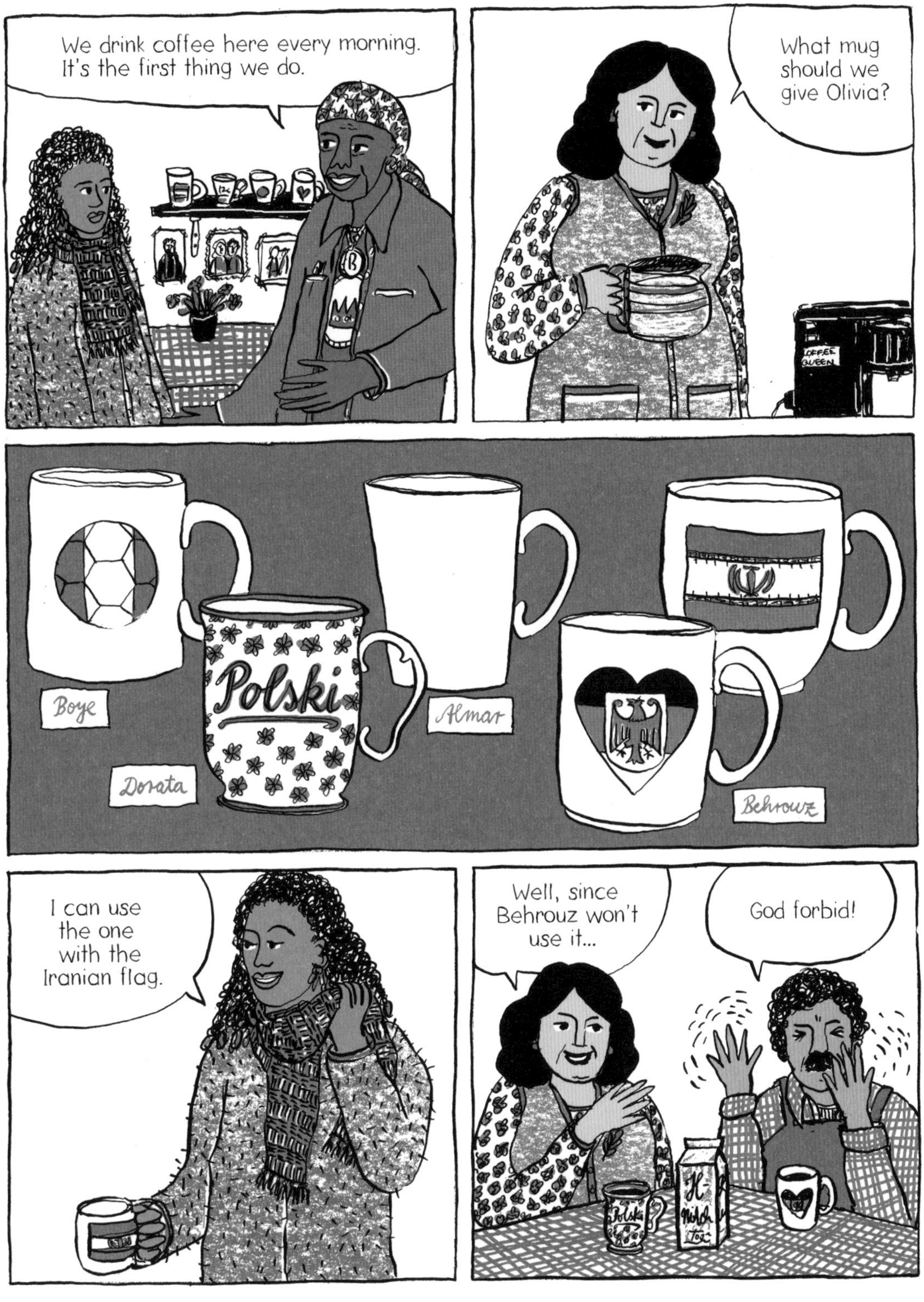
We drink coffee here every morning. It's the first thing we do.
What mug should we give Olivia?
Boye
Polski
Almar
Dorata
Behrouz
I can use the one with the Iranian flag.
Well, since Behrouz won't use it...
God forbid!

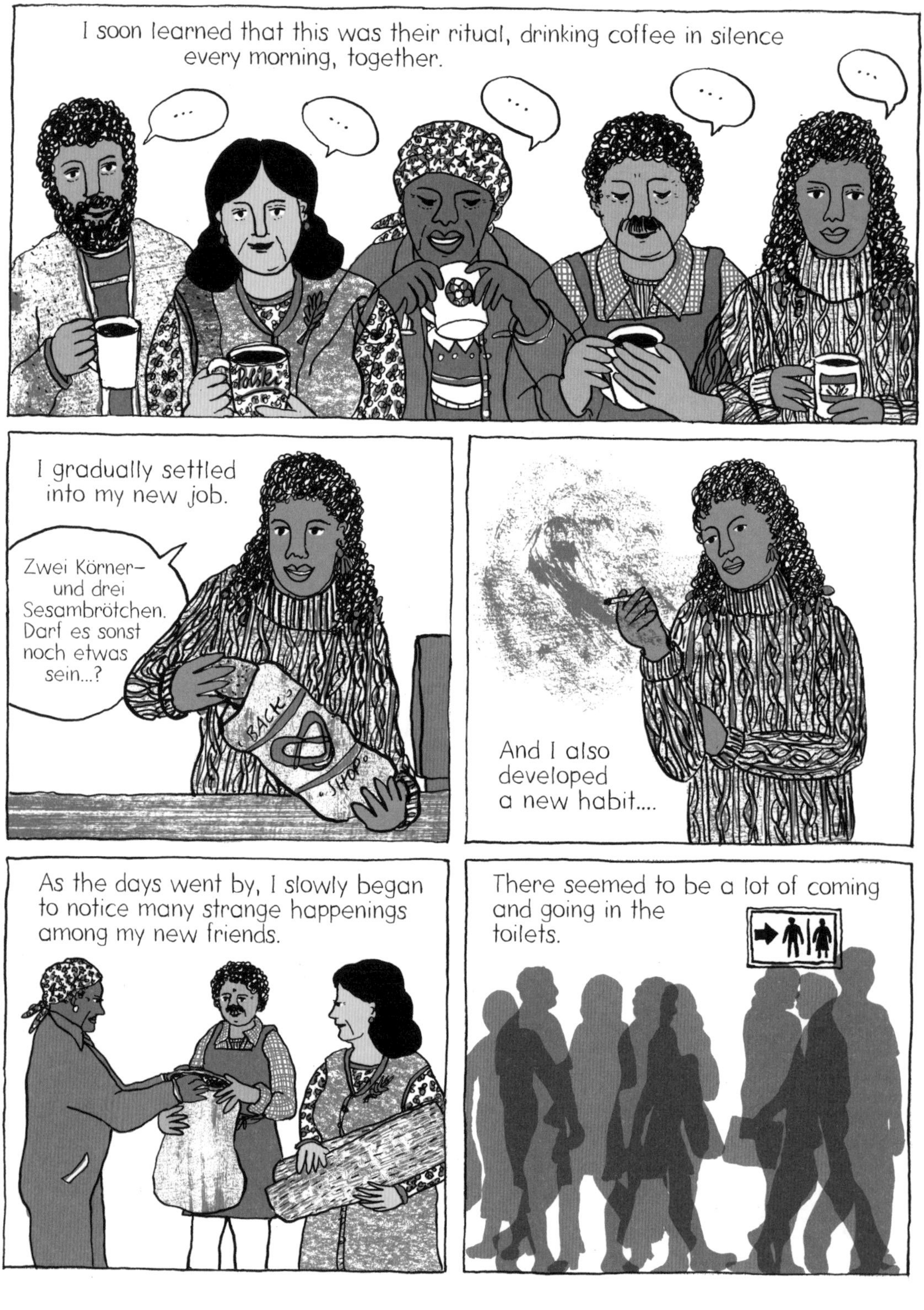
I soon learned that this was their ritual, drinking coffee in silence every morning, together.
...
...
...
...
...
Polska
I gradually settled into my new job.
Zwei Körner- und drei Sesambrötchen. Darf es sonst noch etwas sein...?
BACK SHOP
And I also developed a new habit....
As the days went by, I slowly began to notice many strange happenings among my new friends.
There seemed to be a lot of coming and going in the toilets.

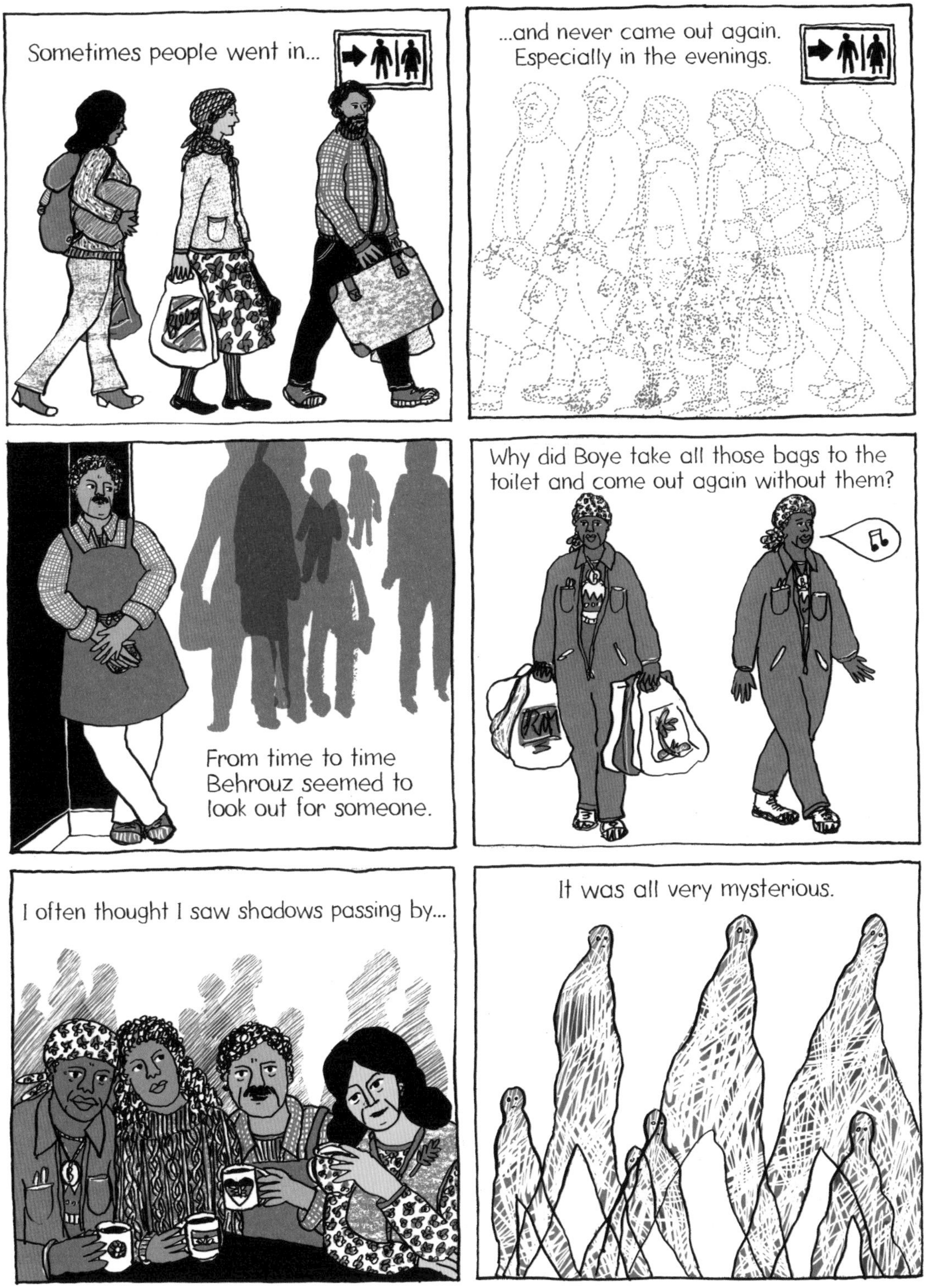
Sometimes people went in...
...and never came out again.
Especially in the evenings.
From time to time
Behrouz seemed to
look out for someone.
Why did Boye take all those bags to the
toilet and come out again without them?
I often thought I saw shadows passing by...
It was all very mysterious.

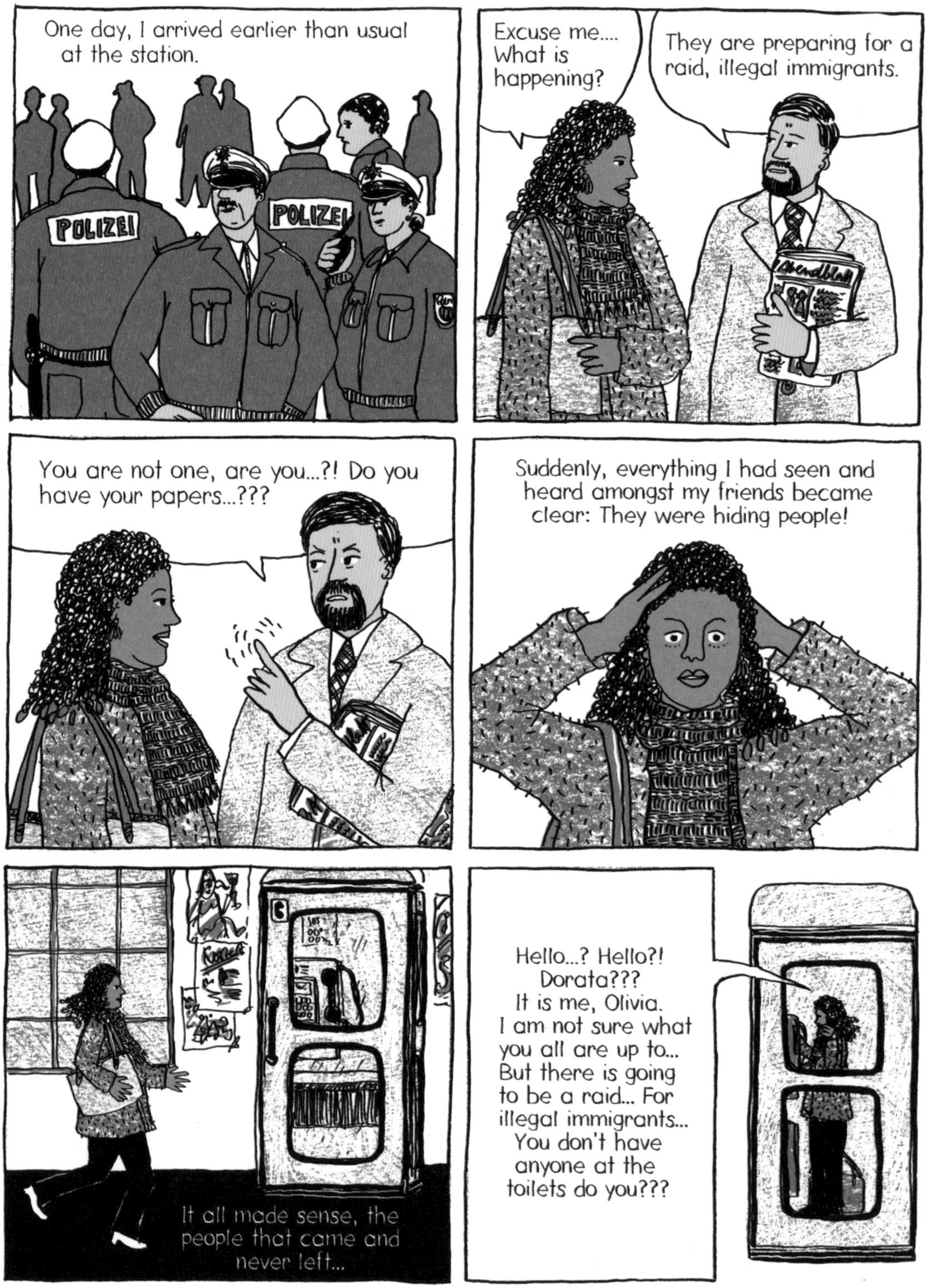

One day, I arrived earlier than usual at the station.
POLIZEI
POLIZEI
Excuse me.... What is happening?
They are preparing for a raid, illegal immigrants.
You are not one, are you...?! Do you have your papers...???
Suddenly, everything I had seen and heard amongst my friends became clear: They were hiding people!
It all made sense, the people that came and never left...
Hello...? Hello?! Dorata??? It is me, Olivia. I am not sure what you all are up to... But there is going to be a raid... For illegal immigrants... You don't have anyone at the toilets do you???

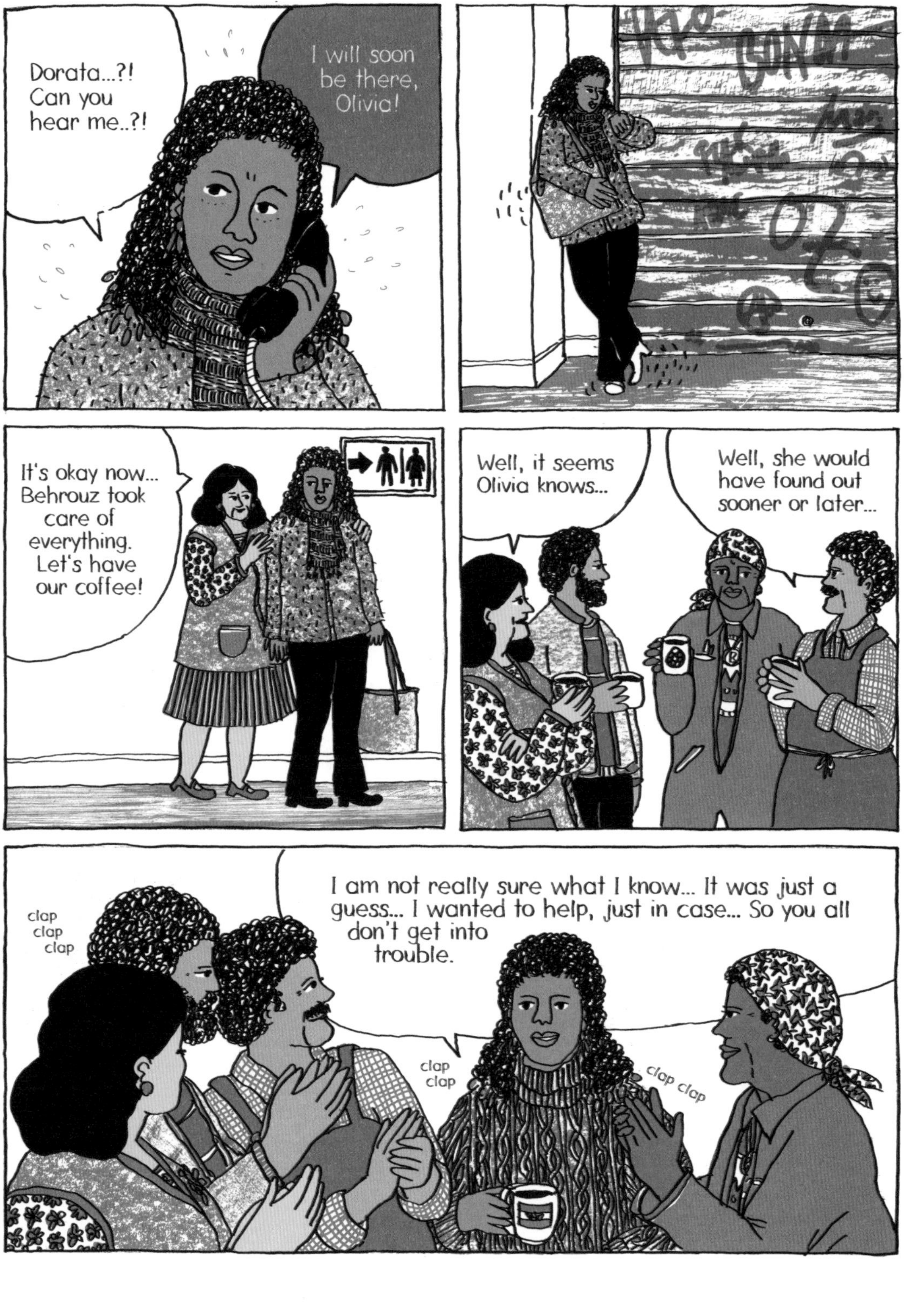

Dorata...?! Can you hear me..?!
I will soon be there, Olivia!
It's okay now... Behrouz took care of everything. Let's have our coffee!
Well, it seems Olivia knows...
Well, she would have found out sooner or later...
clap clap clap
I am not really sure what I know... It was just a guess... I wanted to help, just in case... So you all don't get into trouble.
clap clap
clap clap

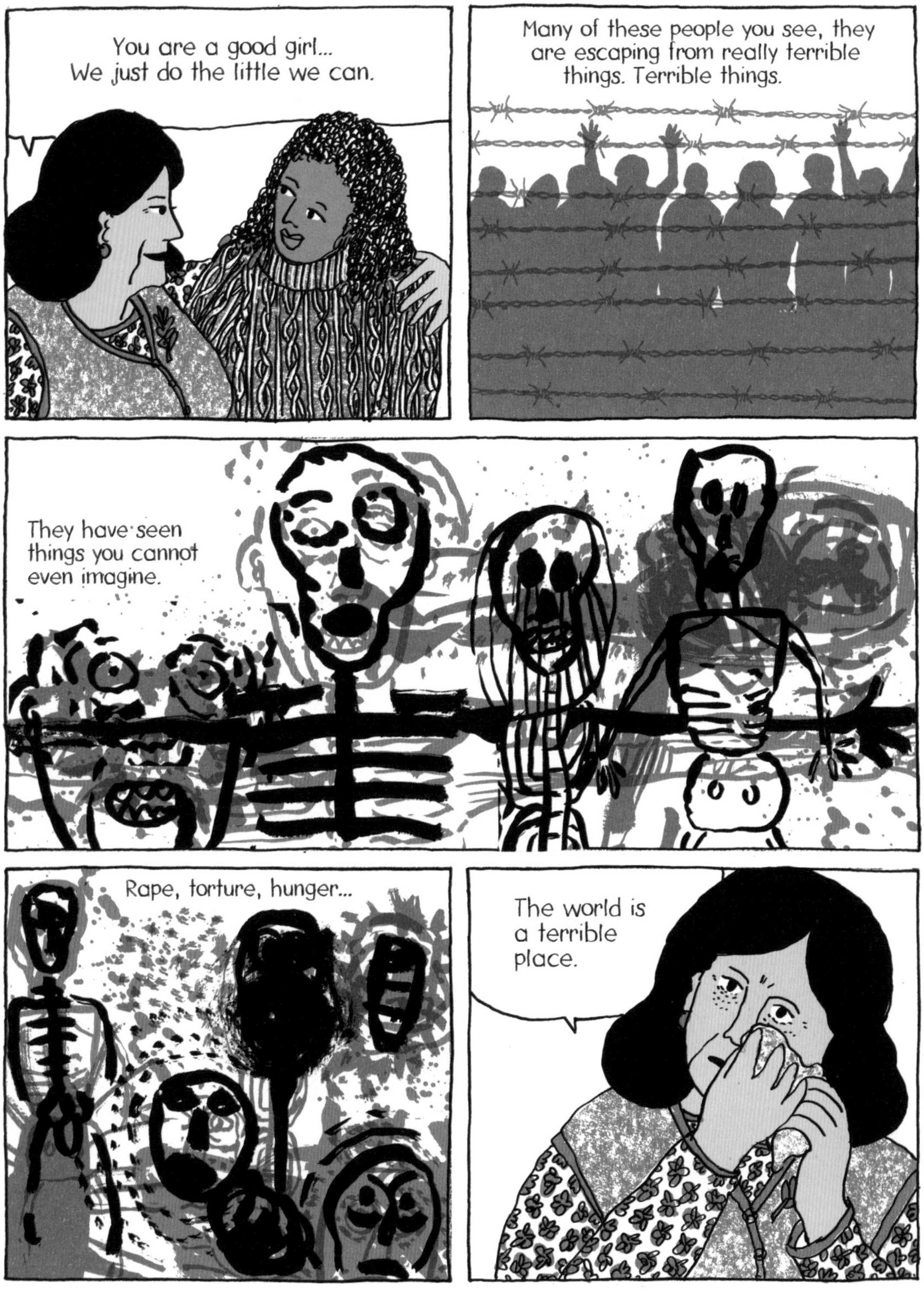
You are a good girl...
We just do the little we can.
Many of these people you see, they are escaping from really terrible things. Terrible things.
They have seen things you cannot even imagine.
Rape, torture, hunger...
The world is a terrible place.

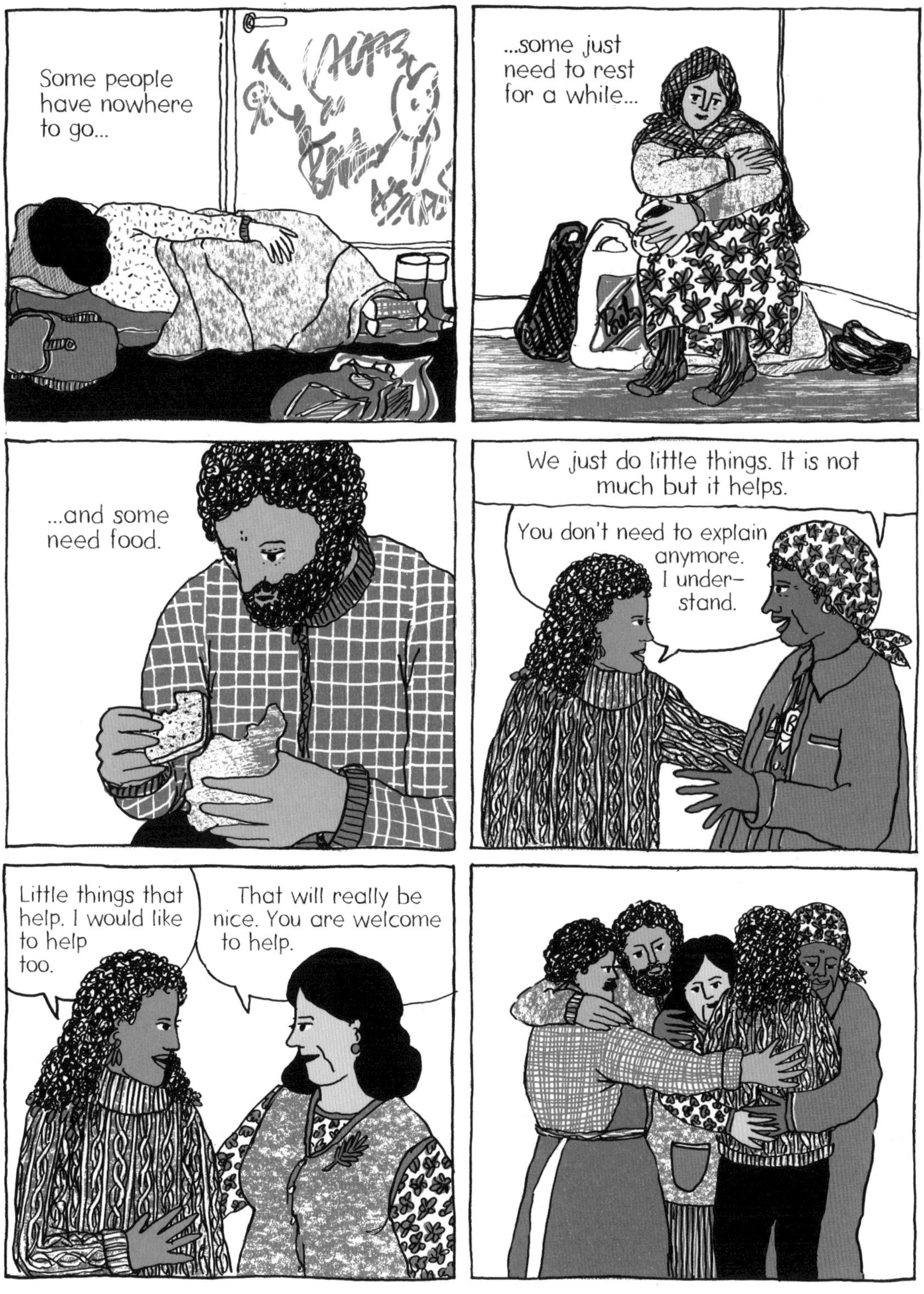
Some people have nowhere to go...
...some just need to rest for a while...
...and some need food.
We just do little things. It is not much but it helps.
You don't need to explain anymore. I under-stand.
Little things that help. I would like to help too.
That will really be nice. You are welcome to help.

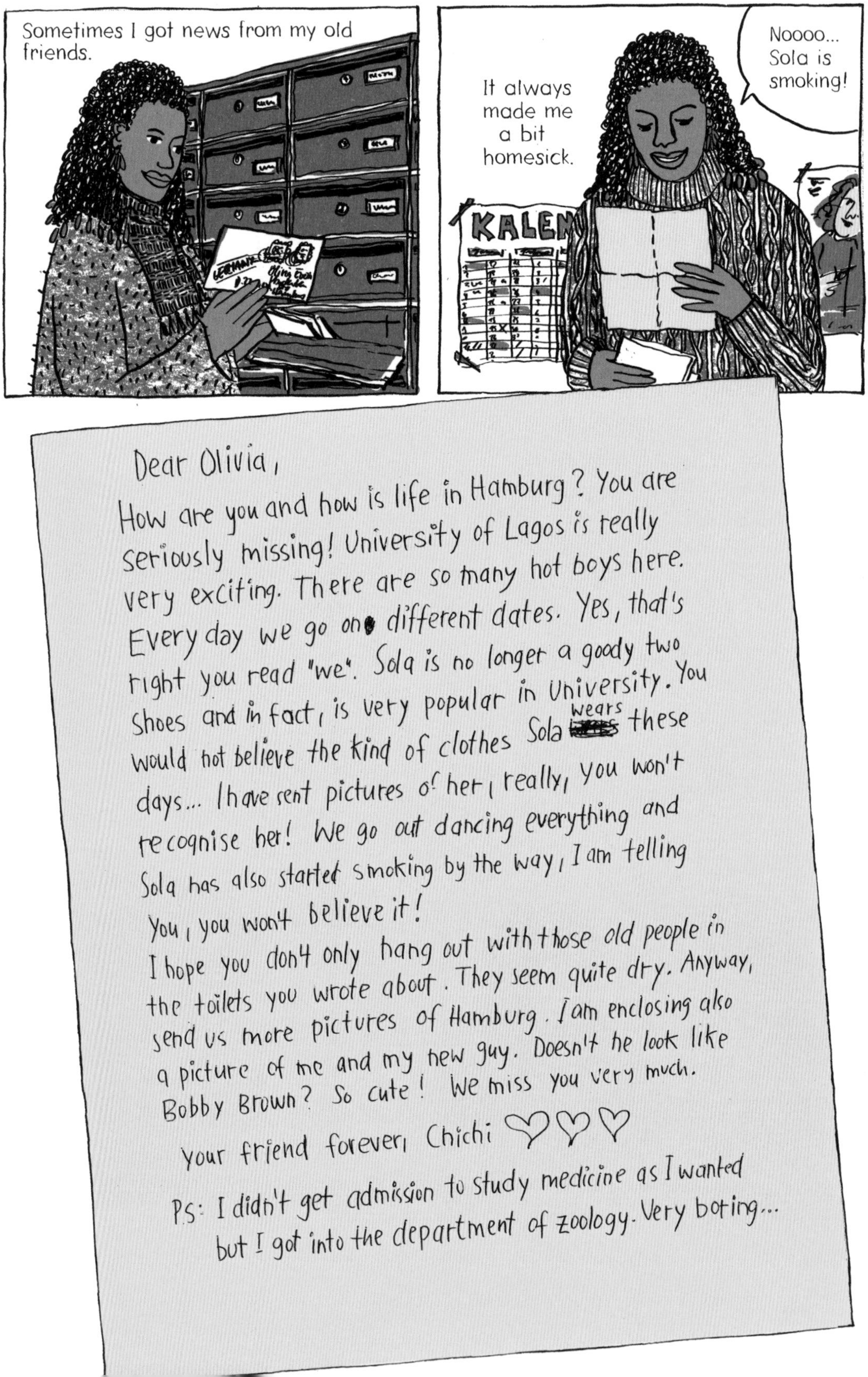

Sometimes I got news from my old friends.
It always made me a bit homesick.
Noooo... Sola is smoking!
KALEN
Dear Olivia,
How are you and how is life in Hamburg? You are
seriously missing! University of Lagos is really
very exciting. There are so many hot boys here.
Every day we go on different dates. Yes, that's
right you read "we". Sola is no longer a goody two
shoes and in fact, is very popular in University. You
would not believe the kind of clothes Sola wears these
days... I have sent pictures of her, really, you won't
recognise her! We go out dancing everything and
Sola has also started smoking by the way, I am telling
you, you won't believe it!
I hope you don't only hang out with those old people in
the toilets you wrote about. They seem quite dry. Anyway,
send us more pictures of Hamburg. I am enclosing also
a picture of me and my new guy. Doesn't he look like
Bobby Brown? So cute! We miss you very much.
your friend forever, Chichi
PS: I didn't get admission to study medicine as I wanted
but I got into the department of zoology. Very boring...

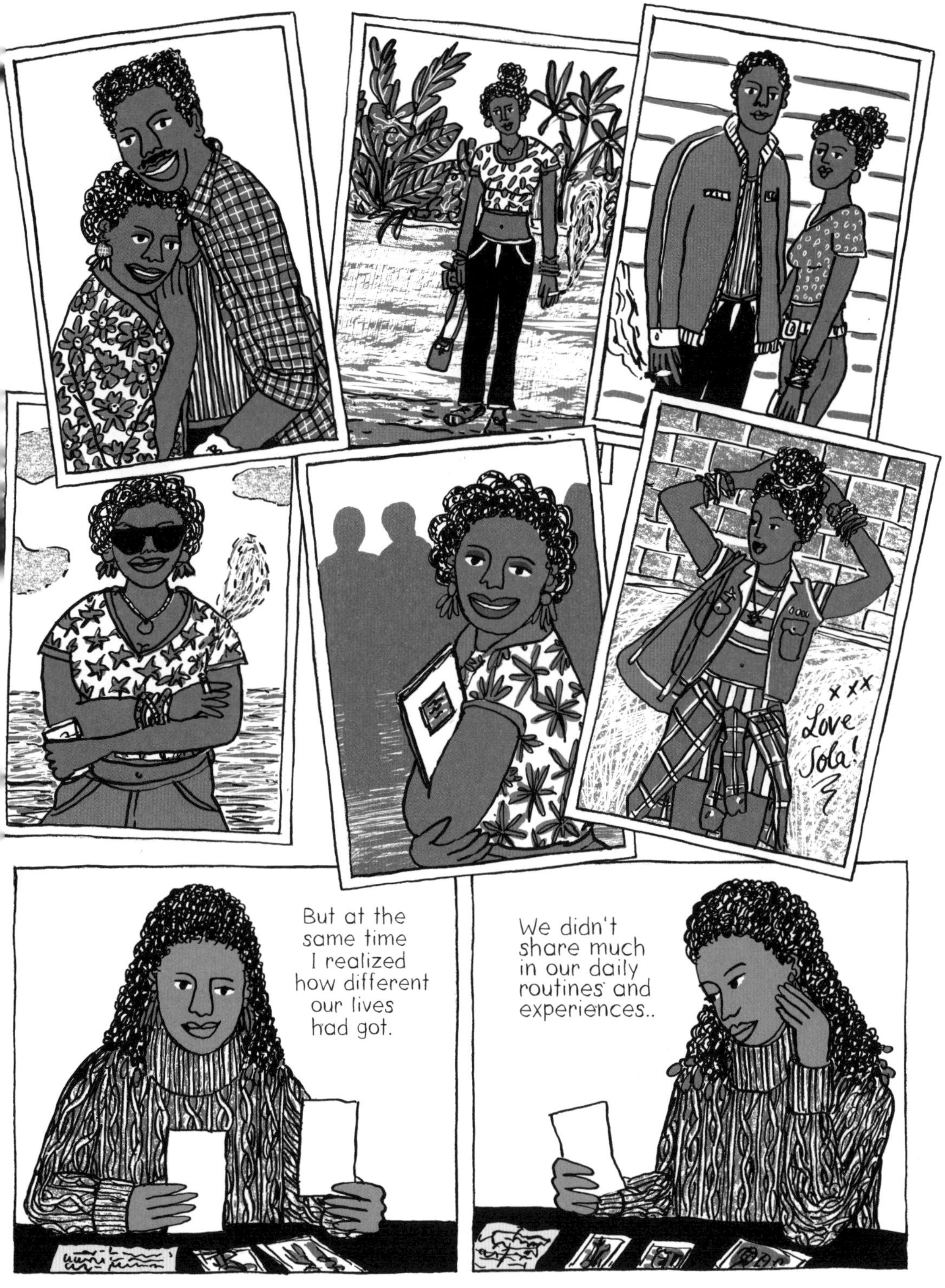
xxx
Love Sola!
But at the same time I realized how different our lives had got.
We didn't share much in our daily routines and experiences..

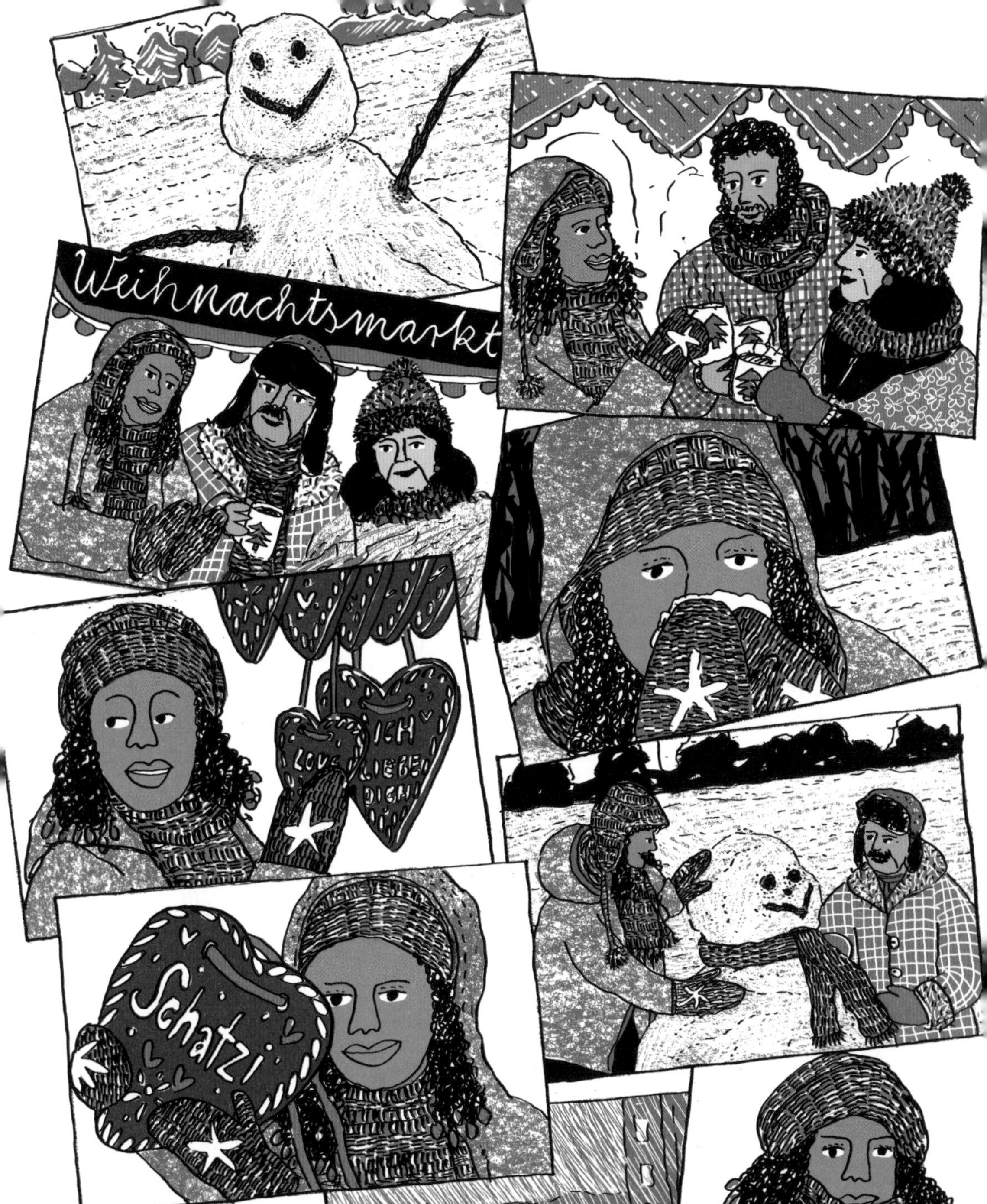
Weihnachtsmarkt
LOVE
ICH LIEBE DICH
Schatzi

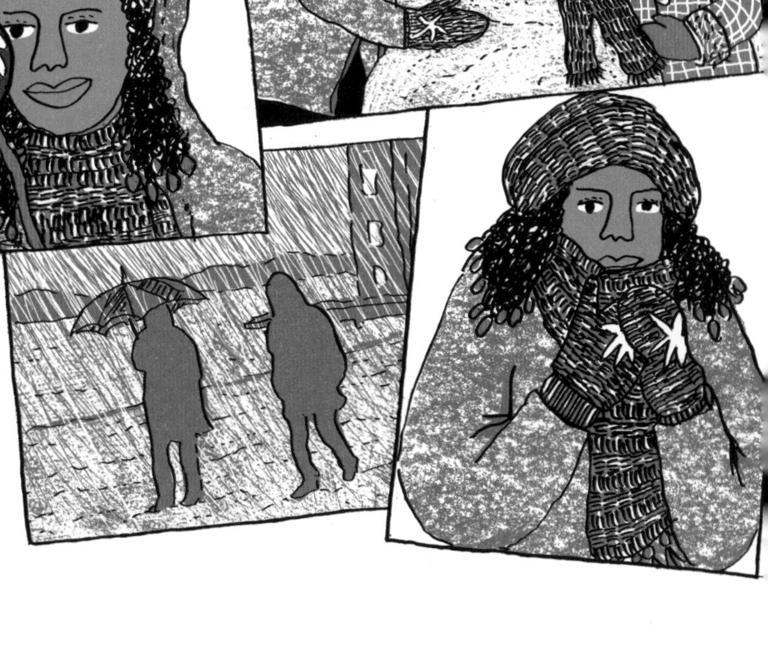

My first winter...

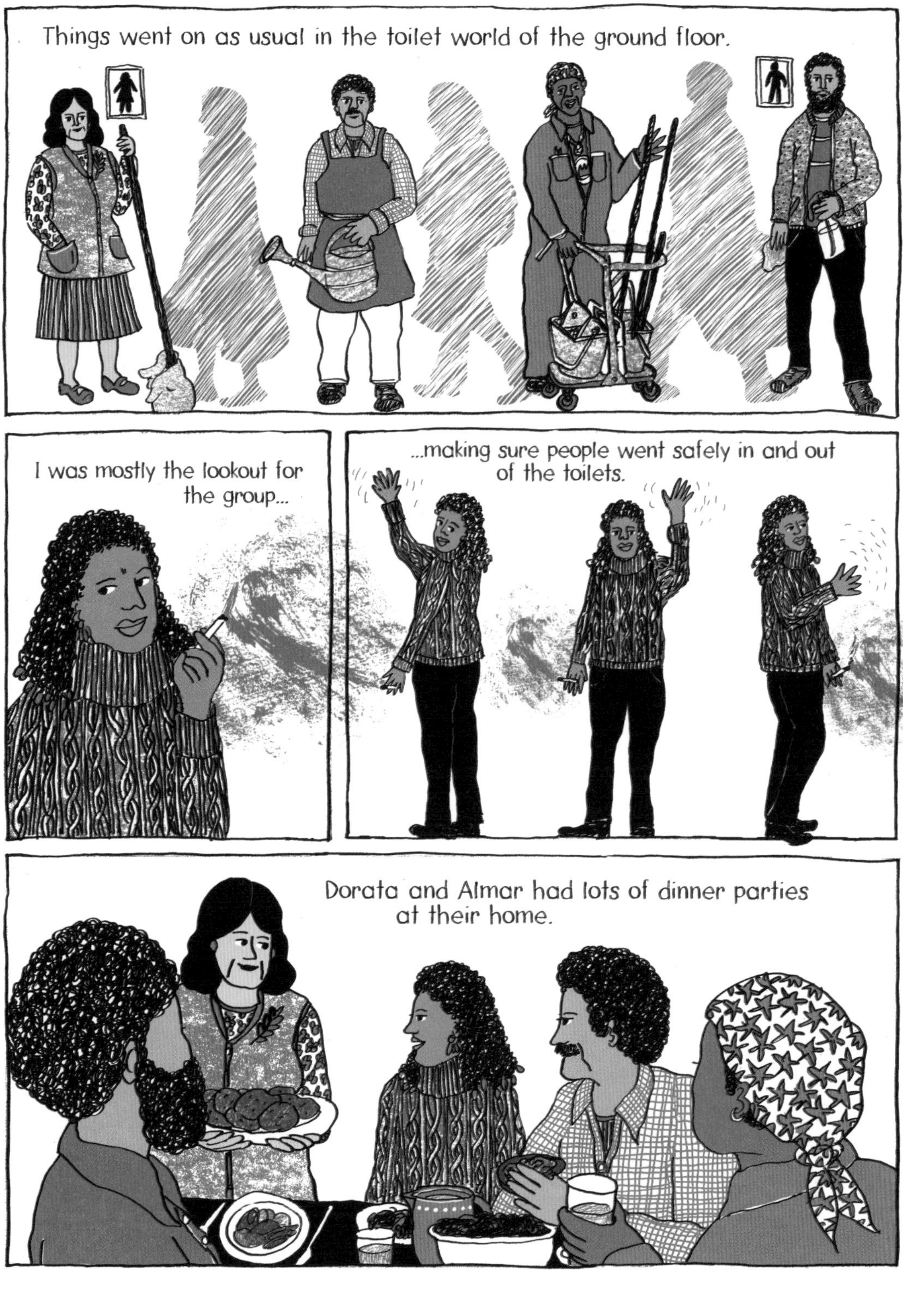
Things went on as usual in the toilet world of the ground floor.
I was mostly the lookout for the group...
...making sure people went safely in and out of the toilets.
Dorata and Almar had lots of dinner parties at their home.

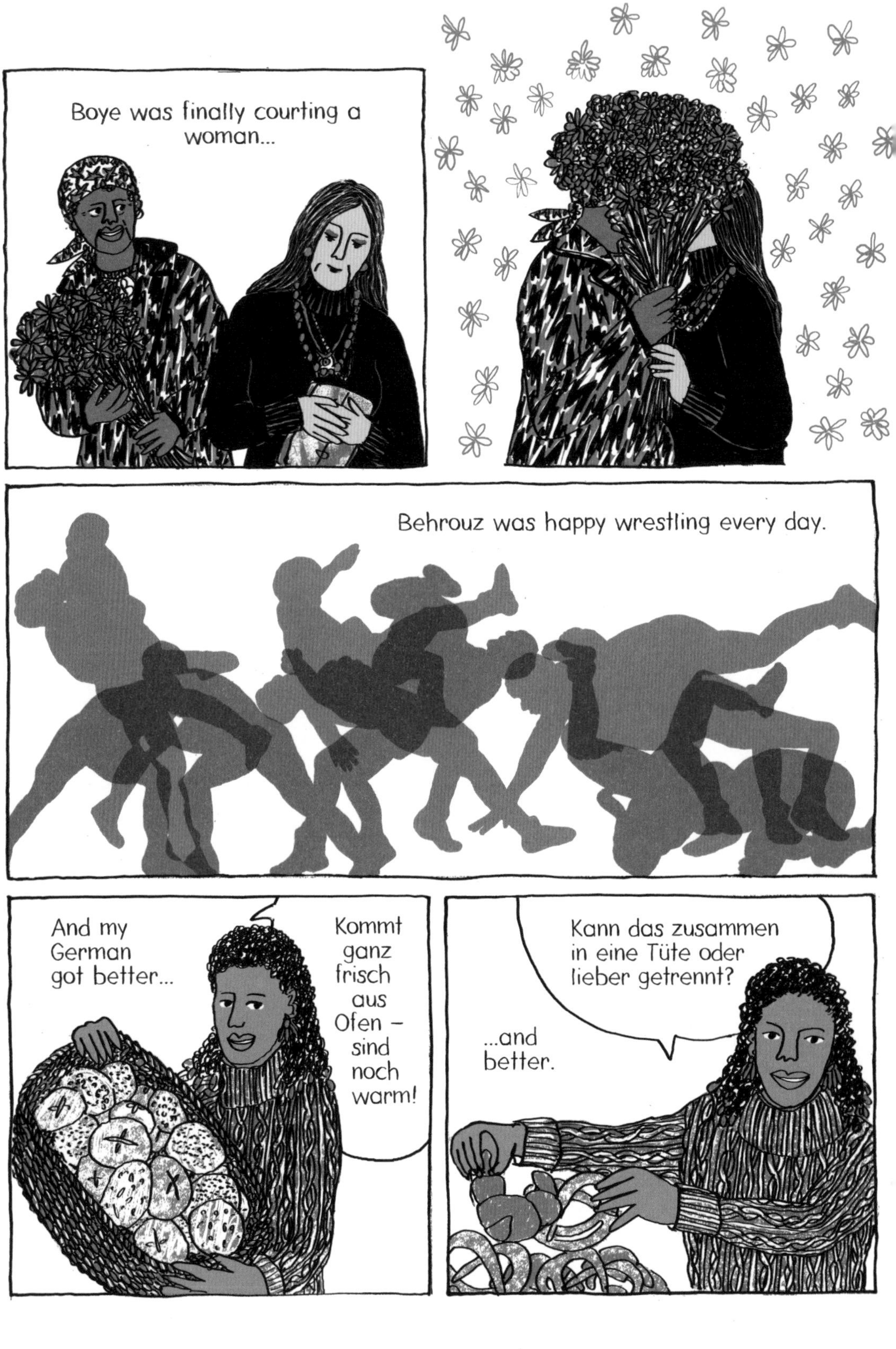
Boye was finally courting a woman...
Behrouz was happy wrestling every day.
And my German got better...
Kommt ganz frisch aus Ofen – sind noch warm!
...and better.
Kann das zusammen in eine Tüte oder lieber getrennt?

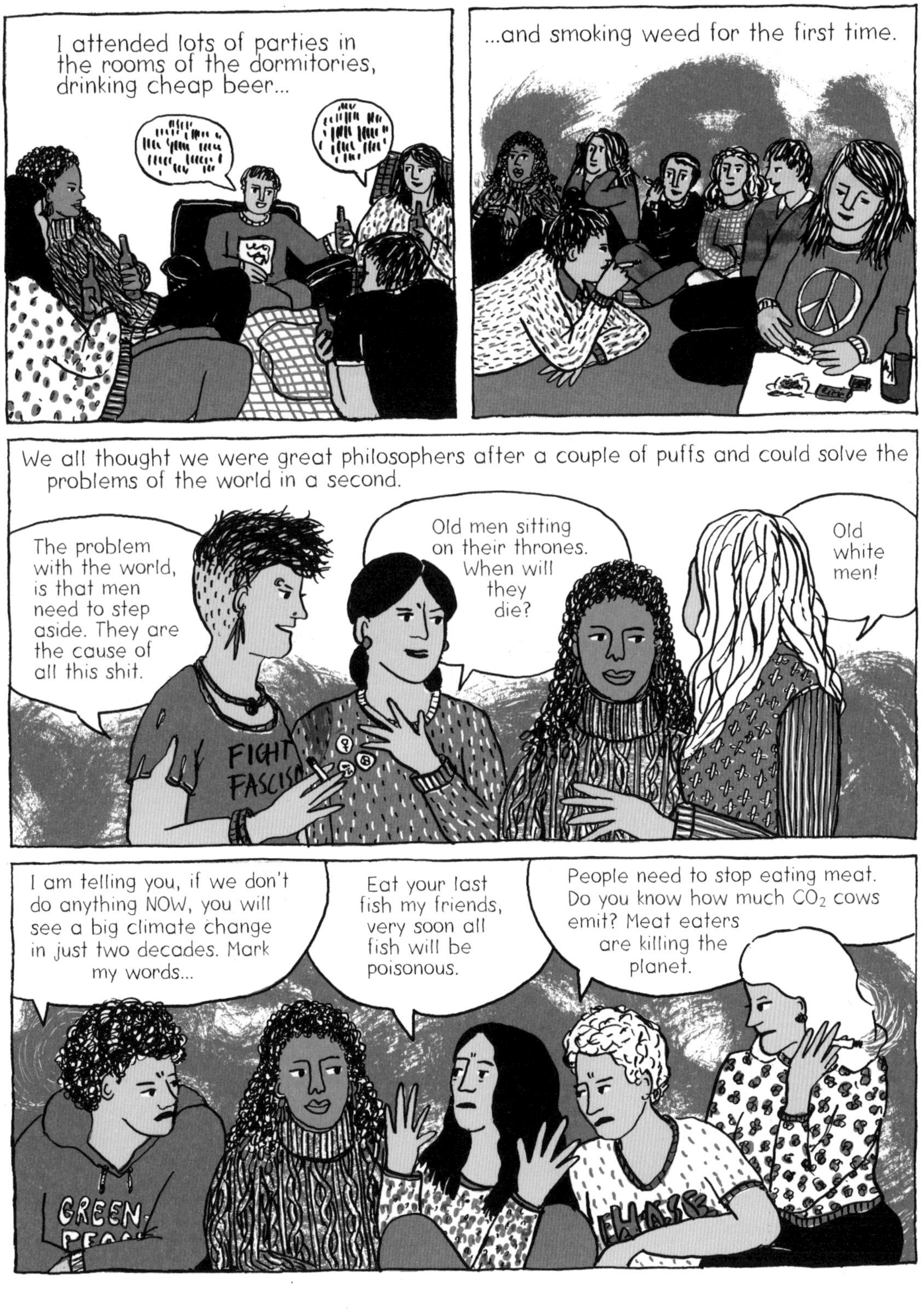
I attended lots of parties in the rooms of the dormitories, drinking cheap beer...
...and smoking weed for the first time.
We all thought we were great philosophers after a couple of puffs and could solve the problems of the world in a second.
The problem with the world, is that men need to step aside. They are the cause of all this shit.
Old men sitting on their thrones. When will they die?
Old white men!
FIGHT FASCISM
I am telling you, if we don't do anything NOW, you will see a big climate change in just two decades. Mark my words...
Eat your last fish my friends, very soon all fish will be poisonous.
People need to stop eating meat. Do you know how much CO2 cows emit? Meat eaters are killing the planet.
GREEN-

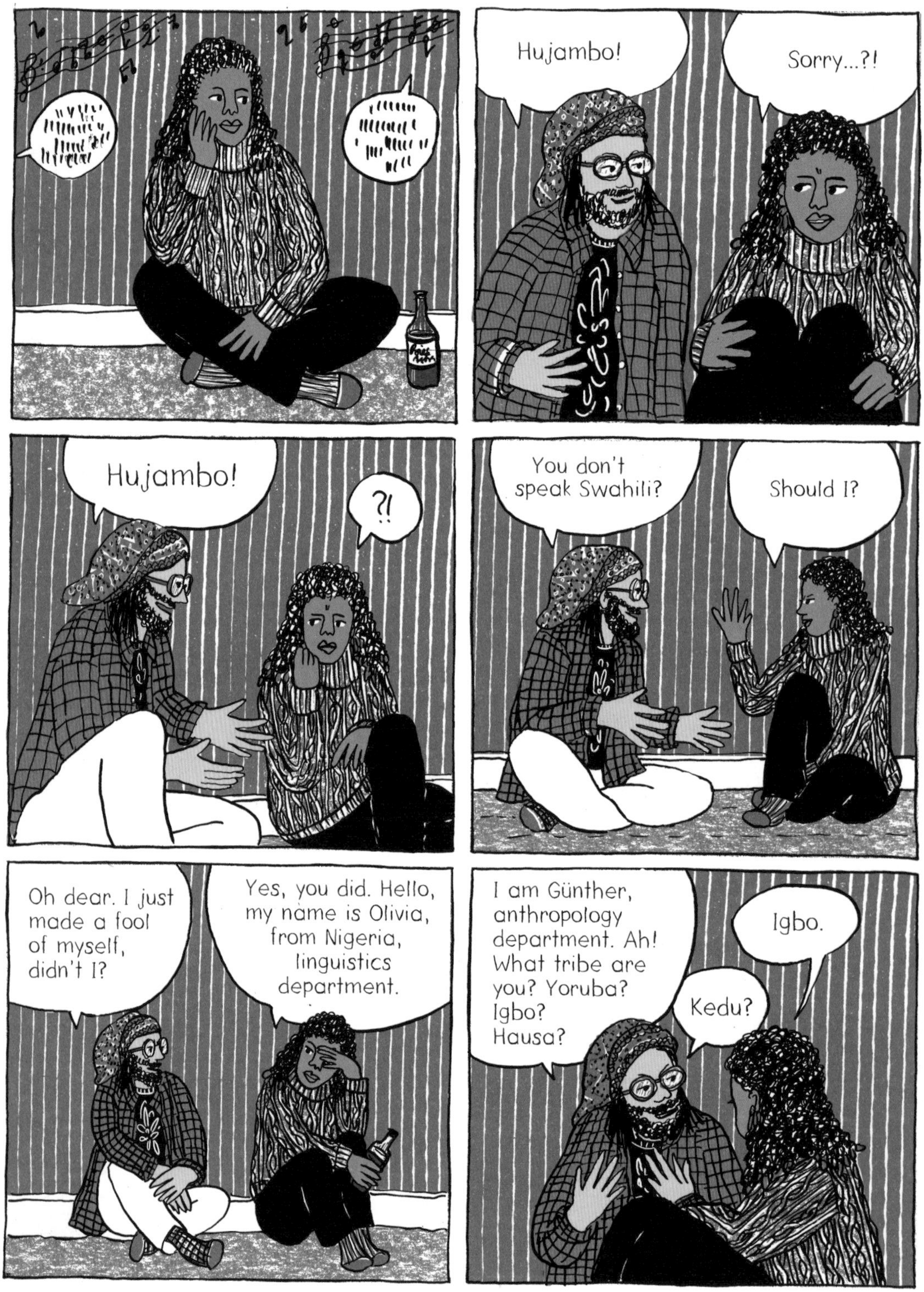
Hujambo!
Sorry...?!
Hujambo!
?!
You don't speak Swahili?
Should I?
Oh dear. I just made a fool of myself, didn't I?
Yes, you did. Hello, my name is Olivia, from Nigeria, linguistics department.
I am Günther, anthropology department. Ah! What tribe are you? Yoruba? Igbo? Hausa?
Igbo.
Kedu?

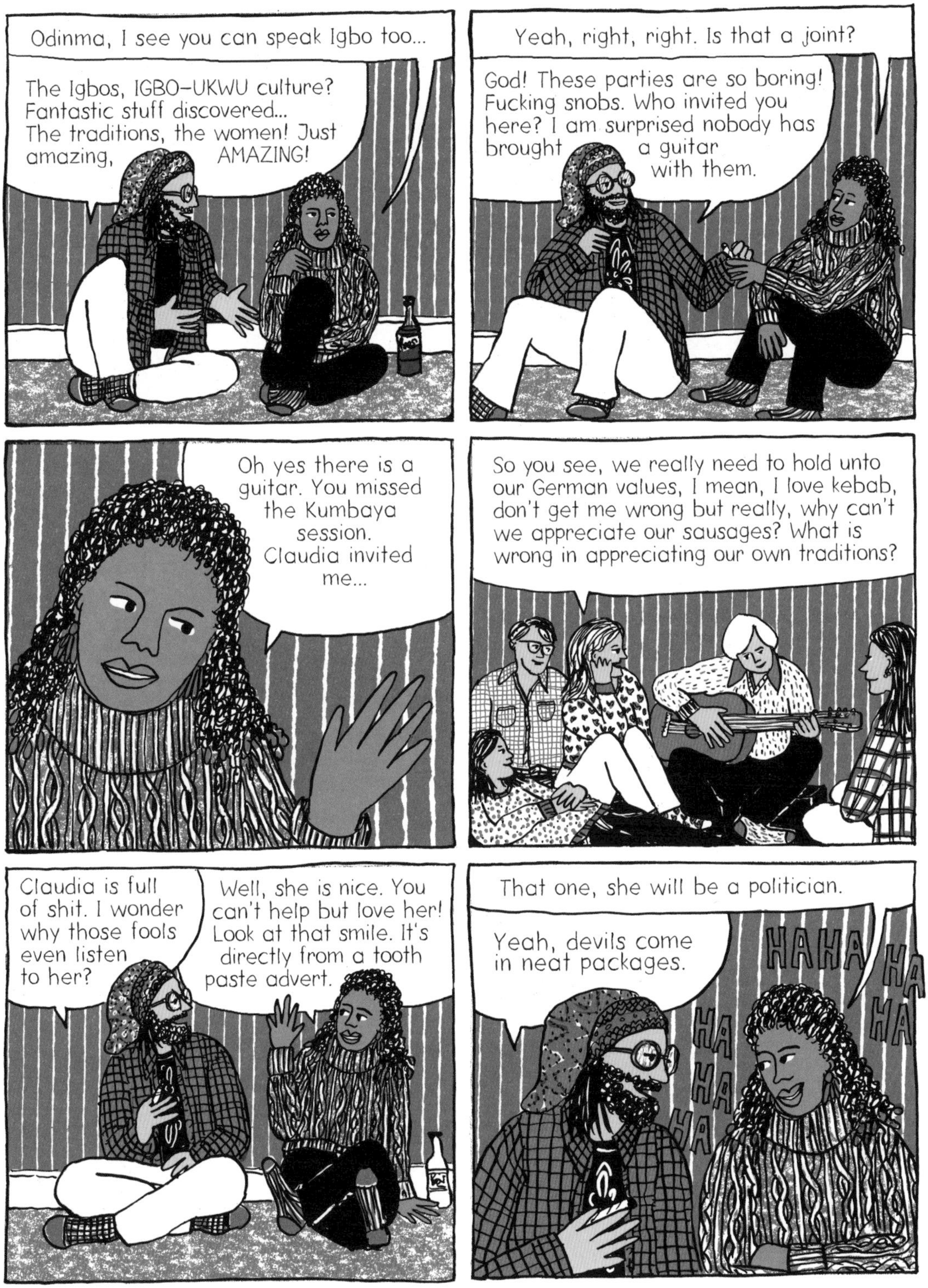
Odinma, I see you can speak Igbo too...
The Igbos, IGBO-UKWU culture? Fantastic stuff discovered... The traditions, the women! Just amazing, AMAZING!
Yeah, right, right. Is that a joint?
God! These parties are so boring! Fucking snobs. Who invited you here? I am surprised nobody has brought a guitar with them.
Oh yes there is a guitar. You missed the Kumbaya session. Claudia invited me...
So you see, we really need to hold unto our German values, I mean, I love kebab, don't get me wrong but really, why can't we appreciate our sausages? What is wrong in appreciating our own traditions?
Claudia is full of shit. I wonder why those fools even listen to her?
Well, she is nice. You can't help but love her! Look at that smile. It's directly from a tooth paste advert.
That one, she will be a politician.
Yeah, devils come in neat packages.
HAHA HA HA
HA HA HA HA

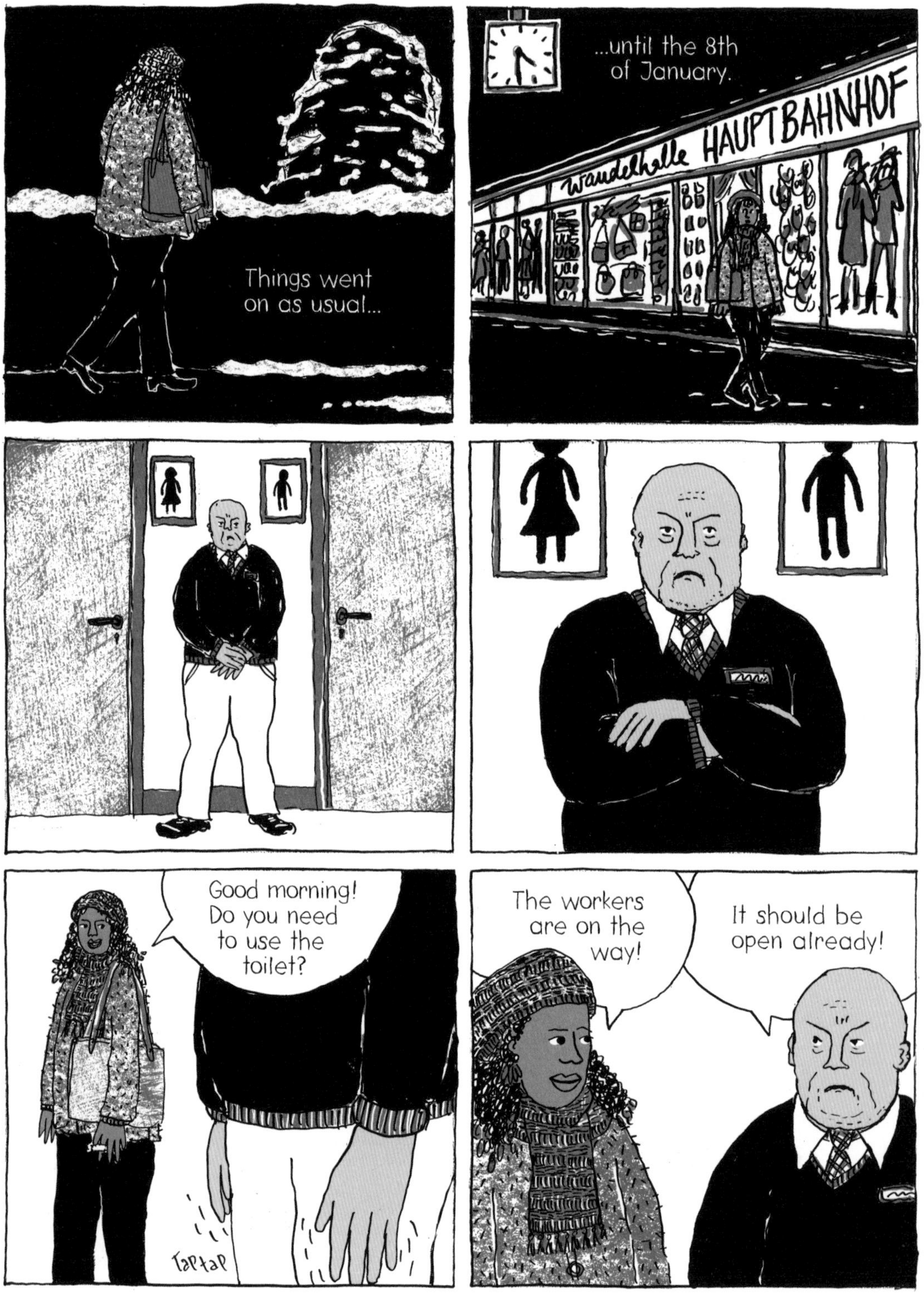
Things went on as usual...
...until the 8th of January.
Wandelhalle
HAUPTBAHNHOF
Good morning! Do you need to use the toilet?
TAPTAP
The workers are on the way!
It should be open already!

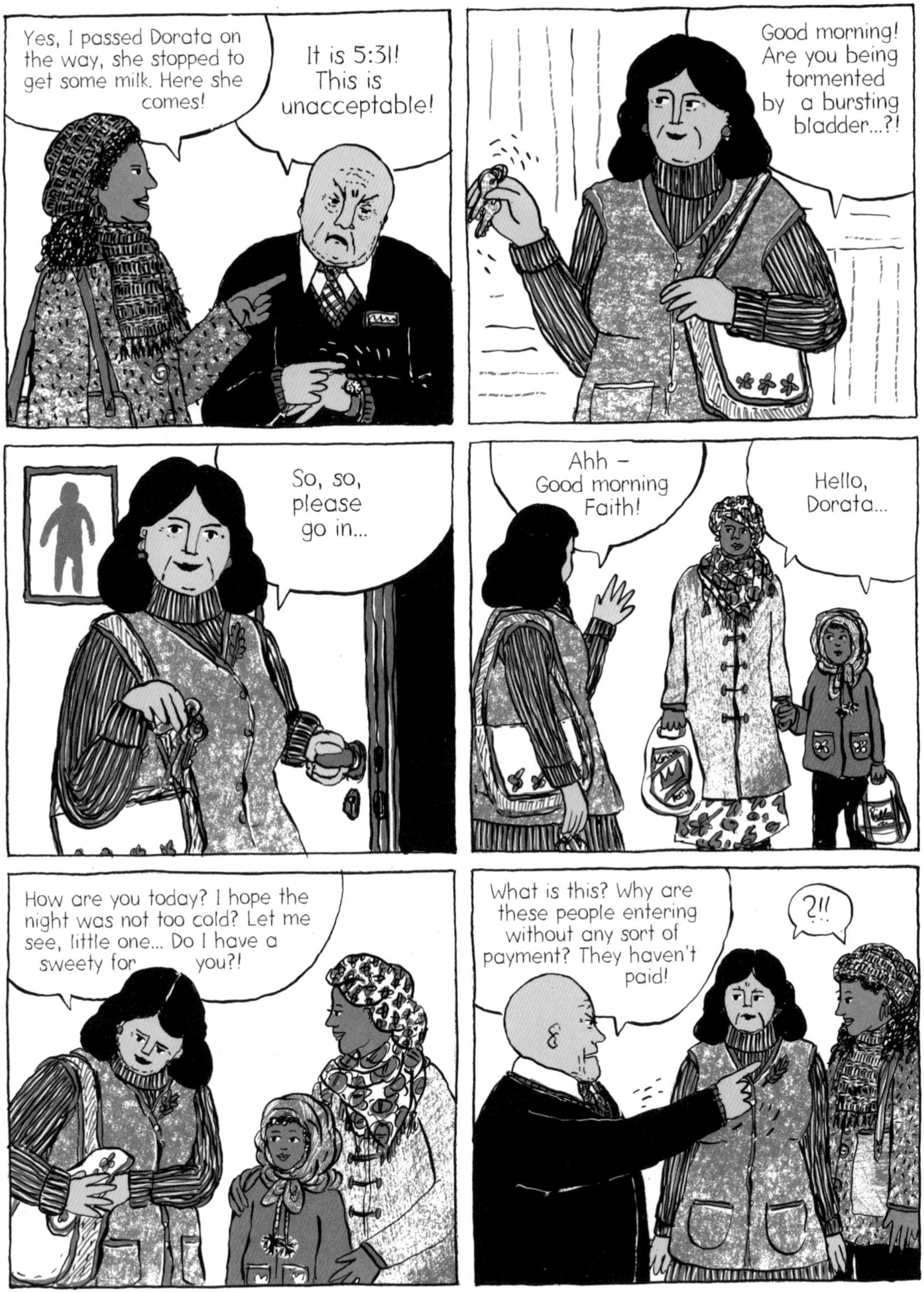
Yes, I passed Dorata on the way, she stopped to get some milk. Here she comes!
It is 5:31! This is unacceptable!
Good morning! Are you being tormented by a bursting bladder...?!
So, so, please go in...
Ahh – Good morning Faith!
Hello, Dorata...
How are you today? I hope the night was not too cold? Let me see, little one... Do I have a sweety for you?!
What is this? Why are these people entering without any sort of payment? They haven't paid!
?!!

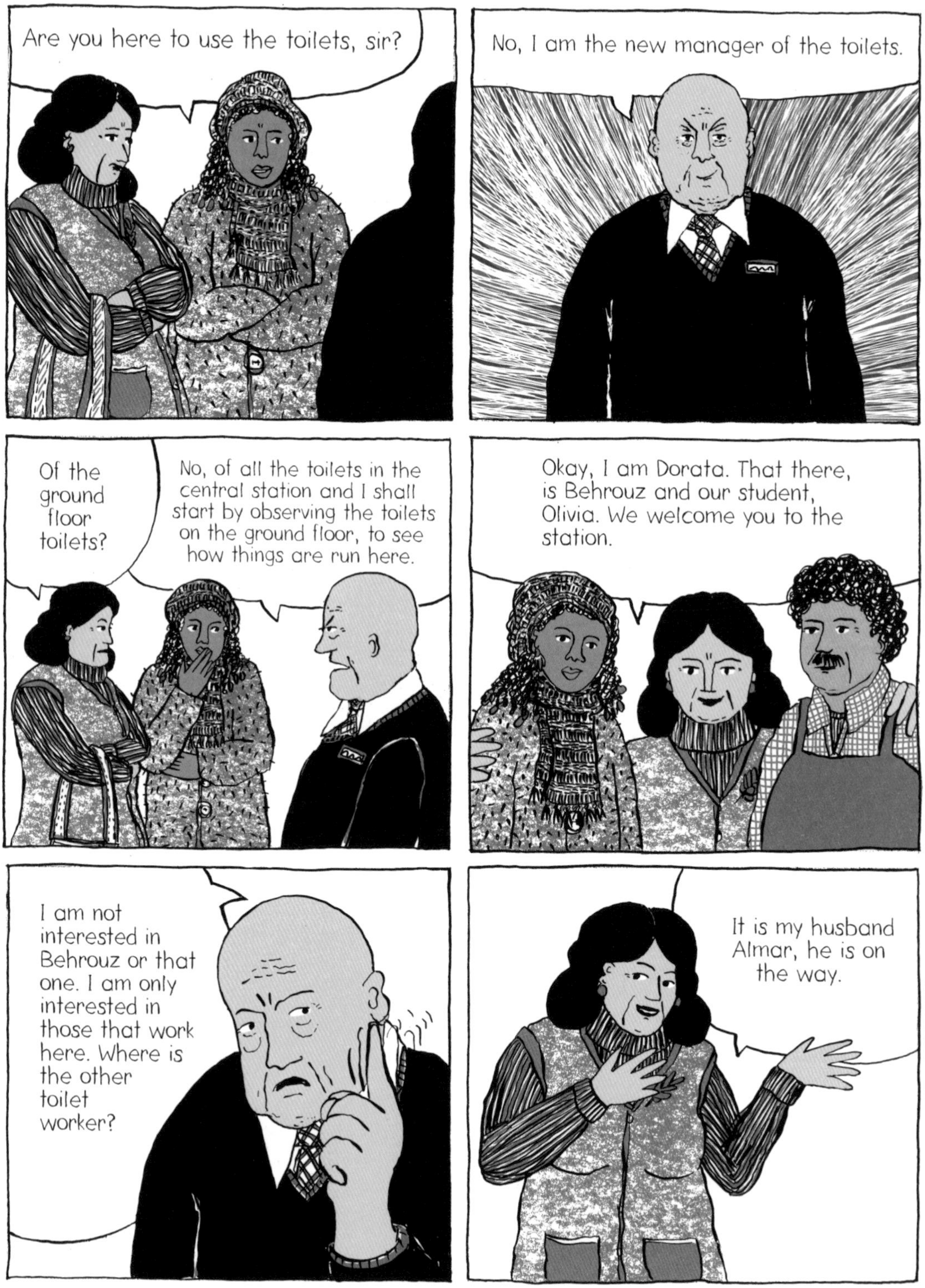
Are you here to use the toilets, sir?
No, I am the new manager of the toilets.
Of the ground floor toilets?
No, of all the toilets in the central station and I shall start by observing the toilets on the ground floor, to see how things are run here.
Okay, I am Dorata. That there, is Behrouz and our student, Olivia. We welcome you to the station.
I am not interested in Behrouz or that one. I am only interested in those that work here. Where is the other toilet worker?
It is my husband Almar, he is on the way.

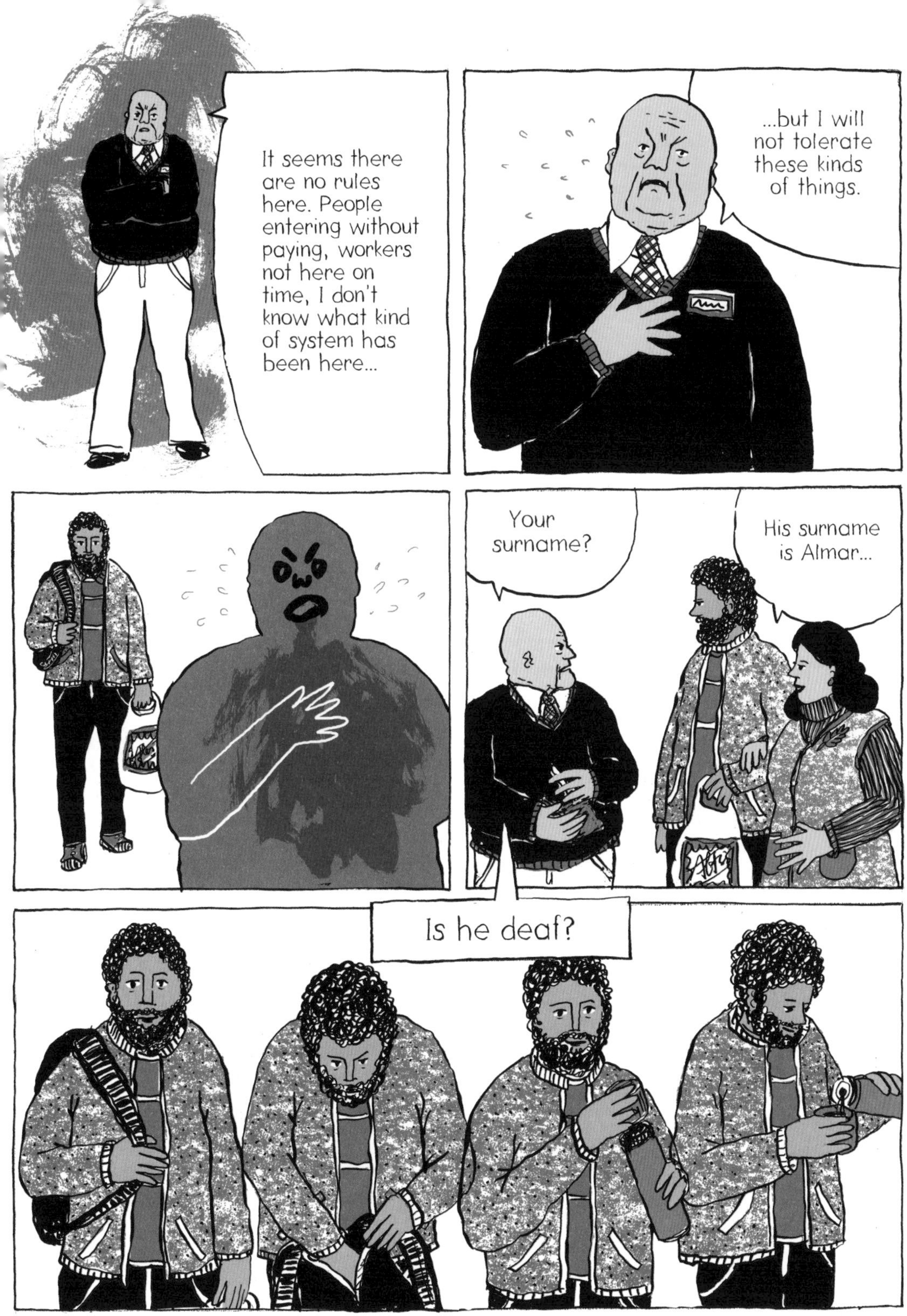
It seems there are no rules here. People entering without paying, workers not here on time, I don't know what kind of system has been here...
...but I will not tolerate these kinds of things.
Your surname?
His surname is Almar...
Is he deaf?

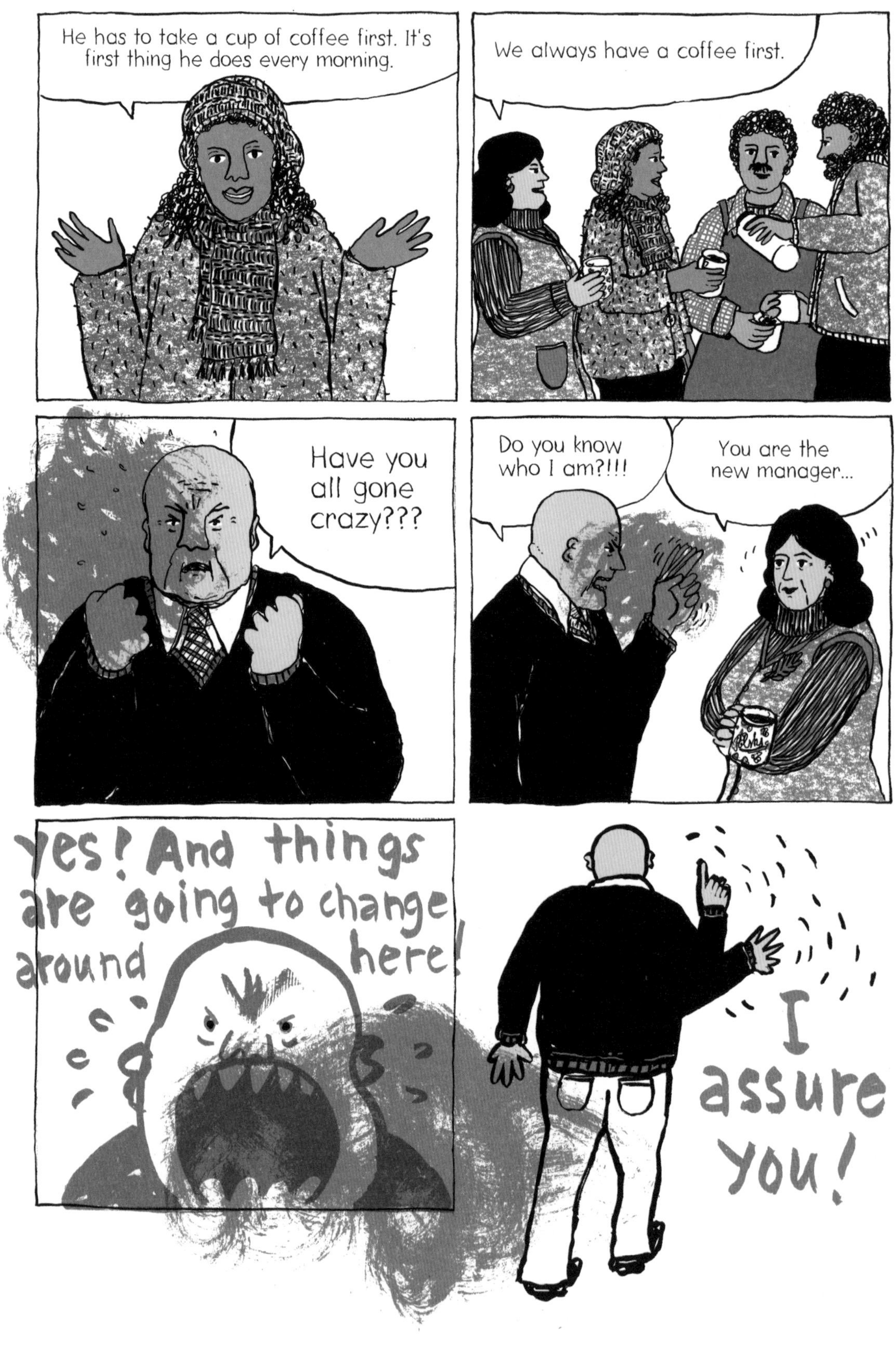
He has to take a cup of coffee first. It's first thing he does every morning.
We always have a coffee first.
Have you all gone crazy???
Do you know who I am?!!!
You are the new manager...
yes! And things are going to change around here!
I assure you!

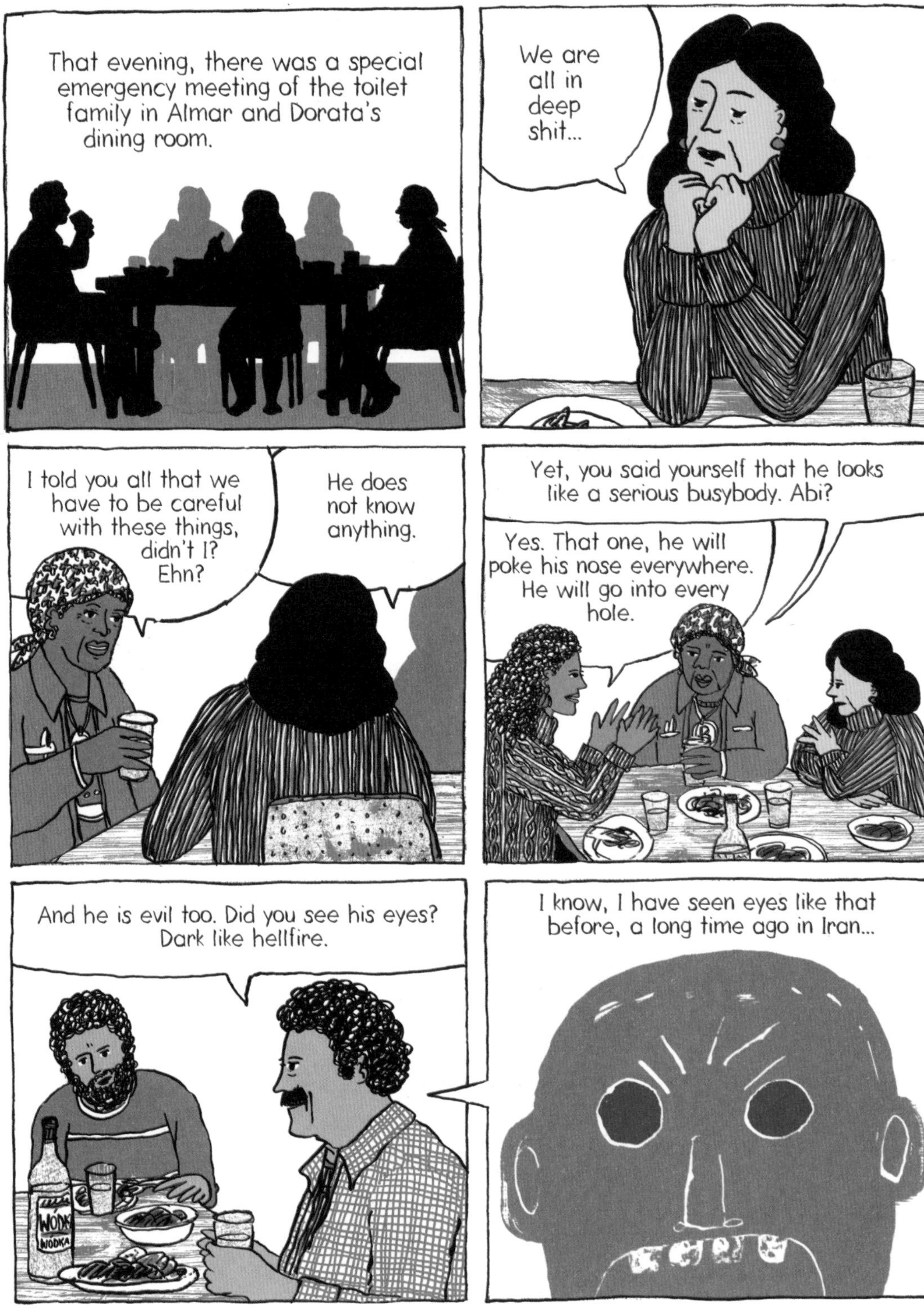

That evening, there was a special emergency meeting of the toilet family in Almar and Dorata's dining room.
We are all in deep shit...
I told you all that we have to be careful with these things, didn't I? Ehn?
He does not know anything.
Yet, you said yourself that he looks like a serious busybody. Abi?
Yes. That one, he will poke his nose everywhere. He will go into every hole.
And he is evil too. Did you see his eyes? Dark like hellfire.
I know, I have seen eyes like that before, a long time ago in Iran...

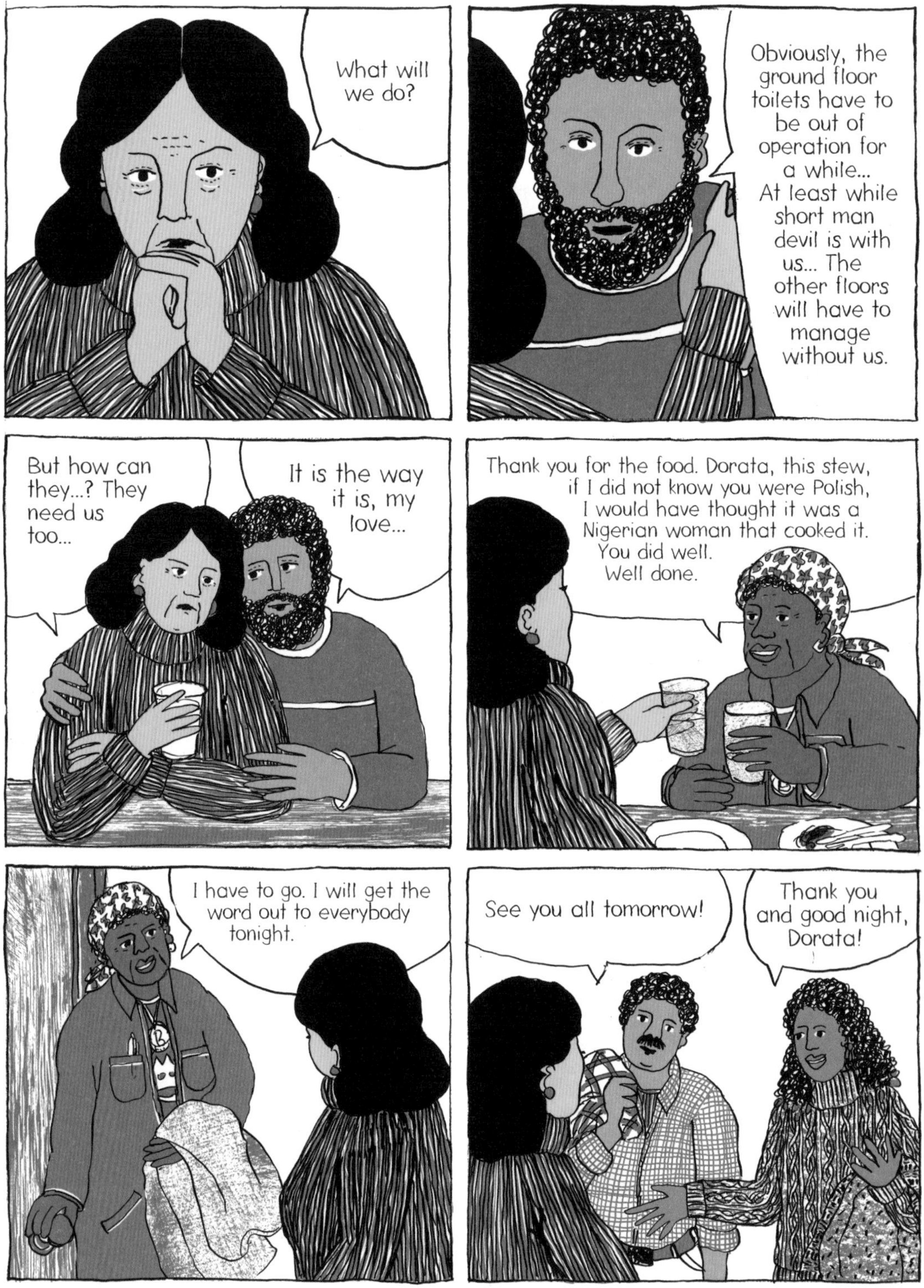
What will we do?
Obviously, the ground floor toilets have to be out of operation for a while... At least while short man devil is with us... The other floors will have to manage without us.
But how can they...? They need us too...
It is the way it is, my love...
Thank you for the food. Dorata, this stew, if I did not know you were Polish, I would have thought it was a Nigerian woman that cooked it. You did well. Well done.
I have to go. I will get the word out to everybody tonight.
See you all tomorrow!
Thank you and good night, Dorata!

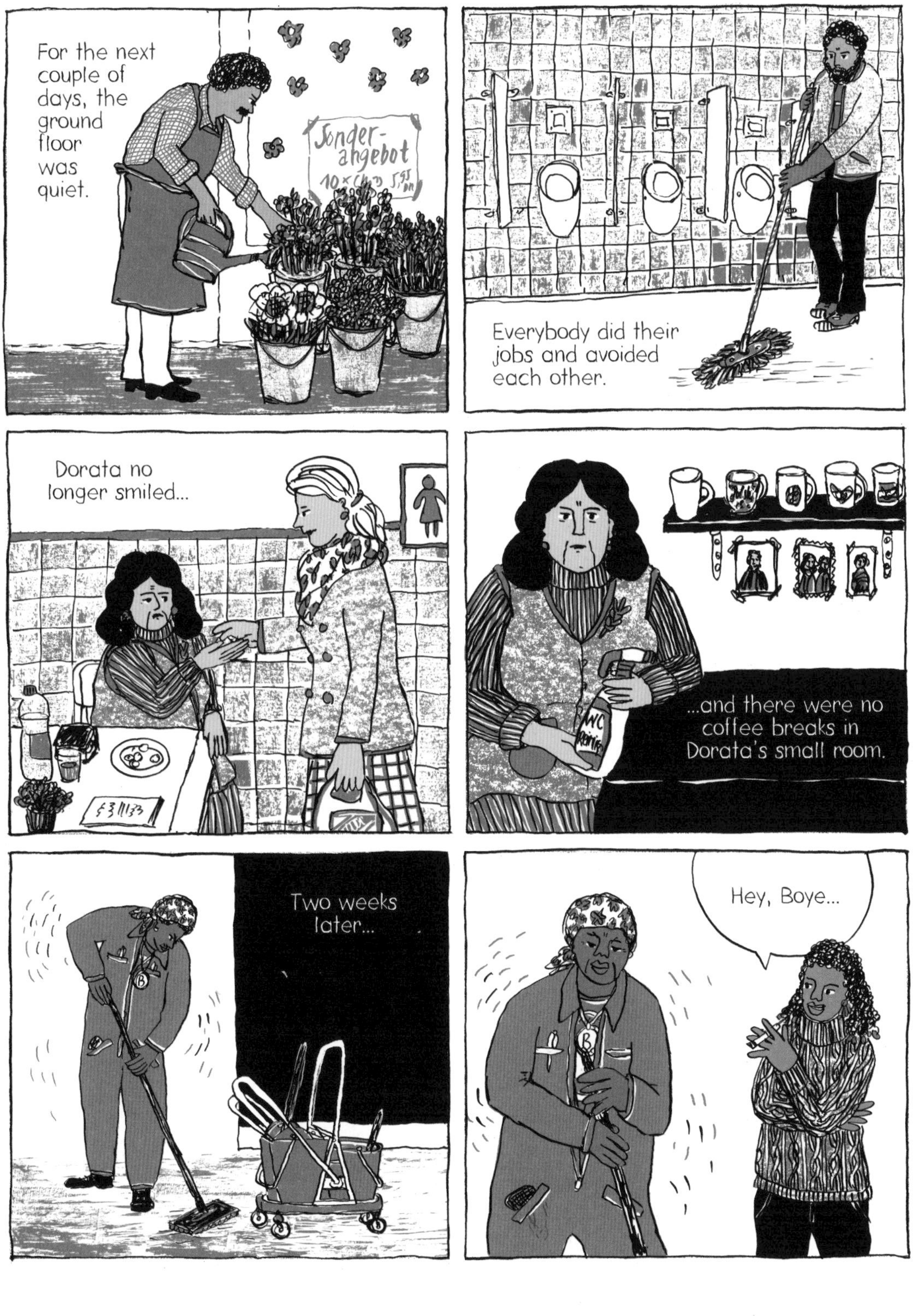
For the next couple of days, the ground floor was quiet.
Sonder-angebot
Everybody did their jobs and avoided each other.
Dorata no longer smiled...
...and there were no coffee breaks in Dorata's small room.
Two weeks later...
Hey, Boye...

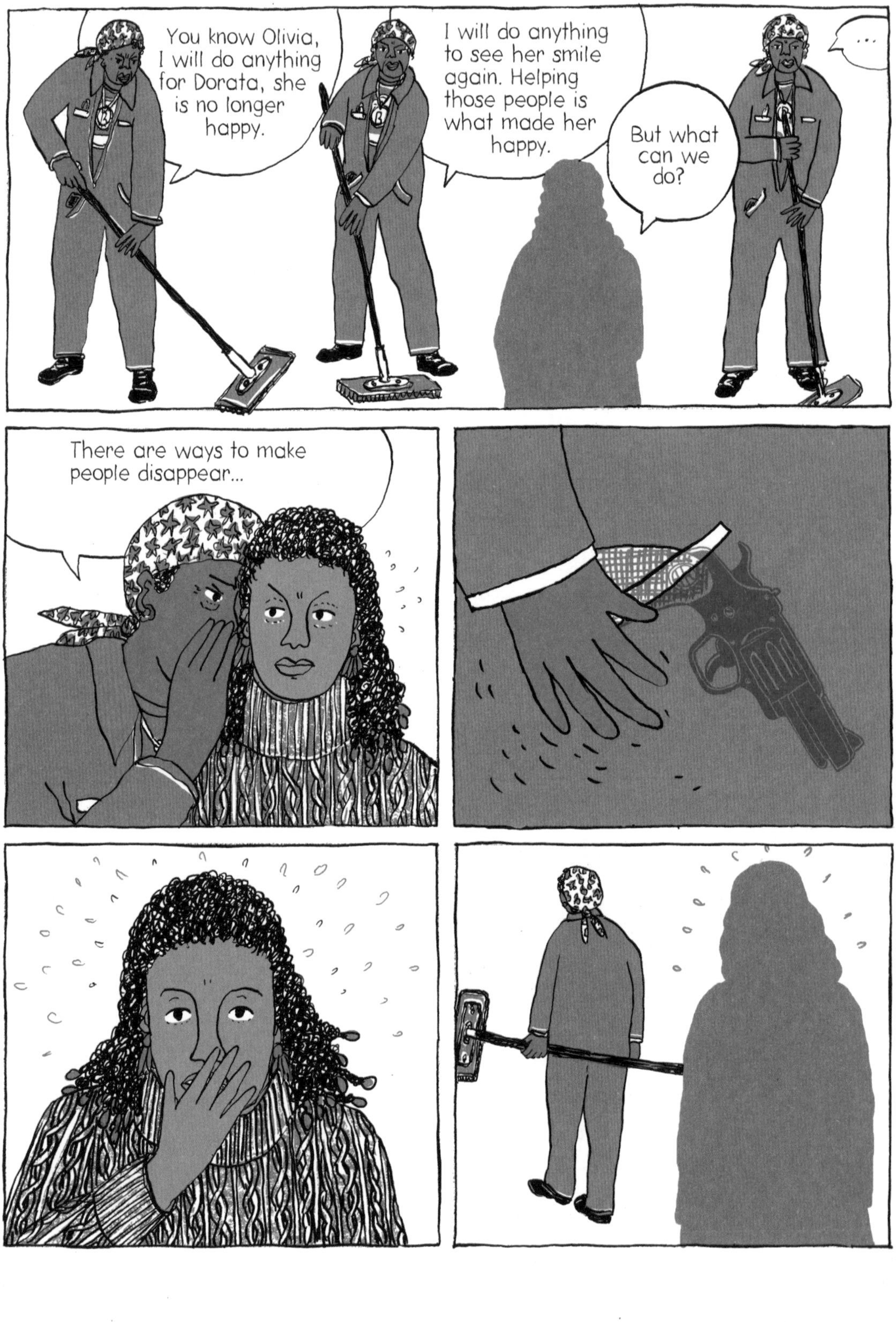
You know Olivia, I will do anything for Dorata, she is no longer happy.
I will do anything to see her smile again. Helping those people is what made her happy.
But what can we do?
...
There are ways to make people disappear...

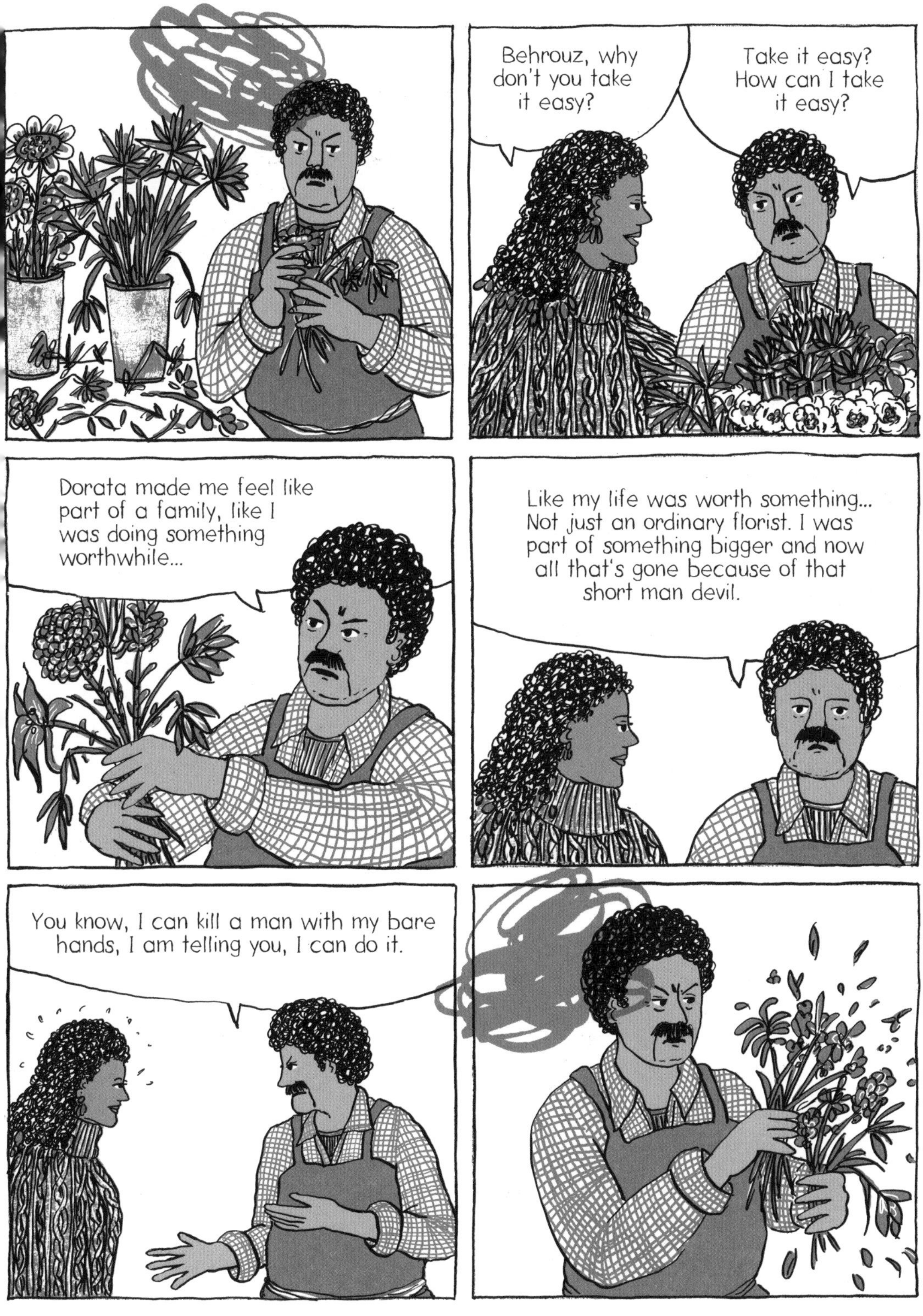
Behrouz, why don't you take it easy?
Take it easy? How can I take it easy?
Dorata made me feel like part of a family, like I was doing something worthwhile...
Like my life was worth something... Not just an ordinary florist. I was part of something bigger and now all that's gone because of that short man devil.
You know, I can kill a man with my bare hands, I am telling you, I can do it.

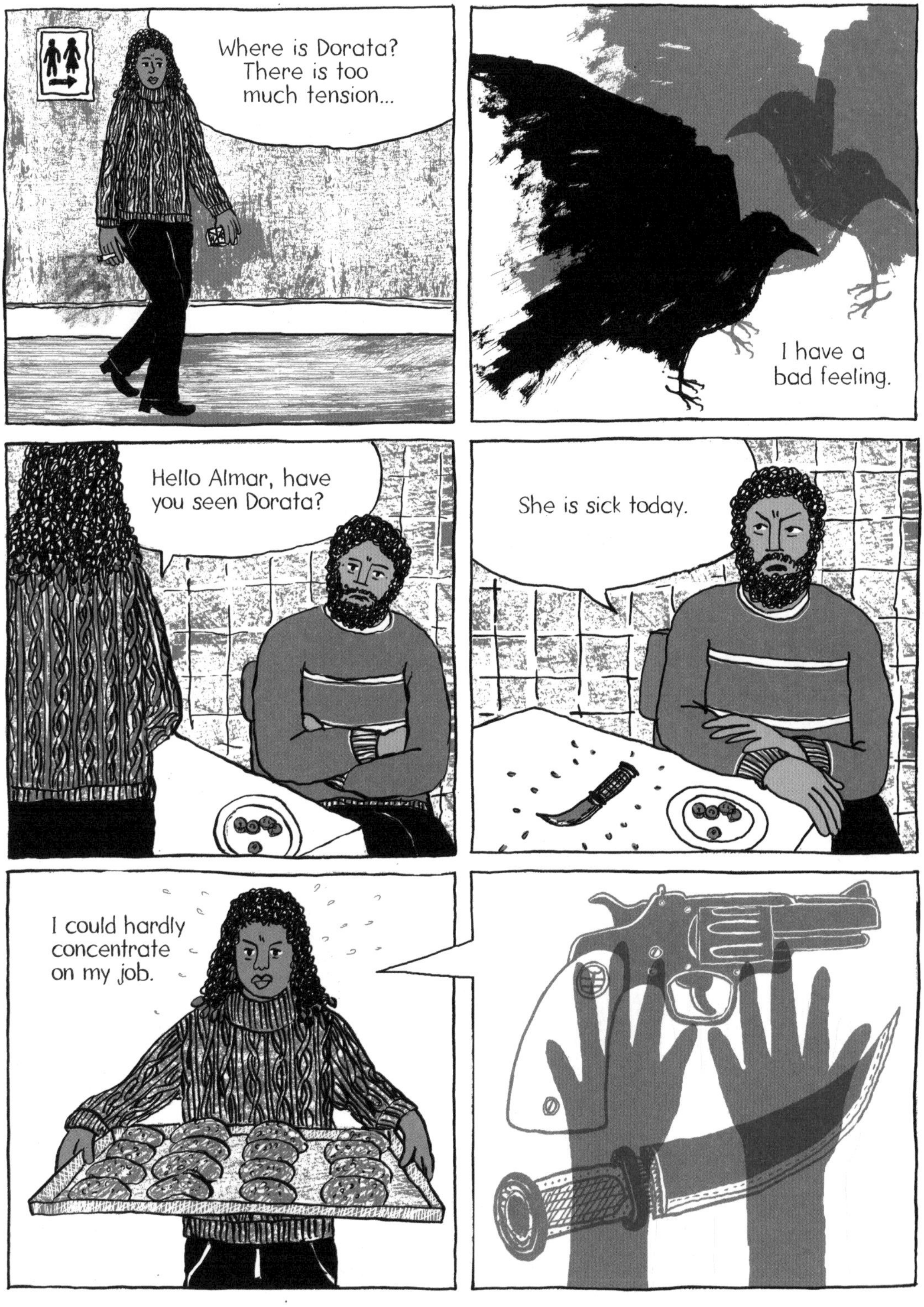
Where is Dorata? There is too much tension...
I have a bad feeling.
Hello Almar, have you seen Dorata?
She is sick today.
I could hardly concentrate on my job.

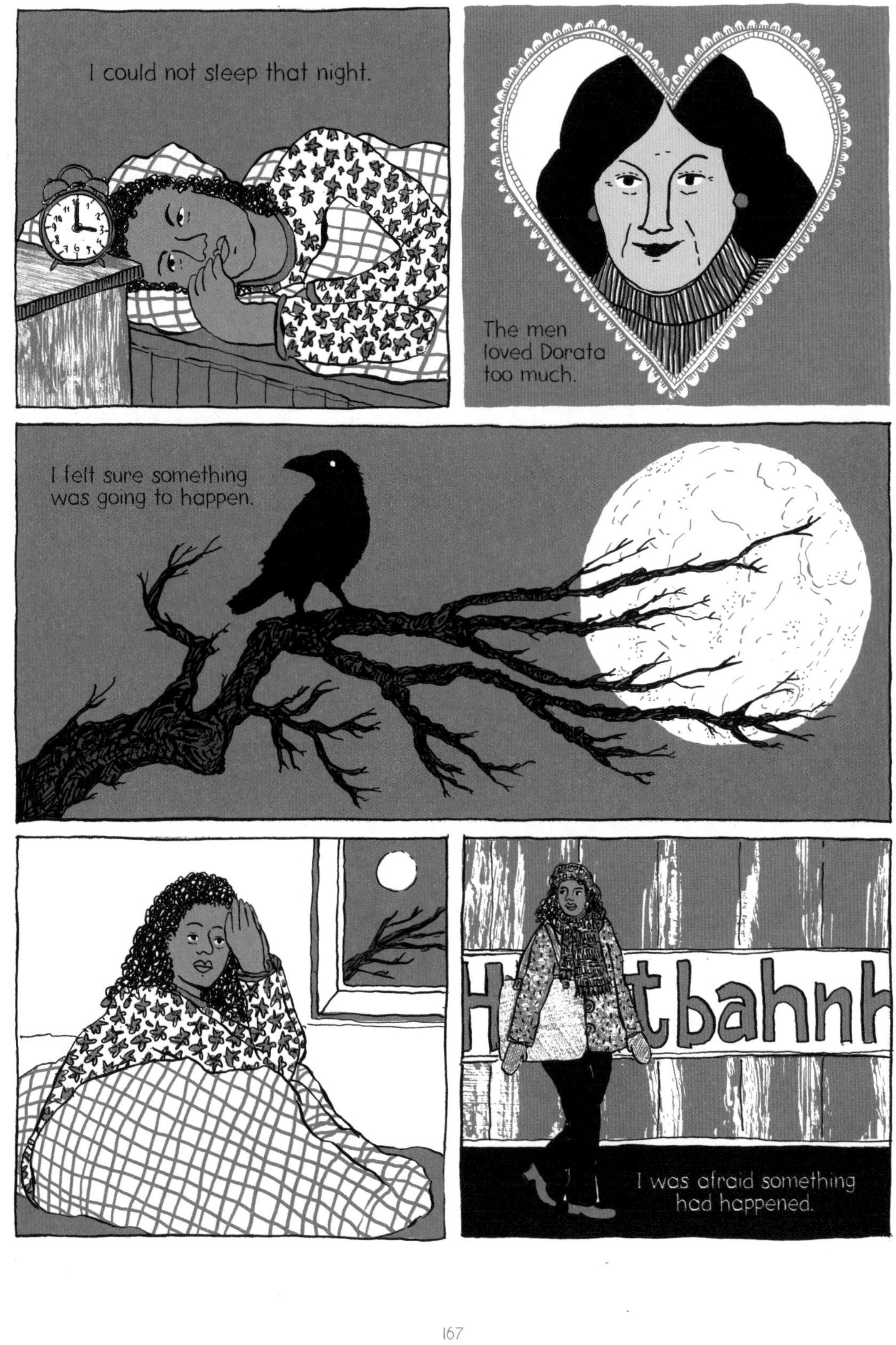
I could not sleep that night.
The men loved Dorata too much.
I felt sure something was going to happen.
I was afraid something had happened.

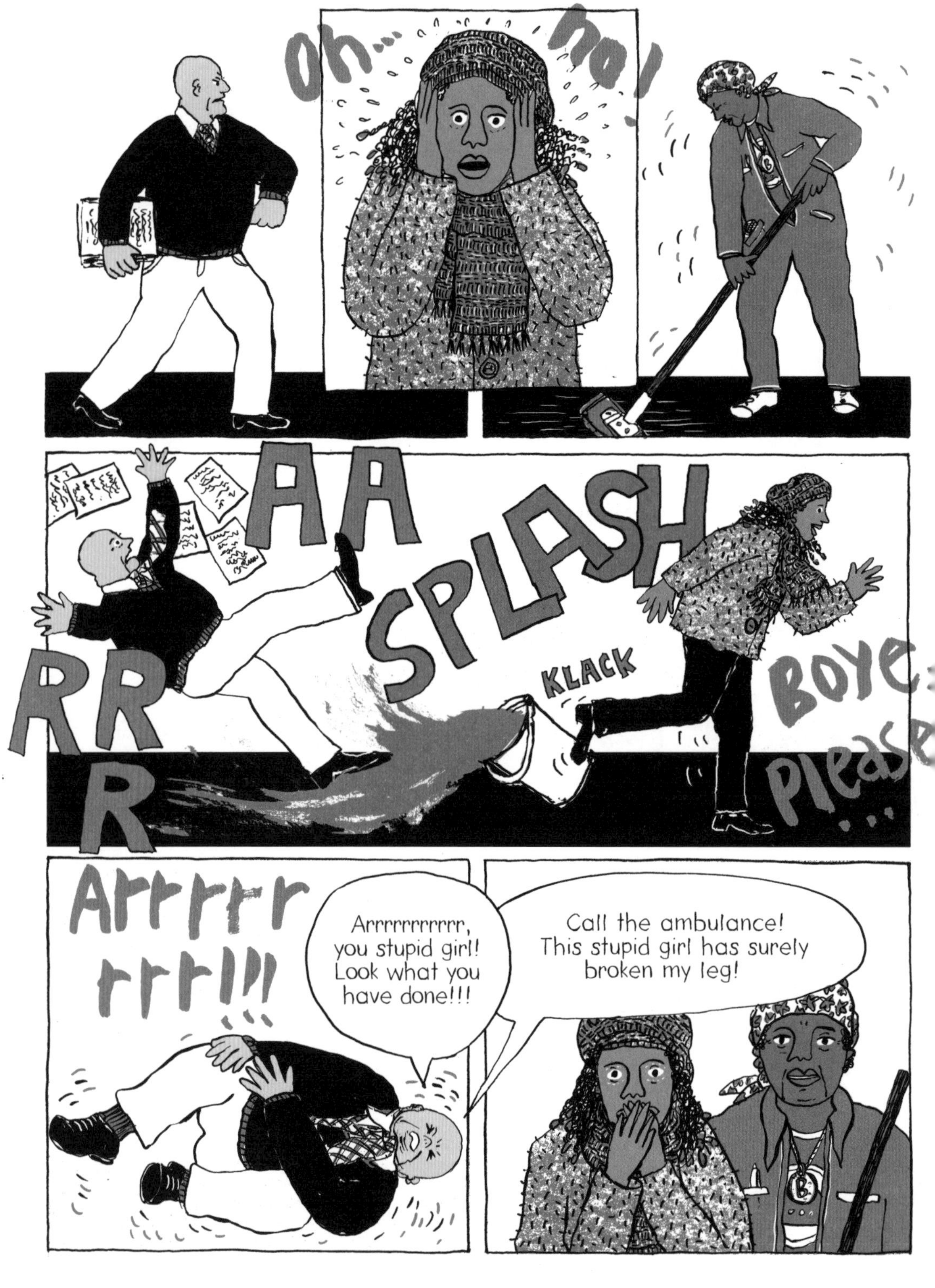
Oh... no!
AA
SPLASH
KLACK
Boye, please...
RRR
Arrrrrrrr!!
Arrrrrrrrrrr, you stupid girl! Look what you have done!!!
Call the ambulance! This stupid girl has surely broken my leg!

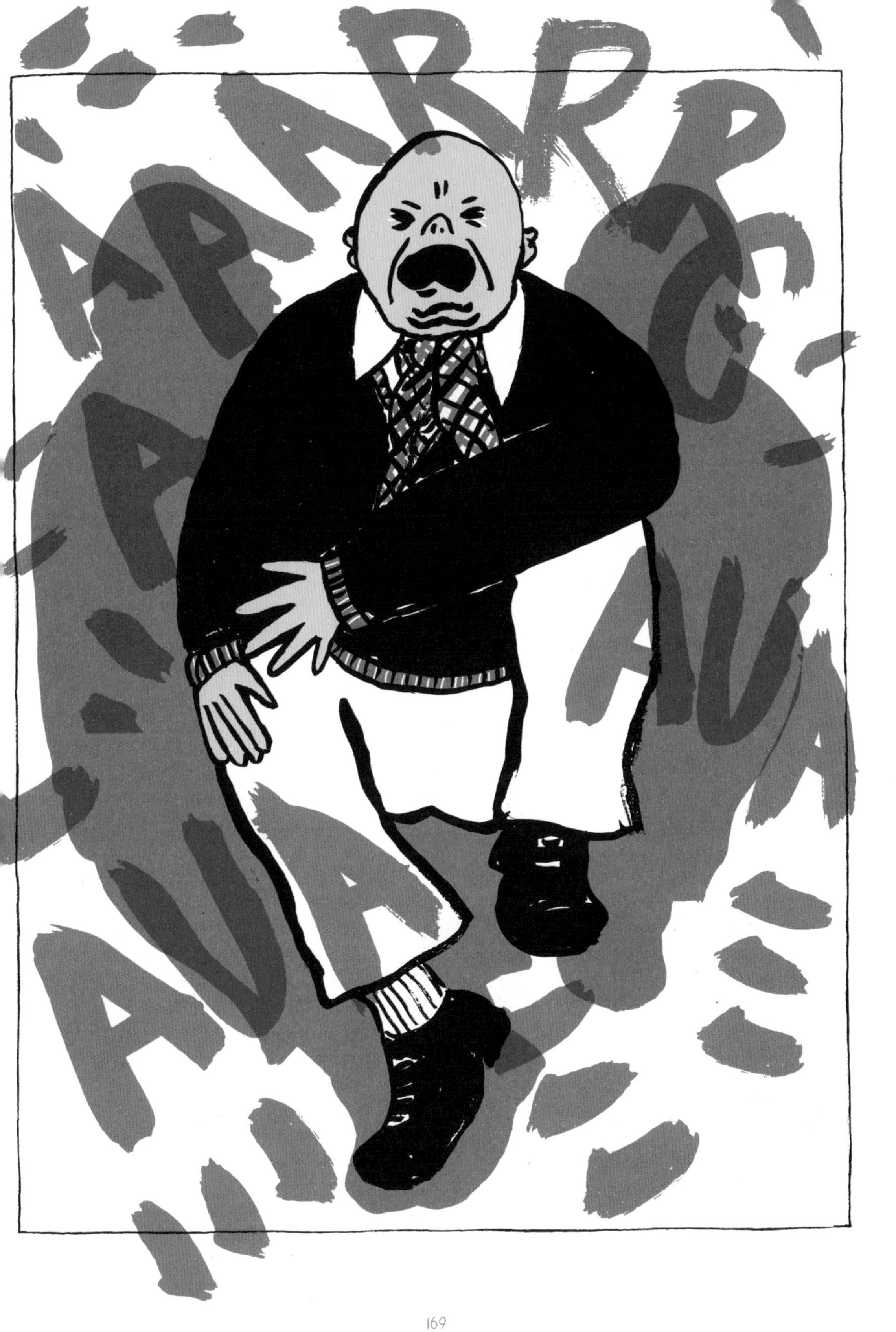

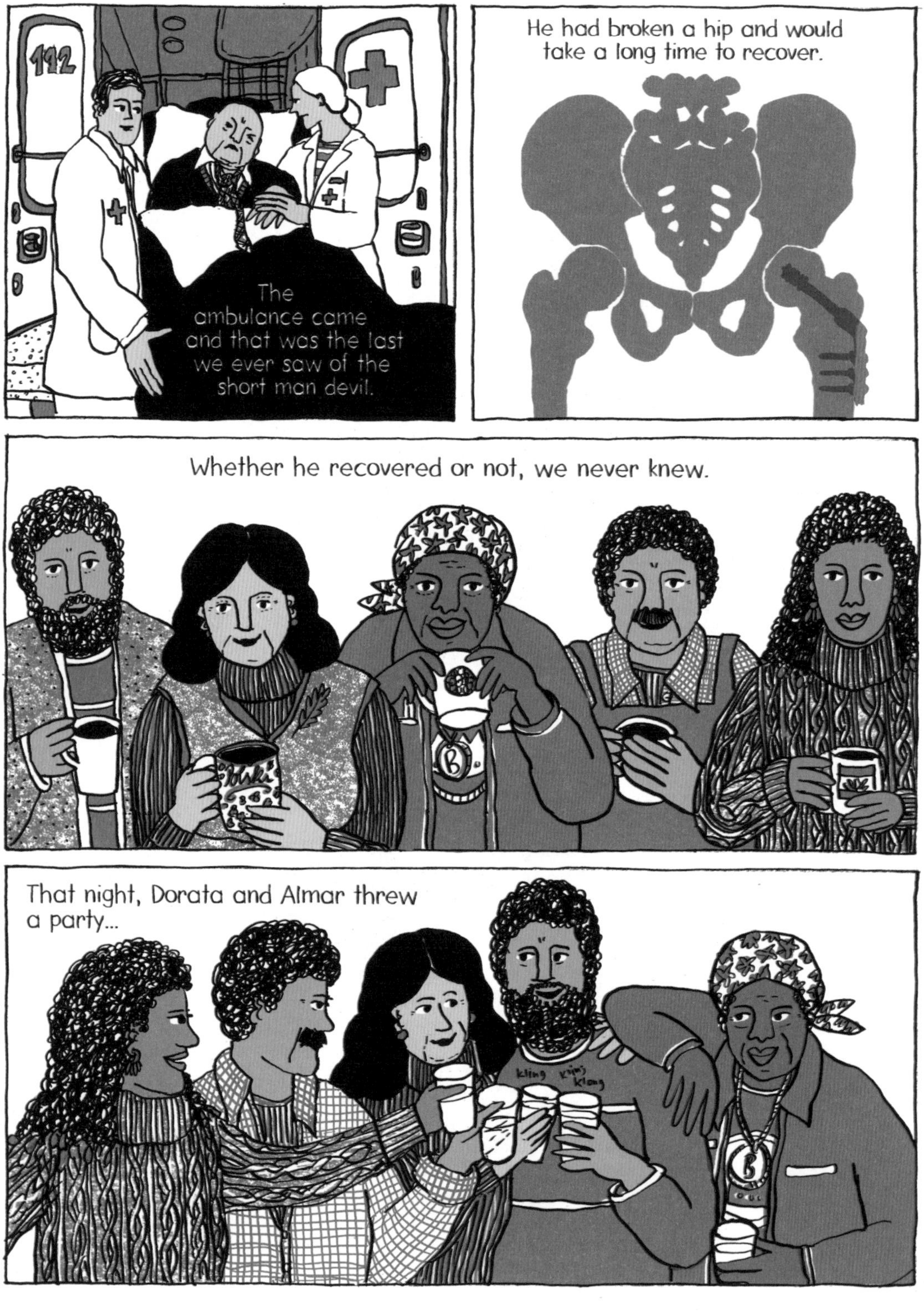
The ambulance came and that was the last we ever saw of the short man devil.
112
He had broken a hip and would take a long time to recover.
Whether he recovered or not, we never knew.
That night, Dorata and Almar threw a party...
kling

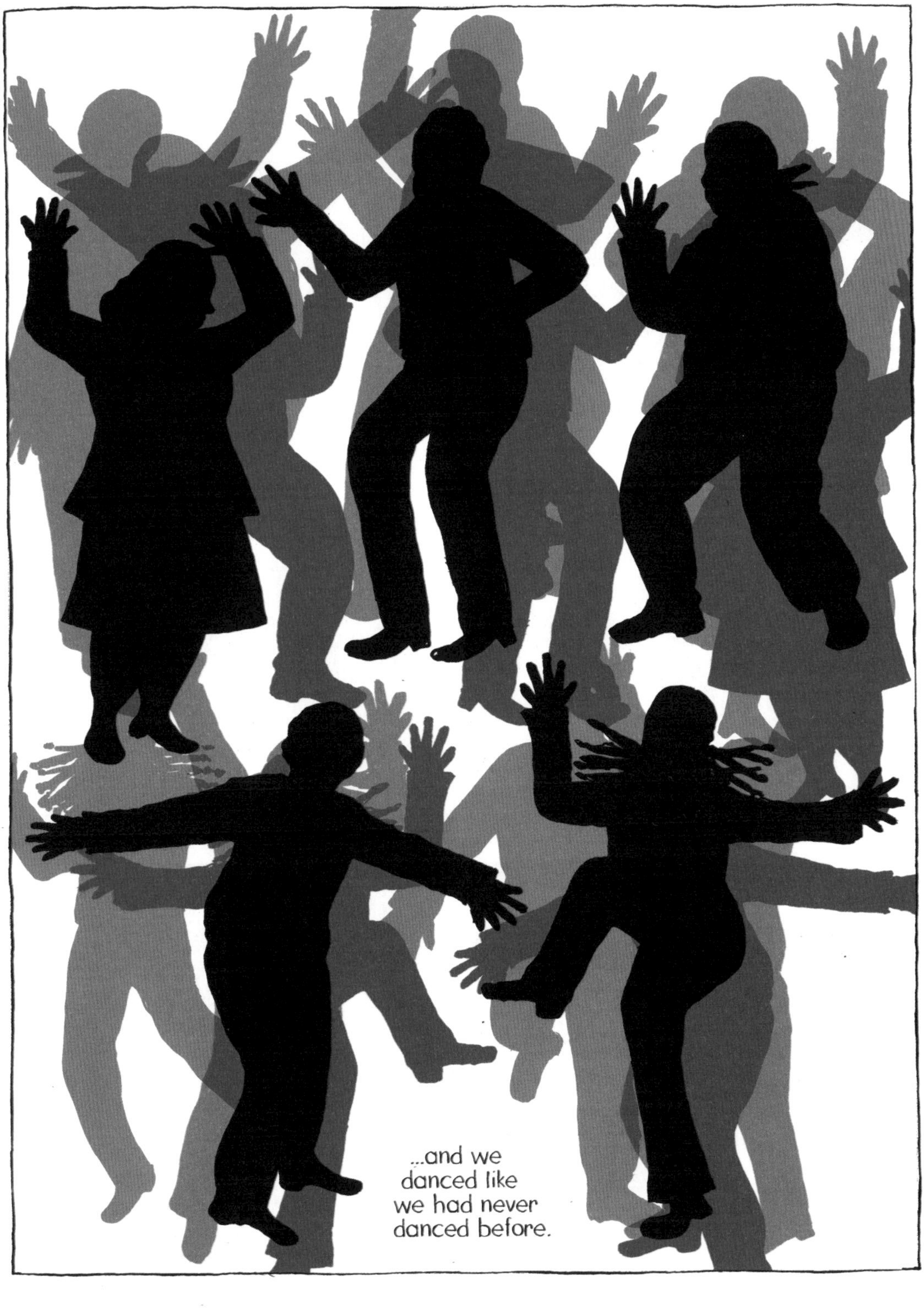
...and we
danced like
we had never
danced before.

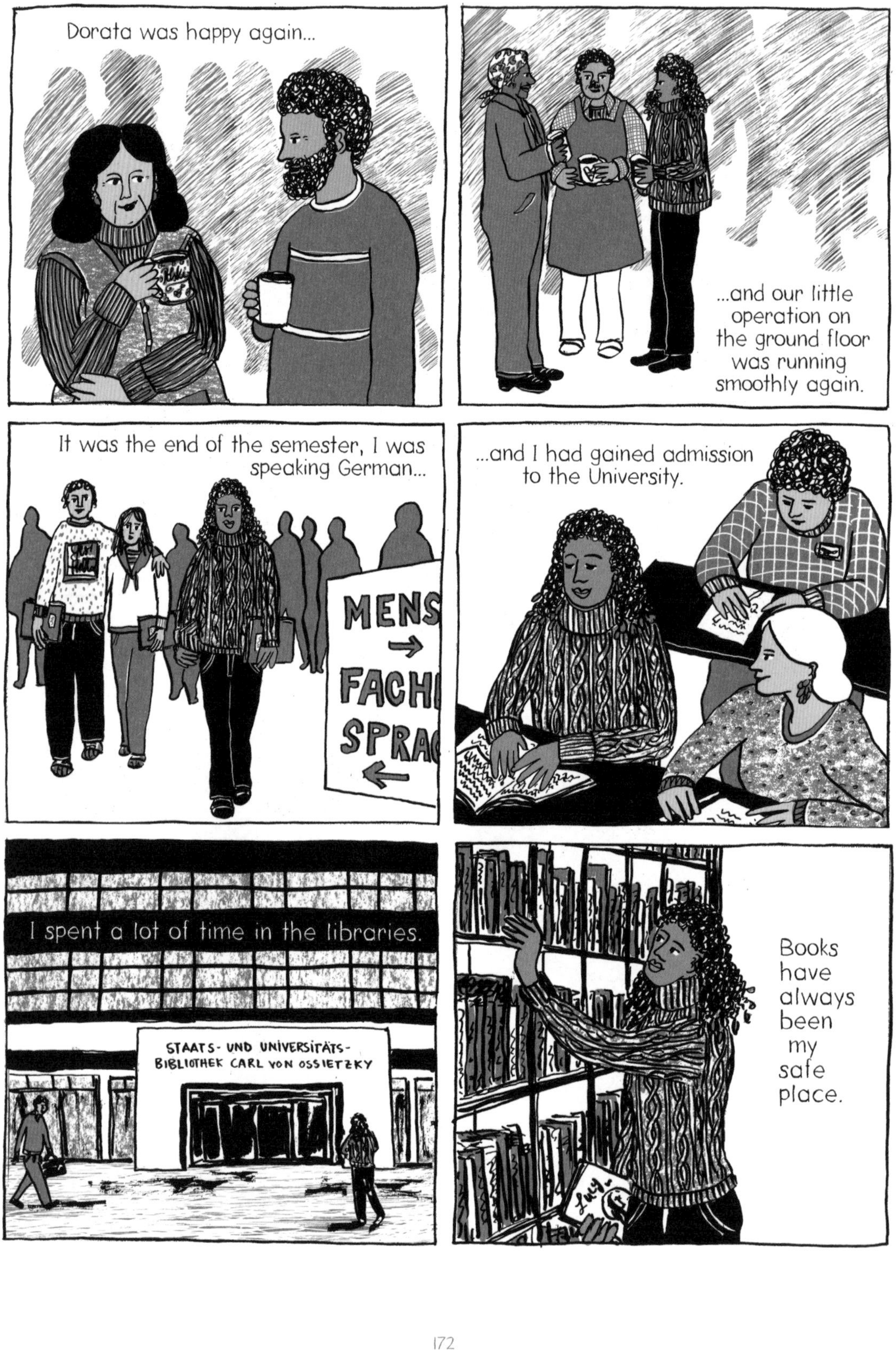
Dorata was happy again...
...and our little operation on the ground floor was running smoothly again.
It was the end of the semester, I was speaking German...
MENS
FACH
SPRAC
...and I had gained admission to the University.
I spent a lot of time in the libraries.
STAATS- UND UNIVERSITÄTS-
BIBLIOTHEK CARL VON OSSIETZKY
Books have always been my safe place.

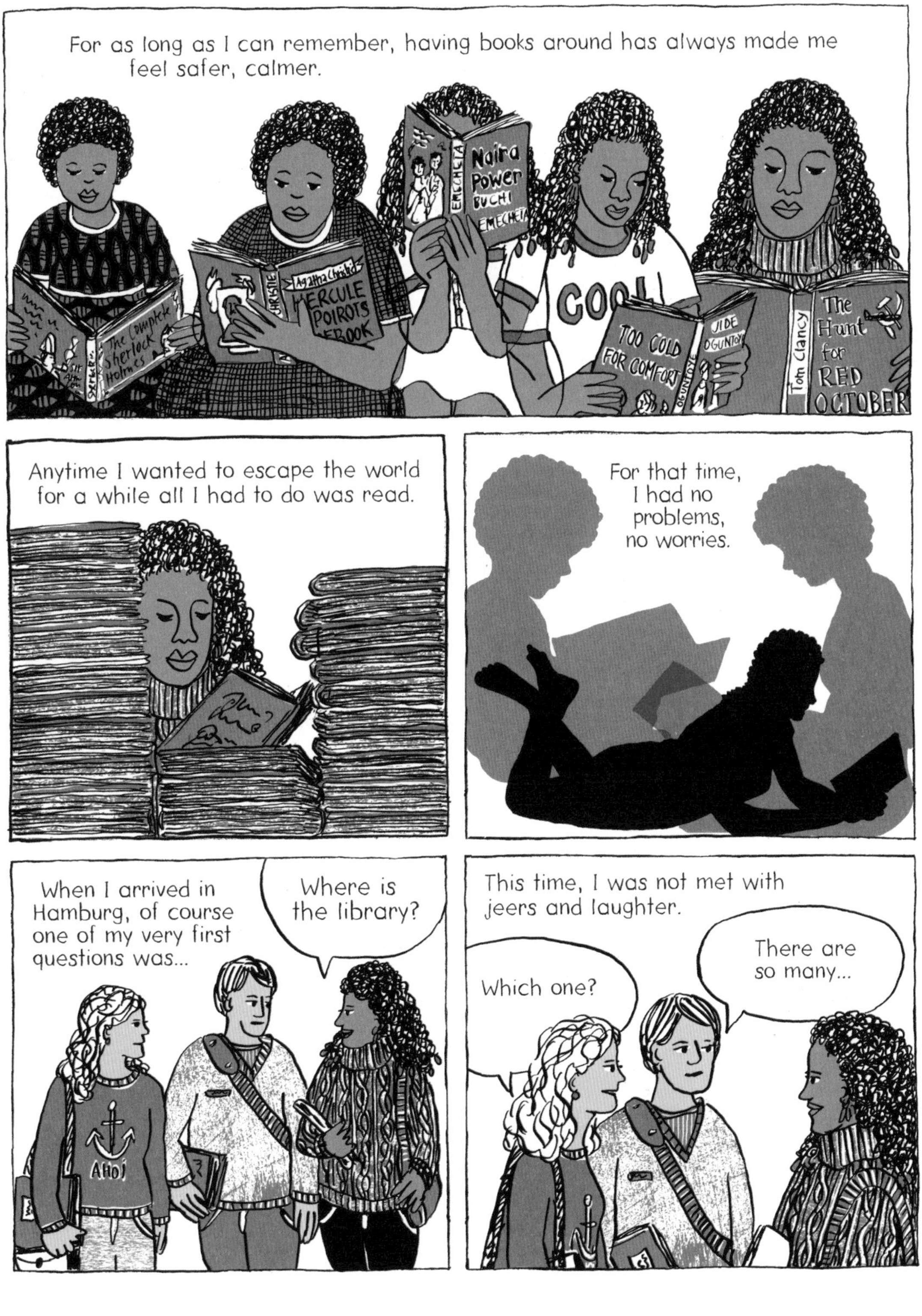
For as long as I can remember, having books around has always made me feel safer, calmer.
Naira Power
BUCHI EMECHETA
TOO COLD FOR COMFORT
JIDE OGUNTOYE
The Hunt for RED OCTOBER
Tom Clancy
COOL
Anytime I wanted to escape the world for a while all I had to do was read.
For that time, I had no problems, no worries.
When I arrived in Hamburg, of course one of my very first questions was...
Where is the library?
AHOI
This time, I was not met with jeers and laughter.
Which one?
There are so many...

STAATS-UND UNIVERSITÄTS
BIBLIOTHEK
HAMBURG
CARL VON OSSIETZKY

BÜCHERHALLEN
HAMBURG

Volksdorf
Billstedt
Dehnhaide
Altona
Eimsbüttel
Wandsbek
Barmbek
Horn
Farmsen
Elbvororte
Eidelstedt

HŒB4U

TUHH
Technische Universität Hamburg

ZBW

Kinderbibliothek Hamburg
Kibi

HIBS

There were too many libraries to go to...

...and too many books to discover.

Lucy A Novel
JAMAICA KINCAID

I found the libraries fascinating.

Amélie Nothomb
HYGIENE AND THE ASSASSIN
Europa editions

SOSEKI NATSUME
I AM a CAT

BELOVED
A NOVEL
TONI MORRISON

The PROPHET
KHALIL GIBRAN

Maxine Hong Kingston
The Woman Warrior
Memoirs of a girlhood among ghosts

The Bo...
Reflections on the...
Kahlil G...

NAWAL EL SAADAWI
MEMOIRS OF A WOMAN DOCTOR

Mystical Poems of Rūmi 1
First Selection, Poems 1-200
Jalāl al-Dīn Rūmi

Imre Kertész
Roman eines Schicksallosen

The Poems of Hafez

I discovered a new world of literature, especially poetry from the middle east.

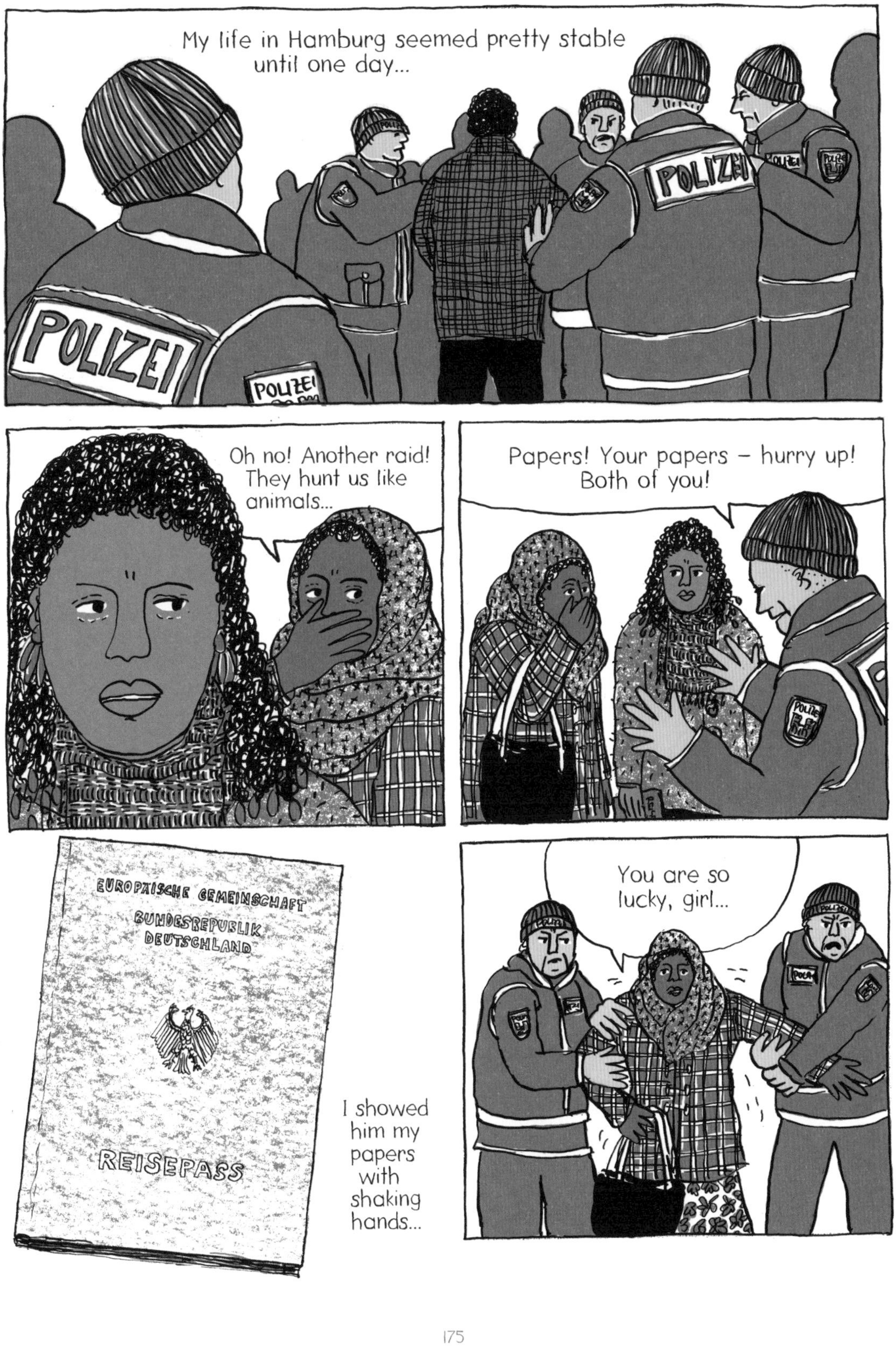
My life in Hamburg seemed pretty stable until one day...
POLIZEI
Oh no! Another raid! They hunt us like animals...
Papers! Your papers – hurry up! Both of you!
EUROPÄISCHE GEMEINSCHAFT
BUNDESREPUBLIK DEUTSCHLAND
REISEPASS
I showed him my papers with shaking hands...
You are so lucky, girl...

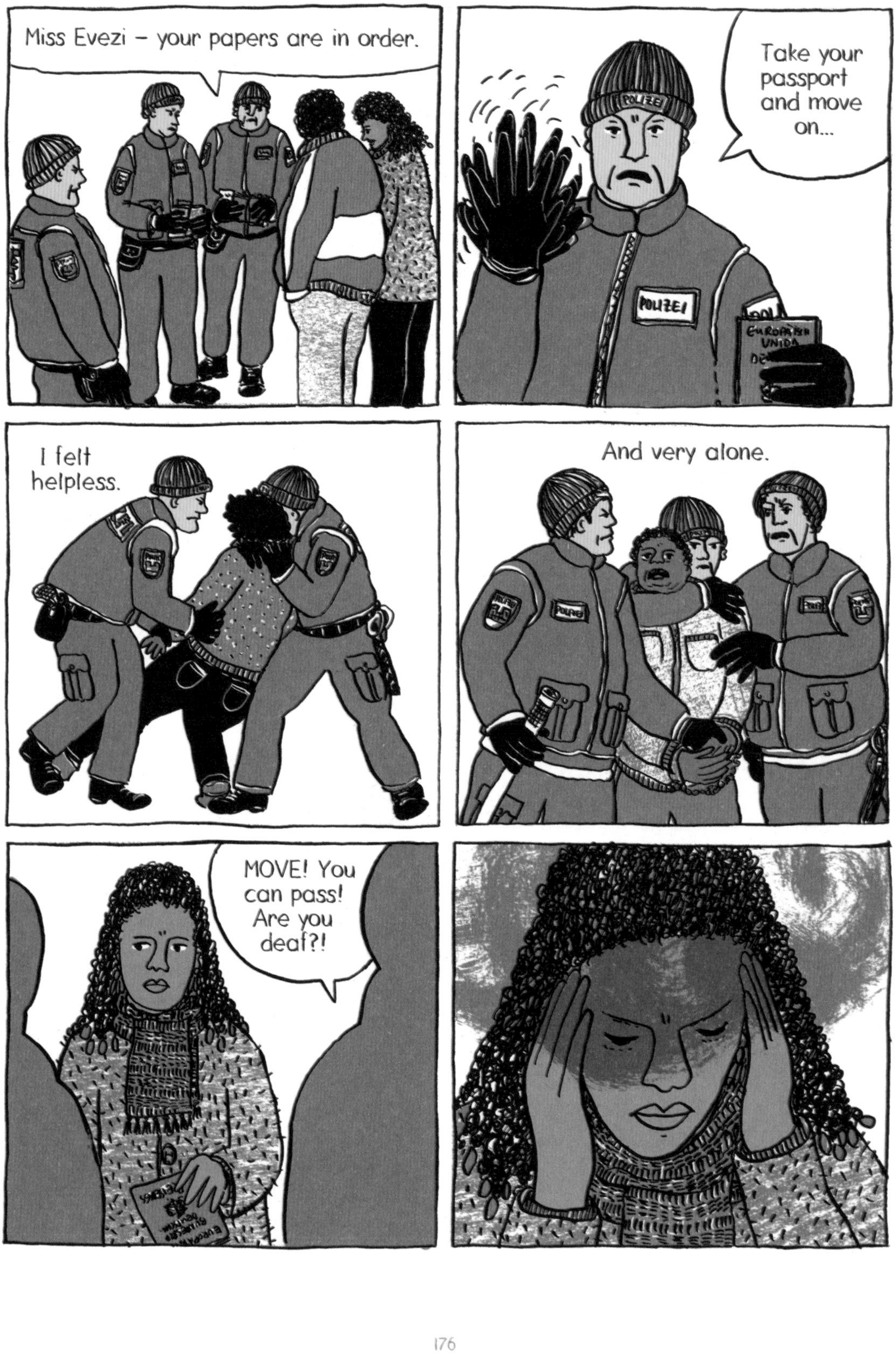
Miss Evezi – your papers are in order.
Take your passport and move on...
POLIZEI
I felt helpless.
And very alone.
MOVE! You can pass! Are you deaf?!

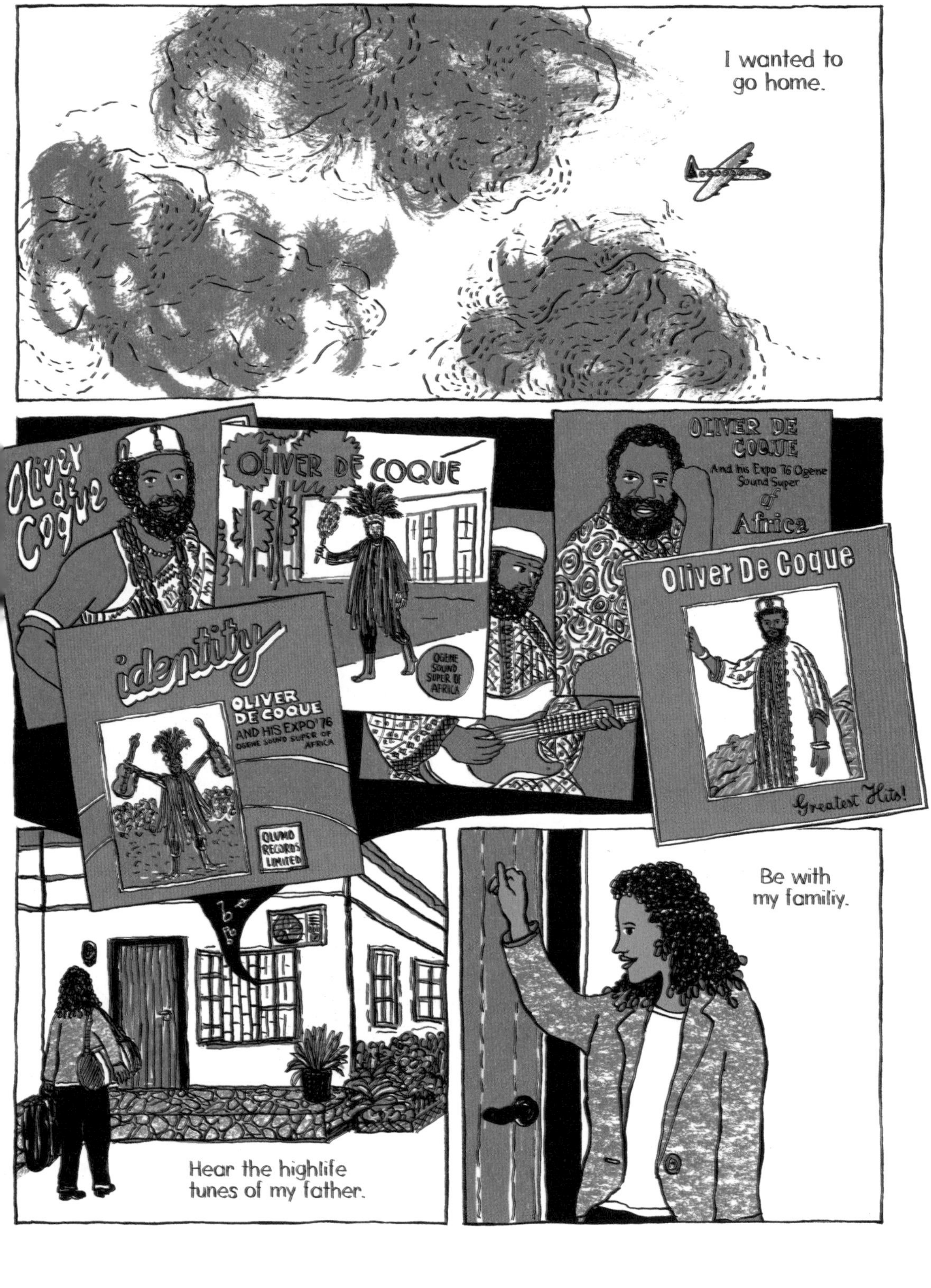
I wanted to go home.
Oliver de Coque
OLIVER DE COQUE
OGENE SOUND SUPER OF AFRICA
OLIVER DE COQUE
And his Expo 76 Ogene Sound Super of Africa
identity
OLIVER DE COQUE
AND HIS EXPO '76 OGENE SOUND SUPER OF AFRICA
OLUMO RECORDS LIMITED
Oliver De Coque
Greatest Hits!
Hear the highlife tunes of my father.
Be with my familiy.

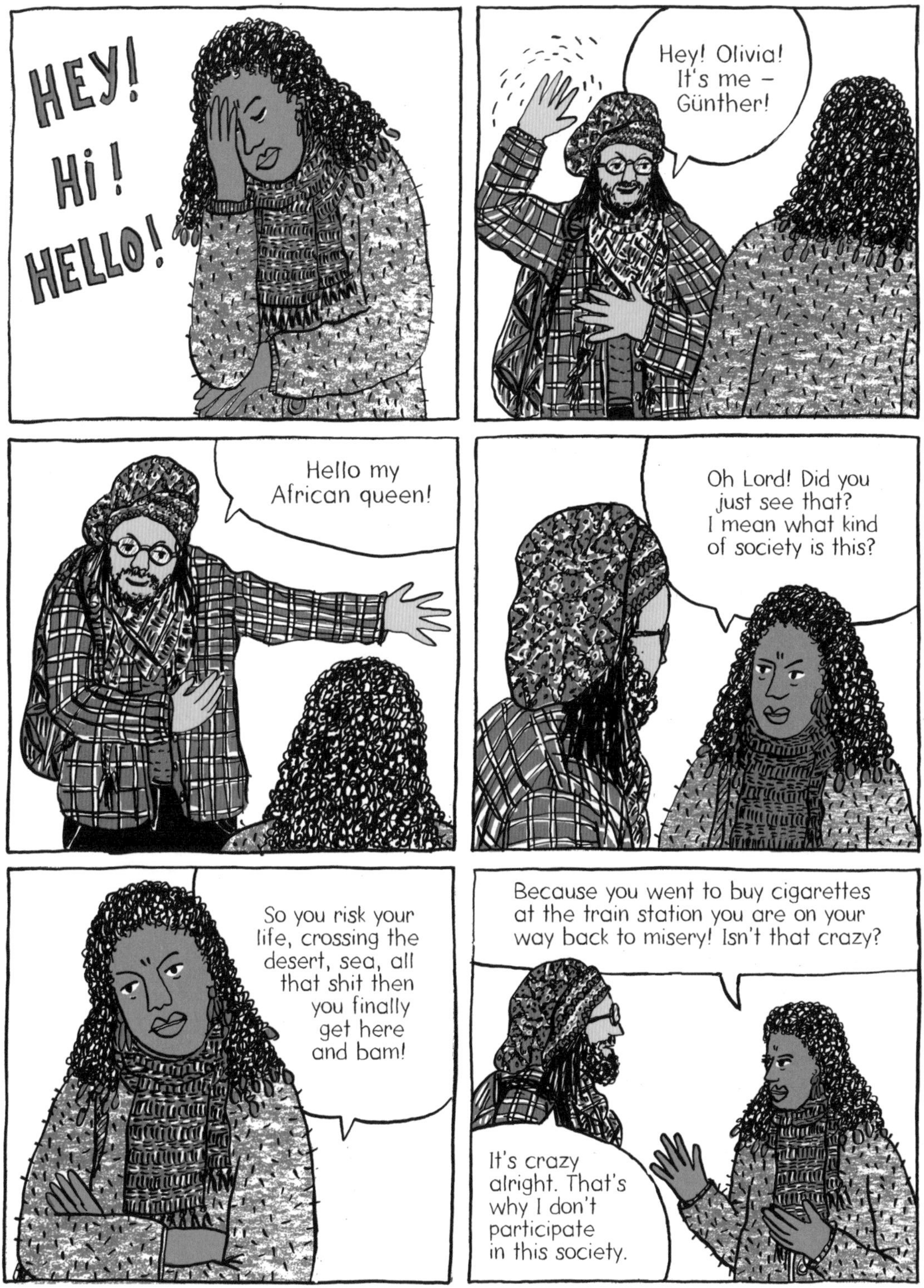

HEY! Hi! HELLO!
Hey! Olivia! It's me – Günther!
Hello my African queen!
Oh Lord! Did you just see that? I mean what kind of society is this?
So you risk your life, crossing the desert, sea, all that shit then you finally get here and bam!
Because you went to buy cigarettes at the train station you are on your way back to misery! Isn't that crazy?
It's crazy alright. That's why I don't participate in this society.

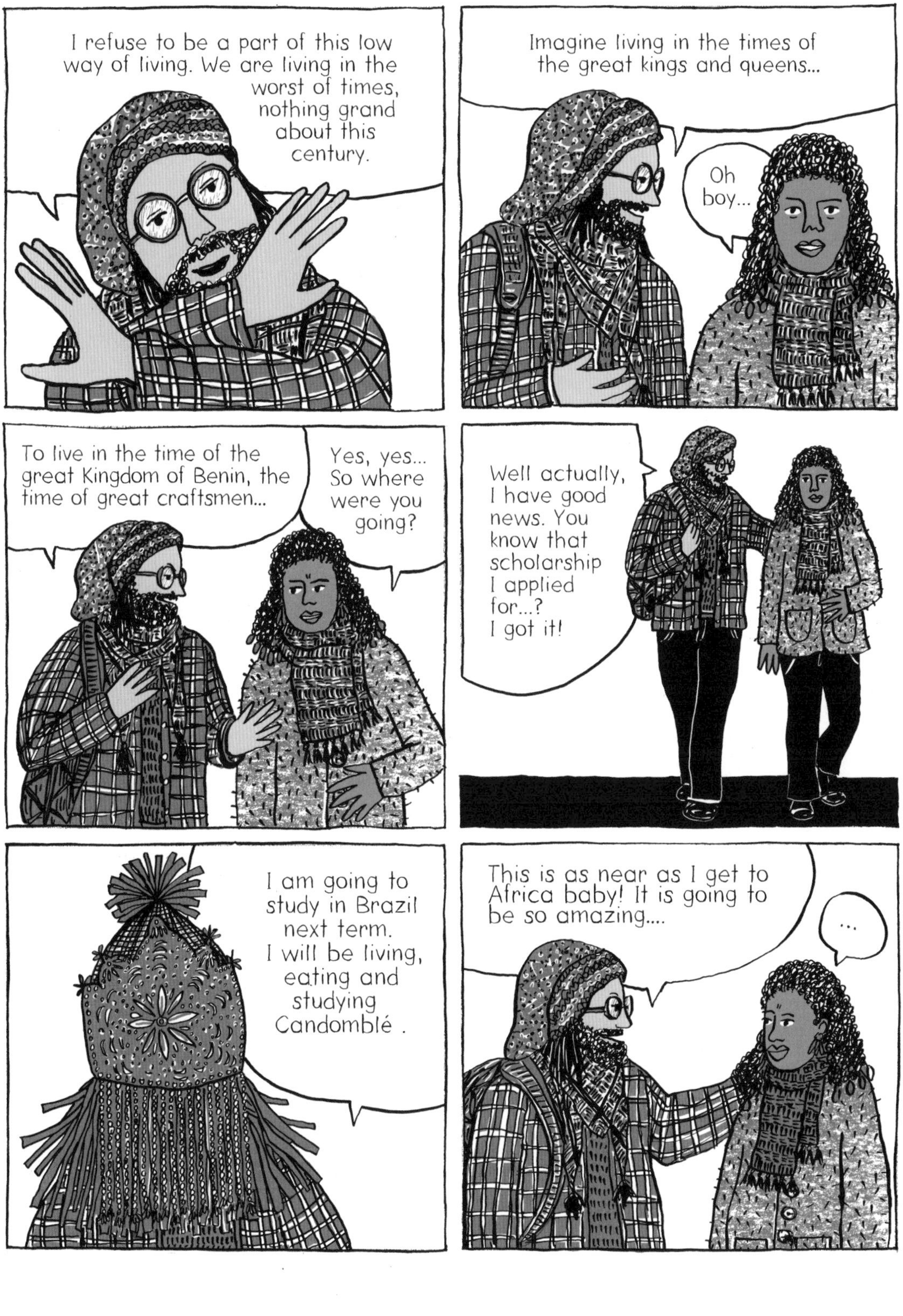
I refuse to be a part of this low way of living. We are living in the worst of times, nothing grand about this century.
Imagine living in the times of the great kings and queens...
Oh boy...
To live in the time of the great Kingdom of Benin, the time of great craftsmen...
Yes, yes... So where were you going?
Well actually, I have good news. You know that scholarship I applied for...? I got it!
I am going to study in Brazil next term. I will be living, eating and studying Candomblé .
This is as near as I get to Africa baby! It is going to be so amazing....
...

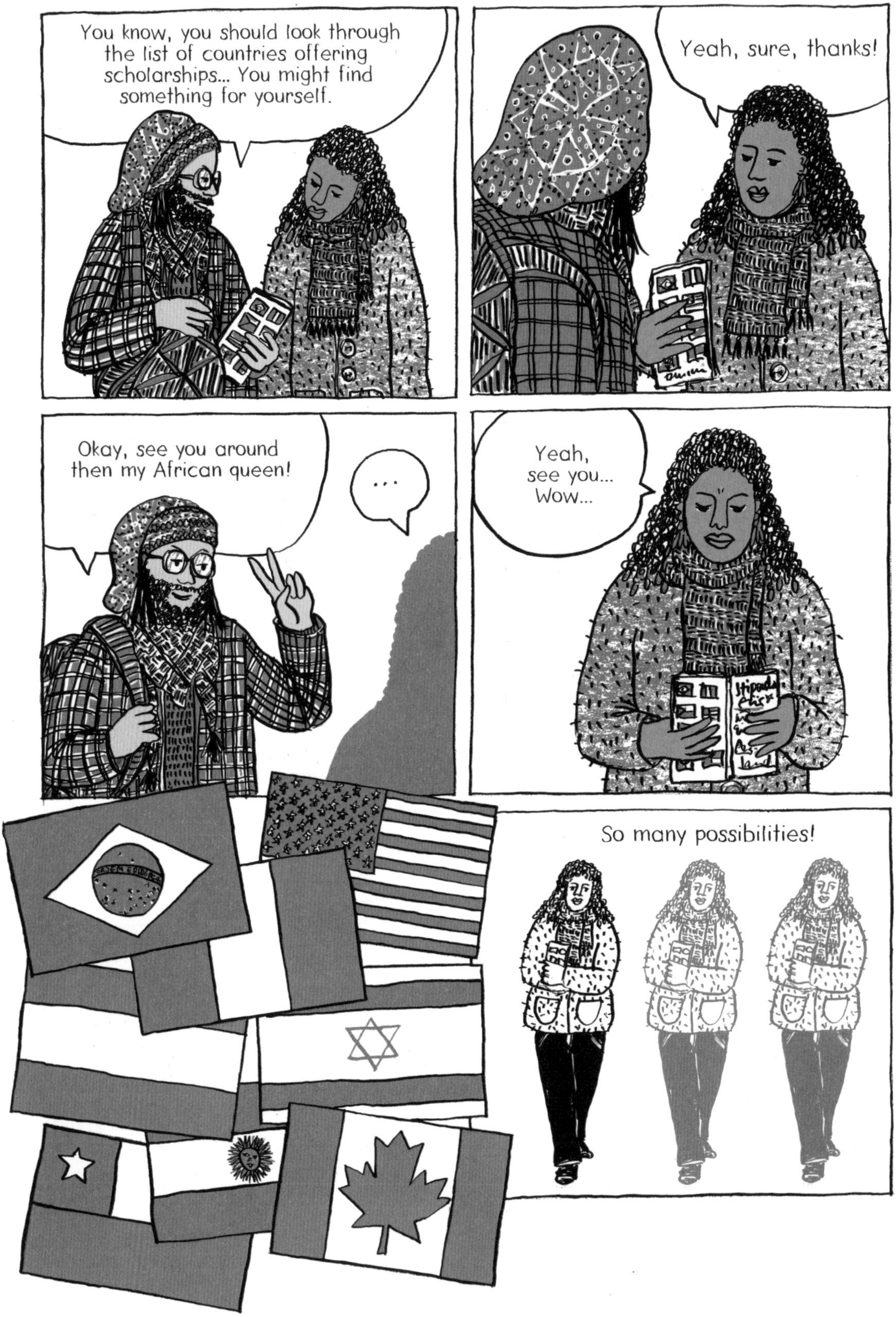
You know, you should look through the list of countries offering scholarships... You might find something for yourself.
Yeah, sure, thanks!
Okay, see you around then my African queen!
...
Yeah, see you... Wow...
So many possibilities!

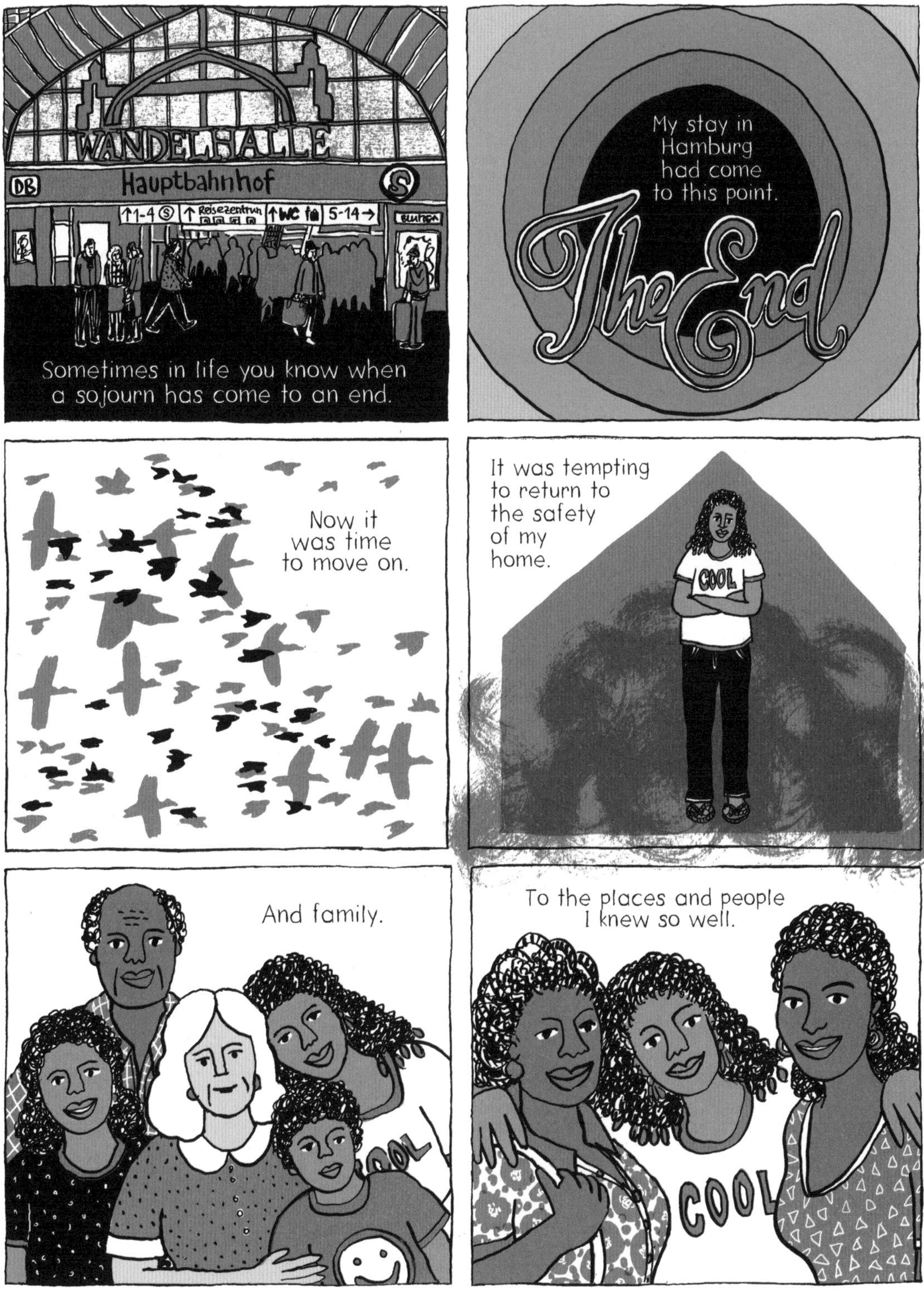
WANDELHALLE
DB
Hauptbahnhof
S
↑1-4 S
↑ Reisezentrum
↑WC
5-14 →
Sometimes in life you know when a sojourn has come to an end.
My stay in Hamburg had come to this point.
The End
Now it was time to move on.
It was tempting to return to the safety of my home.
COOL
And family.
COOL
To the places and people I knew so well.
COOL

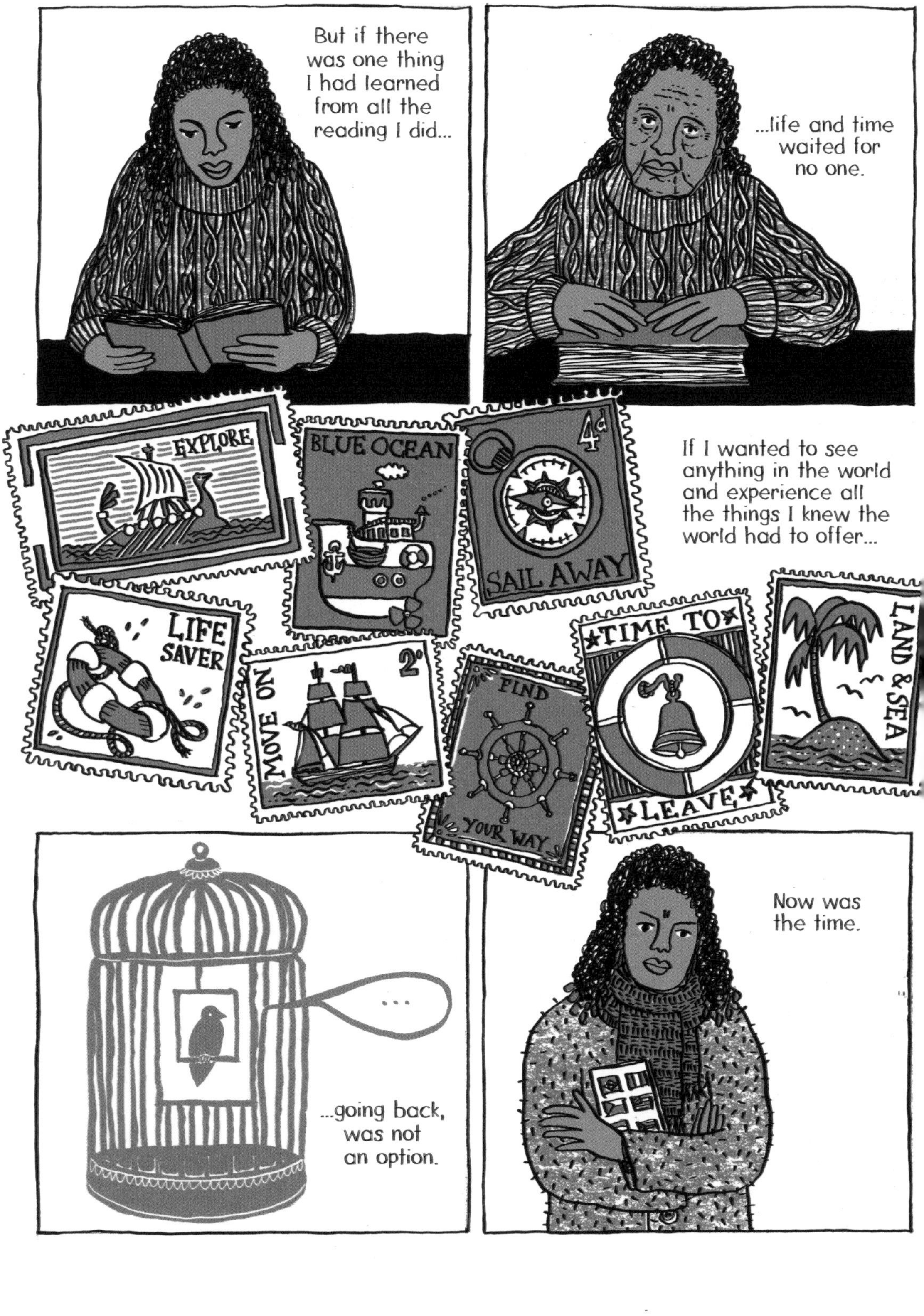
But if there was one thing I had learned from all the reading I did...
...life and time waited for no one.
EXPLORE
BLUE OCEAN
4d
SAIL AWAY
If I wanted to see anything in the world and experience all the things I knew the world had to offer...
LIFE SAVER
MOVE ON
2d
FIND YOUR WAY
TIME TO LEAVE
LAND & SEA
...
...going back, was not an option.
Now was the time.

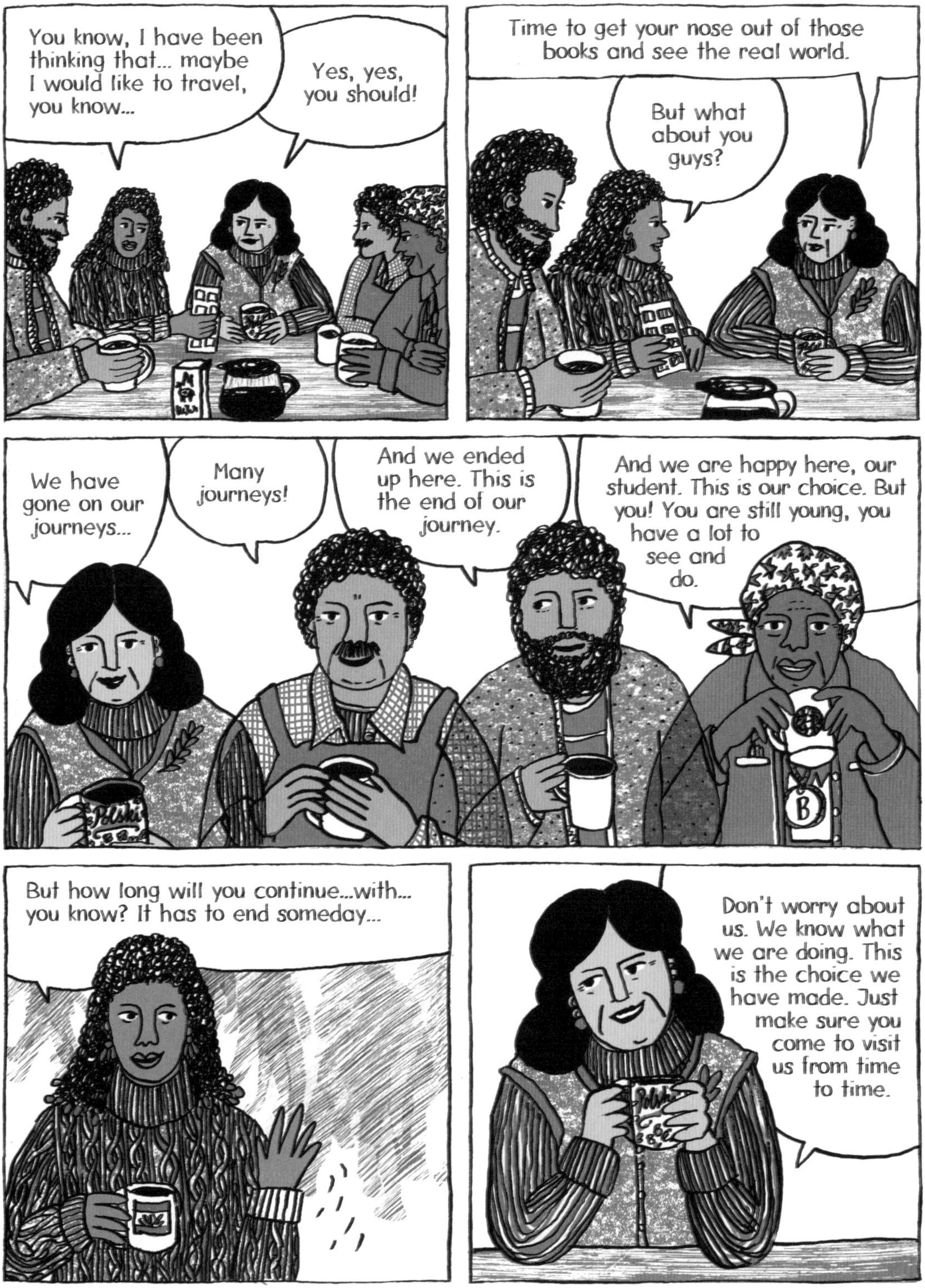

You know, I have been thinking that... maybe I would like to travel, you know...
Yes, yes, you should!
Time to get your nose out of those books and see the real world.
But what about you guys?
We have gone on our journeys...
Many journeys!
And we ended up here. This is the end of our journey.
And we are happy here, our student. This is our choice. But you! You are still young, you have a lot to see and do.
But how long will you continue...with... you know? It has to end someday...
Don't worry about us. We know what we are doing. This is the choice we have made. Just make sure you come to visit us from time to time.

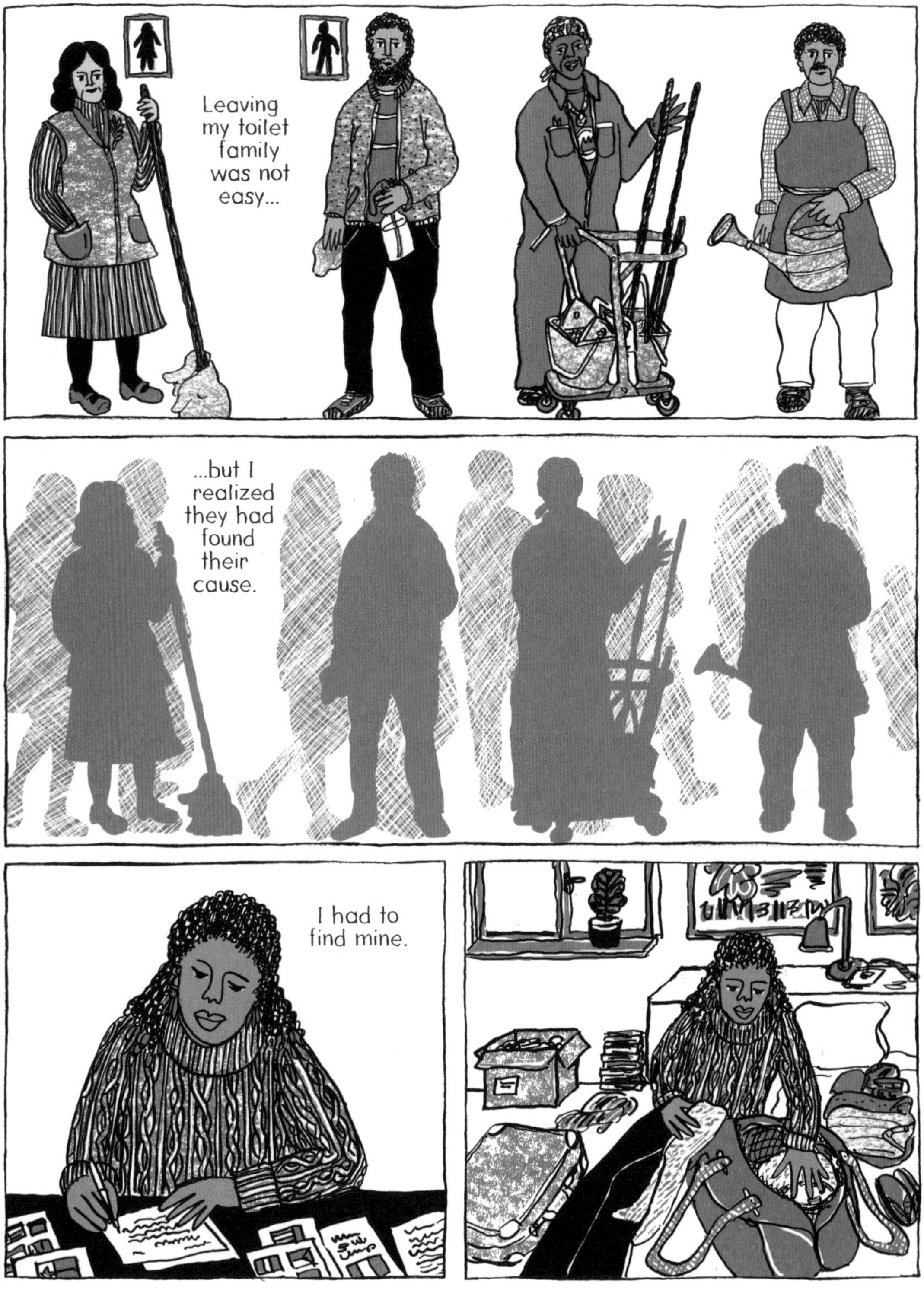
Leaving my toilet family was not easy...
...but I realized they had found their cause.
I had to find mine.

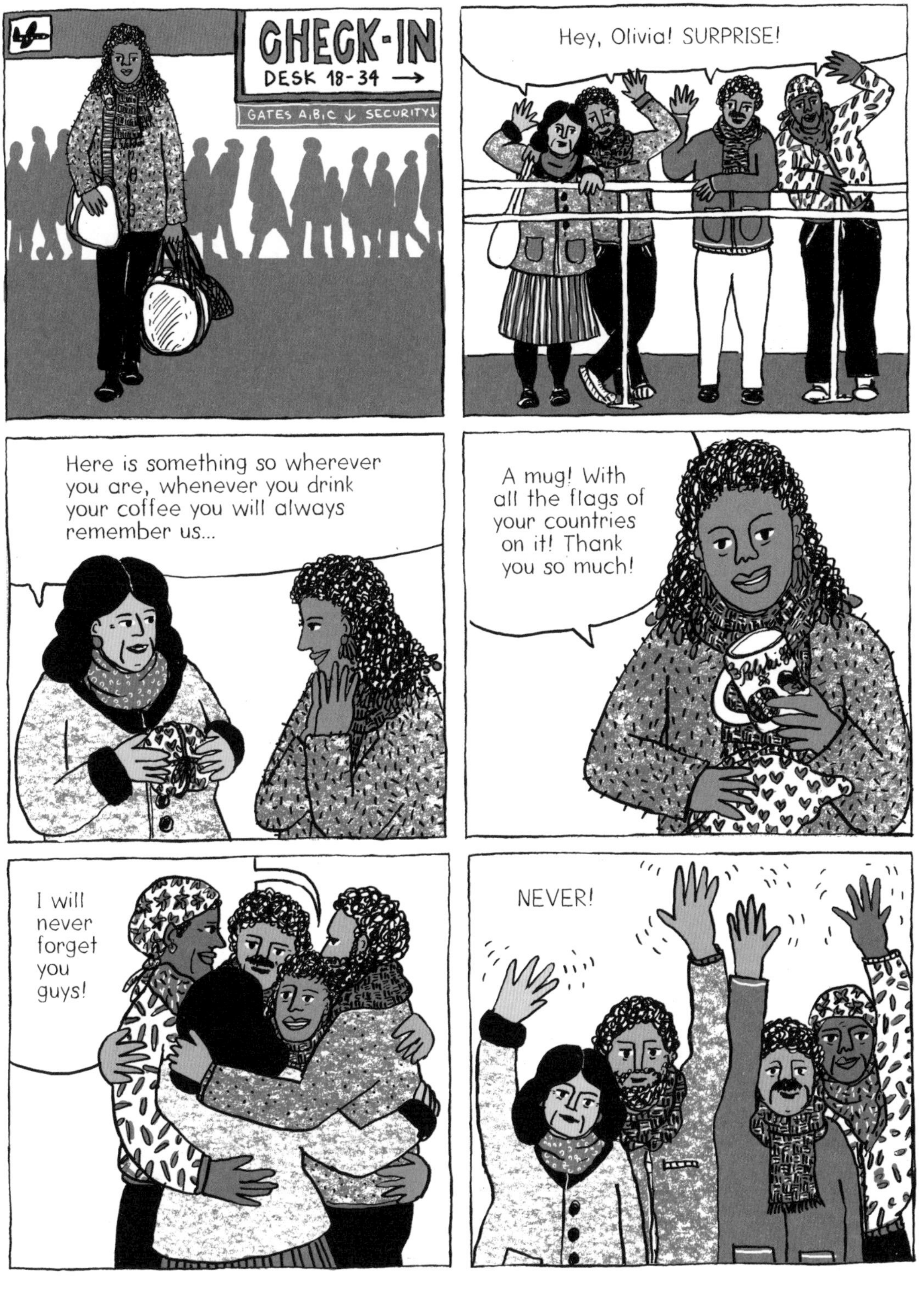
CHECK-IN
DESK 18-34 →
GATES A,B,C ↓ SECURITY↓
Hey, Olivia! SURPRISE!
Here is something so wherever you are, whenever you drink your coffee you will always remember us...
A mug! With all the flags of your countries on it! Thank you so much!
I will never forget you guys!
NEVER!

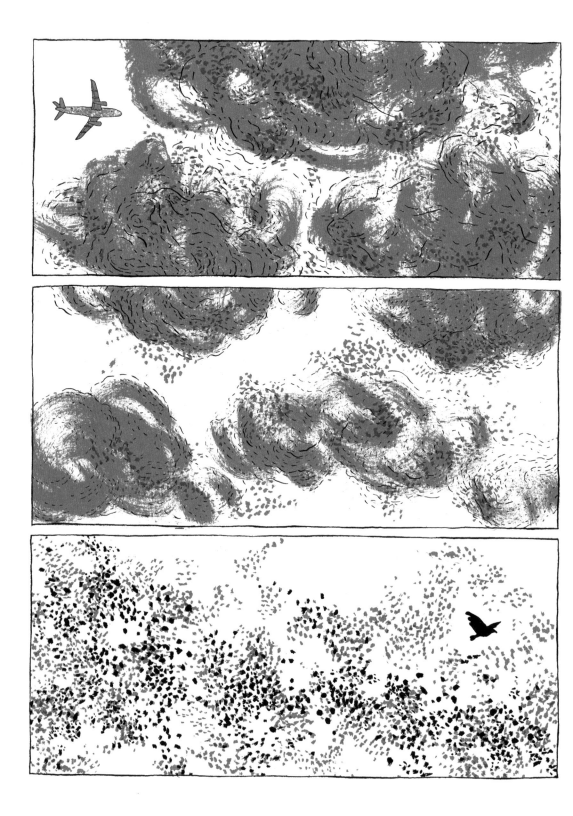

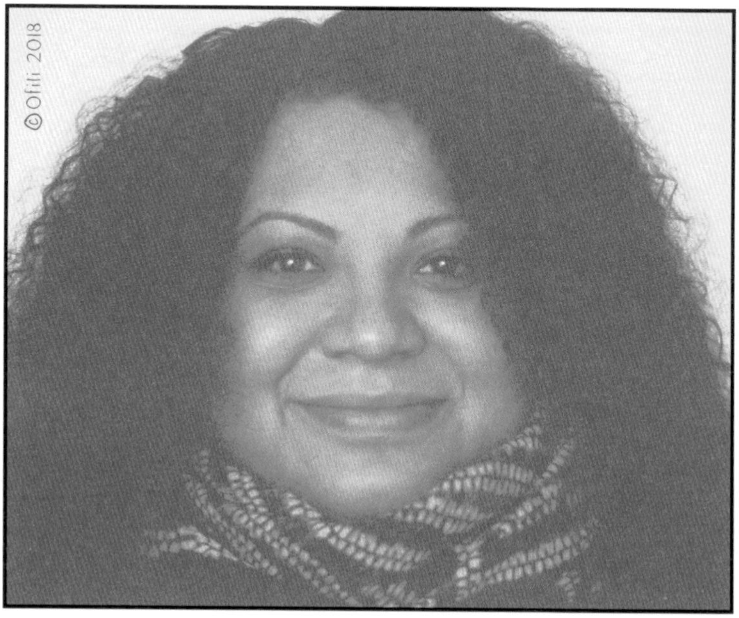
©Ofili 2018

Sylvia Ofili is a writer and teacher currently based in Stockholm. She was born in Lagos Nigeria of Nigerian/ Hungarian parents and her writing has appeared in The Guardian Nigeria and Brittle Paper. She is also known as "the waffarian" and has been writing on her blog for over ten years. *German Calendar No December* is her first full length graphic novel.

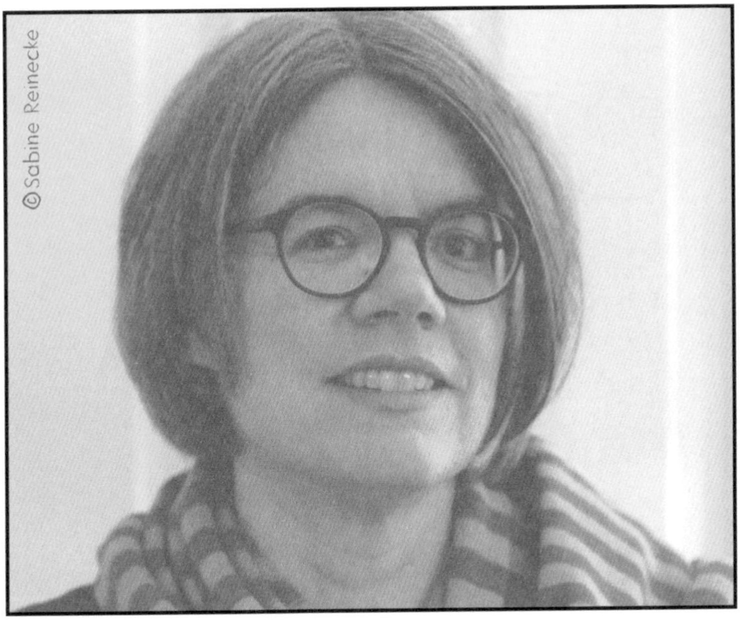
©Sabine Reinecke

Birgit Weyhe is a comic book artist. Born in Munich, she spent her childhood in East Africa before moving back to Germany to study. Her work has been exhibited in numerous European countries and her comics have been published in a wide range of international magazines and anthologies. In 2016, her Graphic Novel *Madgermanes* won the Max-und-Moritz-Prize for best German Comic. She has lectured at various international workshops on behalf of the Goethe Insitut and currently teaches at the Hamburg University.

Acknowledgements

I am grateful to Birgit Wehye for bringing my words to life. Thank you, Birgit. Many thanks to Bibi Bakare-Yusuf for editing, and to Johann Ulrich for providing homes for this book. Thanks to Marc-Andre Schmachtel of Goethe Institute for making this mission possible.

Inspiration: Thank you to the incredibly creative David Liljemark and my teachers in Dynamisk Pedagogik, Eva Borseman and Monica Findahl for introducing me to a world beyond text. Your presence in my life has made all the difference.

"What's happening now?": Thank you for your friendship and following my writing journey over space and time. Desola Ilori, Uyo Ejiofoh, Nadalina Vladic, Martin Arce Lindqvist, Jacqueline Okiemute, Jowhor Ile, Jahman Anikulapo, Stina Grahn, Sandrine Apelbaum and Manan Tuli.
Sylvia Ofili

I sincerely thank everyone that was involved in this project and I am proud of what we have created together.
Birgit Weyhe

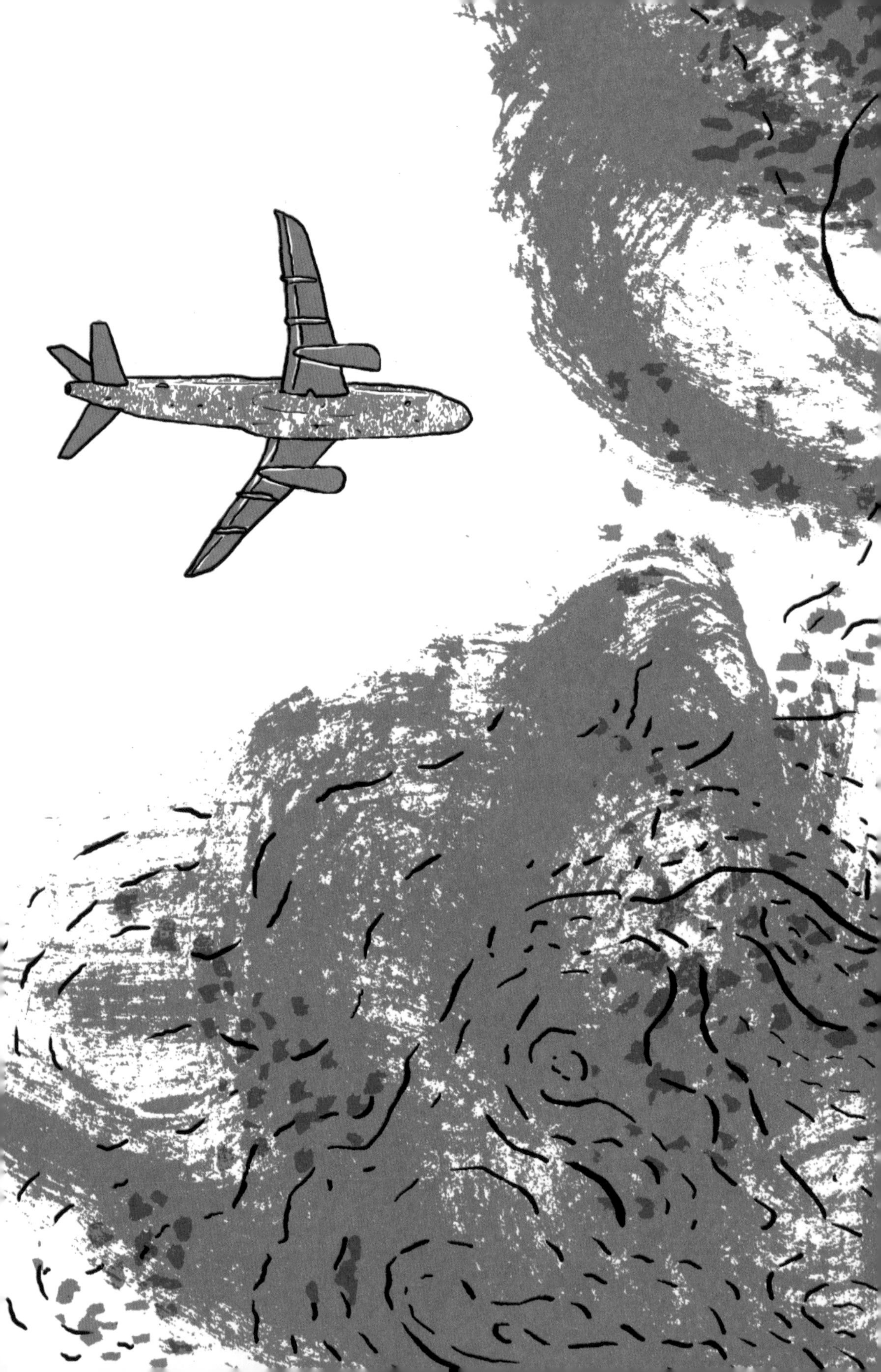

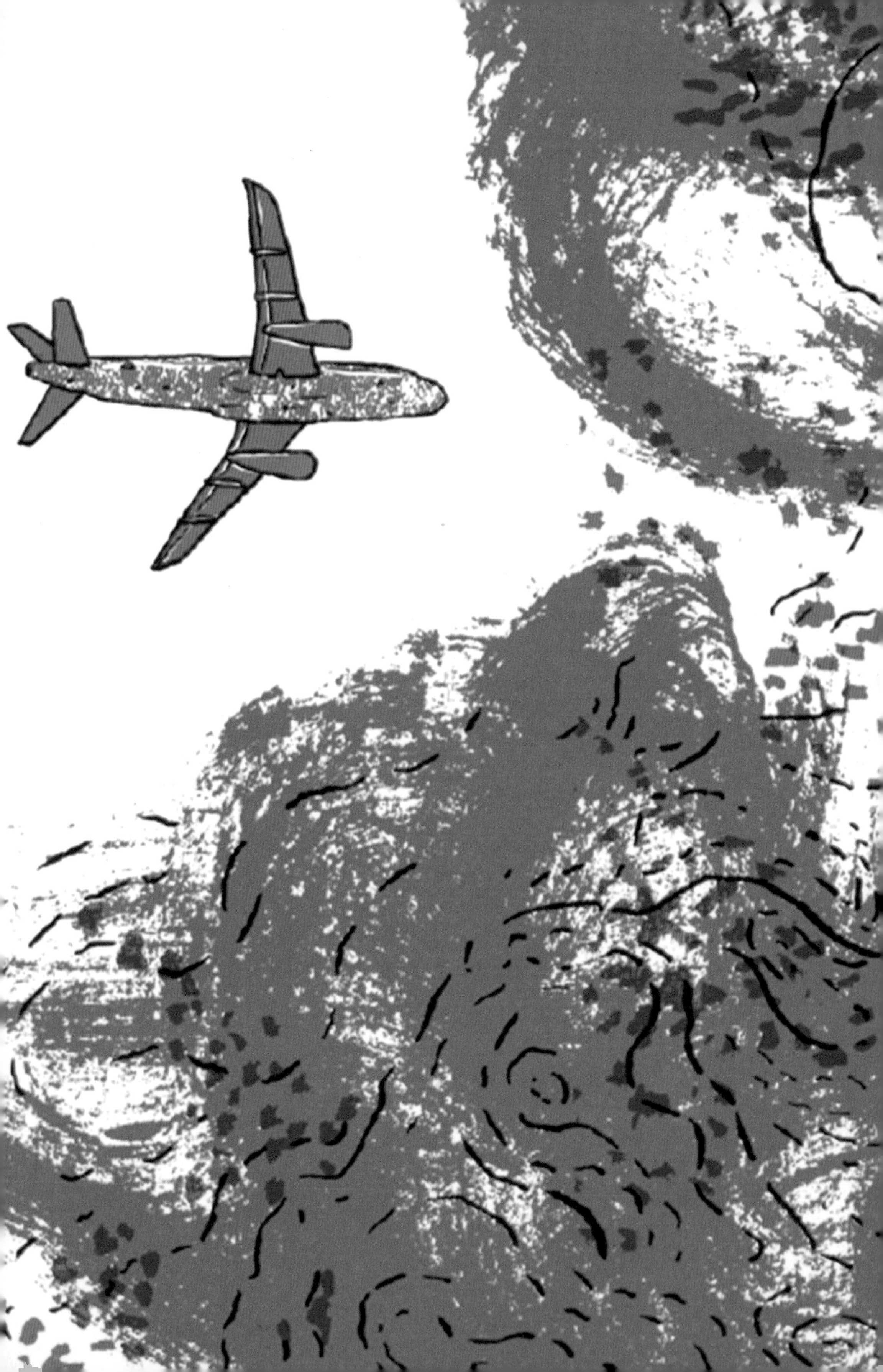